CHAPTER ONE

"The matchmakers call you the perfect gentleman," Sycamore Dorning said. "Now that Tresham has succumbed to a permanent case of marital bliss, the hopefuls turn their lonely gazes to you. I'd envy you, except I know you long for the company of your sheep."

Grey Birch Dorning, Earl of Casriel, pretended to study his program. "Sycamore, you will please keep your ribald innuendo out of polite surrounds."

Sycamore sent a friendly nod to the Misses Arbuckles, twin sisters who looked Grey over as if he might be the answer to a troubling riddle known only to unmarried young ladies.

"I was in complete earnest about the sheep," Sycamore replied. "You name them, you know their birthdays. I daresay you don't know mine."

"May the fourteenth. I recall the occasion vividly. Papa was so relieved you weren't a girl, he became inebriated. One of the few times I knew him to over-imbibe."

Sycamore was nonetheless correct in a general sense. Grey longed to be home in Dorset, where the greenery went on forever, the air was redolent of rural fragrances, and the quiet was profound.

Mayfair by contrast was a hell of muslin, eau de desperation, coal smoke, and violins. And yet, in hell Grey would bide until an heiress or wealthy widow looked with favor upon his suit.

"Papa was drunk on botany," Sycamore said, "just as Will revels in his mutts. I see Miss Hamilton is to perform tonight. Another visit to the punchbowl becomes imperative."

Of all the Dorning brothers—who numbered seven—Sycamore had the most fondness for the ladies.

"If you invite the Arbuckles to sit with us," Grey muttered behind his program, "I will disown you."

"Disowning a sibling who is attempting to mend his ways is frowned upon in good society. I'm safe from banishment until you find your countess."

From the far side of the room, Grey heard familiar laughter—Beatitude, Countess of Canmore, was among the guests. She brought graciousness with her everywhere, also charm and startlingly frank blue eyes. Grey kept his gaze elsewhere, though ignoring her ladyship was like ignoring a beautiful sunset: nearly impossible and inherently foolish, for lovely sunsets were too transitory to be taken for granted.

Sycamore left his program on his chair. "You need a hobby other than counting sheep, Casriel. Old age is making you disagreeable. Shall I bring you a glass of punch?"

"I can fetch my own." Grey rose, his height, as always, making him feel as conspicuous as a bull among spring lambs.

Cam attempted to precede him to the punchbowl, like an outrider who clears the road of potential ambushes, which would not do. Sycamore had matured significantly in the past year—meaning he was no longer an unrelenting disgrace—but Grey was still the oldest sibling, still the head of the family. He maneuvered himself ahead of his baby brother and offered the Arbuckles a nod.

"Now you've done it," Cam said. "I'm not to invite the twins to sit with us, but you just sent them an engraved, perfumed invitation."

"I merely acknowledged them, as manners require a gentleman to do."

A TRULY PERFECT GENTLEMAN

GRACE BURROWES

A Truly Perfect Gentleman is published by Grace Burrowes Publishing

21 Summit Avenue

Hagerstown, MD 21740

graceburrowes.com

Print ISBN: 978-1941419670

Ebook ISBN: 978-1941419663

A Truly Perfect Gentleman by Grace Burrowes

To those who falter but resume the struggle nonetheless

"When you are merely an earl, merely the owner of thousands of beautiful acres, and merely in need of a bride, you show your manners at peril to your bachelorhood. Tresham has arrived. I must speak to him on a matter of some urgency. Best of luck, and find us a wealthy countess who can at least make you smile." Cam patted Grey's shoulder and wound away between chairs, debutantes, and matchmakers.

Find us a wealthy countess. Precisely. That project was off to a slow start. Grey still had a few weeks before the Season ended and the house parties began, but the game became more complicated then, and nothing would keep him away from Dorset as harvest approached.

"Punch, my lord?" a liveried footman asked when Grey had moved to the head of the line.

"Half a glass, please."

"Does my lord enjoy a sprig of lavender or mint with his beverage? Perhaps a dash of cinnamon?"

My lord enjoyed summer ale, fresh bread, and creamy butter from his own dairy, with his own roasted beef and his own baked potatoes. "Plain will do, thank you."

"I'll have the same. Half a glass, plain." The countess smiled at the footman. "And perhaps you know where I might find a pitcher of water?"

The footman glanced around as he ladled out her ladyship's drink from the smaller bowl. "If you ask Harry there by the door, he'll point you in the direction of the billiards room. Should be water on the sideboard."

The Arbuckles were bearing down on the punchbowl with the focus of raptors on the wing. From across the room, their progress was being remarked by Miss Pamela Threadlebaum, who had yet to secure a match despite her fortune. Lady Antonia Mainwaring, rumored to be fabulously wealthy though a confirmed bluestocking, had apparently developed a sudden thirst as well.

"Perhaps your lordship would like to help me find the billiards room?" Lady Canmore asked.

The countess was not wealthy, not flirtatious, not longing to acquire a title. She was, in fact, the very last woman with whom Grey should spend his evening.

"A gentleman never knowingly leaves a lady without an escort," he said, taking the second glass from the footman. "Let's away, shall we?"

She slipped a gloved hand around his arm, nothing possessive in her touch—damn the luck—and made a decorous progress with him toward the door.

BEATITUDE, Countess of Canmore, had made her peace with fate's cruelties five years ago. A widow made her peace because her alternatives—foolishness, the poppy's pathetic oblivion, unrelenting grief or worse—were all defeat of one sort, and Beatitude believed in neither defeat nor surrender.

Neither did she believe in unproductive suffering, which made this stolen moment with Lord Casriel difficult to justify.

"Harry said the billiards room was down the second corridor to the left," Casriel observed. "Perhaps he meant to the right."

Lady Fogerty's sprawling town house was well illuminated in the public areas. One floor up, only the occasional sconce had been lit.

"Perhaps we missed a turn," Beatitude said.

Casriel set both glasses on a deal table positioned beneath a speckled pier glass. Beatitude liked being able to see Casriel both front and back at the same time. He had the renowned Dorning eyes, a soft periwinkle shade between blue and violet. He also had a set of shoulders that likely moved his tailors to raptures. The rest of him held up the promise of those shoulders—he was as tall and as muscular as a plowman.

He carried himself with the quiet self-possession of a lord, and his face was interesting rather than handsome. His features would become craggy with age, the eyebrows a bit bushy, his nose a tad beaky, but for now, he exuded such masculine appeal that Beatitude truly, honestly should not have been private with him.

Private with him *again*.

And yet, his greatest transgression was not robust physical appeal, or abundant good manners, or his title or even his lack of a willowy countess who nodded pleasantly at him across ballrooms, for that's what willowy countesses did.

Grey, Earl of Casriel, was a *kind* man, and thus he threatened Beatitude's resolve, even though she knew his path would diverge from hers permanently and soon.

"We appear to have lost our way," he said.

They weren't nearly lost enough, alas. "If we go back the way we came, we'll come right eventually, my lord."

"We passed a stairway," he said, taking her by the wrist. "I thought I heard a quartet tuning up, though the viola was flat."

Beatitude would not know a viola from a prancing unicorn. "Aunt Freddy said to thank you for restringing her harp." Beatitude refused to be towed along like a tired toddler and laced her fingers with the earl's instead.

"I enjoyed the harp as a hobby for many years, and your aunt sent me a fine old instrument."

His lordship took the left turning at the next intersection, though Beatitude had no idea upon what mental map he'd based his choice.

"Aunt has a whole collection."

He paused. "Of harps? How unusual, rather like your name is unusual."

Even in the dim light of this chilly corridor, Beatitude could see that the earl was genuinely interested. She had never known Casriel to deviate from polite behavior, and she'd also never seen him dissemble.

Which was another grievous fault. Most of polite society believed flattery, white lies, and casual falsehoods were so many dance steps to be executed in the course of an evening's entertainment. Casriel waltzed to his own tune, and Beatitude liked that about him.

That too.

"Aunt was never a very accomplished player," she said, "but she took to rescuing neglected harps before I was born. She has two dozen at least. One doesn't find much occasion to mention such a thing, lest one be associated with eccentricity."

Casriel led Beatitude to the end of a corridor where, to her surprise, a set of steps descended to a well-lit passage below.

"I like a little eccentricity in a person," he said. "Particularly in the elderly. They've earned the right to decide when convention suits them and when it's so much foolishness. If we take those steps and then bear right, we ought to come out on the library side of the music parlor."

"How do you do this?" Beatitude asked. "How do you keep your bearings with nothing to guide you?"

The question was about more than a search for the billiards room, and Casriel's steady regard said he knew that.

He dropped her hand. "I was raised in the country, where a boy can roam freely for hours and never cross the same meadow twice. Keeping my bearings is second nature to me. You should precede me down, as if returning from a visit to the retiring room."

She thought he'd ignore the innuendo in her question, but he stepped closer. "You must not allow a bad moment to overly trouble you, my lady. Lord Davington is kicking his heels in Paris, and if he should stir from that location, I will be certain you are alerted to his whereabouts."

Lord Davington had made a nuisance of himself to Beatitude several weeks ago, importuning her rather forcefully in a dimly lit alcove. Friends had intervened in a timely and discreet manner, and Casriel had seen Beatitude home. He'd been plaguing her imagination ever since.

Though Lord Davington's bad behavior had troubled her as well. "He was not the first to importune me, sir."

"He will be the last." Casriel spoke firmly.

"You are optimistic regarding the state of gentlemanly deportment in Mayfair."

"I have six brothers, several of whom frequent the usual London social outings. I patronize three clubs and have memberships at several others. His lordship's disgrace was made known to all in my ambit, and any man who attempts the same liberties will find himself the butt of unrelenting, even violent, contempt. If you ever have cause to again doubt your safety, my lady, you will apply to me, and the matter will be addressed."

He might have been discussing the price of wool by the pound, though the very blasé tone of his remarks reassured Beatitude. Smacking a presuming disgrace like Lord Davington on the nose was of no great moment to Casriel, all in a day's earl-ing.

"Thank you, my lord."

He studied a shadowed portrait of some bewigged old fellow with a hound panting at his feet.

"Having six younger brothers has given me certain skills where arrogant striplings are concerned. No thanks are needed. The corridor below sounds deserted. You should rejoin the company."

Beatitude should kiss him, a harmless little peck on the cheek that would convey her esteem, nothing more. A kiss needn't be salacious, nor even flirtatious, though Casriel was looking like a man determined to not be kissed. Beatitude had gathered her skirts and had descended three steps when voices floated up from the passage beside the steps.

"He reminds me of a lumbering bear, though no bear ever had such lovely eyes. A pity that the Dorning eyes are wasted on such as him."

Casriel drew back into the shadows above, leaving Beatitude alone on the stairway.

"He's titled," a second voice said. "One must always recall that Casriel is titled."

Beatitude silently retraced her steps, joining the earl in the dim corridor.

"If he weren't titled," the first woman said, "he'd be just another farmer trying to wash the stink of the country from his boots. Papa says we must not consider him. Mama says Papa should leave the matchmaking to her."

Casriel had gone as still as a distant mountain range.

"You'll consider him," the second woman said. "We both have to consider him, but can you imagine the wedding night?"

Beatitude was ready to fly down the steps and scold both of the simpering ninnyhammers into next week, but Casriel put a finger to her lips and shook his head. This talk clearly did not shock him, did not surprise him. He'd likely heard worse.

"They are in their third Season," Beatitude said when the Arbuckle twins had gone tittering and gossiping on their way. "They grow pathetic, and their rudeness is becoming apparent to all."

Casriel offered his arm as he escorted Beatitude down the steps. "My sisters' perspective on a young lady's come out has given me sympathy for those with whom I waltz. Twins would face a dilemma, choosing between loyalty to a sibling and the dictates of well-meaning parents. Family dilemmas are the very devil, don't you think?"

In the distance between one floor and another, Casriel had changed the subject, dismissed several insults, and shown compassion that was damnably appropriate.

"They are well dowered," Beatitude said. "This too is becoming common knowledge. That the twins haven't secured matches in three years of trying reflects poorly on them."

"Then we should pity them. The library is that way and the music room to the right." He bowed, which was Beatitude's cue to curtsey and leave him to his chivalry.

Again.

She was tempted to quit the gathering altogether. Miss Henderson was scheduled to play her flute after the interval. The poor woman ought to have been encouraged to focus on her needle-point for the sake of London's hearing.

Beatitude instead returned to the music room and found a seat among the other widows and wallflowers, who were, after all, the best company to be had.

"Nobody wants to sit with those two," Miss Pansy Miller said, stealing a glance across the audience. "They can stand about smiling at each other until their dimples fall off, and not a bachelor in the house will approach them."

"Exactly what they deserve," Mrs. Palmyra Whitling whispered, nodding behind her fan toward the far side of the room. "Turned up their noses at my nephew Lucas, when the boy's due to come into five thousand a year and a darling little manor house."

The objects of this talk were none other than the Arbuckle twins, who were indeed fanning themselves and chatting gaily two obvious yards from the men's punchbowl.

"They're young," Beatitude said. "We were all young once, and I for one was prone to foolishness."

"Foolishness is understandable," Mrs. Whitling retorted, "but rudeness... Ah, they're to be rescued."

The Earl of Casriel, lone among all the gentlemen, was bowing over Miss Drusilla Arbuckle's hand and then treating her sister to the same politesse. While Beatitude watched, he led them to seats in the third row, where his younger brother rose and greeted them.

"I've always liked the Dorning boys," Miss Miller said. "Their mamas put the manners on them."

"And that Casriel," Mrs. Whitling replied, fanning herself with her program, "is no longer a boy."

Casriel was a gentleman. A true, honest, kind gentleman, and Beatitude must stop thinking about him or she'd go mad.

She left off pretending to study the bouquet on the piano as the earl solicitously assisted Miss Drusilla Arbuckle into her chair. Beatitude hadn't meant to see that, hadn't meant to catch the earl's eye, but his companions were the last of the guests to be seated.

Casriel winked at her—subtly, discreetly—but Beatitude caught that too.

~

"THE SITUATION ISN'T AWFUL," Jonathan Tresham said, passing Grey a sheet of figures. "You're solvent, treading water as they say."

Tresham was a duke's heir and a genius with figures. The latter capability had defined him entirely until recently, when marriage to Theodosia Haviland had brought a more balanced focus to Tresham's outlook.

Grey considered Tresham a close acquaintance, not quite a friend. But then, even close acquaintances didn't generally audit a man's books for him, much less at no fee.

"Treading water won't do," Grey replied. "With Willow married, I still have five younger brothers who are also treading water. They need a start in life, and I'm the one who is supposed to provide it to them. Treading water won't do when a landlord is responsible for every repair and improvement made to his tenant holdings. Treading water won't serve when I'm to take a bride, and my finances will soon be dissected by that lady's family."

Tresham leaned back in his chair. "Have you chosen your countess? You were seen paying particular attention to the Arbuckle twins last night."

"They wanted for company, and Sycamore likes them." Not quite true. They wanted for husbands.

"They want for tutelage in ladylike deportment," Tresham replied. "Theo says they gossip with each other like magpies. Your finances would pass muster with such as them."

"Because of the title. I begin to understand my father more clearly."

Tresham rearranged the papers. "One of the blessings of maturity, I suppose, is to gain insight into one's father's situation. Yours was a botanist, I believe."

Botanist kindly skirted less charitable terms—eccentric, for example. "Papa named his children Grey Birch, Willow, Jacaranda, Ash, Oak, Hawthorne, Valerian, Sycamore, and Daisy. If he wasn't a botanist, he was daft."

Tresham set the figures on the desk. "Was he both?" Tresham's father had been a rogue, indulging in every vice permitted to a duke's spare, and a few forbidden to even those idle creatures.

"At the end, he was more daft than botanist, but you try raising nine children on the proceeds from one glorified sheep farm and see what's left of your sanity." Grey's step-mother had certainly parted with her composure somewhere between sons number three and four.

"Nine is a lot of children." Tresham's observation bore an air of curiosity, but then, he was newly married and doubtless fascinated by the privileges attendant to that station.

"Nine is too many. Ye gods, what if I had more than two sisters? Do you know what an earl's daughter requires in the way of a dowry these days?" Grey knew—he'd done that calculation many times—and he hadn't half those funds at his disposal though they'd doubtless be needed.

Tresham rose. He was exquisitely attired, while Grey was in shirt-sleeves, his cuffs turned back, his waistcoat a plain blue affair chosen for comfort rather than style. All of his waistcoats were blue, because simple gold accessories went well with blue, and yet, he had favorites among the lot.

"I am acquainting myself with what's required for a duke's daughter," Tresham said. "Diana will be raised as if she were my own, and Seraphina will soon make her come out." The new Mrs. Tresham had brought a daughter and a younger sister to the union, and Tresham, naturally, had taken on the expenses incurred by both.

Naturally for him.

He wandered around the estate office, pausing to admire a

painting of Durdle Door. "Who is the artist? This is not the typical seascape."

"I painted it. My brother Oak is the real talent, though." Oak had never tried his hand at the peculiar formation on the Dorset coast that looked as if a dragon were drinking from the sea. "If you were in my shoes, what would you do to improve your finances?"

Tresham moved on to the landscape of Dorning Hall, with the abbey ruins crumbling in the distance.

"I'm not a farmer, Casriel, and your situation is mostly agrarian. Some people advise selling off acres, but in your case, those acres produce income. Others advise borrowing to invest. As a peer, you cannot be jailed for unpaid debt, so the strategy isn't particularly risky, but you are honorable, which means you would never walk out on a commercial venture simply because it proved costly."

If Jonathan Tresham had no idea how to improve the earldom's finances, then the conundrum could not be solved.

"You don't mention marrying for money."

Tresham's next distraction was a set of shepherd's pipes made for Grey when he'd been a boy. "One doesn't want to state the obvious, Casriel. You have a title, you are solvent, you have no direct heir, and you're in London for the Season."

Grey hadn't lasted the whole Season the previous spring. He'd grown too damned homesick and had lacked the fortitude to face the house parties. The mere stink of London—horse droppings, coal, and mud—had brought all of last year's failure rushing back.

I am turning into my father. "I watched while the title-hunters and matchmakers tried to ensnare you," Grey said, rising to take the pipes from Tresham's grasp. "I found a reason to be grateful that I'm a mere earl, not a duke's heir or a marquess. These are fragile, and they have sentimental value."

Tresham's gaze fell on the pile of figures in the center of Grey's blotter. "You don't have to marry at all. If ever an earl had abundant spares, it was your late father."

"Who wanted nothing more than to spend his life communing with trees."

"What happened?"

"I happened." The plain truth, and not even that unusual a truth among British aristocracy or courting couples regardless of station. Except that Mama and Papa hadn't been courting.

Tresham was at a loss for words, which should have been a small victory for earls everywhere, but a tap on the door interrupted the moment.

"Enter."

The butler stepped into the room and bowed. "A lady to see you, my lord. She's brought a harp."

Grey rolled down his sleeves. "If she has wings and a halo, tell her I'm not at home."

Tresham snorted. "His lordship is hunting for a countess and cannot be distracted by celestial intercessors."

Crevey had served the Dorning family since he'd been a boot-boy back in Dorset. He was doubtless withholding the woman's name out of discretion.

"I'll show her to the family parlor, my lord, and tell the kitchen to send up a nice tray. You won't want to keep her waiting."

"Is she pretty?" Tresham asked that ungentlemanly question.

"None of your business." Grey slipped plain gold sleeve buttons into his cuffs, though he couldn't help but hope the Countess of Canmore had come to call. He liked her, though he must not court her and must not mislead her.

"Why not the formal parlor?" Tresham asked.

Crevey sent Grey a look, bowed, and withdrew.

"The formal parlor faces the street." Grey shrugged into his morning coat. "If a lady calls on me, I'd like the option of keeping the visit private, rather than advertise my guest's identity to any passerby."

Tresham batted Grey's hands aside and began doing up his coat buttons. "You're going about this marriage business all wrong."

"How many weeks have you been married?"

"I've been a ducal heir since childhood. You should marry the lady whom you can't imagine spending the rest of your life without. If she's marrying you on the same terms, all will be well."

"I recall a certain gentleman who approached the business with a list and with an advisor from among the widows. He had *criteria*, a schedule, an objective, and a complete disregard for matches based upon sentiment."

Tresham stepped back and held his arms wide. "And look at that fellow now. In charity with life, devoted to wife and family, a friend to mankind."

"And so bloody humble about his undeserved good fortune," Grey muttered, examining his reflection in the cheval mirror.

"That is a disgraceful waistcoat, by the way," Tresham said. "I can give you the name of my tailor."

But not the means to pay the man. "The blue goes well with my eyes. Thank you for your efforts, Tresham, and give mankind a great big friendly kiss on the cheek for me."

Grey saw Tresham off at the front door and turned his steps to the family parlor, where—he hoped—her ladyship might have brought him another harp to be restrung. He'd chosen his oldest blue waistcoat for comfort, and also because it reminded him of her lady-ship's eyes.

His hopes were doomed, as it turned out. The harp was a disaster and Lady Canmore nowhere to be seen. Mrs. Fredericka Beauchamp —her ladyship's Aunt Freddy—had taken Grey's favorite reading chair and demolished half the tea tray by the time he joined her.

"Casriel," she said, half a biscuit in her hand. "Have a seat. This one's in bad condition, but I've every confidence you can put it to rights. These biscuits are too dry. Pour a tired old woman a cup of tea, and I'll tell you all about my friend here."

Casriel wanted to return to Tresham's figures, to visit his horse, to sit down to a meal of more than biscuits and sandwiches. He instead took the place across from Mrs. Beauchamp.

"Ma'am, a pleasure to see you. Tell me about that little beauty, for I'm sure it's a tale worth sharing."

Mrs. Beauchamp finished her biscuit, took a sip of tea, and launched into a recitation that took up the next hour of Grey's afternoon.

CHAPTER TWO

"Casriel's really not that bad," Drusilla said, "and he is an earl."

Anastasia paused in the corridor before the mirror hanging across from their bedroom door and made her Thoughtful Expression. "His lordship knows something about music. We must allow that to be a gentlemanly attribute."

"Don't arch your eyebrows," Drusilla suggested. "You want a pensive quality rather than skepticism."

"Like this?" Anastasia tried again, pursing her lips, gaze downward, eyes serious.

"Exactly like that. Contemplative, as if measuring your words before deigning to share them with the gentleman."

Anastasia pulled her over to the mirror. "You do it."

They spent a few minutes perfecting the Thoughtful Expression. Anastasia set great store by her arsenal of expressions and glances, while Drusilla was the expert on the languages of the fan, gloves, and parasol. Both sisters considered a hearty luncheon important, because Mama and Papa took the midday meal together, one of few times they were in the same room for any length of time.

"You didn't need your reproachful look last evening," Drusilla observed. "Lord Casriel has fine manners."

"I suppose we must account that a gentlemanly accomplishment too. He also has a half-dozen brothers, all in good health. One needn't provide him a spare."

"But one ought to, unless one wants to become an Object of Pity."

Anastasia shuddered. "The very mention of such a fate will upset my digestion, but then the notion of the wedding night..." She wore her Honestly Uneasy Expression, not something a lady had to practice where Casriel was concerned. He was a great strapping specimen of earlhood, and that was fine for when a lady needed assistance into a phaeton, but not so fine when the lady was married to that specimen.

"Mama says the wedding night is quickly over," Drusilla murmured. "Do we know anybody who has visited at the family seat in Dorset?"

"We do not, but Dru, Mama says twins run in families."

"And we know what twins can do to a lady's figure." Mama expounded at great length on that topic. Drusilla paused by the mirror outside the breakfast parlor. "We are in good looks today. Well rested after passing an agreeable evening."

"Agreeable is putting too fine a point on it, Dru."

"Is it? I thought Casriel acquitted himself well enough. He can discuss music, he knew something about Lady Fogerty's landscapes, and his brother is a flirt."

"We aren't supposed to enjoy the company of flirts, sister dearest. You know Where That Can Lead."

Drusilla fluffed her bangs with her smallest finger while she peered at her reflection to check for emerging freckles. She rubbed her skin with a raw potato religiously to ensure freckles did not become a problem.

"Flirtation leads straight to Ruin," Drusilla said. "I suspect Ruin is a village outside of Bath or some other spa town."

They were still smiling over that notion when the footman seated them on either side of their mama, who had donned her usual Serene Expression, while Papa was for once not taking his meal from behind *The London Gazette*.

"I hear my darling daughters shared their evening with an earl," Papa said. "Well done, my dears."

Anastasia waited until the footman had withdrawn, for the meal was taken *en famille*. "I thought you said Lord Casriel was beneath our notice, Papa."

"Your mother has persuaded me to reconsider my opinion of the man, and you know how convincing your mother can be."

Mama placidly sipped her tea. "Casriel has thousands of acres and is said to be a conscientious landlord, not like some who leave the poor tenants to struggle with overgrown hedges and leaking roofs."

Papa sawed away at his ham. "The Dornings are an old and respected family. One of the sisters married a Kettering, another old and respected family. The Dorning spare married a Haddonfield. Lord Casriel's connections are above reproach."

Beyond all things, Papa treasured good connections, and he'd apparently been researching Casriel's—or Mama had.

"The earl has lovely eyes," Mama said. "The Dornings are legendary for those beautiful eyes."

Mama cared nothing for a man's eyes, but she very much wanted her daughters to marry well.

"He's a fortune hunter," Drusilla said, lest Mama wax admiring about his cravat, which had been plain to a fault.

"You said we weren't to consider him," Anastasia added, though last night Mama had bade them accept his lordship's invitation to sit with him and his brother. On the way home, she'd made comments about a lady being at pains to ensure no gentleman felt excluded from a gathering, graciousness to the less well situated, and other nonsense.

This morning, Lord Casriel had lovely eyes and good connections.

"Fortune hunter is such a vulgar term." Mama poured herself more tea, then passed Drusilla the pot. "Let's first determine if his nature is agreeable before we pry into his finances. I want my girls to be happy."

And happiness, as was known to all, depended on being well situated. Ladies married to titled men were Very Well Situated. Papa had no title, which left a daughter with something to puzzle over.

Papa had a fortune, though, as a result of his own antecedents having invested in shipping ventures during the reign of George II. The Arbuckles weren't old money, in other words, but they were eminently respectable and quite well-to-do.

Grandpapa Arbuckle had purchased not one but three country manors, two of which were slated to become dower properties for the twins. To further advance the family's standing in the world, the Arbuckles needed to acquire a connection to a title. Drusilla and Anastasia had learned that lesson before they'd been taught to remember Good King George in their prayers every night.

"Pass the pot, Dru," Anastasia said. "How do we determine if a man's nature is agreeable?"

"You spend time with him," Mama said as Papa picked up the paper. "You converse, you dance, you enjoy a supper waltz if you can. I've been considering your invitations and have decided to make a few changes."

Mama considered the invitations with more focus than Wellington had likely brought to his quartermaster's reports.

"Are we to attend the Hendershots' card party tonight?" Drusilla rather fancied Mr. Xerxes Anderson, even if he had been sent down from university again.

"Possibly," Mama said. "For a certainty you will attend the Bowlers' ball tomorrow night. They are not the best company a young lady could find, but they are decent, and their fortunes are said to be improving."

They were richer than Papa, in other words. More to the point, Lord Casriel was likely to be there.

Drusilla affixed her Cheerfully Agreeable Expression to her features, while Anastasia adopted the same look.

"I love a ball," Drusilla said.

"Who doesn't?" Anastasia added with a bright smile. She picked up her knife and fork and went after the slab of meat on her plate.

Drusilla did likewise, though, really, balls were growing tedious, titled men were growing tedious, and making stupid faces designed to convey false emotions was growing very tedious indeed.

GREY WAS BACK in the estate office, coat off, slipping his sleeve buttons free, when the butler intruded again.

"A lady to see you, my lord. Your luncheon tray was on the way up from the kitchen. I sent it back and told Cook you'll need more tea and cakes."

The thought of yet more tea and cakes made Grey bilious. "Thank you," he said, shrugging back into his coat. "Did the lady give you a card?"

"She did not."

Does she have lovely blue eyes that seem to peer straight into your soul? "After this call, I will not be home to visitors for the rest of the afternoon. My correspondence won't answer itself."

"Very good, my lord." Crevey withdrew, his step obnoxiously sprightly.

Doubtless Mrs. Arbuckle had come to inspect Grey in person. He had spent the longest ninety minutes of his life feeding the twins small talk and compliments the previous evening. He could not tell if the young ladies were silly, shrewd, or both, but their mother had sat across the room, sending Grey speculative looks while she'd tapped her fan against her cheek.

He'd limit this call to the prescribed two cups of tea and then get back to the figures Tresham had compiled. He was an earl, for the love of bonnet ribbons, and pouring scandal broth the livelong day was the province of gossips and matchmakers.

Grey tugged down his waistcoat, said a prayer for patience, and let himself into the family parlor. His caller was across the room, her back to him. The line of her spine and set of her shoulders conveyed displeasure and resolve.

The nape of her neck drew his eye, looking all too feminine and alluring.

"Lady Canmore, a pleasure."

She turned and dropped her arms only long enough to curtsey before resuming the pose of a displeased governess. "My lord. Good of you to see me. I needn't take up much of your time."

"I have nothing pressing this afternoon, and a tea tray is on the way. Won't you stay long enough to at least take a cup with me?"

She wore a simple rose-colored dress with a quilted white spencer. The ensemble showed off her blond hair and blue eyes nicely and did absolutely nothing to distract Grey from the perfection of her figure. Her ladyship was on the petite side and exquisitely curved. She put him in mind of a beautifully carved harp, which conjured music from silence even when sitting idle.

"I did not come here to swill tea and make small talk," she said, stalking away from the window. "I came to apologize."

"In what regard could an apology possibly be owing, my lady?"

She crossed to the sofa, skirts swishing, and took the place in the center. "My aunt has made a nuisance of herself again, hasn't she?"

"Again?"

"Please do sit, my lord, and you needn't feign gentlemanly consternation. I've known Aunt Freddy all my life, and she has about as much tact as a rhinoceros in spring."

"My consternation is genuine," Grey said, taking the wing chair nearest the sofa. The elderly Mrs. Beauchamp bore a slight resemblance to the rhinoceros about the jaw and nose. "Your auntie is a delightful lady, and I can't conceive of how she might be likened to exotic game. Perhaps you could elucidate?"

Her ladyship heaved a great sigh, which strained the seams of her spencer and the limits of Grey's self-discipline. He was not a schoolboy smitten with the parlor maid, to be so preoccupied with Lady Canmore's charms, but neither was his attraction to her merely physical.

Lady Canmore was a stranger to deceit, even the social variety that smoothed superficial interactions and simplified life in polite society. She was neither a merry widow nor permanently cast down with grief. She got on with life, disdaining any of the clichéd roles foisted on women in her circumstances.

She could not be neatly labeled and dismissed, and Grey respected that about her enormously.

"Aunt is growing difficult," Lady Canmore said. "She has always been a determined woman, but then, she's had to be. Lately, she becomes fixed on an objective, and all threats, arguments, and distractions are unavailing. She foisted another of her orphans onto you, didn't she?"

Grey's mind presented him with the wholly irrelevant thought that Lady Canmore would make a fiercely vigilant mother.

"You make it sound as if I've been given lifelong responsibility for somebody's cast-off boot-boy. She's merely asked me to have a look at a damaged harp, my lady."

The countess sat up quite straight. "It is not *merely a harp*. Aunt Freddy has an agenda, one that I am ashamed to discuss with you."

"Then don't. I'll do what I can for a musical instrument in need of a little attention, and she will have her harp back within the week or two. Nobody need admit to or discuss any agendas."

Where was the tea tray when a countess looked as if she'd bolt out the window rather than stay another moment?

"She is *matchmaking*, my lord."

"If matchmaking has become a high crime, then half of Mayfair will soon be housed in Newgate." Should that occur, finding an heiress would become even more challenging, but oh, the peace and quiet...

"Your inherent good manners have blinded you to Aunt's stratagems. She seeks to make a match *between us*."

In no learned tome on gentlemanly deportment could Grey have found a suitable reply to that expostulation. "The notion offends you?"

"Of course... not. Not in that way, but yes. I find the notion troubling." The countess rose and resumed her post by the window. "I don't need my aunt, or anybody else for that matter, meddling in my business."

A woman of fair complexion could not hide a blush, not even by turning her back on her host.

Perhaps this was best. A frank discussion that put to rest all silly fantasies and worries. Grey rose and joined the countess at the window, the weight of duty and decency turning his mood sour. The garden was coming into its late spring glory, with roses blooming white and pink against the wall and heartsease bordering the walks.

All was sunshine and birdsong in the garden. Grey longed to sit out there with her ladyship and listen to her read her favorite French poems. Instead, he'd have an adult discussion with her, offer her a cup of tea, and be about his fortune hunting.

"Mrs. Beauchamp could leave me a different broken harp every day of the week, and I'd never assume that entitled me to a claim on your attentions. I truly was passionate about the harp as a youth, and the occasional music room project is a pleasant diversion."

Her ladyship faced him, the sunlight finding all the highlights in her hair—gold, copper, russet, wheat. Painting her would be like painting a sunset, a thousand details adding up to one memorable impression.

"You don't know Aunt Freddy," the countess said. "She'll hare off to Bath, and when you have the latest instrument put to rights, she'll send you a note telling you to drop it around at my house. She'll have another wounded harp sent to me, with instructions to leave it in your keeping."

Her ladyship wore a subtle gardenia scent, both light and rich, an olfactory oasis of pleasure amid the rank odor of London. Grey had always favored gardenias and was relieved Papa hadn't appropriated that name for a girl child.

The countess was honestly vexed, and that bothered Grey on her behalf. "I see now the unspeakable skullduggery your aunt is capable of, sending broken harps all over the realm, expecting me to pay a call or two on you, and expecting you to receive me, of all the outrageous notions. The shameless baggage should be pilloried for such scandalous machinations."

Lady Canmore aimed the full brunt of her blue-eyed cannon on him. "You are joking, aren't you?"

"I am joking, also sincerely admiring. Last night, I endured an execrable rendering of a Haydn flute sonata while the Arbuckle twins pressed me, one on either side, as if I were the world's largest wine grape. When they weren't dropping their programs, the better to show off their feminine endowments, they were whispering some mangled French inanity directly into my ear. That you witnessed this farce gilded the absurdity with embarrassment. Matchmaking that involves social calls and ailing harps sounds downright dignified by comparison."

Lady Canmore studied him, while Grey studied her. She was no schoolgirl, but she had a vitality and confidence that appealed to him more strongly than any tittering debutante ever could.

"When I said I wasn't offended..."

"Yes, my lady?"

"I didn't mean—"

Whatever she'd been about to explain was interrupted by the damned tea tray.

"Thank you," Grey said as Crevey bowed and withdrew. Her ladyship resumed the place on the sofa, and Grey repaired to his wing chair. "How do you take your tea?"

"You don't want me to pour out?"

He'd amused her, and how he loved that impish version of her smile. "I suspect you are called upon to fulfill that office routinely. I'm a confirmed bachelor of mature years, and if I sat around waiting for somebody to pour my tea, I'd live a pathetic, tea-less existence such as no Englishman could possibly endure."

"Two sugars, no milk."

Grey peered at the tea and decided it needed to steep. "Your expression suggests perplexity, my lady."

She drew off her gloves and set them beside her on the cushion. "I've tried to puzzle out why you are not like the other men cluttering up the ballrooms. You *are* a confirmed bachelor, aren't you?"

He offered her the plate of cakes. She chose the one with lemon icing.

"What do you know of my late father?" he asked.

"Nothing." She bit off a corner of the cake. "I know you have many younger siblings. Six or seven?"

"Eight, including five unmarried brothers." And they were by no means his only dependents. "My father was a botanist. Hence the names."

"Names, my lord?"

"My siblings are Daisy, Jacaranda, Oak, Ash, Valerian, Hawthorne, Sycamore, and Willow."

She dusted her hands. "Might I ask what your name is?"

Her curiosity pleased him. The brisk manner in which she put the question also pleased him. "I was christened Grey Birch Hallowell Runnymede Dorning, and you are...?"

"Beatitude Marie Maude Purvis Canning. You may laugh, but you are sworn to secrecy regarding the Maude part."

He poured her a cup of tea, more touched than amused that she'd given him that confidence. He did not laugh, though he did smile. He added two lumps of sugar and set a spoon on the saucer. "Were you named for somebody, my lady?"

"Aunt Freddy's late sister. Aunt Maude died without issue and left me a competence. I have had reason to be very grateful that her name gave me a connection to her." She stirred her tea and took a sip. "What of you? Were you named for somebody?"

"That brings us back to my father, the botanist. I and several of my brothers were named for his greatest passion, the forests of England. He tramped from one end of the realm to the other, and we have plantings at Dorning Hall from all over Britain. A family was very much an afterthought for him, as if children sprang up in the nursery like volunteer saplings at the edge of an orchard. For most of my life, Papa puzzled me."

She finished her cake. "Which implies that at some point, he ceased to be a conundrum."

"Papa never planned to marry, never planned to have children. He realized the earldom was not wealthy and intended that the title pass to a cousin better situated than he was. I see the wisdom of his scheme now, when I have younger brothers who need a start in the world and the earldom has little means to provide one. If I had only myself to consider, I'd be content to raise my sheep, maintain good relations with my neighbors and tenants, and read agricultural pamphlets of a winter evening."

She took another sip of her tea. "As a younger woman, I scorned mere contentment. Now..."

She gave Grey a smile such as no debutante could have given him. Commiserating, sweet, a little sad. A woman's smile, not a girl's.

"I married for love," she said, "and far above my station. My husband was an earl's heir. I was the outspoken daughter at the vicarage. I was mad for him, and not only because everybody with any sense disapproved of the match."

Grey hadn't known she'd been raised in a vicarage. "And if you had to choose again?"

"No regrets, my lord. I loved my husband, for all his faults, and he saw something in me, despite mine. We were not content, but we did care for each other. Aren't you having any tea?"

Grey poured himself a cup. His appetite for tea was sated until Michaelmas, but this conversation—a little personal, nothing scandalous—was a pleasure.

Also a torment. "I am the sort of man most parents will approve of as a son-in-law. I will provide for my wife and children, I am titled, my estate in Dorset is well cared for, and my nature is temperate. Nobody will regret marrying their daughter to me, and yet..."

She patted his hand. "You like your life as it is. I like my life as well, for the most part. Nobody warns you about the loneliness, though, do they?"

What loneliness? Except, the question had barely formed in Grey's mind and he already knew the answers, plural. The loneliness of a man at the height of his physical powers who had no intimate companion—not simply a mistress willing to tolerate his advances in exchange for coin, but a woman who'd chosen him because she was attracted to him.

The loneliness of an earl without a countess.

The loneliness of a patriarch who had no partner to confide in or with whom to discuss the family's joys and tribulations.

The loneliness of a brother watched beloved family members, one by one, leave the family seat for other horizons. What loneliness, indeed.

"I should not have asked that." Lady Canmore set down her tea cup. "Consider the question rhetorical rather than impertinent. Are we agreed that Aunt Freddy is not to inconvenience you and embarrass me with her little schemes? You must be firm with her, my lord. Tell her the press of business and the obligations of your social calendar do not permit you to take on more of her orphans."

Grey sipped his tea, ignoring the hunger he'd made worse by gobbling cakes for the duration of Aunt Freddy's visit.

"I enjoyed the last project she sent me, and I will enjoy this one as well. I believe the harps give her pleasure, and I like hearing her stories about life in the late king's day. I cannot turn away an elder for the sake of something as paltry as my convenience."

Lady Canmore rose. "You are kind, my lord, but you are also stubborn in your gentlemanliness. I won't waste any more of your time, and I will thank you for the tea and conversation."

Grey got to his feet, her smile making him uneasy. "Have I offended?"

She beat him to the door, their hands colliding on the latch. She stepped back, and he opened the door for her.

"I doubt you know how to give offense."

This too, somehow, was a transgression in the lady's eyes, or possibly a disappointment. Grey escorted her to the front door, telling himself that if Lady Canmore was unhappy with him, that made his life simpler.

"Thank you for paying a call, and when I am finished repairing your aunt's harp, I will return it personally to her."

A parasol of the same rose hue as her dress lay on the sideboard. Grey passed it over, feeling as if something more ought to be said, not knowing what that something might be.

"May I offer your lordship an observation before I go?"

No servants lurked, not even Crevey. "Of course."

"You are a contented bachelor, so naturally the notion of change is disquieting, and yet, here you are in London, looking quite determined to find a bride."

"I haven't made a secret of my unmarried state." Though *determined to find a bride* wasn't exactly how an eligible bachelor wanted to be described. *Dashing* was out of the question for a glorified sheep farmer, but gentlemanly, solid, *honorable*... Those qualities might have come to mind instead.

"If marriage is in your future," her ladyship said, "then might I suggest that marriage to the wrong woman will, indeed, diminish your peace, but marriage to the right woman will increase your joy. I'll bid you good day."

She curtseyed, he bowed, and then the lady was gone, a waiting footman joining her at the bottom of the steps.

What was that about? Grey liked Lady Canmore, and he was attracted to her, but he was uncertain if she liked or was attracted to him, not that her predilections were relevant. He might marry the right woman, he might marry the wrong woman, but at all costs, he must marry a wealthy woman.

And whoever she might be, the next Countess of Casriel would not be Lady Canmore.

～

LADY ANTONIA MAINWARING WAS WEALTHY, attractive, and losing her mind one ball, card night, and boating party at a time.

"Mr. Anderson is coming this way," Beatitude, Lady Canmore, muttered. "We're for the retiring room."

Antonia let the countess link arms with her and turn her toward the steps. "We've already visited the retiring room twice, and both times all we heard was gossip."

"But not about either of us, so those trips were wasted."

The countess had the knack of moving through the crush at the Bowlers' ball without appearing to hurry. She was smaller than Antonia—most women were—and like the British navy faced with the Spanish Armada, agility and purpose accomplished what size and power could not.

"Do you truly lurk in the retiring room to hear gossip about yourself?" Antonia asked as they made a decorous progress up the steps.

"One must remain informed. My old abigail pounded that into my head when I became engaged to an earl's heir. She also told me that my London lady's maid was to wait out a social evening in the retiring room, rather than enjoy the fare below stairs. A maid in plain sight could both suppress gossip about me among my peers and catch the stray slanderous comment from the unwary."

"Let's admire portraits or play cards."

Lady Canmore surveyed the ballroom below with the dispassion of a general. "You're safe. Mr. Anderson has attached himself like a barnacle in rough seas to Miss Drusilla Arbuckle's arm."

Thank God. "Why would a frivolous man seven years my junior think I'd consider his suit?"

Lady Canmore's gaze became sympathetic. "Because he is seven years your junior?"

That was honest, also true. "I'm an earl's daughter, with wealth of my own. He's a coal nabob's insolent puppy with wandering hands." The feel of those hands on Antonia's person was enough to make a nice, quiet nunnery with a decent library look appealing.

"Better him than the coal nabob with foul breath. Even insolent puppies can dream, and being insolent, they usually dream of their own wishes being gratified. Are you considering accepting anybody's addresses?"

"I am content with my present circumstances," Antonia replied as they traversed a corridor between alternating pier glasses and seascapes. "I have independence few women can aspire to at my age, and I manage my funds as I see fit. I have my charities, my literary interests, my cousins..."

"And a herd of puppies slobbering over your hand," her ladyship said, turning the handle of a carved door. "Some would envy you your situation, my friend."

"You haven't remarried."

Lady Canmore had pretty ways. Her smiles were winsome and friendly, her gestures graceful, her walk ladylike, though she was more curvaceous than the standard English beauty. Antonia envied her all of that, but she also envied the countess knowledge only a wife was permitted to gain, knowledge of intimacy that went beyond the bedroom and gave a woman a partner in life.

Though marriage could also inflict an intimate enemy on a lady.

"We are not the first to seek refuge among the portraits," Lady Canmore said, advancing on a tall gentleman halfway down the long wall. "Lord Casriel, good evening."

"Lady Canmore, Lady Antonia."

The earl had been introduced to Antonia at a ridotto several weeks earlier. She always noted the tall gentlemen, because they were potential dance partners. In her first Season, she'd had to endure partnering short men, and they'd invariably spent the entire waltz in conversation with her bosom.

"My lord." Antonia's curtsey was polite, while Lady Canmore's was somehow elegant. "I take it you enjoy art?"

"I do," he replied. "And you?"

Because he was standing near a sconce, Antonia could see what made the Dorning gaze so noteworthy. His eyes were the beguiling hue of periwinkles or violets in bright sunshine. She'd never seen another with eyes that shade.

"I like a good landscape," Antonia said. "Portraits are fine for memorializing a beloved ancestor, but for my parlors and bedrooms, I'd rather not have anybody's countenance gazing at me."

The countess took to smoothing her perfectly unwrinkled gloves, suggesting Antonia's comment had been less than refined.

"I'm of a similar disposition," the earl replied. "I keep a landscape of the family seat in my London office, a reminder of happy times and places. Lady Canmore, what sort of art do you prefer?"

He was an attractive man, not stunningly handsome, not a golden god, not a fop. His hair was brown, perhaps shading russet in the out of doors. His voice was cultured, and he was a baritone, if not a bass.

He was an earl. She was an earl's daughter.

Antonia made these assessments while Lady Canmore prattled on about the honesty of caricatures in contrast to the flattery in most portraits, not a point Antonia would have thought to make. They wandered as a trio from one end of the room to the other, and the elderly couple who'd been chatting by the window left before the circuit of the gallery was complete.

"The supper waltz approaches," the earl said. "If one of you ladies has yet to commit that dance, perhaps you'd consider partnering me?"

How polite he was, how genial and gentlemanly.

The countess spoke up before Antonia could accept. "I believe her ladyship has yet to offer that waltz to anybody."

Was Lady Canmore's good cheer a bit forced?

Casriel smiled, not a hint of flirtation in his expression. "I'm also without a partner, my lady. Might I have the honor?"

Had he been hiding up here, lurking where an older couple would provide him chaperonage? "The pleasure would be mine, my lord. Lady Canmore, will you accompany us back to the ballroom?"

"I think not," the countess said, curtseying again with enviable grace. "I must ensure my coiffure is in good repair before I attempt a waltz. Enjoy the music."

Antonia had observed the earl often enough to know he was competent on the dance floor. He was also gentlemanly, titled, not bad looking, and tall. Tall was important to a woman who'd been referred to as a Long Meg since her eleventh birthday.

So why did she feel as if the earl's invitation had been aimed not at her, but at the countess? And why had the countess, who did not suffer fools, refused a man who was clearly no kind of fool whatsoever?

CHAPTER THREE

"You were very bad, Aunt Freddy," Beatitude said, drawing a finger along the mantel. A smudge developed on her fingertip, meaning another scold was in order for Aunt's housekeeper. "You should not importune an earl to repair instruments that have been broken for ages."

Fredericka Beauchamp had been a great beauty in her day, back when fashion had favored well-curved females rather than the willowy, boyish figure now in vogue. In later years, Freddy had grown plump, and Beatitude had loved her hugs. They were soft and fierce at the same time, and fragrant with the scents of camphor and verbena.

Now, Aunt Freddy seemed to grow smaller each year. Her hugs were still fierce, but they'd become bony, and Beatitude didn't dare hug her back with the abandon of a favored niece.

Aunt Freddy, don't leave me. The same plea Beatitude had made when she'd been banished to boarding school and when Aunt had come to pay her rare calls at the vicarage. *Don't leave me amid these joyless, dour saints who are crushing my spirit one sermon at a time.*

"I have not been bad, Addy mine," Aunt Freddy replied, knitting needles clicking away. "I knew Casriel's parents. Lovely couple, though the earl was a bit distracted with his horticulture. Not *too* distracted. Between his first and second wives, he had a regiment of children, all of them with those lovely eyes. The present titleholder is too serious. He has his papa's focus, but has aimed it entirely at duty rather than at any particular passion."

Casriel was passionate about the harp. Beatitude traced the base of a candlestick and found more dust. "His lordship is an adult, and you must respect his choices." *As I must.*

"Addy dearest, where has my fun-loving, warmhearted girl gone? Did Roger take all of your joy with him when he wrecked his curricle in that ditch?"

The windows were also in need of a good scrubbing, coal dust being a chronic problem in London. Then too, the parlor smelled less than fresh. The carpets needed beating and a liberal sprinkling of dried lavender, while the drapery should have been tied back with verbena sachets.

"I am a widow," Beatitude said. "I loved my husband. Grief changes our perspective." Though that husband had never called her Addy or dearest.

Aunt laughed, her mirth dry and papery. "I've been at widowing rather longer than you, my dear. I loved my darling husband too, and yes, widowhood changes us. It needn't turn us into angry nuns."

"I am not angry." *Though I am as celibate as a nun.*

Aunt put down her knitting needles, struggled to her feet—she boosted herself off the chair arms more than she rose on main strength—and crossed the room.

"Beatitude, I shall soon go to my reward. Please do not trouble what time remains to me with worries for my favorite niece."

Aunt was so tiny, so pale and frail, as if the girl she'd once been was haunting her from within. "You give me this speech every Season, Aunt."

"Not every Season. I waited until Roger had been gone for three years. I like Casriel. A woman can like a man, and a man can like her in return. Casriel knows virtually every tune written for the harp and all styles of crafting the instrument. He sang me a little Scottish air about some fool who'd sold his fiddle for a dram of whisky, and I realized the concert hall is missing a fine talent. Did you know he's a first-rate painter of landscapes?"

He sang for you. Addy tucked the shawl up around her aunt's shoulders. "You can be friends with a man half your age. My options are more limited."

"Quite the contrary. Your options are greater than my own, provided you are discreet. I suspect Casriel was born discreet."

"While you were born with a naughty streak."

"You wanted to grow up to be just like me." Aunt resumed her place in the wing chair, settling into the cushions with a sigh. "When you're staring death in the face, Addy my girl, you will not wish you'd spent more evenings at home knitting shawls."

"No more talk of death, please, and no more inveigling the Earl of Casriel with matchmaking-by-harp. Were he interested in me, he's had plenty of time to make that interest apparent."

Aunt picked up her knitting, arranging the completed portion of the shawl over her knees. The yarn was a soft, lavender blue that put Addy in mind of Casriel's eyes, but then, everything brought the earl to mind. Not since Addy had been smitten with her late husband had she felt this unruly fixation on a male of the species.

"Casriel isn't like that boy you were married to," Aunt said, needles clicking. "Roger clung to the privileges of boyhood, though he was an understandable choice and a charmer. Casriel is a man. He'll not come simply because you crook your finger, and he'll not come laughing in any case."

"When did you become an expert on enticing men?"

Aunt aimed a particularly solemn glance at Addy, her needles moving in the same steady rhythm. Some snippet of mythology tugged at Addy's imagination, the Fates perhaps, spinning out the length of mortal lives.

"I am an expert on living for decades without a companion to share my days, young lady. See that you don't grow up to be just like me in that regard, at least."

That salvo was all the more devastating for being quietly offered. "Casriel needs money, Aunt. I haven't much of that now and never will."

Aunt Freddy flipped the half-made shawl over. "Money is not the only form of wealth a man can appreciate. All aristocrats think they need money, when, in fact, they have a roof over their heads which will stand for centuries, more land to cultivate than the common man can fathom, art treasures cluttering up their attics, and stables that provide better accommodations than some inns. He does not need money, he merely wants it."

If the Earl of Casriel was marrying for money, then he *needed* money. "He doesn't want to marry at all."

Addy made another circuit of the room, concluding that more than a lecture was due the housekeeper. The time had come to issue a threat. The carpet needed beating, the whole room wanted a good dusting, and no flowers had been brought in from the garden to beautify an old woman's day. Creeping damp was the next phase of neglect, and from there, a house could crumble in a very short time.

"Lord Casriel told me his father hadn't wanted to marry either," Addy said, peering more closely at a sketch beside the hearth. "Is this me?" She hadn't noticed the drawing previously, or perhaps it hadn't been on display. "It is me."

The younger version of Beatitude was a little thinner, a little more lithe, and she was radiantly happy. Her resemblance to Fredericka was obvious about the smile and the warmth in her eyes.

"Who did this?"

Aunt did not reply, and her needles had gone silent.

She'd fallen asleep in the middle of a call, a rare occurrence until recently. Clearly, matchmaking had tired the old dear out. Addy extricated the needles from Aunt's grasp, folded up the shawl so the needles were on top, and set the lot on Aunt's knitting basket.

"I'll come again soon," Addy said, kissing her aunt's cheek.

Though visiting Aunt had become a labor of love. She had been Addy's dearest friend and relation, and she was fading.

Addy committed the unpardonable offense of appearing in the housekeeper's parlor without notice and issued a writ of ejection, stayed only by the housekeeper's assurances that Mrs. Beauchamp refused to let anybody clean in her private parlor, and she noticed if the maids tried to dust on the sly.

"Dust anyway," Addy said. "If Aunt has callers, she will be embarrassed by the state of her parlor, and if her parlor is a disgrace, she won't be home to them anyway."

The housekeeper curtseyed until her cap came loose. Addy inspected the rest of the house and found the housekeeper had spoken honestly. For the most part, the dwelling was clean and orderly. Only the bedroom and sitting room—where Aunt spent most of her time—had been neglected.

Perhaps another trip to Bath was in order. That daunting thought occurred to Addy as she met her footman at the bottom of Aunt's porch steps.

"Where to now, my lady?"

"Home, Thiel. I'm only capable of so much socializing in a day, and I'm expected at a card party tonight."

"Pretty day to be out and about, though, ma'am. London shows to best advantage in spring."

A footman typically did not converse with his employer, but Thiel was a holdover from before Roger's death. He'd come with Roger from the seat of the Canmore earldom and declined to return there when Addy had been widowed. He was probably five years her senior, handsome as footmen were supposed to be, and cheerful.

Addy liked him. When she'd first put off mourning, she had wondered if she was attracted to him, but had reasoned that if attraction was a matter of speculation, it wasn't attraction, but rather, boredom, or some other more troubling sentiment.

She *was* attracted to Casriel—no question about that, more's the pity—and she suspected he was attracted to her as well. His lordship was simply too proper to yield to any wayward impulses.

"Looks like you're to have company," Thiel said as they approached Addy's house.

A tall gentleman was striding up the walk. He wore standard daytime attire—breeches, waistcoat, morning coat, top hat, cravat in a simple knot, no ornamentation. His walk was not the gentlemanly saunter, however.

This fellow would arrive at his chosen destination long before the saunterers or strollers. He moved with the purpose of a man who expected to cover miles in the course of a day and who decided exactly where he would arrive and when—and in whose company.

"Lord Casriel." Addy curtseyed.

He swept off his hat and bowed to a correct depth. "My lady. If you could spare me a few minutes of your time, I'd be grateful."

"Of course." Addy took the earl's arm, and Thiel trotted up the steps to open the front door. His lordship's usual genial demeanor had been replaced by a gravity that reminded Addy of Mrs. Palmyra Whitling's words.

Casriel was not a boy.

"Shall I ring for tea?" Addy asked when Thiel had taken his lordship's hat and walking stick.

"Tea will not be necessary. A word with you in private would be appreciated."

"This way." Addy led him not to her formal parlor, but to her personal sitting room. She wanted to see him among her favorite artwork and comfortable furniture, wanted the quiet available at the back of the house.

"How are you?" Casriel asked. The question was nearly fierce.

"I am well, and you?"

"In good health, thank you." He stared down at her. "I am not like Tresham, who needed the services of a matchmaker to find him a suitable lady."

This was interesting. "But you are angry."

"Frustrated, my lady."

"With me?"

"Because of you."

"Should I be flattered?"

Casriel ran a hand through thick chestnut hair. "Probably not, but with ladies, a gentleman can never be certain."

"Might we sit?"

"I can't stay long."

"But you won't leave without saying your piece, so let's be done with it, shall we?"

THE COUNTESS EXUDED SERENITY, while Grey felt torn between foolishness and determination. He'd slept badly, then his horse had thrown a shoe in the park at first light. What should have been a good gallop had become a hike through Mayfair's streets towing a gelding who had perfected the art of the theatrical limp.

Grey had attempted to deal with his correspondence, because he was two weeks behind with the steward's reports from Dorning Hall, but Sycamore had wandered by, intent on discussing his new business venture. The morning had been a waste, and luncheon at the club had seemed like a small consolation.

Ha. Grey had been unable to enjoy his steak in a dining room that still reeked from last night's smoking in the cardroom across the corridor. He'd made the mistake of glancing at the betting book on his way out the door, and his day had gone from trying to impossible.

Her ladyship took a seat, making a portrait of feminine contentment in a wing chair near the window. She clearly wasn't afraid of sunlight, though that thought brought a question. What *did* she fear? What could ruffle her composure? What preoccupied her when she laid her head on her pillow and waited for sleep to come?

Not you, old chap.

"My club keeps a book," Grey said, rather than attempt any small talk. "The ledger records wagers of all kinds." He wanted to pace, but this little parlor would afford him about two strides in any direction. The appointments were comfortable and pretty, also delicate enough to be easily smashed by a heedless earl.

The mantel held a series of porcelain figures in gilded pastels—a laughing shepherd boy, a girl in a straw hat with a goose curled adoringly against her skirts, another girl who was barefoot and leading a small cow. Sheep figured among the collection, as did a white donkey with a blue butterfly on its nose.

Whimsical, bucolic choices for a Mayfair countess, and the sight of them helped settle Grey's temper. This might have been a series of scenes from the home farm in Dorset, where Grey could return when his task in London was completed.

"Are you the subject of a wager?" Lady Canmore asked.

"I am the subject of a host of wagers, all of them recent and inappropriate."

Her ladyship looked as if she were studying a hand of cards, deciding what to toss and what to keep. "I was married to a man who took enthusiastically to life's joys. I am familiar with the mechanics of conception. I know that across the street and three doors down, a pretty woman of years comparable to my own maintains a common nuisance. From my morning room, I can see who patronizes her establishment. I know who spends the entire night there, and who is in and out—so to speak—in less than half an hour."

Grey left off admiring the figures. "You are saying I needn't be delicate."

"My husband liked to drink to excess. He dabbled in nitrous and opium and occasionally shared a pipe with me. He teased me into trying his cigars and laughed uproariously when I nearly coughed myself to perdition on the first puff. He read me naughty poetry and had a wicked imagination, which he did not keep to himself in the presence of his wife."

This recitation had Grey taking the other wing chair. He could not tell if her ladyship missed this man, judged him for his vices, neither, or both.

"So, my lord, tell me of these wagers."

Grey didn't want to, but as he'd stomped from the club and endured the knowing smirks of a few passing acquaintances, he'd concluded that he must.

"Some of the wagers are merely unkind, betting that I will propose to an Arbuckle before King George's birthday. Others are less innocent."

"Welcome to the entertainments of the idle, wealthy male, my lord. For my part, I usually find the sums involved more obscene than the wagers themselves."

Excellent point. "The wager gaining the most attention says I'll make you my mistress before I leave Town, brideless, one assumes, though some are betting that I'll propose to Miss Sarah Quinlan, and others have put their faith in Lady Antonia Mainwaring's charms."

Those bets made Grey uneasy. The one regarding Lady Canmore infuriated him.

"You cannot *make me* your mistress, my lord. That is an office I must choose for myself." She offered this observation with a baffling touch of humor, not quite smiling, but communicating mirth with her tone of voice.

"You will forgive me, my lady, if I don't refine on that point to the idiots at my club. A lady's good name should be protected at all costs. I'm tempted to resign from the damned organization before sundown. The Arbuckles are in precarious standing, from what I understand, being unpopular and without any offers in their third Season.

"I cannot speak for Miss Quinlan's situation," Grey went on, "though I suspect she is an heiress of some renown. Lady Antonia cannot help that she is tall, any more than I can help that I am tall, and yet, her appearance was referred to unflatteringly in the ledger book."

Lady Antidote. Did young women make up sly names for the

gentlemen? Grey hoped they did, because such puerile tricks deserved retaliation.

"You are an earl. Height is manly and unwomanly at the same time."

Her calm baffled him. "Why have I spent my youth and adulthood pounding, lecturing, and threatening my brothers into a semblance of gentlemanly conduct, only to come to London and find this, this... vulgarity from men who are supposed to manage the affairs of the realm?"

The countess smoothed a hand over her skirts. "You are concerned your brothers will learn of these wagers."

Well, yes, though Grey hadn't come to that realization until her ladyship had spoken. "Sycamore hears everything. He's like a damned house cat, always where he isn't supposed to be, always listening and plotting secret mischief. Lately, he's taken up the habit of correspondence, which is enough to give me nightmares. Hawthorne regards Town as Sodom-on-Thames, and I suspect Ash, Oak, or Valerian will come on an inspection tour any week now. They expect better of me."

Her ladyship rested her chin on her palm, gazing out the window. "We could have an affair."

Grey responded before the import of the words fully registered. "No, we could not—I mean, such an undertaking would doubtless be delightful, but one doesn't, or rather, I haven't, or not very—what the hell kind of suggestion is that, Beatitude?"

Had she been teasing him?

And when had the adult male cock become an auditory organ? Her outrageous notion sent desire pooling where it wasn't easily hidden. Grey considered crossing a knee over an ankle, but Lady Canmore had apparently enjoyed a very modern marriage.

He did not cross his legs, or fidget, or for one instant allow the possibility of an affair to consume his imagination. Instead, it sat like a cat in a shadowed corner of his mind, licking its paws and switching its tail in a knowing fashion.

"People do," she went on, brows knit. "Have affairs, especially people who like each other. Ever since you escorted me home from Lady Bellefonte's ball, I have held you in high regard."

This conversation was unlike any Grey had had with anybody, including his horse, including those discussions undertaken with his married brother, Willow, while drinking from the bottom quarter of the decanter.

"I hold you in utmost esteem, my lady, which is why I will decline to have an affair with you." Grey did not look at her décolletage, though he esteemed that abundance right along with the rest of her.

The situation was hilarious, also sad. He was an adult, he desired her madly, respected her tremendously, and she apparently did not find him objectionable. A courtship might have started under those circumstances, but for his lack of funds.

"No affair, then," she said, as if choosing a velvet fabric over a muslin. "I suppose that leaves a warm friendship, if we're to scotch the gossip."

"What is a warm friendship?" A *warm friendship* probably involved such public tortures as being seen with the lady in casual conversation, sitting out a set with her, perhaps taking her driving during the carriage parade.

Grey hated the carriage parade with a passion that exceeded his loathing for foot rot and dull shearing blades.

"I don't envision anything too onerous," her ladyship replied. "I'll partner you at whist, you'll stand up with me for a supper waltz. We might ride out together for an early morning hack and indulge in a bit of flirting where others can admire your wit and my smile. Aunt Freddy will be delighted if she gets wind of these doings, but you mustn't encourage her daft notions. The idea is that we behave with cordial good cheer toward one another, and in a few weeks, another wager will have caught the attention of the buffoons at your club."

To waltz with her, to see her first thing in the day amid the foggy beauty of the bridle paths, to gaze at her across a card table, sending subtle signals regarding the hands in play...

"How do you advise me to act toward the other ladies?"

"Oh, much the same. They aren't widows, though Miss Quinlan is something of an original, so the demands on you will be fewer. Aunt Freddy always says the best response to idle talk is no response at all, and she has weathered many a Season."

Grey had probably flung that maxim at his brothers over the years, for which he deserved to be punched by each of them in succession. "I still want to resign from the damned idiot club."

Lady Canmore patted his wrist. "You are doomed to be a good example to your peers. Sainthood is a thankless burden, but you might like having me for a friend."

The cat in Grey's mind purred at that thought. He mentally nudged the randy beast through the nearest window. "Will you enjoy having me for a friend?"

"I believe I shall, though ladies are known for their changeable opinions."

"You are teasing me." Nobody teased the Earl of Casriel. He wasn't sure he minded it—from her. "How do we embark on our warm friendship?"

She rose, and Grey came to his feet as well. "Are you attending tonight's card party?"

"I am."

"Try not to sound so overcome with joy, my lord. I will partner you for the second half of the evening, and we will bicker over farthing points, as friends do."

"I'm to *bicker* with you? A gentleman does not argue with a lady."

She smoothed his cravat. "I'm afraid you must."

"I refuse to sink to such an ungentlemanly—" He was *bickering* with her, and she was grinning at him, looking delighted with herself while she *petted* him. "Very well, a little friendly bickering."

She linked arms with him and escorted him to the front door. "If you'd ever like to reconsider, let me know."

"Reconsider?"

She passed him his hat, her expression solemn. "About the affair, of course. I haven't much experience with such adventures, but one doesn't forget the basics. I'm sure I could muddle along fairly well once we got past the first few trysts."

Minx. What a lucky man her husband had been. "If I ever reconsider, you will be the first to know." And because she'd been entirely too serene, confident, and charming for the duration of this awkward interview, Grey bent close and pressed a kiss to her cheek. "You must promise to do likewise—let me know if something more than a warm friendship would be to your taste."

She touched her fingers to the spot he'd kissed. "That is estimable flirting for a man who professes little interest in frivolous undertakings. I account myself impressed."

But not tempted, which should have been a relief. He bowed over her hand. "Until this evening, when we will plunder our opponents' coffers and flirt the evening away."

"Plundering sounds delightful. Until this evening, my lord."

"PAPA, I have told you and told you: I refuse to discuss a baronet, and I certainly won't settle for a musty old knight. A mere baron won't do either, and a viscount hardly bears consideration. I want an earl, at least. If the only available marquess were less than forty years of age, I'd consider him, but alas, he's doddering, and even my ambitions must be bounded by common sense."

Charles Quinlan shot his wife a pleading look, but Edna was absorbed with spooning peas onto her plate.

"Have you settled on a particular earl?" Charles asked his only child. Sarah was nothing if not confident in her schemes. Also beautiful.

Her beauty bewildered him, for neither he nor his dear wife were particularly attractive people. They looked, he supposed, just as a wealthy ironmonger and his lady ought to look in midlife. Comfortable, well fed, well dressed. Mrs. Quinlan had been handsome as a younger woman, her figure matronly even before she'd become a mother.

Charles had liked her figure then and liked it still, though he daren't say as much except in a whisper late at night under private circumstances.

Sarah, in contrast to her mama, was gorgeous and heard about her various stunning attributes from any callow swain with the ability to form a fatuous rhyme. Her glossy sable hair, cameo-perfect features, and stunning green eyes came together in a symphony of feminine pulchritude. The standard English roses paled in comparison to her, and when she smiled, confirmed bachelors stopped what they were doing and reconsidered their options.

"Pass the butter," Sarah snapped. "No lady of refined sensibilities can possibly endure peas without butter, and no, I have not selected a particular earl, not yet."

Edna set a plate of butter pats impressed with the letter Q at Sarah's elbow. "Surely, darling, you recall the list of names we discussed this morning? The Season is half over, and you'll want to be about your choice."

Sarah stabbed a buttery Q with a delicate silver knife, also engraved with the letter Q. "You need not remind me of the date, Mama."

Charles set down his utensils. "You will address your mother respectfully, miss, or leave the table until your disposition is equal to the challenge of a civil meal."

He rarely rebuked his daughter—of late, he rarely saw her, for that matter—but week by week, Sarah became less the little girl upon whom his sun had risen and more a petulant virago whose whims dictated the mood of the entire household.

"She meant nothing by it," Edna murmured, passing over the salt cellar.

More than Sarah's moodiness, Edna's subdued demeanor tore at Charles's composure. He'd married a quiet, dignified lady who had nonetheless brought good cheer and wifely affection to the union. Edna's counsel had proven valuable in many regards, though now she seemed reduced to *yes-dears* and *of-course-dears*.

"Do you think it's easy," Sarah began, "being paraded before the eligibles night after night? Asking over and over about favorite composers, preferred season of the year, or most delicious flavor of ice? I'm expected to be charming and gracious at all hours, even to plain-faced misses and mere misters who haven't a spare groat. I bear up despite exhaustion and the strain to my nerves, and you scold me as if I were six years old." She rose, tossing an imperious look at her parents. "Send a tray up to my room, then, for a meal in such impossible company has lost its appeal."

She stormed out, slamming the door and leaving blessed quiet in her wake.

"I was a plain mister without a spare groat," Charles observed, taking his daughter's full plate and exchanging it for his empty one. "She conveniently forgets that."

Edna took a sip of her wine. "Our beloved child disappoints me. She never sits out a dance, and her reputation as a beauty grows apace, while her recall of her manners falters."

"Perhaps we should leave Town?" Charles loved his sprawling acres up in Cheshire. He hadn't been born in the countryside, but the increasingly crowded surrounds of his native Manchester had made him appreciate open spaces and clear skies all the more.

"We cannot blow retreat at this point, sir, else all of these weeks of paying calls, staying up until all hours, and buying out the shops will have been for naught."

"We can't simply try again next year?"

Edna offered him a wan smile. "Sarah would disown us. The

young ladies are all feeling cast down because the Quimbey heir chose a widow, and not even a titled, wealthy, beautiful widow."

Charles finished the last of Sarah's peas. Cook had prepared them in fine butter sauce, which Sarah's discerning palate had apparently failed to detect, and good food should not go to waste.

"If I were a young lady of untitled pedigree," he said, "the notion that a ducal heir could plight his troth with a woman of modest origins would cheer me considerably."

Edna drew a fingertip around the rim of her wineglass. "You are not a young lady, and neither am I. They all dreamed of wearing Jonathan Tresham's tiara, and now they must endure the rest of the Season knowing they've been passed over. Sarah considered herself the best candidate to become the next Duchess of Quimbey."

"Then Sarah's wits have gone begging. No ducal family would ally itself with us, even if I had all the money in Manchester." Quinlan didn't blame the aristocrats for sticking to their own kind. He certainly preferred the company of men who understood business and weren't terrified of change.

Edna set down her drink, and by the light of the candelabra, Charles could see both the girl she'd once been and a wife growing weary of fashionable Society.

"You underestimate the extent to which these bluebloods need cash, Charles. The land rents have done nothing but drop, enclosures cost a king's ransom, and the Corsican is no longer keeping our factories humming the livelong day."

Charles had taken some military contracts, when he could do so at a handsome profit, but he'd refused the lure of becoming dependent on warfare for his livelihood. His employees had grumbled at the time, but many of them were now the sole support of cousins, parents, and in-laws who'd not been as fortunate.

"I have more money than we can possibly spend. If it will make Sarah happy, I'll part with the lot of it, as long as you stay with me."

Edna held out her wineglass, and Charles poured her another

half serving. "I married a romantic. I think you mean that, about the money."

The door was closed—Sarah's tantrum hadn't been overheard by the servants—and thus Charles spoke honestly.

"I have concluded that unless Sarah is happy, you cannot be happy, Edna. If you're unhappy, I'm unhappy too. London is all well and good, but it's not for us."

He served himself more wine. This was doubtless an expensive French vintage, chosen by an expensive French sommelier. To Charles, the wine was simply a drink to wash down the peas. Ale would have done the job just as well and more enjoyably.

"Nobody snubs Sarah directly," Edna said. "She's too pretty for them to risk that, and you are too well-to-do. The gentlemen like to be seen with her, and she is trying to be agreeable."

"But nobody befriends her, and nobody befriends you." The sooner Charles could return his family to the north, the better, though if Sarah had her way, she'd probably never set a dainty boot in Cheshire again.

Edna lifted her glass in a salute. "The titled families will befriend her settlements."

The table was laden with costly silver, French porcelain, and Venetian glass. All so much dross, from Charles's perspective, trappings to be endured until Sarah had what she craved. His greatest treasure sat at his right hand, finishing her dinner and keeping him company.

"Sarah's ambition impresses even me," he said. "She'll be ridiculed, mocked behind her back, and viewed as a sorry deviation from standards by the next three generations of her own progeny, even as her money funds their foolishness, and yet, she will have a title."

Edna patted her lips with her table napkin and sat back. "Perhaps she'll be able to make the leap, from a cit's pretty daughter to an aristocrat's wife. Sarah is determined and shrewd in her way, also beautiful, and her papa is wealthy."

Her mother was also determined and shrewd, something even Charles could lose sight of. "You've found her a viscount?"

"Two possible viscounts, and there is an earl..."

"Younger than forty? Not given to debauchery? Even for a title, I won't allow my daughter to marry a wastrel."

"The Earl of Casriel is not much past thirty, sober, responsible, reasonably good-looking, and in need of coin. He might not be able to make Sarah happy, but he could make her a countess. At the moment, she thinks that's better than happiness."

Sarah would learn otherwise, but this earl would certainly need heirs, and children might do what a title and wealth could not.

"Mrs. Quinlan, if it wouldn't be too great an imposition, perhaps you'd like to accompany this plain doddering mister above stairs, where we can discuss Sarah's situation privately."

And discuss this impoverished earl. They'd consider that gentleman until Charles knew how many sheep, acres, poor relations, and teeth he had, as well as all of his vices and his virtues. His lordship would need an abundance of virtues if he was to marry dear, sweet Sarah.

And her settlements.

CHAPTER FOUR

"You've seen Lady Canmore at her worst," Jonathan Tresham said, "and your protective instincts were stirred. That's not the same thing as"—he waved a hand in circles—"that other nonsense that can afflict a man in the presence of a woman."

"You're in my light, Tresham." Grey had appropriated the Earl of Bellefonte's woodworking shop for purposes of repairing Mrs. Beauchamp's harp. Like most repair jobs, this one was proving more complicated than it had seemed at first glance. At least in Bellefonte's workshop, Grey was surrounded by the scents of varnish, beeswax, and sawdust, which he associated with honest industry and rural pursuits.

Tresham shifted, taking up a stool farther down the workbench. "When I said your financial circumstances were not that bad, I didn't mean you could flirt with whomever you pleased."

"A gentleman can always flirt with whomever he pleases, provided he's doing so within the bounds of friendship and good manners. Where is my—? You moved my awl. If you value the present arrangement of your features, don't touch my tools."

The harp needed reconstruction, from the soundboard to the

pegs to the strings. The wood itself was in adequate condition, but the glue, screws, and strings were beyond salvation. To make music, a harp needed resonance, and resonance required sound construction.

"When you flirted with the Arbuckles at a musicale," Tresham said, "nobody thought anything of it. They are well dowered, though one can't exactly have an intelligent conversation with them, which leaves flirtation."

"I expect *one* has never attempted to have an intelligent conversation with them. Hand me that—" Grey swiped a soft cloth from Tresham's end of the bench. "I did not flirt with the Arbuckles. They flirted with me, or tried to. They doubtless found the task very uphill work."

"While Lady Canmore made you laugh, in public, more than once over nothing more than a hand of whist. She's not a sweet young thing, she isn't wealthy, and—one hesitates to mention this when sharp objects are at hand—she might not be able to provide you an heir."

Grey considered the pieces strewn about on the bench before him. He would have to put in hours of work to restore the harp, hours when he ought to be squiring Lady Antonia about, plowing through his steward's reports, or getting himself introduced to... What was her name? Quintet, Quotient, Quixote? Ah, Quinlan. That was it.

"What do you know of Miss Sarah Quinlan?"

Tresham spun on his stool, like a small boy bored with his lessons. "*Lasciate ogne speranza, voi ch'entrate.* Even I didn't consider her."

Abandon all hope, ye who enter herein. Dante's inscription over the gates of hell. "Unkind words to say about a young lady, Tresham."

"She is not a kind young lady. Her papa's an iron nabob, she's pretty, and she has no siblings to keep her conceit in check."

Siblings surely did perform that office. "Some people attribute the same factors to the aristocracy—endless self-importance, arrogance, vanity."

Lady Canmore wasn't vain, self-important, or arrogant. When

she made a droll observation, nobody's dignity suffered, nobody's feelings were hurt.

"What is this?" Tresham asked, picking up the pile of letters, invoices, and reports Grey had brought with him.

"Correspondence. Quaint English custom. Perhaps, having kicked your heels in France for so long, you're not acquainted with it. A man travels up to Town to enjoy the stink of London and bask in the gossip and buffoonery of his peers. To ensure he brings all of his rural troubles with him while he navigates the ballrooms and bridle paths, the king's mail kindly delivers bundles of problems, miseries, and laments from home."

Grey rubbed the cloth across his tin of beeswax and ran the rag over a carved piece of maple wood that would form a part of the harp's shoulder.

"The king's mail is very efficient," he went on, "if the objective is to plague a fellow no matter where in Britain he finds himself. I'll take that lot of bother to my club when I'm finished planning this repair."

"You are trying to change the subject," Tresham said, leafing through Grey's letters. "Lady Canmore is not a suitable *parti*, given that a titled man ought not to engage in trade, and you have many younger siblings who will expect your support as they embark on professions. Lady Canmore plucked your heartstrings when Lord Davington insulted her, and now you think you're smitten. The wounded dove has ever—"

Grey pitched the rag at Tresham's handsome head.

"Davington not only *insulted* her, he *assaulted* her. Tore her clothing and made lewd advances. Why you did not lay him out flat on the carpet, I will never know."

"Are all the men from Dorsetshire so violent? I was tempted, but the ladies were present."

"The men from Dorsetshire with six younger brothers learn that a certain brevity of expression, such as that afforded by a few blows, can save a lot of wasted time and noise when a contentious matter must be settled. Give me back my rag."

Tresham tossed it back and resumed sorting papers. "One generally puts correspondence in date order, Casriel."

"No, one does not. The various botherations *arrive* in date order, and then one sorts them in order of priority. My brother steward reports every lame lamb, loose-boweled calf, and discontented tenant to me, though my brother Hawthorne is on the premises at Dorning Hall to deal with the lot of it. The solicitors provide only monthly updates, but their letters convey the state of my funds and thus merit immediate notice."

"About Lady Canmore..."

Tresham was newly married and therefore an expert on everything. Babies, courting, the funds, flirting... Grey would trust Tresham with his life, but in his present mood, he could not trust himself to go a few rounds with Tresham at Jackson's.

"Fortune-hunting does not agree with me," Grey said. "Friendship with a sensible, mature, pretty woman as I navigate the business of ending my bachelorhood seems a harmless comfort amid many tribulations."

"You ask about Miss Quinlan," Tresham said. "She's tribulation in a ballgown. Her store of conversation is limited to inane questions about ices at Gunter's, which is a lure to get you to invite her for an outing there. She might inquire about your favorite season of the year. When you reveal to her what you typically do and where you will be during that season, she can plan to attend the same house party, for example. If you disclose a favorite composer, she'll learn something he's written for a soprano or for the pianoforte, and they all apparently wrote for both."

The old wood took the wax well, though several more applications would be required. "Miss Quinlan sounds pragmatic and determined."

Tresham tidied up the letters, tapping them into a neat stack against the worn and pitted bench.

"And shall you cuddle up to all that pragmatism and determination for the next twenty years? Shall you offer it a big, friendly kiss on the cheek each evening? You might muss her hair and be banished to the dressing closet for months."

"I have been sleeping in the dressing closet, so to speak, since I came down from university. It's no great hardship."

Tresham set aside the papers. "That is unnatural, Casriel. You're in your prime, a vigorous specimen, and marriage is designed to be an intimate undertaking, at least in the early years."

Perhaps this lay at the bottom of Grey's discontent. "My marriage need not be very intimate—I have a half-dozen brothers who are also vigorous specimens—but it must be lucrative."

"So you'll take a mistress?" Tresham inquired casually. "Use Miss Quinlan's settlements to live separately from your own countess?"

"Don't be distasteful. Many couples live apart for much of the year, and you are wrong about Lady Canmore."

Putting the harp together would take days, because the project could proceed only at the pace allowed by the old wood. Grey would much rather spend his time with the harp than dancing attendance on well-dowered young ladies.

"In what regard am I wrong about the countess?" Tresham took the top letter from the stack, a literary peregrination from Dorning Hall's land steward that Grey had been avoiding for two days.

"I did not see Lady Canmore at her worst when Davington so grievously disrespected her, Tresham. On the coach ride home, she was shaken, of course. What woman expects to be criminally assaulted at a Mayfair ball? But she was... ferocious, dignified, articulate, and altogether impressive. You won't have to call Davington out if he returns to England. Her ladyship will draw his cork with a quip and a cut direct."

Such a woman wouldn't disdain a man's company because he'd been in the shearing shed all morning, sweating, swearing, and wrestling indignant sheep. She wouldn't be cowed by a lot of unruly brothers-in-law, and she'd easily earn her welcome among the gentry whom Grey called neighbors.

"This is serious," Tresham muttered, staring at the letter.

"Her ladyship and I have a warm friendship," Grey replied, closing the tin of beeswax. "Our dealings are not serious, and we are agreed they cannot become serious."

"I wasn't referring to your flirtations," Tresham said. "Your dower house has burned to the ground, Casriel. Nobody was hurt, and no other buildings were damaged, but the dower house is a complete loss."

Grey snatched the letter from him and began cursing in French, English, and Latin.

"YOUR LORDSHIP IS PREOCCUPIED TODAY," Addy observed. The earl did not appear bored—Casriel was too well mannered to evidence boredom in a lady's company—but neither was his mood tease-able.

"I am returning to Dorset in the morning."

Hence the restlessness that lay more in his gaze and his tone of voice than any movement or mannerism.

"Have the charms of London paled already, my lord?"

The occasion was a picnic styled as a Venetian breakfast and thus held in the afternoon. Thank heavens the weather had accommodated the hostess's plans. Small groups of guests lounged about the lawn in wicker chairs and on blankets. A string quartet lilted through Haydn on the terrace.

Addy had been surprised to find Lord Casriel outside the conservatory, listening to another peer's harangue regarding the Irish question. She'd been even more surprised—and pleased—to accept the earl's invitation to admire the roses.

"London's greatest charms are limited to present company," he said, "and Hyde Park on a sunny morning."

Addy examined her escort more closely, noting faint lines of fatigue around his eyes and the beginnings of grooves bracketing his mouth. He had apparently offered her honesty, which in its way was more flattering than flirtation.

"You are homesick," she said. "Heaven knows I grow homesick for Surrey. I sometimes tell the maple at the foot of my garden how badly I miss an honest forest. All we have in London are the lone specimens permitted to give shade, provided their roots don't disturb any walls or foundations. Hyde Park is an exception, but it's often a crowded exception."

"And noisy," Casriel muttered, "and heavily scented with coal smoke, and yet, homesickness is not what sends me back to Dorset. My dower house was struck by lightning and is a charred ruin. The storms in Dorset are magnificent, though from all accounts, it hadn't even begun to rain."

"Hence the fire was unchecked by a handy downpour. I am so sorry. Let's sit a moment, shall we?"

The garden was peaceful, the roses not quite in their glory. An occasional precocious bloom waved gently in the sun, though most buds were yet furled. Casriel found a bench in the shade and—surely this was a coincidence—out of view of the house and lawn.

"Tell me about your dower house, my lord."

He stretched out long legs and rested an arm along the back of the bench, a man settling in to weave a story.

"We played hide-and-seek in the dower house by the hour as children, and when my grandmother was alive, we learned the tea ritual in her parlor. She taught us manners and made it a game, or not a one of us would be received in polite society. My sister Jacaranda and I learned to dance in that parlor, while my grandmother called the steps from the pianoforte."

"Happy memories, then."

"For the most part. Grandmother could be very articulate regarding a boy's lapses in decorum, but by nature she was loving and merry. She gave me my first harp and insisted Papa hire a proper music master when I began to show an affinity for the instrument. She died the year I went to public school."

His first harp, his first dancing lessons, his first course in manners... No wonder Aunt Freddy's company appealed to him.

"I hope that harp survived the fire."

He crossed his legs at the ankles. "I sold the harp. It was an antique, more beautiful in appearance than in musical ability. The proceeds went to repairing the dairy and the laundry on our home farm."

A valuable harp, and one that had to have carried sentimental weight. Let that be a warning to any woman setting too great store by casual friendship.

"Did you replace your first instrument with another?"

"We still have a great harp in our music room at Dorning Hall. My sister Daisy occasionally plucks out an air. She lives not far from the family seat. My brothers call upon her when I'm in need of a lecture, and Daisy obliges over tea."

Casriel missed this sister, he missed Dorning Hall. The wistfulness with which he spoke of them was as plain as the grass growing up through the brick cobbles of the garden path. Relentless, and both obvious and easily overlooked by passersby.

"If you travel to Dorset, will you return to London, my lord?"

"I must."

Addy waited, because this was a conversation between friends, not vacuous small talk. Clearly, Casriel had considered abandoning London altogether and had scolded himself out of the notion. For him, she was disappointed. For herself, she was pleased.

"I attended this gathering," he said, "because the thought of truly fresh air, fragrant with the scents of the garden and field, appealed strongly, also because Tresham agreed to introduce me to Miss Sarah Quinlan."

Pain lanced through Addy, useless and undeniable. "Miss Quinlan is very pretty." An Incomparable, though would Miss Quinlan have earned that appellation without incomparable settlements? Without youth, which promised many fertile years to whomever she married?

"Dorset is prettier."

Addy laughed. "You are a squire in earl's clothing. Maybe that's what I like about you. I was raised in a country vicarage, and I miss it sorely. I knew who I was there, didn't have to convince anybody of my status, over and over. Beneath my finery, I'm a vicar's hoyden of a daughter, not some widowed countess with a Mayfair abode."

"At heart, you are a delightful woman. Have you no dower property of your own?"

Every rose has its thorns. "The current titleholder is my husband's younger twin brother. They were not cordial. Shall I introduce you to Miss Quinlan?"

Perhaps Casriel wasn't that eager to meet Miss Quinlan of the gorgeous settlements. He stayed right where he was, as did Addy.

"Is that unusual, for twins to be estranged?" he asked.

Addy never discussed this aspect of her marriage. Not with her friends, not with Aunt Freddy, not with the maple at the foot of the garden.

"For twins to be at daggers drawn is unnatural, I think. I told my husband as much, but on this point, he could not be swayed."

"I cannot fathom estrangement from a sibling. Did their father divide them?"

Perceptive man. "Emotionally, geographically, every way he could. From the time they left the nursery, the old earl treated Roger as the heir and Jason as an upper servant. I gather the boys were close once, but that ended when Roger was sent to public school, and Jason remained at home with the occasional tutor. Jason did not accept his fate passively, and thus the competition began."

Though Jason made a conscientious earl, and Addy's refusal to occupy the dower house was not for lack of an invitation from the current countess.

"My brothers compete," Casriel said, "but in the face of a threat, they become a Roman guard of shared fraternal honor. All for one, and so on, until there's only one biscuit left, and then it's back to fisticuffs and insults."

"You miss them, and their fisticuffs and insults."

Addy caught a whiff of his lordship's shaving soap as he reached past her to snap off a white rosebud. "I will miss you when I'm back in the wilds of Dorsetshire, though Dorset hasn't any real wilds. We have some dramatic seacoast, but the rest of the county is tame by the standards of any self-respecting adventurer."

Addy took the rose, though the bloom should be put in water. "You're flirting again. That suggests the loss of the dower house is a setback, not a tragedy. How will you explain your absence from Town?"

He resumed frowning, which was easier for her to bear than his flummery. "The loss of the dower house is a considerable setback. For the past ten years, if we had coin to spare, I spent it mostly on restoring the dower house."

"Are you giving up on your quest, then?"

"My quest?"

"To find a bride."

"Why would I give up...? Damn. I take your point. No prospective countess worth her coronet should favor the suit of an earl without a dower house. I could fall off a haystack next summer, and then where would she be?"

He climbed haystacks, which in some parts of Britain were piled higher than houses, though they weren't nearly as sturdy.

"What purpose will a trip to Dorset serve, my lord? Surely your family and your staff have the matter in hand."

This question occasioned a brooding glance. "My brothers have penned letters, warning me not to come around, kicking at the wreckage and muttering. They claim I'm needed here more, particularly if Sycamore bides in London."

"But you want to go home." While Addy wanted him to stay, which was very foolish of her.

"I am the earl. When I mutter and muck about at Dorning Hall, my tenants and family know that all will proceed in a predictable fashion. I'm not shy about getting my boots dirty either."

"You work in the hayfields?" She'd like to see him, chaff in his hair, coat off, a touch of sun burnishing his complexion.

Shirt off...?

"I typically fork the hay up from the wagon to the stacker because height is an advantage for that task. Ash and Willow are also forkers, Thorne has the knack of stacking, Valerian hangs about in the shade and gives orders, while Oak prefers to drive a team. You must never tell a soul that the Dorning brothers labor beside their tenants. We also assist with shearing, though I leave plowing to those born to the art. We brothers compete, but it's friendly competition. I'm sorry your husband and his twin were not close."

He was offering Addy an opportunity to share a confidence. He was also refusing to let a difficult subject drop.

"Roger died in a curricle accident."

"My condolences. They are notoriously unstable vehicles."

Also very light, which made them ideal for racing. "He was trying to beat Jason to Brighton, and he had a substantial lead. He would have won, though he took a curve too fast at the bottom of a hill. He lived for a few hours, long enough to pen me a note. I kissed him good-bye one morning expecting he'd return within the week, and I went to bed that night a widow."

Addy often recounted the circumstances of her husband's death —an unfortunate, though not uncommon, accident—but she'd never brought up Jason's role in the tragedy.

"That is a stupid, irresponsible, unpardonable way to die. Are you still angry with him?" Casriel's vehemence revealed a sternness behind his polite conversation and pretty gestures. Sternness was attractive on him, damn the wretched luck.

"One doesn't speak ill of the dead, my lord."

"One doesn't dissemble before one's friends, Beatitude."

She liked it when he used her name, liked it rather too well, and yes, she had been furious with Roger, but not for an accident that might have happened to anybody.

"My husband thrived on taking risks, testing limits, and breaking rules, else he'd never have married an unsuitable woman. Shouldn't you be searching out Mr. Tresham?"

"Tresham is easy to find." Casriel rose. "One simply looks for Mrs. Tresham, and there he'll be, simpering witlessly at his wife."

"Are you envious?"

He smiled and extended a hand. "Torn up with jealousy. You?"

She took his hand and stood. "Witless simpering has never been my preference from a man, but Miss Quinlan might find it attractive."

"That would be unfortunate for my aspirations," Casriel said, tucking Addy's fingers over his arm. "I'm good with a hay fork, can coax a tune from a harp, and hold my own in the shearing shed, but the witless simper has eluded me."

"That is *not* unfortunate." Addy had to stretch up to kiss his cheek, but she managed it. "I'm sorry about your dower house. I won't say a word to anybody." She gave him a squeeze, because some of his dearest memories were now charred ruins.

"Thank you." He held her for a moment, a bit closely considering the embrace was merely a friendly hug. "We'll manage. The Dornings always do."

She stepped back and passed him the rosebud. "Best of luck, my lord. Safe journey to Dorset."

He tucked the rose into his lapel. "I don't suppose I'll be traveling to Dorset after all. That would announce my bad fortune to all my prospective countesses and their mamas. They'll disdain my addresses in favor of the handsome baronets."

He was half joking; Addy was half angry at him for that. "Heaven forbid that a woman should see you as worth marrying, despite your lack of a cottage or two. Good day, my lord."

She did not hurry, or flounce, or stomp away—only young women engaged in such foolish dramatics—but neither did she turn around to take a final, admiring glance at the rose garden.

"THE DOWER HOUSE is the first edifice a visitor sees when calling on Dorning Hall," Grey said. "I wanted the interior to live up to the promise of the exterior."

Mrs. Fredericka Beauchamp twitched at a paisley shawl of green, gold, and blue. "In my youth, I spent a few days with your grandmother. She was the countess then, very much in love with her earl. I was the unfortunate, untitled, unwealthy young woman who had failed to merit Society's notice in either of my first two Seasons. The countess was quite kind."

Mrs. Beauchamp had received Grey in a little parlor that felt rife with memories. Sketches adorned the walls, a sampler or two among them. Above the fireplace, cutwork had been framed behind glass, the paper yellowed with age, the glass dingy. The carpet wanted beating, and the hearth was overdue for sweeping. The room smelled of dust and ashes, making Grey wish he'd brought fresh flowers.

"Grandmother was a dear," Grey said, "and she loved the dower house. The third earl had it laid out in the Elizabethan E, though she used only one wing."

Now, visitors would see a scorched pile of bricks, stone, and lumber when they turned through the front gates to the Hall. Ash had sent another letter, detailing the damage. The building was gone, not a wing left standing.

"Can you rebuild?" Mrs. Beauchamp asked.

"Not any time soon. We have a handsome cottage, Complaisance Cottage, that my sisters claim will do should we need a dower house."

Grey's hostess gestured to the tea tray. "Perhaps you'd pour out. That teapot is heavy."

The teapot was delicate porcelain, very likely antique Sèvres, based on the glazing. Grey obliged, serving the lady a cup not quite full. Her hand shook minutely, a characteristic Grandmother had developed toward the end of her life.

"You must first find a countess before anybody can need a dower house," Mrs. Beauchamp said. "I hear you are seeking to address that oversight."

Had Beatitude told her that? Lady Canmore, rather. Grey must not think of her as Beatitude. He did, however, think of finding a countess as remedying an oversight, which flattered neither him nor his prospective wife.

"The earldom's finances needed improvement before this fire, a goal marriage can often address. I had planned to let out the dower house later this year, and the attics contained considerable inventories of furniture, art, and appointments."

All gone, and the loss was sentimental as well as financial. The greatest blow, though, was to Grey's pride.

"You blame yourself," Mrs. Beauchamp said, pouring half her tea into the saucer and then back into her cup. She set the cup down without taking a sip, a few drops having splashed onto the tray. "You are a dutiful man, so you feel responsibility for what can only be called an act of God. Why do the great minds of the day tell us women are the fanciful gender?

"I always thought dower houses were uncivilized," she went on. "A woman gives her best years to raising a family, and then, just as the grandchildren come along, she's relegated to a moldering pile out of sight behind the stables, with only the lazier servants for company."

"You say that to be shocking, madam. I owe my countess a dower house, a place of quiet respite when her children are grown."

The old lady fished around between her hip and the chair, producing a set of knitting needles trailing blue yarn.

"Oh, right. Did you ever ask your grandmother if she'd prefer to dwell where her grandchildren were growing up, rather than at the foot of the drive? Did you ask her whether she wanted to be parted from her firstborn son and sent packing just as he took a bride who could have used an ally? Of course not. Your grandmother went quietly into old age, because she was another dutiful Dorning. Your mother let her go, because God forbid a young woman new to marriage should enjoy a bit of decent company among strangers. Have some tea."

Grey poured himself half a cup, casting around for a change of subject. He had not devised the customs of the aristocracy regarding aristocratic widows. He was merely heir to them.

"Your harp should be ready next week."

"That harp actually belongs to Beatitude, though she prefers the pianoforte. I gave it to her when she was twelve, and nobody has looked after it."

The harp had been in sorry condition when gifted, then. "Why pass along an instrument that's not at its best?"

"You haven't heard that harp, my lord. A humble appearance can hide a mighty soul. I suggest you indulge in a few airs before you return it to me." Her knitting needles moved in a steady rhythm, while her conversation was becoming a series of lectures.

"Do you know of a Miss Sarah Quinlan?" he asked.

Mrs. Beauchamp whisked the scarf or shawl or whatever she was creating across her lap. "An Incomparable, by all accounts, which usually means the lady is pretty, vain, and well dowered, also in her first Season. When all those assets fail to win her a match, she must cede the field to the next Incomparable, to whom she will invariably *be* compared. You should drink the tea if you pour it out. Only old women dwelling alone on limited means pour tea back into the pot."

Grey took a sip. "So you don't know Miss Quinlan personally?" He hadn't yet been introduced to her, Tresham and his lady having left yesterday's Venetian breakfast by the time Grey had abandoned the rose garden.

Mrs. Beauchamp's needles stilled. "Oh, I know Miss Quinlan. Her poor mother sits among the dowagers and wallflowers while Miss Quinlan reigns on the dance floor. The girl is spoiled, immature, and not that pretty. Her eyes are an interesting color, granted, but they look out on the world without kindness or joy. I suspect the bills she runs up at the modiste are incomparable. She will develop some humility over the next few years, if the bachelors are sensible enough to avoid her."

Sensible and *bachelors* did not strike Grey as a likely pairing. He mentally shuffled Miss Quinlan to the bottom of his deck of potential countesses and felt ungentlemanly for even that much selfishness. If needs must, he'd marry the devil's handmaiden, lest innocents suffer because he'd shirked his duty.

Though what sort of mother would the devil's handmaiden make for his offspring? "What of Lady Antonia Mainwaring?"

Mrs. Beauchamp resumed knitting. "Lovely woman. She's refined, gracious, of an appropriate station, and wealthy in her own right. Quite well read too."

So why did the notion of winning her favor leave Grey so unmoved? "I ought not to be discussing this topic with you, but a man likes to know the particulars before he attempts to socialize."

And he could not ask Lady Canmore.

Mrs. Beauchamp snorted. "Your grandmother would have scouted the terrain, cleared out the hostile parties, and saved you a good deal of waltzing and whist."

Grey had yet to waltz with Lady Canmore and had promised himself he'd avoid that torment. "You've been very helpful, ma'am. Shall I ring for somebody to take the tea tray?"

"No, thank you. Just about the time it's cool enough to drink, the maid will come for it. If you are determined to repair the earldom's fortunes through an advantageous match, you must be considering the Arbuckles."

They figured in Grey's nightmares. "Lady Antonia seems more likely to find happiness dwelling in Dorset."

Mrs. Beauchamp yawned behind her hand. "I have not met such a gentlemanly specimen as yourself in quite some time. You put me in mind of my dear Romulus. Such a fine man, but it wasn't meant to be."

What was she going on about? "I'll take my leave of you," Grey said, rising. "Thank you for your time."

"Dash off if you must, young man, but mark me on this: There is more to life than duty, and marriage is for a very, very long time—especially if you make the wrong choice."

"I'll remember that." He bowed his farewell and saw himself to the front door, finding no servant on duty there. In more modest households, the housekeeper often answered the front door, and it might be half day for Mrs. Beauchamp's butler, porter, or footman.

Grey retrieved his hat and walking stick and took himself out into afternoon sunshine, which could never match the Dorset sun for brilliance. At least today's breeze blew the stench of the river away from Mayfair rather than directly at it.

Please God, let the courting soon begin, for Grey honestly detested spending time in London.

Lady Antonia Mainwaring was lovely, in her way, and of a suitable station to become his countess. The Arbuckles were a more daunting prospect, and—based on Mrs. Beauchamp's advice—Miss Quinlan was not to be considered.

Grey set his mind to planning out a courtship of Lady Antonia, complete with whist and waltzes. His good intentions were repeatedly nudged aside by the memory of Lady Canmore kissing his cheek, then leaving him alone in the garden to practice his witless simpering.

CHAPTER FIVE

"I know now why you considered a repairing lease in Hampshire," Addy said.

Theodosia Tresham opened her parasol. "The charms of London can pale."

Addy opened her own parasol, linked arms with Theo, and set a course for the ornamental lake at the foot of the grade. Lady Brantmore's fête was an annual institution, and Addy usually enjoyed a day away from London.

The gathering began with a luncheon al fresco, graduated to an afternoon of outdoor entertainments, and finished with a ridotto. Guests arrived and departed throughout the festivities, depending on whether their tastes ran to archery, picnics, dancing, or gambling.

Through it all, people laughed, flirted, and wandered in couples and small groups along the nature walk and into the vast, rambling Brantmore country house.

Addy was wandering as well, along the edges of melancholy and annoyance.

"The Season always arrives as such a relief," she said. "After the dreariness of winter, London comes back to life. Parliament sits, the menfolk argue their politics, the dancing begins, and..." And she watched another crop of young people make the same mistakes she and Roger had.

"And then you realize," Theo replied, "that the discussions at the formal dinners closely resemble the discussions held for the past five years. The gossip all begins to sound the same as well, and you're listening mostly to make sure your own name doesn't come up. How are you, Beatitude?"

Lonely. Upset. Unable to stop searching the crowd for a certain tall, determined earl.

"I am well." Addy didn't need to ask how Theo fared. Marriage to Jonathan Tresham had put a bloom on Theo's cheeks worthy of a debutante at her presentation ball. "Aunt Freddy is fading."

"I'm sorry. She has been a fixture for so long, it's hard to imagine her spirit diminishing. She will be much missed."

That response was characteristic of Theo: kind, pragmatic, less comforting than Addy might have wished.

"Her situation makes me realize that I don't want to become a fixture myself, Theo. You kept your hand in with the social nonsense because you have a daughter and sister who will eventually make their bows. I look around at the same inane activities year after year, see most of the same people, and wonder: What am I doing here?"

She fell silent as Mr. Fortunatus Tottenham strolled around the turn of the path, Lady Demeter Montgomery on his arm. They made a beautiful couple, though the lady was a good ten years her escort's junior.

Tottenham bowed, and as always, his gaze made Addy uneasy. She smiled and curtseyed, plagued by the same thought a Tottenham sighting always provoked: How much had Roger told him about the realities of marriage to a vicar's bumpkin daughter? How much had Roger told any of his endless legion of cronies and intimates?

The couple continued on their way. Rather than resume progress around the lake, Addy took the side path that led to a shady bench.

"You don't like him," Theo said. "Mr. Tottenham seems agreeable, but then, a certain variety of male excels at seeming agreeable."

"I have no reason to dislike him. He and Roger were great friends, and Mr. Tottenham was solicitous during my period of mourning."

Theo settled on the bench, and even in that casual movement, she displayed more grace and relaxation than she'd had as a widow on the fringes of polite society. "Did you consider marrying Mr. Tottenham, Beatitude?"

"Never." *Nor will I ever.*

"Are you considering marrying Lord Casriel?"

Addy had not allowed herself to ponder that question. "One cannot consider marrying a man whose only interest in one is friendship. Attempting to do so embarrasses all concerned."

Theo closed her parasol and propped it against the bench. "I recall a certain widowed countess telling me that we'd grieved our first husbands long enough, that we were due for a little *adventure.* Can Casriel serve in that capacity?"

"I haven't inquired." Addy had made a passing joke, and Casriel had not been amused.

"You want to."

Wasn't this what a close friend was for? Sorting out difficult emotions, offering well-intended advice?

"I watched my husband racket from one adventure to another, Theo. He had a talent for embracing life, ignoring talk, and leaping into every day. His joy remained unabated, whether he won or lost, looked a fool, or prevailed against daunting odds. I loved that about him." *At first.*

"While you were the sensible one. Sense makes a dull bedfellow."

"This is true." *Had Roger felt that way?*

"You are tempted by Lord Casriel."

"Casriel is not merely dutiful, Theo. He's honorable. He will try his utmost to be a worthy husband to any woman he marries, whether she sincerely esteems him, or has accepted his suit simply so that her daughters will have the title of lady."

"A fortune hunter with a conscience. A rare breed."

A conscience, patience with little old ladies, loyalty to his many siblings, a way with a flirtation... "Theo, I am at risk for foolishness."

No sooner had Addy admitted that than the inspiration for her restless dreams ambled around the bend in the path. Lord Casriel escorted Lady Antonia Mainwaring, an earl's daughter who had an independent fortune, and who appeared all too comfortable at Casriel's side.

"Ladies." His lordship bowed. Her ladyship curtseyed.

Lady Antonia was damnably pretty when she smiled.

"Mrs. Tresham," her ladyship said. "I have been hoping to cross paths with you. Did you know that my favorite lending library is on the very next street over from Mr. Tresham's town house?"

Theo rose, and Addy got to her feet as well, rather than feel as if the other three were talking around her.

"I have visited the library once," Theo said. "The ducal collection is notably devoid of recent novels."

Lady Antonia unwound her arm from his lordship's. "If you will excuse me, my lord, Lady Canmore, I would like to abduct Mrs. Tresham for a short chat about the library's Neighborly Committee."

"What an interesting name for a committee," Theo replied.

"Nearly a contradiction in terms," Lady Antonia said. "May I explain?"

Theo and Lady Antonia were soon strolling in the direction of the lake, deep in conversation, leaving an odd silence behind.

"We have been abandoned in one another's company," Lord Casriel said. "Are you pleased or vexed?"

"Both. You?"

"Lady Antonia is all that is gracious," he said. "She's also quite knowledgeable regarding Greek and German philosophers, medical science, and female theologians of the Middle Ages."

He sounded bewildered, and Addy's mood lifted marginally.

"Did you regale her with your expertise on sheep farming and hay stacking?"

"One had not the opportunity. Would you care to view the lake with me?"

That small, sharp pain Addy was coming to associate with him pricked her heart. "I should demur on the grounds that Mrs. Tresham forgot her parasol, and I must return it to her."

"I see. Well, then, shall I escort you back to the house?"

Perhaps Casriel did see and was again being every inch the gentleman. Addy treasured him for his honorable nature, though she could not endure another moment of his gentlemanly politesse.

"I would like to have an affair with you, my lord. Are you similarly inclined toward me?"

"HIS LORDSHIP IS VERY PLEASANT COMPANY," Antonia said. Casriel was also wonderfully tall and solid, not a maypole of a man. "He's a patient listener."

Mrs. Tresham paused and looked around. "I forgot my parasol. Jonathan gave it to me, and I'd rather not lose it."

Oh, to be sentimentally attached to a parasol. "I can assure you, Mrs. Tresham, Lord Casriel will see to your parasol. He'll likely return it to you personally, not send it 'round with a footman or porter." The earl had that attentive, hovering quality good escorts were supposed to have. Lady Antonia esteemed him for it, truly she did.

She and Mrs. Tresham came to a rise in the path that overlooked the ornamental lake, a small body of water gleaming blue under sunny skies.

"I'm told the Dorning menfolk have fine manners to go with their distinctive eyes," Mrs. Tresham said. "Jonathan and Lord Casriel are cordial, though I'm not well acquainted with the earl."

Jonathan this, Jonathan that. Newlyweds were charmingly devoted.

Drat the lot of them.

"The Dornings have interesting names as well," Antonia said, though this idle talk was not getting Mrs. Tresham to accept a place on the Neighborly Committee. "I can't recall them all. Willow is the fellow who likes dogs, isn't he?"

"Willow Grove Dorning. Seems a pleasant sort and devoted to his lady. There's an Ash, a Sycamore. One of the sisters is named Jacaranda."

A future duchess would take note of such things. Antonia was more interested in enjoying a rare day away from Town and recruiting for the library committees. The path ringed the lake, and between clumps of trees and scenic breaks in the shrubbery, other guests could be seen taking the air.

"Would we scandalize the company if we took off our boots and cooled our feet in the water?" Antonia asked.

Mrs. Tresham was a pretty, dark-haired woman, though even besotted with her husband, she had a serious air. "Is that why you dragooned me away from Lady Canmore's side? To coax me into getting my toes wet?"

To add a future duchess to the Neighborly Committee, Antonia would do much more than dip a toe in the lake.

"You're a respectable widow now married to a ducal heir. If you got your feet wet, nobody would remark it. I'm an unmarried heiress. If I did something so bold, everybody would comment, but the bachelors would still leave me no peace."

Mrs. Tresham took up a perch on a slab of granite at the edge of the trail. "Was Lord Casriel disturbing your peace? Is that why you seized upon my company? He strikes me as a decent sort, not the type a woman must flee."

And therein lay the problem. "He likely is a very decent fellow, but I can sense when a man is interested in me and when he's trying to be interested in me. I maundered on and on about Galen and

Paracelsus, Hildegard von Bingen and Héloïse d'Argenteuil. Then I brought up the Stoics and Marcus Aurelius, thinking surely Lord Casriel would have an opinion or two to defend, for the classics are part of every university education."

Mrs. Tresham undid the lace of one boot. "You said he is a patient listener."

"Do you like it when a man listens to you patiently?"

Mrs. Tresham toed off her boot. "Better than impatiently. Why aren't you removing your boots?"

Antonia took the place beside Mrs. Tresham. "Are those our only options? Patience and impatience from men? Are we children? Doddering dowagers? Why could his lordship not argue with me on any point? Why not challenge my opinions regarding women as the proper stewards of theological thought?"

Antonia yanked at her boot laces, surprised at her own ire.

"A gentleman does not argue with a lady," Mrs. Tresham said, setting her boots aside.

"Do you argue with Mr. Tresham?"

The great Leonardo da Vinci would envy Mrs. Tresham her smile. "Oh, definitely, and we make up. We also agree to disagree and we tease and twit one another. Jonathan has a subtle but wicked sense of humor, which can make disagreeing with him quite entertaining."

The surface of the lake was a calm mirror, into which Antonia longed to toss her boots and Mrs. Tresham. *I want to drop my husband's name all over every conversation. I want to love even the ways he aggravates me.*

"If I were to look for a man," Antonia said, "note the conditional, I'd look for a man who listens to me, not out of duty or manners or in preparation for flattering me, but because he enjoys my company. That wish is absolutely reasonable." She got her boot off and started on the second one.

"You have concluded, after half a circuit of the lake, that Lord Casriel is not such a man?"

"I concluded as much before we'd finished our first waltz. He's polite, even charming, and next Season when I see Miss Quinlan swanning about as his countess, I will wish I had encouraged him."

Mrs. Tresham reached under her skirts to peel down her stockings. "You're sure you and Lord Casriel wouldn't suit?"

"We would suit—merely suit. I would gradually learn not to inflict my philosophers on him. He would give up discussing politics with me—if that's what holds his fancy. I could end up with a daughter named Lady Dandelion Dorning, and that would drive me to establishing my own household in Paris. He'd visit me in spring and tell me how his personal hedgerow of brothers fares."

Civilized, pleasant, and utterly inadequate compared to Antonia's dreams. She wasn't sure Lord Casriel had dreams, other than perhaps a new roof for his hall.

Mrs. Tresham draped her stockings over her boots. "Then you must be frank with his lordship, if you think he has courtship in mind. Tell him you are not interested."

Antonia rolled down her stockings and stood barefoot on the cool grass. "I would like to be courted, in theory, though not by him. Is that frank enough?"

"Tell him that. You and he would not make each other happy, and you wish him every joy, but you cannot be the woman to share a life with him."

"Rejection sounds very sensible, even kind, coming from you."

Mrs. Tresham advanced toward the water gently lapping against the sandy bank. "Tell him you are enamored of a Frenchman, somebody his lordship has likely never met."

"Somebody named Abelard?" A philosopher, theologian, and fool.

"Abelard will do nicely. Now, let's enjoy the water, shall we? Jonathan has paid more than one compliment to my ankles, if you can believe that."

"Somehow, Mrs. Tresham, I can believe your husband has done exactly that."

~

THE SUN SHONE at the same angle as it had a moment ago, the water on the lake rippled beneath the same gentle breeze, and yet, Grey's world had endured a seismic shock.

"You would like to have an affair with me," he said slowly. Then, to make sure he hadn't indulged in wishful hearing, "An intimate affair?"

Lady Canmore glowered up at him. "Is there another kind?"

"I would not know."

She stalked along at his side. "You've *never* enjoyed the company of a woman outside the bounds of wedlock?"

"By London standards, I am retiring when it comes to those sorts of amusements. I have learned to be, and I have my reasons."

Lady Canmore took him by the hand and dragged him down a barely visible side trail. For a small woman, she was strong.

"The hermit's folly is this way," she said. "What do you mean, you have your reasons? Reasons to be a monk? I have been a monk for the past several years. Monkdom loses its charms. If you think that makes me fast or vulgar or unladylike, then I think such an opinion makes you a hypocrite. There's not a man in Mayfair who doesn't indulge his appetites to the limit of his means, and a few beyond their means. Roger told me swiving is all many men think about."

"I most assuredly think about it." That admission was not polite. Not gentlemanly. Not... what Grey had intended to say.

Her ladyship came to an abrupt halt in the middle of the trail and let go of his hand. "You do? You think about it with *me*?"

Oh, how that smile became her, how that light of mischief transformed her gaze. "You have broached this topic, my lady, but are you certain you want to pursue it in present company?" A gentleman had to ask, for the discussion would soon pass the point where her overture could be dismissed as a jest or flirtation.

"You haunt me," Lady Canmore replied, clearly displeased with her own disclosure. "Men I've been dancing with for the past eight years now strike me as lacking stature, though I myself am short. When I arrive at a gathering, I look for you, even though all the way to the venue, I tell myself I must not do that. You and I are engaged in a semblance of a friendship, I remind myself, only a friendship. Which reminds me. Are there any new bets?"

She resumed walking. Grey fell in step beside her.

"Your strategy has been successful," he said. "No new wagers, save for one that involves my brother Sycamore. His notoriety has made him Peacock in Residence at my town house, and he wasn't a pattern card of humility to begin with."

Lady Canmore took a turn off the path that Grey would have missed. She knew where she was going, while he was increasingly lost.

"I don't want to be your mistress," she said. "I want to be your lover."

Grey almost sagged against the nearest oak. "Do you frequently make such announcements in the same tone of voice most people reserve for discussing the Corsican, long may he rot in memory?"

The way ahead opened into a clearing that held a small three-sided stone edifice on a slight rise. The surrounding woods had been carefully manicured to give the folly three views. One looked out over the lake, another toward Brantmore House. The third faced the woods sloping away to the east.

A circular portico framed the interior of the folly, where benches provided a private place to rest.

"I am not happy with myself for becoming interested in you," Lady Canmore said. "But there it is. You are kind, gentlemanly, and a fine male specimen. Your flirtation is original without being prurient or presumptuous. You dance well. You humor Aunt Freddy. You love your siblings. You are not afraid of hard, physical work. In fact, I think you need it to thrive."

She paced before the folly, listing attributes that made Grey's heart ache. She *saw* him, saw him clearly, and appreciated who and what she beheld.

"You are the comfort of your aunt's declining years," Grey said, "a ferociously loyal friend, a minister's daughter who has learned how to manage polite society without being seen to do more than smile and chat. If I had to choose one word to describe you, that word would be courageous. I can't help but watch you, even when you dance with others, because you have such inherent grace. I see you walking away, and I know I have nothing to offer you, but I want to call you back, every damned time."

She came to a halt before him. "My lord, what are we to do?"

"My name is Grey, and as for what to do... I would like to kiss you."

The anxiety and bewilderment cleared from her gaze. "Excellent idea, for I'd like to kiss you too."

NOTHING HAD BEEN RESOLVED by this excursion to Lady Brantmore's folly, but Addy gazed up at Lord Casriel—Grey, he had given her leave to use his name—and a sense of rightness edged out all doubts and frustrations.

A kiss was harmless, precious, or nothing. A kiss was whatever she and Casriel chose to make of it. A kiss was a place to start or a farewell, but it was a kiss, and she'd share that much with him at least.

Her perceptions sharpened, gilding the moment with possibilities. The scent of the lake was a mere undertone, overlaid with the lush aroma of the forest in spring. The fragrance of Casriel's shaving soap blended with the scents of greenery and sunshine, adding a faint tang of sandalwood.

Amid the quiet of the trees, the air stirred, leaves fluttered, birds flitted overhead. A forest was a busy place despite the sense of privacy. Nestlings tried their wings this time of year, babies ventured forth under the eyes of cautious, watchful parents.

Addy stepped closer to Casriel, more aware than ever that he was a fine specimen indeed. Roger had been athletic, but slimmer, shorter, less muscular. A genteel example of manhood, not this robust, unapologetic masculinity writ large.

"Ladies first," Casriel murmured. His gaze was somber, though his eyes told another story. He was teasing her, *daring* her even.

She kissed his cheek. He remained unmoving, apparently determined that she decide when and how the journey began. She liked that, liked that he had the self-restraint to be still while she explored. On her next foray, she pressed her mouth to his, then she slid an arm around his waist inside his coat, seeking the warmth and shape of him.

He was hard muscle and soft wool, shelter and temptation.

"You torment me," he said, hands still at his sides. "I will have revenge, Beatitude."

"May you have it soon and often." She wrapped her arms around him and settled in for an adventure.

Casriel enveloped her in an embrace, drawing her against the unyielding plane of his chest. Addy could not have wiggled free if she'd wanted to, and she did not want to, not ever.

His hold on her was implacable, strong enough that dammed-up yearning broke free inside her.

"Casriel, I want..."

He seemed to know what she needed, bringing their bodies together in a fashion that left no doubt that he desired her.

Oh yes, please. To be held securely, to share the madness of mutual plundering. Addy opened her mouth, ready to devour Casriel until she'd satisfied an appetite years in the making.

He rallied, drawing back slightly, kissing the corner of her mouth. "We're in no rush."

His revenge was patience, stealth, and the slow slide of his hands over her back and bottom. All the while, he kissed her, sometimes lazily, sometimes voraciously, until Addy could only hold on to him and endure the pleasure.

I needed this. I needed this with him. The thought wafted by as desire crested higher, followed by the idea that Casriel was wearing too many clothes. The damned man seemed to sense even that thought, for he gently seized both of Addy's hands in his, stepped back, and rested his forehead against hers.

"You are a formidable kisser, madam."

She had been married, and Roger had had a rake's full complement of expertise in the bedroom. A single kiss should not have stolen her wits and left her breathless.

"I thought I wanted to have an affair with you," Addy said.

"And now?"

He wasn't even winded.

"I know I do."

Casriel straightened, kissed Addy's hands, and moved away. He smoothed his fingers through his hair, putting right what Addy had mussed.

"An affair would not be wise, my lady."

And now, when she needed him to tease her—she was almost certain teasing came after kissing—he was back to being the serious, polite earl. The change was so sudden and absolute, Addy had to prop her back against the solid granite of the folly.

"When is any affair wise?" she asked. "I do not understand you, my lord. You kiss me like a soldier returning from years at war, and I kiss you back in the same fashion. You desire me, and I..." Drat the man, she *more* than desired him. She longed for his company, loved to hear the sound of his voice, wanted to fall asleep to the rhythm of his breathing. "I want you."

Worse than that, she *trusted* him in some fashion that could not end happily.

Casriel came close enough to tuck a lock of her hair behind her ear. "For me, it's worse than simple wanting. I want an apple. I want a nap. When it comes to you..."

He was unhappy about his feelings, which cheered Addy. "So we will become lovers?"

He dropped his hand. "I would like that, if I might be permitted an understatement, but you must know that I bring nothing of value to such an arrangement, and nothing can come from it."

Addy waved a hand. "I don't want gifts and jewels or evenings at the theater causing talk and speculation. I want—"

His gaze was so solemn, caution stopped her from elaborating.

"My lady, while I respect you greatly and desire you madly, I must inform you that my affections are claimed by another, and in all fairness…"

He ran his hand through his hair again and looked about, as if not sure how he'd come to be in the middle of the woods, alone with a woman.

His words rang in the quiet, and Addy reeled with their impact. *My affections are claimed by another? By another?*

"You kiss me like some… some… oversized lordly houri, when you esteem another woman? Did you misplace that esteem in the undergrowth, Casriel? Leave it back in the men's retiring room? You esteem *another*?"

She drew back her hand to deliver a stinging slap, not only on her own behalf, but on behalf of the woman who'd been betrayed by that passionate kiss. The *other* woman who'd been betrayed by that kiss.

Casriel caught her by the wrist, his grip firm without hurting. "Beatitude, let me explain."

"I will have no explaining, my lord. If you are secretly married, have a mad wife living in the attics at Dorning Hall, or you became engaged as a boy, that is no concern of mine. I was under the impression you were considering marriage as one possible future option. You *gave* me that impression, and I concluded that you are as yet free to enjoy my company. I was wrong."

He still held her wrist, though Addy knew she could free herself with a raised eyebrow.

"I don't refer to that sort of affection. I am unmarried, I have not proposed to anybody, and I an not engaged, but I have a daughter. She holds my heart in her dainty palm, and if my brothers and tenants weren't reason enough for me to go courting a fortune, hat in hand, then Tabitha alone would inspire my efforts."

Two thoughts whirled through Addy's mind, neither of them happy. Of course he had a daughter. The sense of purpose, the focus, the patience, the maturity... He was a parent. Addy had been attracted to those qualities without considering the whole constellation of characteristics.

The second thought was unworthy of a lady, but honest. *I might have competed with a fortune for Casriel's affections, with a woman who held a higher status, a prettier woman, a younger woman.*

I cannot compete with a daughter.

"Will you please allow me to explain, my lady?"

The *please*, the polite, gentlemanly, earnest *please*, penetrated Addy's hurt. "You may explain, and then we must return to the gathering."

She retrieved her hand from his grasp and fixed her gaze on the smooth, blue expanse of the lake in the distance.

"HE'S HERE," Drusilla murmured. "A man that tall stands out, and I know I saw him on the far side of the lake."

"With Lady Antonia," Anastasia replied. "A woman that tall stands out too. Is that your second piece of cake, Dru?"

Her third—the pieces were small. "Mind your own portions, sister. I'm not worried about Lady Antonia. If she sets her cap for Lord Casriel, she'll go about it carefully and discreetly. It's *La Quinlan* who concerns me. She'll pounce like a wolf, and we'll never see her spring."

Anastasia pushed her strawberries around with a silver fork. "We could try to compromise him. I'd be willing to kiss him."

Anastasia had been willing to kiss more than one gentleman last Season. She'd kept her willingness under wraps so far this year, much to Drusilla's relief.

"We're too petite." Not short. *Never* short. "For you to kiss Lord Casriel in a compromising fashion, he'd either have to be willing, or you'd have to stand on a chair and grab him by the ears. One can't compromise a man while appearing ridiculous." Drusilla doubted Anastasia had much insight into how to *make* a man willing to be kissed.

"We could tell him about our settlements."

Mama had made sure both of her daughters knew what they were worth, and they were worth a good deal. "That's not good *ton*, to discuss money. We're barely twenty. We aren't desperate."

Anastasia set aside her plate. "I am desperately bored, Dru. Looking pretty, batting my eyelashes, waltzing with whoever presumes to ask... This is not how we discussed being out. Not how we discussed it at all."

Drusilla picked up the discarded plate and dumped the strawberries onto her own. "Our ballrooms were awash in crown princes. We wore only gorgeous dresses, danced to only full orchestras, and rode in only magical coaches that we shared with the noblest, handsomest, best-dressed, and best-natured of the princes, but we are not princesses, Ana."

Ana plucked at her spencer. She'd chosen the blue today, which went nicely with her eyes. Drusilla had taken the green, though it washed out her complexion. Tomorrow was Drusilla's turn to have first pick of outfits, though that whole business struck her as childish.

If Papa was so wealthy, why couldn't each daughter have a separate wardrobe?

"Lord Casriel isn't a prince either, Dru. I'm willing to see him married to you, but I cannot abide the notion that Miss Quinlan gets him."

"He's not a pretty bonnet in a shop window. Maybe none of us will get him." None of them had earned Mr. Tresham's notice, which still made Drusilla uneasy. Perhaps mental instability ran in the Tresham family, for the current Mrs. Tresham was neither beautiful, nor wealthy, nor young. She did not have a gorgeous voice. Her family was not high up in government. She'd been a complete nobody making up the numbers and had stolen a march on all of polite society.

Anastasia rose and opened her parasol. "Casriel must marry somebody. Mama said, and she is never wrong. Let us enjoy the fresh air, and we're bound to cross paths with his lordship not far from the house. The lake is only so large, and even Lady Antonia can walk only so slowly."

Drusilla downed a handful of strawberries all at once, grabbed her parasol, and linked arms with her twin. She nearly choked on the strawberries, but no ripe fruit should be allowed to go to waste. Mama said that too.

CHAPTER SIX

How could Grey explain what he'd never had to put into words before?

"Her name is Tabitha," Lady Canmore said, no trace of emotion in her voice, which was in itself telling. Her ladyship took the sun-dappled bench that faced the woods, the best choice for privacy. Grey came down about six inches from her, a distance between presuming and polite.

How fitting that he and Lady Canmore have this honest, intimate discussion in a setting that offered relief from London's unrelenting stench and stupidity.

"Her name is Tabitha Ann Dorning," he said, "though we call her Tabby. She is fourteen years of age, the product of a youthful departure from all good sense and moral decorum. Tabby went off to a private school in the midlands last autumn, the better to form the sorts of acquaintances that will help her overcome the stigma of her birth."

He hated even saying those words. *The stigma of her birth.* Why didn't Society refer to a child bearing the stigma of a father's selfish stupidity? Her mother's rash impulse?

"You did not want her to leave your household."

"Rather like Wellington did not want to be defeated by the French, but Tabby was lonely at Dorning Hall, her harp her only consolation. No cousins, no siblings, and she's too well born to make friends with the tenants' children. The gentry households welcome her, but only as a favor to me, not because they'd allow their daughters to genuinely befriend her."

Lady Canmore's profile was a perfect study of female repose, save for knit brows. "What brings you great joy—to rusticate with your herds and siblings—brings your daughter sorrow. That must be painful."

Grey's brother Willow might have noticed that heartache, but he would never have spoken of it.

"Tabby's governess tried to tell me that I could not protect my daughter forever, and the sooner Tabby found a place in the world, the better off she'd be. I did not listen. Then I came upon Tabby practicing the hairstyles she'd seen in some ladies' magazine. She was thirteen, and I thought of her very much as my little girl. With her hair up in curls and ringlets, I saw that I was wrong. My little girl—who likely is as tall by now as you are—had already departed from Dorning Hall. Her ghost was wafting about, waiting for me to grieve my loss."

"How did you ever let her go?"

"I made a complete hash of it, of course." The recollection still hurt like hell. "I escorted her to her school, saw that her trunks were carried up to her room, lectured the headmistress at length about the standard of care I expected for my daughter, kissed Tabby on the forehead, and told her to be good and to write to me."

"And then?"

"I returned to my coach, very much on my dignity, and tried not to look back."

"But you did look back?"

"Waved my damned handkerchief out the window like a shipwreck survivor trying to flag down a rescue vessel." Grey felt compassion for that poor papa with the ache in his throat, wanting to protect, needing to let go. The memory was touching without quite being humorous.

"I realize," he went on, "that five years from now, I might be walking my darling child up the church aisle, handing her happiness into the keeping of some spotty boy. The notion is insupportable. I was a spotty boy and not worth a place on the bottom of most women's slippers."

Lady Canmore patted Grey's thigh. "Tabitha has six uncles, my lord, and her father is an earl. Not just any spotty boy will take on those odds."

Her touch was brisk, meant to comfort—and it did. "I hadn't thought of that, that my brothers would for once serve a greater purpose than to vex me and burden the exchequer."

"Is Tabitha's school expensive?"

"Dreadfully." Which admission came close to whining. "The headmistress educates the girls as if they were the legitimate offspring of their titled parents, and the students include the children of many wealthy gentry and cits. No appointment is spared: dancing masters, language tutors, drawing masters, a stable of good horseflesh so the young ladies will learn to ride and drive if they don't already have those skills. Tabitha is encouraged to continue her devotion to the harp, though she must acquire other graces as well. I inspected the premises thoroughly. No child is housed in a musty garret, though the girls do sleep six to a room."

"You chose well."

Nobody had said that to him, not ever. "I chose carefully. I visited twice without notice, and both times, Tabby was pleased to see me and also—I fear—relieved to see me go."

"Someday, my lord, you might feel the same about Tabitha, or about your grandchildren when they visit with their mother. I gather Tabitha's situation is part of the reason why you are determined to marry lucratively."

Lady Canmore offered no judgment with that conclusion, though

Grey judged himself. "Tabby will need a substantial dowry. She is an earl's daughter who cannot claim the title lady. On that one word, her fortunes can fall."

"I see." Carefully neutral, suggesting Lady Canmore did not see at all.

"I know what you're thinking," Grey said. "I've had nearly fifteen years to set aside funds for my daughter. Even a modest amount in the cent-per-cents would grow over that length of time. I set aside what I could. When Tabby was three, the steward ran off with the entire contents of our safe. When she was five, I had to settle my late father's debts, which were substantial. When she was ten, a dam broke on a neighbor's property, and half my water meadows became swamps. I had to buy fodder or watch my herds starve over a particularly hard winter, then we had failed harvests. In every case, the only reserves I'd managed to save were those funds set aside for Tabby."

The air was soft, the sun gentle, and Grey did not want to return to the gathering. His disclosures to Lady Canmore had been painful, but not for the reasons he might have anticipated. She did not castigate him for his folly, did not ask for the stupid details of his youthful error. She listened, and she took his situation to heart.

Would the woman he eventually proposed to do as much?

"Perhaps Tabitha's lack of fortune is for the best," her ladyship said. "You want Tabitha to be happy, and marriage to a man who looks only at her settlements won't guarantee that."

A nightingale sang out, a rare sound in daylight, except for those few weeks when the unmated male sought to woo a lady. The song was poignant and clear, a beautiful solo against the backdrop of the forest breezes.

"I do want Tabby to be happy," Grey said. "I all but insist upon it, though my arrogance on the matter doubtless tempts the Almighty to dash my hopes. Any number of men could make her happy, but without a substantial dowry, her choices will be unnecessarily limited, for many of those men come from families who won't consider her separate from her settlements. Then too, a dowry's purpose is to secure a woman's well-being for the entirety of her life and even to add to the fortunes of her offspring. For that reason too, I want Tabby to be well dowered."

"Your intentions are good," Lady Canmore said. "We can't say the same about mine."

She was smiling, a little sheepishly, which made Grey want to either kiss her or thump his head against the granite wall.

"Are you plotting to overthrow the Crown, my lady?"

Her smile dimmed. "I invited you to have an affair with me."

"Is the invitation still open?" Grey wanted it to be. Wanted to have some happiness and comfort—some damned intimacy and pleasure—before going meekly to his fate.

And he wanted Beatitude to rescind her offer, because as surely as Tabby's funds kept disappearing into the bottomless pit of Dorning Hall's expenses, an affair with the countess would be painful to conclude.

Though conclude it Grey would, and before he so much as offered for another.

"The invitation is still open," her ladyship said, as the nightingale fell silent. "Until such time as you are obligated elsewhere, I would like our friendship to become discreetly personal."

Her neck turned pink, then her cheeks, while Grey found pleasure in the moment. The countess listened to him. She knew the truth of his situation and didn't see him as some princeling on a snorting charger.

Even so, she sought his intimate company.

"I don't think you need to worry that I might present you with another dependent," she went on. "I was married for five years to a very vigorous man and never conceived. Roger's mother said that was God's judgment upon me for getting above myself."

"Roger's mother was a damned idiot."

Lady Canmore brushed a shy glance over him. "I thought so too, but I was raised in a vicarage. My ability to blaspheme wants work."

Grey rose and offered his arm. "I do not blaspheme when I say spite is the province of small-minded fools. For all your mother-in-law knew, her precious son was the party upon whom the Almighty was casting judgment, if judgment was cast on anybody. How do we go about having an affair?"

He ought to have been blushing as well to speak so bluntly, but the question wanted asking. It very much wanted asking.

"I am not sure."

He drew her ladyship down the steps, but she stopped two higher than he, so she was eye to eye with him.

"This is your first affair?" he asked.

She nodded, gazing off toward the lake. "I haven't been a very merry widow. Haven't been tempted."

"This will be my first affair as well. Tabby's mama was a maid at the local tavern to whom I, in a fit of seventeen-year-old dementia, proposed marriage. She was several years my senior and had no intention of giving up her freedom when she could instead line her purse as my paramour. She ran off with a tinker when Tabby was eleven months old, and her family presented me with the child. My papa didn't so much as blink. He took the baby, pronounced her a Dorning, and passed her to me. I've had encounters since then, never an affair."

"I am your first?" Lady Canmore asked.

"And I am yours."

Not a first love, not a first spouse even, but they were something new and special to each other. Grey took comfort from that, while Beatitude grabbed him by the hair and helped herself to a kiss.

"COME, Mama. It's time we take the air." Sarah Quinlan grasped her mother's elbow quite firmly and headed north on the lakeshore path.

"My dear, we have been taking the air for half the afternoon."

Mama was short and thus had to be encouraged to walk more quickly.

"Of course we have been taking the air. The rumors are apparently true regarding Casriel. He prefers outdoor activities, which is perfectly acceptable to me, when a husband and wife living in each other's pockets is most unfashionable. His lordship went this way, Lady Antonia on his arm. Lady Antonia just went into the house with Mrs. Tresham, meaning his lordship is either unaccompanied, or he's taken up with that plain, chubby widow Lady Canmore."

To make matters worse, the Arbuckle twins, joined at their matching reticules as usual, had disappeared onto the lake path not fifteen minutes past. Sarah would have gone in search of the earl herself, except a young lady didn't dare traverse a woodland trail without a companion.

"The advantages afforded to widows are really most unfair," Sarah said. "Mama, please stop dragging your feet. I have an earl to catch."

Mama came to a halt. "Daughter, mind your tongue."

Oh bother. Mama still occasionally tried to assert parental authority, as did Papa. A countess need not listen to anybody, which was half the reason Sarah had fixed her sights on Casriel. That, and he promised to be manageable. Everybody said he was a truly perfect gentleman, which was what they had to say when he was a truly rolled-up gentleman with a title.

Sarah tossed out a placatory smile and resumed walking. "Mama, nobody will hear me, and we have always been honest with each other. Casriel needs me. He needs a wife who knows how to manage a large household, who won't bother him when he wants to go shooting for weeks at a time, or spend his evenings with the House of Lords. I do fear my darling earl will end up with an Arbuckle or Lady Antonia if I'm anything less than diligent about my pursuit of him."

"Honesty and cruelty are worlds apart, Sarah. Lady Canmore wasn't born to a title, and she has suffered a bereavement. She has no children to comfort her, and she is very attractive in a way a mature man would appreciate."

Mature was a problem. Casriel wasn't ancient, exactly, but Sarah wanted to get the heir and spare part of the marriage over with before he became much older. One had to be practical about those matters.

"I'm sorry, Mama. I should not have been so blunt, though you must admit, blue-eyed blondes are plentiful, while my looks do set me apart."

Mama had never been a beauty. She did not grasp what a burden befell a woman who turned every head in the room, some with appreciation, many with envy, a few with the wrong sort of covetousness. Sarah occasionally danced with the covetous men simply to torment them, which was... the closest she came to diversion at a formal ball.

"If you are not careful, Sarah, you will be set apart by your waspish tongue and the desperation with which you seek to gain the notice of your betters."

Mama had become tiresome within two hours of Sarah's return from finishing school, though recently... tiresome was a vast understatement.

"Waiting for a duke or marquess to wander my way hasn't worked, Mama. I thought perhaps Mr. Tresham would take notice of me, but his tastes are apparently not as refined as I'd hoped." Another plain widow had snabbled the ducal heir, more's the pity.

Good heavens, what if marrying widows became *fashionable*?

"Sarah, you are young," Mama said, another one of her frequent laments. "Your father and I did not marry until I was one-and-twenty. You have time. There are other earls, other heirs. If you focused instead on developing an acquaintance with men of suitable station, a proper friendly acquaintance, of course, rather than poring over Debrett's and reading the scandal sheets, perhaps—"

Mama stumbled, probably because she was a little out of breath from trying to keep up with Sarah's longer stride while she lectured.

"Mama, do be careful. This path is not well maintained, considering the traffic it must bear. Where can Lord Casriel have got off to?"

And where were the Arbuckles? At the very worst possible

moment, they'd doubtless come giggling and bouncing from behind a tree, spoiling the day with their sly innuendos.

"I believe that's his lordship on the bench up ahead overlooking the lake," Mama said, "sitting with Lady Canmore."

"Then we are not a moment too soon. Look as if you are fond of me."

"I *am* fond of you, for the most part. Your father—"

"*Not now*, Mama." The less said about Papa, the better. Sarah adored him, of course, and was very grateful that he'd managed to pile up a lot of lovely money—about which one must never speak—but Papa was common, blunt, and plain. He had the fashion sense of a dead mackerel and grumbled about every expense. The less he was mentioned in proximity to the earl, the better.

"Good day," Sarah called, waving gaily. "Lady Canmore, my lord." She and the countess had been introduced, as had Mama and the countess. Now the countess would have to introduce Sarah to the earl.

How perfect.

Casriel rose and bowed. "Ladies. It's Mrs. Quinlan, if I'm not mistaken, and Miss Quinlan."

Oh, he was being a bit bold, dispensing with the introductions, but then, this was not a formal gathering, and he was *an earl*. Perhaps he was eager to make the acquaintance of the Season's most eligible heiress?

Lovely thought. "My lord." Sarah swept her most graceful curtsey. Mama ruined the effect by bobbing at the same time. "A very great pleasure to meet you. Have you been enjoying the beauties of nature?"

He and the countess had been sitting a proper distance apart on the bench, not even speaking. When a woman hadn't any conversation, what else was there to do, except admire the scenery?

"I have indeed," his lordship replied. "The wonders to be found in the immediate surrounds bring joy to my bucolic soul."

Lady Canmore's lips quirked, though his lordship's comment had not been humorous. It had, in fact, been moderately adept flirting, considering that Sarah was the only wonder in the immediate surrounds.

More loveliness. "I have ever enjoyed fresh air and sunshine," Sarah said. "Mama says young ladies must mind their complexions, but I say that's why we have parasols."

"That reminds me," Lady Canmore said. "I should return Mrs. Tresham's parasol." She brandished a lacy affectation.

"Allow me that honor," his lordship said, plucking the parasol from the countess's grasp. "I'll leave you ladies to enjoy the view."

Bowing and curtseying ensued, though Sarah did not like the look on her ladyship's face. For an older woman, the countess had a nice smile, and her eyes... They were plain blue, but they sparkled like the lake beneath the afternoon sun. Perhaps age did that for a woman, gave her sparkly eyes as a consolation for sags and wrinkles.

"Oh, look, Anastasia!" a voice cried. "We'll have company for the rest of our walk."

Drusilla the Dragon churned up the path, Awful Anastasia at her side, while the earl remained with Lady Canmore by the bench.

Her ladyship smiled at the twins as if she was honestly glad to see them. "Miss Arbuckle, Miss Anastasia. Good day. I was just about to return to the house. Perhaps you'd like to join me."

"A fine idea," the earl said, "though perhaps Mrs. Quinlan and Miss Quinland would like to continue around the lake?"

"I rather would," Sarah said, sending him her best limpid gaze. "The day is so lovely and the company fine."

"Then I'll leave you and your mother to the fresh air," he said. "Lady Canmore and I can return to the house with the Arbuckles."

He bowed, offered Lady Canmore his arm, and Sarah was left with nothing to do but curtsey and smile as if her dearest wish had just been granted.

"Come, Mama," she said. "If we want time to rest before tonight's dancing, we must be on our way. I do hope to see you on the dance floor, my lord."

He was not a particularly bright man, for he appeared puzzled rather than pleased. "I'm afraid I cannot stay for the evening's dancing. A debate on the Corn Laws demands my attention. Perhaps another time."

The Arbuckles were looking mutinous, which was delightful. Lady Canmore was smiling vapidly, and Mama's gaze promised more lectures.

Sarah curtseyed. "I will look forward to the happy occasion of a shared waltz at another time, my lord."

Much bobbing of bonnets transpired, and then his lordship was sauntering up the path in the company of not one but three women, all of them eligible in the strictest sense, and yet, Sarah considered the encounter a victory.

"You are happy with that exchange?" Mama asked.

"Most assuredly. I made a positive impression, and his lordship was so enchanted with the prospect of gaining my acquaintance, he did not wait for proper introductions. That is very encouraging."

Mama set a spanking pace now, when Sarah's stays were digging into her sides and she needed time to ponder this opening skirmish.

"You believe the earl to be enchanted with you?"

"He is reputed to be a perfect gentleman, Mama. What perfect gentleman ignores a countess when she's on hand to make introductions? We know Lady Canmore, she knows him. She should have introduced us, but his lordship didn't want to bother with the niceties. Normally, I would take such presumption as disrespect for me, but we are at a glorified picnic, and everybody knows who I am."

"I'm not sure I know who you are of late."

The path took a turn, which let Sarah steal a peek over her shoulder. The twins were gamboling along like puppies behind their elders, while Casriel politely escorted the countess as the senior female.

A husband with a title and manners would never unduly impose on his countess, and though Mama might profess some confusion on the matter, Sarah knew exactly who she was.

She was the next Countess of Casriel. Let there be no mistake about that.

"NO PROGRESS WITH MY HARP, THEN?" Aunt Freddy asked, twitching at the quilt over her knees.

"I did not discuss your harp with his lordship," Addy replied, rearranging the various scent bottles, brushes, and combs on Aunt's vanity. She had received Addy in her boudoir, a custom that had been popular during an earlier age. A lady would entertain even gentlemen callers in her bedroom of a morning and chat over tea while her toilette progressed.

Back when ladies and men could be friends without causing raised eyebrows and unkind talk.

"What did you discuss with Lord Casriel, Addy? If you say the weather, I will cut you out of my will."

That frequent threat sat ill now. Aunt Freddy was pale, even for her, and the armchair by the window gave her a translucent quality, as if she'd already sent part of her spirit on to another realm.

Addy took the other armchair. "Lord Casriel has a daughter, Tabitha. She's only a few years from leaving the schoolroom and the darling of his heart. She's apparently something of a harp virtuoso in the making. Would you like to work on your knitting?"

"You shall take up my knitting for me today. One heard talk, ages ago, that the eldest Dorning had been a tad indiscreet. Some of those boys are wild—that Sycamore is a throwback to his great-grandfather —but the rest of them seem susceptible to domestication."

Based on Aunt's tone, she was not complimenting the majority of the Dorning brothers.

"I suspect Lord Casriel might have been a throwback too," Addy said, "but then the younger siblings kept coming along, his one venture into wild behavior resulted in a child, and he became a good example instead."

A good example whom she had propositioned. "He kissed me, Aunt." Addy hadn't meant to say a word about her tryst with Lord Casriel to anybody.

"About time somebody kissed you. Roger has been gone long enough. I hope his lordship's overture was welcome?"

"The overture was mine. His lordship's attentions were very welcome." Addy had remained with him in the folly, kissing and kissing and kissing like a couple new to courting. He was patient, he was plundering, he was inventive and determined, finding sensitive places on Addy's body that surprised her.

The inside of her elbow, the hollow of her throat, the nape of her neck. Casriel's hands were callused—she loved that his hands were callused—and yet, his touch could not have been more tender. In bed, he would be... beyond words.

"Addy, you have not worn that look since you and Roger courted, if even then," Aunt said. "Perhaps you should marry Casriel."

"He needs money. I haven't but my widow's mite." A comfortable mite as mites went, along with the London house, a matched team of solid bays to pull the Town coach, a riding mare, and a standing invitation to Canmore Court, but nothing an impecunious earl should marry for. "I have no interest in remarrying, Aunt."

"You have an interest in Casriel and in his kisses. Marriage generally starts out exactly like that. Do you like him, Addy?"

The question was far from prosaic, no matter how innocently Aunt tucked her shawl about herself.

"Who would not like a gentleman with perfect manners, a title, and such an attractive countenance?" Not handsome in the refined sense, but a face that had been lived in and would weather well.

"Brummel was a good-looking devil with exquisite manners," Aunt said, "also an utter toad on occasion and a profligate rake. Nobody was sorry to see him decamp for France."

"Except his creditors, who were legion." Which was the aspect of Casriel's situation that made Addy also not like him. He was determined to marry for money. Her rational mind understood the utter necessity of having coin enough to provide for dependents, especially for a young female dependent. Her heart, though... Her lonely, stupid heart... She wished for his sake that he need not be so mercenary, and she wished that she could afford a more sentimental view of life too—not of marriage, but of life in general.

"A man must provide for his family, Addy. You cannot in one breath admire Casriel's paternal devotion to a by-blow and in the next castigate him for taking responsibility for the child. She's a girl, which is lucky. She'll marry well enough."

Addy opened Aunt's workbasket, which sat between the chairs, and took out the current knitting project. "Tabitha will marry well if Casriel dowers her well."

"Just so, particularly if he marries a woman both sensible and well born. That color blue goes with your eyes."

Casriel had lovely eyes, not only for their color, but also for the emotion they conveyed. He had a sly sense of humor—admiring the wonders of nature, indeed—and he knew how to keep the upper hand with Miss Quinlan. He did not know how to go about having an affair, and neither did Addy.

"Aunt, how does one conduct a liaison?"

Freddy yawned behind a pale hand and closed her eyes. "In your situation, one conducts a liaison discreetly. Back in my day, we weren't such possessive fools about marriage. Men did not treat their wives like chattel to be locked away in the attic until the right holiday came along to put the wife on display before the relatives. We were friends with our spouses, allies, companions, and lovers as well."

Roger had endorsed such an approach to marriage, calling Addy the family nun when he was feeling like a brat.

"I'm sure everything between the genders was conducted more sensibly back in the day, but how does one conduct a discreet *affaire de coeur* now?"

"That Casriel doesn't have the whole business planned is a point in his favor."

I know that. "That I don't have the whole business planned must be a point in my favor, then."

Aunt opened her eyes and studied Addy. "The trick is to be casual, but not too casual. Careful, but not too careful. Either excessive sneaking about or excessive flamboyance will cause notice, and notice will cause talk. Casriel can simply pay a call on the servants' half day. Nobody will be above stairs save yourself, and you can receive him at the door as you would any caller when the staff is employed with other duties. If you can't puzzle out the rest—"

"You will disown me."

"In addition to cutting you out of my will. Is today Tuesday?"

"Wednesday."

"Then dear Mr. Ickles will be calling this afternoon. What time is it?"

The clock on the mantel was easy enough for Addy to see, though Aunt's eyesight was apparently not equal to the task. Her solicitor was a good ten years her junior, meaning he was venerable rather than ancient.

"Not yet noon."

"Then I have plenty of time to make myself presentable. Send the maid to me in an hour or so."

Addy finished off the row of stitches and rolled the half-finished shawl around the needles. "Aunt, did you eat breakfast today?"

"I would not know. Ask the housekeeper. I usually do, and I am not hungry, so one concludes I ate recently. Did Roger ruin you for any other man's attentions, Beatitude?"

Another question more complex than it sounded. "I esteemed my husband greatly and welcomed his affections."

"Silly girl, do you think it's impossible to esteem a man greatly and want to strangle him in the same hour? Roger was not a bad man, given his privileges, but he lacked exactly the quality you find so attractive in Casriel. Casriel grasps that with privileges come respon-sibilities, and he does not shirk his responsibilities."

Not quite accurate. "Roger desperately wanted an heir. That was very responsible of him. I could not provide one." Three short sentences that waltzed over years of unspoken disappointment on Roger's part and then arguments, tears, and miserable silences.

"Roger had a brother and a fraternal nephew," Aunt observed. "He thus had an heir and spare. He had no need to worry for the succession."

Roger also had no by-blows that Addy knew of, suggesting that Casriel had been right: Paternal limitations had prevented concep-tion, rather than anything amiss with Addy. The issue had not been the succession, however. The issue had been Roger's pride and the need to best Jason at every turn.

"I'm having the kitchen send you up a luncheon tray," Addy said. "Don't let Mr. Ickles overstay his welcome. You need your rest."

Aunt waved a hand. "Go prepare for your torrid assignation, my dear. Casriel looks like a man of healthy appetites. You'll need your rest."

"Naughty, Aunt Freddy." Addy kissed her cheek and left her sitting in the midday sun, pale as a ghost and already nodding off again.

The conversation saddened Addy and hadn't offered her much enlightenment regarding the specifics of a discreet affair. Despite Addy's assurances to Casriel, she needed to take precautions that would make conception less likely and had little idea what those precautions might be.

Theodosia Tresham would know. Of all the ironies, Theo had dreaded the prospect of a second child during her first marriage. Paying a call at midday was not quite the done thing, but Theo was a dear friend, and time was of the essence.

Casriel did not need another by-blow, and Addy would not wish illegitimacy on any child, though she longed to be a mother. Six months before his death, Roger had given up on that dream, at least as it related to Addy becoming the mother of the next Earl of Canmore.

She gave the maid instructions to fetch Aunt a full lunch tray, allow the older woman an hour's nap, and then to make sure Mr. Ickles did not stay more than thirty minutes.

CHAPTER SEVEN

"But how does one conduct such a liaison without starting talk?" Grey asked. "My last venture into an intimate arrangement had unintended consequences, not the least of which was years of gossip."

Tresham was trying to teach a very large dog to roll over. The beast—Comus by name—was trying to teach Tresham to surrender bits of cheese for no more effort than a raised paw or thump of the tail.

Grey's money—if he'd had any to spare—would have been on the dog.

"What sort of consequences?" Tresham asked, making a gesture with his hand. "Sit, Comus."

Comus woofed encouragingly.

"The sort of consequences that go off to finishing school and then make a quiet come out without being presented at court."

Tabitha was approaching adulthood at the speed of a galloping horse, or Grey might never have gone fortune hunting. One of his sisters, Jacaranda, had married well enough to assist with Tabitha's introduction to Society, but Jacaranda had her hands full with her own family.

More to the point, she hadn't offered to help and she bided in London less and less.

"You have a by-blow?" Tresham asked. "Sit, Comus."

"I have a daughter born outside of wedlock. The term by-blow sits ill with me. At the time, I intended to marry her mother and live happily ever after." The words of a naïve and randy youth.

"What did her mother intend?"

"To live happily on a lifetime of lordly largesse, kicking her heels with whichever local lads caught her fancy, apparently. She ran off with a tinker before Tabitha could walk. I've been sending her parents a quarterly sum to compensate them for the loss of their daughter's labor at the posting inn, but that's hardly restitution for the mischief I caused."

Comus was enjoying himself thoroughly, from all appearances, swishing a plumy tail and propping on his back legs.

"Casriel, do you honestly think a tavern wench several years your senior took you for her first lover?"

Grey moved a small porcelain figure taken from Botticelli's *Venus Anadyomene*, complete with clamshell. He set her on the mantel out of tail-swishing range, and though she was pretty enough, Lady Canmore had more generous breasts, sturdier shoulders, and altogether lovelier eyes.

Her ladyship also had a fine sense of the absurd and wasn't shy about letting a man know he was desired.

"Whether Tabitha's mother chose me as her first or her fortieth is hardly a relevant or gentlemanly inquiry. I chose her, and my choice had consequences."

"A liaison could have consequences. This is the most dunder-headed canine ever to chase a rabbit."

The notion of a child with Lady Canmore troubled Grey, not because more progeny would be inconvenient and expensive—all family was inconvenient and expensive, also dear—but because Beatitude would be a wonderful mother. He would never try to entrap her into marriage, nonetheless...

A man could still dream, apparently, all practicalities to the contrary. "If you have no useful advice to impart, I'll be on my way. Please don't forget to give Mrs. Tresham her parasol."

"I have advice," Tresham said. "Don't marry for money, or not only for money. Marry for friendship, attraction, and joy."

"None of which will rebuild my dower house, pay for my daughter's come out, or put new roofs on my tenant cottages, all of which are pressing. How is Sycamore managing at The Coventry Club?"

Tresham shoved the dog's hindquarters to the carpet. "Sit, damn you."

"Woof." *Pant-pant-pant,* while the dog resumed capering about.

"Why don't you ask your baby brother, if you're curious about his fledgling efforts to manage a club?"

"A gaming hell, you mean. I don't ask because Sycamore's pride is delicate, and one doesn't want to pry." One feared to pry, because Sycamore might view a casual question as an opening to ask for a "small loan." When made to Cam, those loans never, ever seemed to be repaid.

And yet, Grey recalled too well the years of being a young fellow without means, one who was expected to comport himself about Town as a well-dressed, sociable sprig.

"I don't pry either," Tresham said, waving a piece of cheese before the dog's nose. "Sycamore must run the club as he sees fit, without unsolicited meddling from me."

The dog's great head wagged back and forth, attention fixed on the cheese like Sycamore fixed on a pretty woman.

"So you have no idea how he's doing? You still own The Coventry, don't you?"

"I own the property and fixtures, but my posture is that of landlord. I've asked the staff not to involve me beyond that role, and they have respected my wishes. Theodosia has set notions about gambling establishments, and I have set notions about keeping my wife happy."

"I wish you better success with that endeavor than you're having as a trainer of dogs."

Grey's brother Willow was a trainer of dogs, and a damned good one. Will had imparted enough knowledge that Grey had to take pity on the poor dog, who was being patient beyond anything Tresham deserved.

Grey plucked the cheese from Tresham's grasp. "Comus, sit."

Comus cocked his head, then sat.

"Good boy," Grey said, hunkering to put the cheese at carpet level. "Down, Comus."

Comus went down on all fours. Now came the delicate part. Grey moved his hand as if about to rub the beast's belly, and Comus obligingly rolled to his back. A slight temptation with the cheese and the roll continued to complete a side-to-side half circle of very large dog.

"You *rolled over.*" He gave the dog the cheese and a pat on the head. "Excellent work, Comus. Good boy for *rolling over.*"

Tresham scowled thunderously, while Comus adopted the hopeful look of patient dogs the world over.

"If you conduct a liaison," Tresham said, "with as much confidence and dispatch you show when handling that mastiff, the object of your affections is a very lucky woman indeed."

"I'm rather hoping *she* will go about the business with confidence and dispatch, while I do the tail wagging and panting. I'll see myself out."

Tresham resumed being trained by the dog, while Grey counted the visit a general waste of time. He'd returned Mrs. Tresham's parasol, learned nothing of Sycamore's financial situation, and gleaned even less about—

He stopped on the landing of Tresham's stairs, for a lady had come to call and was removing her bonnet.

"Lady Canmore, good day."

She beamed at him, and his heart sped up. Stupid, stupid, stupid, but there it was. If he'd had a tail, it would have been wagging hard enough to topple furniture.

"My lord, this is a pleasure. I had intended to call upon Mrs. Tresham."

He descended step by step when he wanted to leap the distance or slide down the bannister. "I believe Mrs. Tresham is from home. Might I escort you to your next destination?"

The butler remained discreetly silent, holding her ladyship's bonnet. Perhaps Mrs. Tresham was out. More likely, a ducal butler had more sense than Grey's servants.

Which was a problem when a discreet liaison sat at the top of a man's list of immediate priorities.

Her ladyship took the bonnet back from the butler. "Thank you, my lord. Today is half day for my servants, and I'm sure my footman would rather while away the afternoon with a pint at the pub than indulge my social schedule."

That was for the benefit of the butler, surely. Grey accepted his hat and cane, escorted Lady Canmore to the walkway, and waited while she dismissed a sizable fellow in livery. The footman gave Grey a dubious look, bowed, and marched off as ordered.

"*Is it* half day at your abode?" Grey asked, when he should have been inquiring about the lady's health or the weather or some damned pleasantry.

God, she smelled lovely. All flowery and wonderful, like Papa's scent garden on a still summer day.

"Today is half day for all but one kitchen maid, my lord, and she does not move about above stairs unless specifically summoned."

Grey offered his arm. "Beatitude?"

She sauntered along, her arm entwined with his. "Perhaps you'd like to come in for a cup of tea, or share a plate of sandwiches?"

"Most kind of you. As it happens, my schedule allows me that pleasure."

She slanted a glance at him under the brim of her bonnet, and Grey sent up a prayer that he could escort her to her doorstep without breaking into a dead run.

"WE SHOULD TELL GREY." Ash Dorning tossed a pencil onto the blotter and stared at the stack of calculations before him. Neither he, Oak, Valerian, or Hawthorne had taken the seat behind the desk. At Dorning Hall, they gathered in the earl's study out of habit. They yielded Papa's chair to Grey out of an instinct for self-preservation.

He who occupied the earl's chair carried many burdens.

"Maybe Sycamore will have the needed funds," Oak ventured. "He's good with figures and works his skinny arse off when he's motivated." Oak was the natural administrator of the group, able to see how a project ought to go, step by step. He didn't begin an endeavor until that path was clear before him. He painted in the same fashion, staring into space for hours or days before embarking on the simplest landscape, which invariably turned out to have details and subtleties that revealed themselves only upon careful study.

"Sycamore larks the day and night away when he's not motivated," Valerian replied from a worn chair before the desk. "He was last motivated months ago, when the issue was leaving university for the blandishments of Town."

"Cam is new to managing The Coventry," Ash said. "He won't have the sum needed."

"That leaves us." Hawthorne was the only one of them taller than Grey and more muscular. He was their plowman, the voice of truth amid a lot of banter and horseplay. Thorne had always been a bit apart, just as Sycamore was always in the thick of things.

"How bad is it?" Oak asked.

"Merely terrible," Ash replied. "I had hoped we could rebuild on the remaining foundation for the southern wing. The engineer's report says that wing experienced the worst subsidence of the whole lot. If we rebuild the dower house anywhere, it shouldn't be on the existing foundation, and that means more expense."

Dorset was wonderful sheep country, but in places it was also riddled with caves, bogs, and other features that made building large edifices merry hell when those edifices were expected to stand for centuries.

"Doesn't seem fair," Valerian remarked, propping his boots on a corner of the desk. Valerian always had the newest boots, though even his were showing a want of polish today. "We have a bloody big pile of bricks, stones, and even timbers, and no place to put up a proper dower house. I had plans for that dower house."

They were all eager to leave Dorning Hall, all hopeful that soon they'd be able to make their own way in the world rather than linger here. The polite fiction was that they assisted with running the estate. The truth was Grey had scrimped and saved to give his brothers a gentleman's education, and the lot of them—save Will and now Sycamore—were little more than poor relations making work for the maids.

"We should write to Will," Oak said, not for the first time. "Will's sensible, and he's earning some blunt with his dogs."

Will had married an earl's daughter, and her settlements were likely all that stood between him and poverty. Raising and training working dogs, training aristocrats in the management of their kennels, and otherwise working from dawn to midnight was in Will's nature, provided the work involved canines.

"Will must contemplate supporting a family," Ash said, taking another turn pacing a hole in the already threadbare carpet. "We can't expect him to keep doing our thinking for us."

"We have the cottage," Thorne pointed out. "Complaisance Cottage has a spectacular view of the valley and the sea, and the roof is mostly sound."

Ash was learning to hate roofs, foundations, bearing walls, and pipes. He truly hated pipes. "I refuse to pester Grey with all of this when he's supposed to be courting a bride."

"Grey won't thank us for hiding bad news," Valerian said. "He's the earl. Is he supposed to bring his bride home to a smoldering ruin for a dower house, leaking cottages, and tenants in revolt?"

"The rain put out the last of the fire." The rain had also necessitated putting off the haymaking, which meant the crop would not be as nutritious when made.

At least they'd have a crop. Some years...

"How does he do it?" Oak muttered, going to the window. "How does Casriel persist in the face of unending setbacks?"

"Setbacks must become normal after a time," Valerian said, tipping his chair onto two legs. "I hope Casriel's having better luck with his courting."

Thorne shoved away from the bookshelf where he'd been leaning. "We are not dashing off to London to meddle in his courting. Any proper lady will take one look at us and marry the nearest cit rather than give Casriel a chance to pay his addresses."

"We're not that bad," Oak said. "I could take up work as a drawing master. I've been meaning to send out inquiries."

He'd been meaning to send out inquiries for years. Oak was shy, and drawing masters were supposed to be charming rather than talented.

Valerian could have been a tutor, not that he was particularly academic, but after Grey, Valerian was the closest they had to a well-bred gentleman. He had charm, small talk, subtle graces on the dance floor, excellent command of foreign languages, and all manner of talents a young man going up to university needed to know.

Valerian could spot a card cheat, knew the *Code Duello* by heart, and sensed how to diffuse awkward moments so that a pair of loaded Mantons were never needed. He was a dead shot, an excellent horseman, and knowledgeable about men's and ladies' fashions.

Dorset society had no need for a male finishing governess, though, or even a female one.

Thorne was slipping into the role of over-steward, supervising the house and land stewards, which had been mostly Will's responsibility.

While Ash's job—keeping Sycamore alive and out of jail—had become less pressing now that Sycamore was playing at managing a gaming hell.

"We might have to visit London," Ash said. "Only Grey can make some of these decisions. The land and fixtures are his, and he'll be the one left to clean up the messes we make."

As usual. The words remained unspoken, even by Thorne.

"We should write to Will and let him know what we're up against," Oak said. "Not to beg money from him, but to ask for suggestions. He knows all the tenancies, knows every field and fen we own, every brindle cow and one-eyed cat. He might have some ideas."

"Then we write to Sycamore as well," Thorne said. "At the club, not at the town house where Grey will see the letter and possibly open it. We write to keep him informed, not to beg money. Sycamore is a wily devil, and he listens at the damnedest keyholes."

Because we taught him that. "I'll go over the figures again," Ash said. "But the rain is not only reducing the quality of our hay, it's affecting the corn crops. We're not looking at a failed harvest, but we're not looking at bumper crops either."

"The growing season is still early," Thorne said, heading for the door. "Write to Will and Cam, tell Grey all is proceeding as usual here and best of luck with his courting."

Oak shuffled out after Thorne, leaving Valerian scowling at the empty hearth and Ash scowling at his calculations. All that brick, all that timber and rubble, and nowhere stable to rebuild the dower house? Perhaps that was for the best when there was no money to pay an architect, much less a builder.

"How is the book coming?" Ash asked, because that's what one asked Valerian. He was compiling an etiquette manual for young gentlemen, which was ironic. Of all the Dorning brothers, Grey alone was fit to write such a volume. Valerian had the manners, turn of phrase, and fashion sense. Grey had the soul of a gentleman.

"The manuscript is coming along nicely." Valerian's standard answer.

"I pray to God that Grey's courting is coming along better than nicely," Ash said. "I pray he's sitting at this very minute with a tea cup balanced on his lordly knee, a wealthy heiress simpering at him from every compass point."

"And their doting mamas beaming at him from across the room. We live in hope."

They lived in fear. What if Grey could not marry well? What if lightning struck Dorning Hall itself? What if the rain resumed?

"I know something I did not know before," Ash said.

Valerian peered at him. "Never say you're considering holy orders. Matters aren't that dire, are they?"

They hadn't been before the fire, before the rain, before the subsiding foundation, before leaking roofs...

"I could never, ever be the earl," Ash said. "I used to wonder... I'm in line behind Will and Grey, but under no circumstances ever, at all, to any degree, do I want the title. I'd go barking mad in a week."

"Three days," Valerian said, rising. "If I'd last even that long. Thorne could endure possibly a fortnight. Oak wouldn't manage a day."

"We need Grey to find that heiress, the sooner the better. I don't care if she's a harpy with horns and a tail, if her money can spare Grey this lot of tribulation, I will be her most devoted servant and say nice things about her too."

"I'll dedicate my book to her in a sonnet worthy of the Bard. Is there any brandy left?"

A fine suggestion. "Sycamore's not here to steal it all. Pour me a tot as well, and we'll drink to our next countess."

NOW THAT THE moment to embark on the intimate part of this liaison was upon Addy, she was torn between eagerness and something else.

Not caution. As a young bride, she'd benefited from Roger's experience and learned that lovemaking was supposed to be pleasurable. For a time, it had been. Then Roger had become preoccupied with siring an heir, and Addy had frequently found herself against a wall, sprawled on a desk, or hauled into the servants' stair. For a time, that too had at least been novel.

"I am telling you the plain truth," Casriel replied, "when I say that a cup of tea or a plate of sandwiches would be enjoyable." His lordship was apparently content to stroll along, a gentleman matching his steps to a lady's stride.

"You are hungry? I can see you fed."

"My appetite is for your company, my lady. We need not begin our time together in the bedroom."

At first, Addy thought he meant they should climb to the hayloft in the stables, or avail themselves of the settee in the library, but Casriel wasn't being sly or naughty.

He was being considerate.

"Is there a discussion that comes before the bedroom part?" she asked. "Something about rules, duration, days of the week?" Something tawdry but practical, perhaps?

"I am unaware of any such requirement, though I am honestly happy to discuss any topic you wish. I also contemplate—with utmost joy—shedding every article of clothing from my person and divesting you of your own *habillement*. From there... I thought we did rather well with the kissing part. Perhaps you have some ideas for what comes next?"

Addy's belly did a little somersault that landed in an ache. "You would like to kiss me when I'm unclothed?"

"When *we* are unclothed. If modesty on your part renders that prospect uncomfortable, then I'd like to kiss you when you're wearing nothing but your shift, so only a thin layer of cotton comes between my touch and your tender flesh. I want to learn your curves and contours with my eyes closed, and I want your hands on me *everywhere*."

Addy tried for several steadying breaths. A pair of dowagers toddled past, and Casriel politely touched his hat to them.

"*Everywhere*, my lord?"

He waited with her at a street corner while a hackney rattled by. "Everywhere. I particularly enjoy how you pull my hair and clutch my bum. A man appreciates a good, ferocious bum-clutching, under the right circumstances—in case you were wondering."

Addy was wondering how she'd last the next two streets to her own door. "And how does a man feel about having a lady's mouth on various parts of his person?"

Casriel patted her fingers where they were curled about his arm, a friendly gesture to any passersby.

"When considering such a pleasure, this man is tempted to hoist the lady over his shoulder and sprint for the nearest bed. That option being unavailable, I can assure you that such a notion will render him speechless with delight."

"Not appalled?" She'd been married for six months before Roger's coaxing and teasing had finally overcome her reluctance regarding this intimacy.

"Would you be appalled to know that I long to pleasure you in a similar fashion? I want your thighs over my shoulders. I want the taste and scent of you filling my being while my cock fills your sex. I want *you*, Beatitude. All of you. Body, mind, fears, and frolics. This is to be an *intimate* liaison, is it not?"

That blunt speech rendered in such cultured, conversational tones had an impact that similar words whispered behind a locked door would lack.

Then there was Casriel's question about *intimacy*. His inquiry pointed to a shortcoming in Addy's marriage that she hadn't found words for. Roger had been forever strutting around without his clothes. He'd been an enthusiastic and inventive lover. He'd shown Addy a side of life few proper ladies, and very few vicar's daughters, ever saw, all without jeopardizing her social standing.

But at some point, the erotic joinings had stopped being intimate. The whole marriage had stopped being intimate, if it ever had been.

Intimacy—the intimacy Casriel described—took courage, and in some regard, Roger had been a coward. That insight nearly had Addy stopping in the middle of the street.

"My lady? Have I offended?"

"You have inspired. If this is your version of conversation with a lover in broad daylight, I eagerly anticipate further discourse with you in private."

His marvelous gentian eyes danced, though his pace remained decorous. "Eagerness must be in the air today, for I am similarly afflicted."

Addy was ready to toss him over her shoulder, or simply start the clutching and kissing on the walkway, but oh, *the glee*, the sheer, adult delight of knowing that anticipation was a mutual torment. Roger had been the type to look up from his noon meal, send the footman at the sideboard a dismissing glance, and then lock the door before Addy had taken the first bite of her raspberry fool.

That Casriel would use the length of four streets to tease and flirt was a degree of loverly expertise Addy had yet to encounter. She'd probably never find its like again, and that thought—a little sad, a lot honest—helped her identify the feeling that walked arm in arm with her eagerness.

She was determined—that was the word, *determined*—to indulge in this affair to the fullest. Casriel had turned her head, which was bad, because he wasn't meant for her. But nobody else had gained her notice to the extent he had, and Addy would sample his charms thoroughly before commending him to the company of his heiress.

For once, she would think of herself, and to blazes with everything else.

Her house came into view, and it was *her* house, not a dower property. Roger had done that much for her, or one of his late aunts had.

"If you were in earnest about the tea and sandwiches," Addy said, "now is your last chance to make that clear. Once I get you behind my door, you will be clutched within an inch of your lordly life."

He tipped his hat to an elderly couple doddering along.

"I live in hope, and I am desperately earnest, my lady—not about the sandwiches."

GREY WAS ABOUT to make love with a woman not his wife for the first time in... He could not make his mind function. His last tryst —a tipsy mutual groping at some house party—had been an appalling several years ago. Before foot rot had followed his flooded water meadows, after the failed harvest.

He had no idea of the when or who, and not much idea about the why. Lust and stupidity explained a seventeen-year-old's idiocy, but a titled man with scores of dependents could not be a slave to lust or even its occasional bond servant.

He could, though, find a lady's company exceedingly agreeable. Lady Canmore—Grey liked thinking of her in polite terms almost as much as he enjoyed using her given name—sashayed along at his side, enjoying a pleasant spring day, not a care in the world.

To appearances. Meanwhile, she spoke of intimate pleasures that ambushed his reason and made him ache. He hadn't planned this assignation, but half day was half day, and what was there to plan, really? Nature mapped out the whole business, but for the details.

They approached her ladyship's town house, a solid, elegant structure in a solid, elegant neighborhood.

"I can leave you at your door if you'd rather," Grey said. "We did not intend to encounter each other today." She had fallen silent, else he would not have made the offer. A lady could have second thoughts.

"I would *not* rather. Would you? Rather leave me at my door?"

A gratifying hint of a grumble accompanied that question, though Grey could answer with only qualified honesty. He'd rather this was not a moment stolen from impending obligations. He'd rather this was a step in a courtship.

"What I would *rather*," he said, leading her ladyship up the porch steps, "had best be discussed behind a closed and locked door from this point forward, or all who behold me will know exactly what I'm thinking."

She darted a glance downward to the vicinity of his falls. "Oh." Another glance, now that they were under the awning of her porch. "I see. Good tailoring leaves a man little privacy."

"You see. I ache."

"Delighted to hear it." Her ladyship stepped back, allowing Grey to open the door for her.

She took off her bonnet. He kept his hat and walking stick, lest some caller dare to stop by. "Shall we to a guest room?" Grey asked.

"No guest room," she said, peeling out of her spencer.

Grey assisted, mostly for the pleasure of brushing his hands over her shoulders. The sight of her ladyship's nape lifted erotic stirrings to outright desire, and had she not preceded him up the steps—foolish, foolish rule that said a woman should go first up a stairway—he would have commenced kissing her in the foyer.

Instead, he trailed her onto the higher floor, arousal creating a pleasant yearning to go with... What, exactly, did he feel about this encounter?

Joy, of course. What man didn't joyfully anticipate gratification of his animal spirits?

A touch of shame, perhaps, to be sneaking around on the servants' half day, departing from the path of strict propriety?

But no, not shame, exactly. He owed no woman fidelity—yet—and the highest stickling hostess wouldn't hesitate to seat him at her right hand, even if an affair with the countess became an open secret. The same hostess would receive Lady Canmore graciously, or become an object of gossip herself.

Still...

The thought trailed away as Beatitude led him into a sitting room done up in blue, white, and gold. Elegant, like her, but a bouquet of fragrant pink sweet peas sat on the windowsill where Grey would have expected roses. An embroidery hoop had been left on the sofa, with the side of the fabric exposed that showed all the knots and loose threads.

A book lay open on a low table, and a pair of worn slippers sat one across the other beside the sofa.

"Your personal sitting room?"

"The very one," she said, closing and locking the door. "Through that door is my personal bedroom. I am not at home to callers on half day, so we are as alone as two people can be in the middle of Mayfair."

And yet, she wasn't grabbing his bum, or any other part of him. He set his hat and cane on the sideboard. "Would you think me very forward if I asked to kiss you, Beatitude?"

"Addy," she said. "My closest friends call me Addy. All, save Theodosia, who calls me Bea."

"I am Grey."

They'd had that discussion, and yet, this time the exchange had the lady smiling. Grey held open his arms, and she crossed the room, straight into his embrace.

"I am at heart still a vicar's daughter," she said. "Roger despaired of me."

"Orgies were beyond you? I've always found them rather tedious myself."

The comment was meant to be humorous, a means of reducing awkwardness, but Addy ducked her face against his chest. "Something like that. He was not merely a hedonist. He thrived on novelty and adventure. If we'd seen to the succession, he might well have been one of those explorers who disappears into the wilderness and grows a beard while subsisting on bear meat and poetry."

From what Grey understood of the New World trappers, they generally had more than one family, and their hygiene departed from gentlemanly standards by the distance of half a continent, which was probably intended to prevent bears from snacking on *them*.

"I do not thrive on novelty," Grey said, stealing a kiss to the lady's cheek. "I thrive on order and hard work, with the occasional leavening of good company and bodily pleasure. The only adventure I seek now is the adventure to be had in your bed."

She sighed against his neck. "You truly don't care if I'm wicked or boring, as long as I'm willing?"

Roger had doubtless been young and spoiled, so Grey withheld a more plainspoken reply. "If you are willing and our dealings are boring, then I, as the only gentleman participating in the proceedings, must hold myself accountable for your disappointment."

The dialogue should have progressed along a predictable script from there: *Shall I unlace you, my dear?* A bit of kissing. A rampant cockstand. Smiles and touches, the lady disappearing behind the privacy screen, the gentleman wrestling off his boots and thinking happy, naughty thoughts while glancing at the clock.

Grey remained in the middle of the parlor, his arms around Addy, breathing in her gardenia scent. He would forever associate that fragrance with joy and a sense of sanctuary from life's demands.

"I did not thrive on novelty either," Addy said. "I learned to tolerate it for my husband's sake, up to a point. These are not trysting thoughts."

"Here's a trysting thought." Grey kissed her gently, without hurry. They had all afternoon, and probably other afternoons besides. Gradually, Addy became more enthusiastic, tasting him, getting a hold of his hair. Her participation struck him not as flirtatious so much as determined.

"My hooks," she whispered, drawing close enough that his arousal had to be apparent to her. "If you please."

He reached behind her and unhooked her dress while she stood with her arms around him. "Your laces?"

"I'm not wearing any. I wear two chemises and seldom go out without a spencer. My modiste knows I don't like to be trussed up and reinforces my bodices accordingly. For evening occasions, of course, I must bow to convention, but during the day..."

He rubbed her back, and she wiggled, like a cat enjoying a caress.

"That feels good," she said.

"Indeed, it does."

Ah, there. A soft, stroking pat to his backside. Her mood was improving.

"Come to bed, Grey," she said, leading him by the hand into the bedroom. The appointments here were unremarkable. Blue bed hangings over a large expanse of blue counterpane, an Axminster carpet in blue and cream with touches of pink. A comfortable reading chair by the window, a vanity and privacy screen along the wall opposite the windows. A rocking chair near the hearth, which was unusual outside of a nursery.

This space had less of *her* about it, and that troubled him. No flowers, no books, no workbasket or forgotten tea cup. Perhaps the room wanted happy memories, and maybe he could give those to her. "Shall I take down your hair?" he asked.

Blond brows rose, then knit. "I can manage," she said, moving to the privacy screen. "Do you need help with your boots?"

He was to undress, then. "I'm not that fashionable. My boots are comfortably made and allow me to retire without bothering a valet. Shall I turn down the bed?"

"Please."

Addy disappeared behind the privacy screen, her manner puzzling. A tryst should be lighthearted, friendly, a shared delight. Her mood was becoming serious, and that troubled him too.

Grey sat and took off his boots, then stood to remove his coat and waistcoat. He'd put his handkerchief on the bedside table and was down to his breeches and bare feet when a sound escaped the privacy screen.

"Beatitude?"

"I cannot believe this."

"Addy?"

"My body hates me. I am a woman cursed. I cannot..."

She emerged from the privacy screen wearing only a shift, her hair a thick golden rope over one shoulder. She was holding a white linen cloth, staring at it incredulously.

Grey approached, at a complete loss. "*I* certainly do not hate your body. I am rather taken with it, along with your many other fine attributes. What has upset you?"

She bunched up the cloth. "I thought I was nervous, a bit unsure. I thought perhaps my nerves... My courses are about to arrive, two days early."

Her... *courses*. The great indisposition about which Grey's sisters were too blunt, the symptom a woman endured when she was not expecting a child.

"Bloody bad luck," he muttered, then realized what he'd said. Not even when all but naked in the bedroom should a gentleman use that language before a lady.

"Well, yes, to be shockingly vulgar about it." Addy was smiling. A rueful smile, true, but genuine. "I do apologize."

"What can you possibly have to apologize for? Nature does what she pleases with all of us. Here I stand, ready and randy, for example, though we've barely kissed."

Not merely randy, hard and aching.

"We are not off to a very passionate start, are we?" Addy said, tossing the cloth over her shoulder. She stepped close and wrapped her arms around Grey. "I am sorry."

She felt good in his embrace, warm and lithe, real. "I am not put off by a little reproductive biology, Addy. If you're interested, I'm still... I have an idea."

She did not like novelty, she'd said. Based on her expression, novelty had served her several bad turns. "What sort of idea?"

"May I finish disrobing?"

She stepped back and flipped down the bedcovers. "I was rather hoping you would. I'm not a mess, not untidy—yet."

But she was unhappy to be denied her intimate interlude. Disappointed. Grey could work with that. He peeled out of his breeches and let the lady have a look.

"You do enjoy physical activity, don't you?" She drew a single fingertip up the length of his cock, which was angled in the direction of true north.

"I thrive on hard work," he said. "Strenuous physical labor being one sort of hard work. You can clutch and pinch and pull on me all you like, and I'll like that too. Come be with me, Addy."

He climbed onto the mattress and lay flat on his back.

She stood on the step beside the bed. "Where does one...?'"

"Here," he said, patting his cock. "You can ride me without taking me into your body. I'll show you."

Lord Roger, Earl of Adventure, had apparently overlooked a few of the pleasurable measures a couple could take to avoid conception. Grey knew them all, though none equaled actual coitus for satisfaction.

"Straddle me," he said, lifting the lady over him. "Tuck in close and prepare to enjoy yourself."

She looked uncertain, a songbird ready to take flight, so he leaned up and kissed her, assaying a glancing caress to her breasts at the same time.

"I like that," she murmured against his mouth.

"This?" He cupped her breasts.

"Mmmmm."

That, accompanied by Addy arching her back, was a yes. Her shift did not unbutton all the way down, so Grey stroked, teased, and fondled with the aid of the thin cotton to enhance the sensation. By degrees, Addy settled herself over his cock.

He was not inside her. He was instead at heaven's door, while she ran her slick flesh along his length. The sensation was exquisite torture, and she was barely getting started.

"Ride me," he said, urging her down. "Ride me as long and as hard as you please, and we'll find pleasure along the way."

Pleasure, not quite consummation.

Addy was a fast learner and a dedicated equestrian. She soon found a rhythm and pressure that tried Grey's restraint to the utmost and set the bed to rocking gently.

"This is…" she panted against his neck, "interesting."

Interesting was a balm to Grey's soul, for he was not an interesting man. He was polite, he was dutiful, he was a good farmer, a loyal brother, and a conscientious landlord. Nobody had ever described him or his ideas as *interesting*.

And with her, *he* was barely getting started. "Don't think, Addy. *Feel*." He raised his hips, meeting her on her next undulation, anchoring her with an arm at the small of her back.

She moved more quickly and more firmly, until he knew she was close—he was close—but the moment wanted… He brushed her shift aside, got his mouth on her nipple, and bit gently.

"Yes." A soft groan, a hard push from her hips, and he could feel the pleasure coursing through her. "Like that," she murmured. "Oh ye gods, exactly like that."

He held back. He held back as a gentleman must when pleasuring a lover, though the effort nearly cost him his back teeth, and then Addy was a panting bundle of feminine repletion on his chest, her braid tickling his shoulder.

"You have the knack now?" he asked, stroking her hair.

"I have the knack. It's a lovely knack, Grey, though I can't grab your bum this way."

Give me strength. "Perhaps another time we'll include that on the agenda. Fortunately, I can grab yours." He obliged, firmly, not too firmly. "Ready to go again?"

She peered at him. Her braid was a bit frazzled, her cheeks pink. "*Again?*"

"Of course again. By the grace of God and a typical Englishman's unrelenting self-discipline, I haven't spent."

She raised up enough to peer down at his member, which was joyfully ruddy, glistening, and hard as a Dorset fence post.

Also aching like thunder.

"Thanks be for an Englishman's unrelenting self-discipline," she said, kissing him soundly.

Grey lasted, somehow, through her next gallop, then rolled with her to spend on her belly. When he could move again and had used his handkerchief on the resulting mess, he shifted to his back and pulled a warm, limp Addy over him, then used his foot to get the extra quilt within grabbing range.

Addy dozed on Grey's chest as the bed curtains shifted gently in an afternoon breeze, and he wallowed in the happy relaxation that followed a good bout of lovemaking.

She burrowed closer, and he wrapped her in his arms, kissing the top of her head.

Addy was precious and dear, and those were not sentiments born of a mere afternoon romp. They were the tip of a complicated iceberg drifting closer to a rocky shore Grey could not at the moment bring himself to examine. He knew this, though: He and Addy were not yet lovers in the technical sense, and that occasioned a puzzling but unmistakable sense of relief.

CHAPTER EIGHT

"Do come in," Theodosia Tresham said. "I was sorry to miss you yesterday, but thank you for sending Lord Casriel around with my parasol."

Addy passed her bonnet to Theo's butler. "His lordship came of his own accord, and he and I met here by happenstance."

"I was sorry to miss you both," Theo said, setting off down the corridor. "Come with me to the library. I'm organizing the collection, which hasn't been done since the Crusades. Jonathan peeks in every so often, then slips out hoping I don't put him to work scampering up and down the ladder."

Casriel would be like that—peeking in—but he'd be happy to impersonate a footman, happy to lug boxes and scale ladders, even as he also discussed the various horticulturalists on his shelves.

And offered scandalously erotic observations all the while.

I have misplaced my wits.

"Will you be at tomorrow night's ball?" Theo asked. "I'm organizing Jonathan's dance card. He's willing to stand up with the young ladies for the quadrilles and minuets, but would rather not waltz with them. Perhaps you could save him your supper waltz?"

Addy neither liked nor disliked Jonathan Tresham. He'd intervened when Lord Davington had pawed her in a secluded alcove, then Tresham had dispatched her into Casriel's company. To Addy, trouncing a complete ponce was useful, but dealing with an upset woman took *courage*.

That again.

"You are quiet today," Theo said, opening the door to the library. "When we strolled by Lady Brantmore's lake, I suspected you were ready for a respite from the socializing."

"A respite?"

"A visit to Bath, Harrow, somewhere peaceful, perhaps Canmore Court. Shall we sit?"

The last place Addy would go for a respite was Canmore Court. "Let's have some fresh air," she said, crossing the library to a set of open French doors. "We'll be cooped up for half the night, and the day is lovely."

"The ball isn't until tomorrow."

"The card party is tonight." Addy had considered sending regrets, but Grey was likely to attend. She should have asked him what his plans were, though that might have been intrusive.

"We can sit in the shade," Theo said, descending the steps of the back terrace. "Shall I ring for a tray? I should have brought my workbasket."

So domestic, so *happy*. "Theo, might we simply sit and talk?"

They'd done a great deal of sitting and talking when they'd both been widows managing their own households. Theo in particular had had to practice economies, though Addy was by no means a spendthrift.

"Of course," Theo said, taking a chair at a grouping in the shade of a stately maple. "How are you?"

Theo's expression was friendly and interested, not concerned, not the perceptive friend who grasped subtleties without a word being spoken. Where had that friend gone, and would Addy ever see her again?

"I am in need of information."

Theo's gaze sharpened. "Is Mr. Tottenham bothering you again?"

"He keeps his distance." Like a wolf kept to the shadows as long as the campfires blazed. Roger had not been discreet about his pleasures. Addy doubted he'd been discreet regarding his marital frustrations.

"Davington has taken rooms in Paris," Theo said. "He won't be a problem."

Casriel had told Addy that. "Good to know, but that's not the information I'm seeking. How do I prevent conception, Theo?"

Theo sat back. "Keep your distance from men?"

"I'm serious."

Addy's hostess gazed out across the garden, a lovely expanse of tidy parterres, classical sculptures, and beds abloom with daisies, roses, and lavender. The scene was both soothing and relaxing, and it also struck Addy as *wealthy*.

A rich man could afford such gardens, and Tresham was rumored to be very rich.

"Keeping your distance from men is the only sure method of preventing conception," Theo said. "I made a study of the matter."

"I know you did. If I send for a midwife to enlighten me, the staff will notice."

"And a midwife might talk, however innocently, about the fine widowed countess who asked such curious questions. Are you with child, my friend?"

Addy rose rather than face the concern in Theo's eyes. "I am most assuredly not, and glad of it. For years, Roger counted days, consulted physicians, read arcane texts, all in an effort to ensure conception. I know all of the strange notions, myths, and folklore intended to result in a child, and I know none of them worked."

"If you cannot conceive, then why...?" Theo waved a hand.

"Why not enjoy myself? Because what if the fault lay not with me, but with Roger? He indulged in many vices, and I have wondered if something—excessive drink, opium, a great fondness for hashish, his sexual recreations—might have impaired his virility."

Theo's scowl boded ill for Roger's memory. "I thought he was faithful."

"I believe he tried to be, at least as regards women. I didn't pry."

"As regards *women*?"

"Roger wasn't a puritan." Though at the end, he'd accused Addy of being one. "The point is, none of what I learned as Roger's wife has given me insight into how to prevent conception should the need arise."

Theo was quiet, doubtless shocked. Addy had been shocked for the entire first year of her marriage, though she'd always told herself that Roger cared for her, in his way.

"This has to do with Casriel, doesn't it?" Theo asked.

Now Theo's instincts were roused? *Now* she turned up perceptive? "It might. I like him and esteem him."

And *that* was the worst problem of all. Addy had considered the occasional romp with the occasional rake, widower, or lonely bachelor. Her eye was drawn to mature men who knew how to conduct themselves discreetly. Men unlike Roger.

"You've liked and esteemed other fellows," Theo said. "Why Casriel?"

"Why not Casriel? He's comely and handles himself well."

Theo was a mother, and thus she had an ability to compel truth from those reluctant to part with it. She didn't have to say a word. Her gaze was sufficiently patient that Addy went on speaking.

"I've never been tempted to the point of indulging, Theo. Marriage to Roger provided me endless opportunities to appease my erotic curiosity—what little I had—to the point that the whole business became tedious. Then he grew fixated on having an heir of his body, and tedious became tiresome. With Casriel, I face a paradox. I want to have an illicit affair with him because he's so decent."

Theo's smile was wan. "Only you, Beatitude, could arrive at that reasoning. Casriel is also no threat to your independence."

Addy resumed her seat in the shade. "What does that mean?"

"He's not exactly rolled-up, but he and Jonathan have discussed finances. Casriel could be comfortable, but for the fact that he's a rural earl with a regiment of brothers to launch. Most of them are done with university and ready to become established in a profession."

Casriel had been forthright about his circumstances, which was no comfort at all. "Launching young men takes influence, which a rural earl might not have much of, and coin. There's also a daughter."

"An illegitimate daughter?"

"Afraid so. Casriel would dote on her, but his common sense allows him only to cherish her from a careful distance. She will need a dowry."

Theo brushed her fingers over a purple heartsease sitting in a pot on the table. "A fire has reduced the Dorning Hall dower house to rubble, Addy. That's not common knowledge."

If Theo knew of it, word of the fire would soon reach others in Town. "What else aren't you telling me?"

"Sycamore Dorning has taken over management of The Coventry Club. When Jonathan offered him that role, he expected one or two of the older Dorning brothers to assist, but so far, young Sycamore has been the only one to take an interest in the place."

Theo was trying to make a point too subtle for Addy to grasp. That earlier comment, about Casriel being no threat to Addy's independence, demanded consideration.

"Is Mr. Tresham concerned for the club?" Addy asked.

"Sycamore Dorning is young, hotheaded, impulsive, and opinionated. Running a gaming hell takes tact, self-possession, experience of the world, and restraint. Jonathan hasn't said anything, but I'm sure he's concerned. A gambling establishment can quickly end up under the hatches, no matter how handsome, bold, and charming the proprietor is."

And again, Casriel had kept this worry to himself. "You hate that place. You'd be pleased to see it fail."

"I don't hate The Coventry Club. I simply don't want the ducal finances to rely upon it, and Jonathan respects my wishes."

If Theo was being honest, her view of recreational wagering had become vastly more tolerant since marrying Mr. Tresham.

"You're saying Sycamore Dorning might need his older brother's financial help."

"Possibly. The spare—Willow Dorning—has begun some venture to do with hounds or dogs. I'm not sure what. He too will rely on Casriel's backing if that enterprise fails to thrive."

The reality Grey faced became more stark the longer Theo spoke. Addy had danced with Sycamore Dorning. She'd been introduced to Willow Dorning and seen him in Hyde Park, walking his dogs while other men galloped their blood stock. She'd partnered Ash Dorning at cards.

These were worthy men who'd simply been born with more pedigree than pence, and they all looked to Casriel for support, influence, and entrée.

"I came here to ask you about preventing conception," Addy said. "I will leave wondering how Casriel has time for frolics when so much responsibility rests on his shoulders."

"When the world gives us the least joy is when we need our comforts the most," Theo said, rising. "I have a book you should read, not from the ducal library."

"About?"

"The author is a French midwife, and the general topic is women's health, but I bought it for the chapter on conception. I am confident every scullery maid and laundress knows the basics before she puts up her hair. We ladies are too delicate to understand how our own bodies function."

"I suspect the physicians are largely guessing," Addy said, getting to her feet. "They had no useful answers for me when I desperately wanted a child, though they certainly charged a pretty penny before they admitted as much."

"That must have been difficult, but then, I gather you've not told me the whole of your situation with Roger."

That was an invitation Addy would have to decline. "In some ways, I was the worst possible wife for him. He thrived on adventure and exploring the unknown. My ignorance was simply one more novelty to him. He'd never met a woman as unworldly as I."

Theo escorted Addy not directly back to the house, but along the garden path that led to the focal point of the landscape design, a fountain in the center of the largest parterre. The sculpture in the middle was a pineapple, the symbol of hospitality. Water gushed from the top, creating a blend of stone foliage and cascading rivulets that drained into a wide circular basin. The result was pretty and different, exactly the sort of eccentricity a ducal garden could turn to good effect.

"You mentioned that Roger was not unfaithful with women," Theo said. "Were there men, Addy?"

"At university, I know there were. Thereafter...? My imagination boggled at some of the sexual escapades Roger described in the most prosaic terms. His younger self amused him, while I..."

She'd been appalled, fascinated, worried. How could a man who'd done such things be content with a church mouse for a wife? He couldn't be, was the honest answer, though he had tried for a time.

"You simply wanted a child," Theo said, "which was a reasonable desire for an earl's wife. I'm sorry your marriage was so lonely. You and Roger seemed like such good friends."

"I worked hard to be my husband's friend. I could hardly hope to hold his interest on any other ground, could I? He tried to be my friend too." He'd betrayed that friendship at the end, if a friendship it had been.

The sound of water trickling over stone fruit filled a sad silence. Addy had awoken with such a sense of well-being and happy possibilities. She'd felt not wicked for having shared an interlude with

Casriel, but fortified. His intimate consideration was balm to her soul, his hands...

She'd dreamed happy dreams about Casriel's hands. This conversation had eroded her good spirits and given her much to think about.

"Come," Theo said, taking Addy by the wrist. "Let's find you that French treatise I mentioned. You are entitled to enjoy Casriel's company on any terms you please, and devil take the hindmost. He'll be married by the end of the Season, and you might as well have your pleasure of him while he's yet unattached."

There was the pragmatic, blunt Theo whom Addy loved, so why did Addy wish that comment had gone unsaid?

"I won't see you tonight," Theo went on when they'd returned to the library. "Jonathan and I try to stay in one evening a week other than Sunday. This is the volume you should read. You need not return it."

Because Theo had no need to prevent conception. Just the opposite.

"Thank you," Addy said, tucking the little book into her reticule. "I'll see you tomorrow night, then, and if Mr. Tresham needs an ally for the supper waltz, let me know."

For Casriel would doubtless stand up with Lady Antonia or Miss Quinlan, perish the pair of them and their fat settlements.

"Jonathan will be relieved. Shall I see you out?"

"I know the way. Enjoy reorganizing." Addy kissed Theo's cheek, wanting to be away to somewhere quiet and private. She had to wait at the front door for Thiel, and even his company on the walk home was a weight on her mood.

She had recently labeled Roger a coward, because his version of marital intimacy had been largely limited to copulation and other pleasures of the flesh. He'd never invited a conversation about the sorrow of childlessness. He'd never spoken openly of the rift with his brother. He'd never admitted that, in the midst of a marriage that looked to be a match of affection and liking, he was lonely too.

Perhaps he hadn't been.

Was an affair with Casriel merely a safe frolic, with a guaranteed parting in the near future? Was that what Addy wanted?

Thiel bowed her through her own front door. "Will we be going out this evening, my lady?"

To watch Casriel partnering Lady Antonia? To see him endure the flirtations of the Arbuckle twins? To smile as Miss Quinlan hung on his arm and flaunted her fortune at him?

"I believe I'll send regrets, Thiel. I'd like to catch up on my reading. We'll attend tomorrow night's ball, though. I've already promised my supper waltz."

Thiel closed the door with a decisive snick. "My lady should do as she pleases."

Casriel had said the same thing, telling Addy to look to her own wishes, as had Theo. That raised the inconvenient question, though: What did she want, and was an affair with Casriel bringing her objectives any closer?

ADDY WASN'T COMING. No matter how many times Grey glanced at the door of the cardroom, Addy wasn't coming, and she wasn't among those already at the gathering.

Grey wasn't exactly disappointed, and he wasn't exactly relieved. He wanted to see her, but more than that, he wanted to be *with* her, to spend time conversing or even being silent. Touching, talking, learning her mind and body, as he'd said.

Finishing the intimate journey they'd started also figured on his list of aspirations where Lady Canmore was concerned. Avoiding her gaze across a cardroom full of gossips would have figured among his notions of purgatory.

"If I partner you for the second half of the evening," Sycamore said, "I'll lose what little coin I have left." He accepted a glass of punch from the footman ladling from the men's bowl, took a sip, and passed Grey the goblet. "You are about as focused on the cards as I was on classical philosophy at the age of thirteen."

"The Arbuckles will put a few extra groats to good use," Grey replied. "I'm sure they have bonnet ribbons to purchase. What of you? Can you stand the loss?"

The mid-evening break had begun, half an hour to take the air, move about, and dine on sandwiches and tattle. The opportunity to brace Sycamore about his management of The Coventry might not come again soon, for Grey's youngest brother often slept for much of the day and was out for most of the night.

"You are trying to be delicate," Sycamore said, moving toward the doors to the terrace. "You want to know if I'm about to fall on my handsome arse before all of polite society. You are gently inquiring whether, in a few short weeks, I've taken an enterprise that all but mints money and driven it into ruin."

"Your aggrieved tone suggests my fears are grounded in possibility, if not fact." For Sycamore excelled at protesting too loudly.

The terrace was cool and quiet compared to the cardroom. Grey searched the shadows for Addy, though he knew that was pointless.

"Your unwillingness to drop the subject," Sycamore muttered, "suggests your real concern is the loan balance I ran up at university. I'll pay you back, Casriel. I've always said I'll pay you back."

All of Grey's brothers *always* said they'd pay him back.

"Of course you will." His standard reply. "The family resources are for the family's use. I merely sign the bank drafts." And merely watched the bank balance decline, season by season. "But I must warn you, Cam. My larking about in London has cost us the rent we usually make when we let out the town house for the Season. Lady Warwick has already told me she won't be leasing from us again."

Her ladyship had been a reliable and conscientious tenant for eight years. This year, she'd had to rent elsewhere and had informed Grey—on three separate, public occasions—that she was exceedingly pleased to be dwelling at a "less quaint" abode.

"I hadn't..." Sycamore propped a hip on the stone balustrade. "I'd forgotten we usually lease out the town house. I can sleep at the club."

But would Cam send his tailor's bills to the club? Stable his horse at the club? Would Cam *sleep*? Would he *eat*? Or would he subsist on worry and fine brandy while he watched a profitable enterprise crumble before his young and proud eyes?

"If you remove to the club," Grey said, "your employees will never get a rest from you. You'll be like Papa, always tromping across the tenant farms, dropping in for a chat when a man has fields to tend, or telling a diker how to mend a wall before the fellow even has his tools assembled."

Sycamore made a handsome picture silhouetted against the garden shadows. He was filling out, adding muscle to his height, growing into the Dorning frame.

But was he maturing?

"Do you know why I've bided in London, Casriel?"

Because you could not tolerate the discipline of university. "I spent my three years at Oxford, Cam. Papa wasted a great deal of coin in the hopes that I'd form lasting friendships with men of influence. I'm not sure what the other fellows were doing there, besides drinking, wagering, and pestering the tavern maids, but they weren't forming a lasting association with yet another impoverished Dorning heir. You were bored." *So was I.*

"I am in London taking my turn at nannying you. We didn't precisely draw lots, but when Ash went back to Dorning Hall and Will abandoned us for the charms of his lady wife, the duty of ensuring you don't make a complete cake of this courting business fell to me."

I am making a cake of myself, nonetheless. "I account myself touched." And Cam was in utter, exasperated earnest. This realization was amusing, upsetting, and surprising.

What did Cam know of courting a proper female, but then, what did Grey himself know?

"Ash wrote to me," Cam said. "The brothers are managing,

though they complain about everything from the weather to the teams pulling the hay wagons. Do you know how lovely it is that they are complaining *to* me rather than *about* me?"

"You left the letter on the piano," Grey said. "I recognized Ash's handwriting."

Cam's smile was patient. "And you did not read my correspondence, because you are a gentleman."

"Also because Ash has terrible penmanship, and I'd rather work on Mrs. Beauchamp's harp." The instrument could take only so much reconstruction at one time. Glue must dry, wax must be absorbed, old wood must be given time to adjust to new pressures and stresses.

Cam folded his arms, stretching the fabric of his coat across broad shoulders. "Your damned decency also means you do not sneak about The Coventry, making sly inquiries or tempting my staff to bear tales. I will put you out of your misery: The Coventry continues to thrive under my able and enthusiastic management."

Meaning Cam was most definitely floundering. "Glad to hear it. If that ever ceases to be the case, you will apply to me for sympathy, if not a loan. I know more than any one man should about ventures that refuse to come right."

"Like your courting efforts?" Cam pushed away from the railing and strolled to the steps. The garden was lit with torches, though Grey would never have ventured onto the paths by himself. Not when Miss Quinlan had been eyeing him the way a feral cat prowling outside the dairy eyes an open window.

"My courting efforts are proceeding well enough," he said. "Witness, we partnered the Arbuckles earlier this evening." For the longest hour and a half of Grey's life. The twins had taken turns brushing slippers over the tops of his boots, pressing their persons against his arm, and smacking him with their fans.

"They are too young for you, Casriel, and whichever one you married would insist that her sister dwell with her. You'd be left with double the bills from the modistes, twice the expense from the milliners, and only half the joys of marriage."

Sycamore's casual prediction had a disquieting ring of probability. An unmarried sister frequently joined the household of a married sibling.

Well, damn. "Do you have a preferred candidate for our next countess?"

"My preferences ought not to matter, Casriel, else I could be doing your courting for you."

For Cam, that was uncharacteristic diplomacy. "Lady Antonia Mainwaring seems an agreeable sort." Grey hadn't noticed whether she was present among tonight's crowd.

"Agreeable." Cam made the word a pejorative. "God save me from a lifetime commitment to a woman who finds my company merely agreeable. Do you suppose Papa and his countesses had nine children on the strength of agreeableness?"

The evening was cool, meaning few people were enjoying the torchlit gardens. Grey kept his voice down, nonetheless.

"Papa and his first countess were forced to tolerate each other as spouses because I came along and took away their options. His second venture to the altar was necessary to provide a step-mother for his bereaved children, though I daresay he chose in haste. I will make my choice based on factors other than lust and hurry."

Cam jammed his hands in his pockets. "You'll make your choice based on duty and stupidity, which strikes me as an even worse bargain. Have you ever wondered where your eight siblings came from? Papa had his heir, he had nephews. He and his countesses need not have troubled each other to the tune of additional children."

Hawthorne was a by-blow, though Grey would pummel any who said that aloud. "I cannot answer your question honestly without insulting our parents, Cam, and this discussion has nothing to do with my marital prospects."

Cam's expression put Grey in mind of their sisters, a long-suffering pair of ladies. "Lady Antonia would make a lovely countess, but I don't see her being the wife for you. Miss Quinlan has been casting lures at you all evening. I suggest you partner her while I'm on hand to chaperone, or I'll be writing to the brothers with unfortunate news indeed."

That Sycamore was giving out sound advice should have inspired a fraternal insult, a comment about flying pigs or blind hogs, for example.

Cam was right, however. Grey should be playing cards with Miss Quinlan, he should be waltzing with her. She was clearly ambitious, and though not as agreeable as Lady Antonia, she had been sending Grey glances, whereas Lady Antonia waxed eloquent about some brilliant medieval nun named Hildegard.

"We should go back inside," Sycamore said. "If we tarry here, we'll be stuck partnering the elders, and while they have all the best jokes and know all the best stories, that will not advance your marital aspirations."

The Arbuckles, arm in arm, perched at the top of the porch steps, smiling ferociously.

I cannot endure another eternity of assault by fan and flattery.

Grey was worried for Sycamore, who was about to ruin his first commercial venture. He was worried for the brothers back home, who were complaining to Cam while maintaining an ominous silence toward Grey. He was tired. He was...

He was longing to spend a quiet evening with Addy, reading her poetry, perhaps. Rubbing her feet, being irresponsible, and doting.

Miss Quinlan emerged from the house on the arm of Mr. Thomas Blessingstoke. Blessingstoke was a decent sort and an earl's heir. His carefully pleasant expression turned to unmistakable relief when he spotted Grey.

"The Dorning brothers, my dear," Blessingstoke said, patting Miss Quinlan's hand. "Mr. Sycamore Dorning is noted to be a dab hand at the cards. Lord Casriel, I believe you and Miss Quinlan have been introduced."

No, they had not, not formally. Time to stop dodging that inevitability. "Perhaps you'd oblige?" Grey said. "I have admired the lady mostly from afar." Too afar, considering his objective for coming to London.

Blessingstoke scampered through the introductions, clearly preparing to bolt before partners were chosen for the second half of the evening.

Miss Quinlan's curtsey was exquisite. Her attire was memorably elegant. Her manner was gracious toward Grey and condescending toward Sycamore without being arrogant. She smiled beautifully, she laughed beautifully, she accepted beautifully when Grey extended the obligatory offer to partner her.

As he cast one last glance around the cardroom, confirming again that Addy was not present, he caught sight of his reflection in the mirror over the mantel, Miss Quinlan at his side. She was gazing in the mirror as well, her expression speculative, as if she were considering a new bonnet, but wasn't quite happy with the angle of the feathers.

As soon as she noticed the direction of Grey's attention, she smiled brilliantly, pressed closer to his side, and patted his arm.

He nearly shook free of her grasp and excused himself.

Lady Antonia it would be, then, particularly if she was amenable to a courtship that progressed at a decorous pace and was followed by a long engagement.

THE PREVIOUS EVENING, Addy had danced with Jonathan Tresham and she'd avoided dancing with anybody else. She'd sat with the dowagers and ignored the sight of Grey Dorning enjoying the supper waltz with Lady Antonia.

His lordship had made the taller half of a perishing, dratted lovely couple.

Addy liked Lady Antonia, she more than liked Casriel, and if marriage to Roger had taught her one thing, it was the folly of possessiveness. She was determined not to call on his lordship to inquire about Aunt Freddy's harp, determined not to go whining to Theodosia, who'd never had an affair and clearly never would.

She was thus whiling away her afternoon, perusing Theo's helpful little book, when Thiel rapped on the parlor door. "You've a caller, my lady. Lord Casriel is asking if you're at home."

She'd taken the precaution of placing her book within the folds of a fashion magazine, a trick Roger had taught her. Half the time when he'd appeared to be poring over some treatise on the profitable cultivation of mangel-wurzels, he'd been enjoying salacious French sketches.

"You may show him up, Thiel."

"We dusted the formal parlor just this morning, my lady, if you'd like to receive him there."

"I have fresh flowers here," Addy said. "Please have the kitchen send a tray as well."

Thiel withdrew, though Addy would bet her most comfortable pair of slippers he'd deliver that tray himself.

"Lord Casriel, my lady." Thiel's announcement was made a bit too loudly. He bowed and withdrew, leaving the door to Addy's personal parlor wide open.

And Grey Dorning filled the doorway. His lordship made an elegant figure in evening attire, but in the more relaxed and individualistic morning attire, he was truly delectable.

"My lady." He bowed. Addy got to her feet to curtsey.

"My lord. A pleasure to see you. A tray should be here shortly." *In case you were interested in a torrid kiss, even though Thiel—I should dock his wages—left the door all the way open.*

"I came by to let you know I'll be at least another few days with Mrs. Beauchamp's harp. My progress is of the slow and steady variety, which is typical of me."

Was Casriel nervous? Addy was, also pleased and annoyed. He'd come to call. He'd not attempted to kiss her. *I am no longer sixteen years old and smitten with the earl's dashing young heir.*

"Aunt Freddy will be pleased to hear you haven't given up. Won't you have a seat?" Perhaps Casriel was waiting to *be* kissed? Perhaps he'd come to cry off, so to speak?

"I stopped at Mrs. Beauchamp's house, though she was not receiving. With the elderly, one never knows whether to pay a call earlier in the day when the mind is more alert, or after noon, though naps are typically taken at such a time." He took a seat at the end of the sofa closest to Addy's wing chair. "How are you?"

Glad to see you, I think. "I am well, and you?"

Why is this so awkward?

Rattling and tinkling came from the corridor, followed by Thiel pushing the tea cart. In the space of a few moments, the kitchen had assembled a midday meal and prepared the good tea service. Not the formal service, which Addy hadn't used in years, but a porcelain ensemble she usually reserved for her monthly at homes.

Thiel set the plates on the table one by one, making quite a production of arranging dishes. He finally withdrew, again failing to close the door.

"Here's my theory," Casriel said when they were alone. "The female staff, meaning the cook, housekeeper, and the maids, hope I will offer you marriage and are thus exerting themselves to impress me. The footman—who is too handsome by half—has a different explanation for my interest in you and is letting me know that I'd best watch my step."

"I made up the bed," Addy said, softly. Another lesson from Roger. "After your most recent call, I made the bed myself, smoothed the covers, refolded the quilt. The staff can't know anything for certain, and I'm not about to tell them."

Casriel accepted a cup of tea, though Addy had forgotten to ask if he'd like sugar or milk. "You are not happy. Having second thoughts, Beatitude?"

She adored his eyes, adored the patient honesty in them, the hint of self-deprecating humor and weariness.

"Watching you waltz with Lady Antonia was difficult."

He held his cup and saucer without taking a sip. "Playing cards with the Arbuckles was difficult. Partnering Miss Quinlan was a penance of proportions a gentleman ought not to admit. She is already choosing the guest list for our engagement ball, unless I am very much mistaken, and I should not be burdening you with any of this."

Casriel would hate having an engagement ball. "Hence you turn your attentions on Lady Antonia."

"Lady Antonia's company is agreeable, even if she does have odd notions regarding who is supposed to lead on the dance floor, but might we change the subject?"

His question assured Addy he was in difficulties too, which was some consolation. "I'd like to close the door."

He rose and not only closed the door but locked it, then resumed his seat. "Better?"

"Somewhat. I am still indisposed. Will you drink your tea?" Addy had gone for five years without blushing, but in Casriel's presence, all of her savoir faire deserted her.

"Not until you pour some for yourself. One assumed you were still plagued by your lunation."

"And yet, here you are." She poured herself a cup, mostly so she'd have something to do with her hands besides touch her guest.

"I've missed you." Casriel rose again, this time going to the window and unfastening the drapes. Nobody ought to be peering into a second-floor sitting room, but Addy appreciated the precaution.

Also the admission. "You saw me two days ago."

"I saw you last night, flitting about on Tresham's arm, flirting with old Quimbey." He turned to face her, his smile crooked. "Driving me mad."

Addy set down her tea cup, the day brighter despite the closed curtains. "I hate Lady Antonia."

He held out his arms, and Addy was in his embrace. "You don't hate her, please tell me you don't hate her, and then we will speak of more cheerful matters while we have the privacy to do so."

"I don't hate her." *But I will if you marry her.* "I've been reading."

"You weren't at the card party. I assumed your indisposition troubled you. Perhaps a lurid novel kept you company?"

To wrap Casriel in her arms, to have a conversation while embracing, felt wonderful. He wasn't aroused, and neither was Addy, but still... The scent and feel of him assuaged a longing of the heart and comforted the body.

"What do you know of lurid novels?" Addy asked.

"I've read everything Mrs. Radcliffe has written. Life in Dorset is prosaic on a good day, and a bit of mortal peril and derring-do make for fine entertainment." He turned Addy under his arm and escorted her to the sofa, then came down beside her. "I take it Mrs. Radcliffe wasn't entertaining you."

"Theodosia Tresham lent me a little French medical tome about ladies and babies."

"I adore your blushes, Beatitude, but I'm a farmer at heart. I know where babies come from, though I suspect you're reading about how to prevent conception."

She adored *him*, adored how he could balance blunt speech with true consideration, fine manners with common sense. Addy snuggled into his body heat, trying to hoard affection and closeness, which was pointless. She didn't want a few stolen embraces. She wanted emotional and social *carte blanche*.

"You say things other people only think, my lord, and yet, you say them kindly."

"A gentleman is kind and honest. I honestly missed you at the card party, then was tormented at last night's ball. I had not planned on... had not foreseen becoming... That is to say..."

He kissed her, thoroughly, deeply, and—how was this possible?—thoughtfully. His kiss was gentle and relentless, searching and respectful. He cradled her cheek against his warm palm, stroked his thumb across her nape.

Casriel broke off the kiss, his chin resting on Addy's crown. "I had envisioned a pleasant, pleasurable association with you. I still want that, but such matters are supposed to end with a smile and a fond wave. I cannot see myself managing such a fiction."

He was brave to trust her with that truth, or maybe this was more of his kindness. "I've missed you too," Addy said. "You'll come by on half day next week?"

"King George can declare martial law and I will still find a way to be with you. Tell me what else was in your French book. Was there a mention of vinegar and sponges?"

"Yes, and lemons and limes cut in half, and herbs."

He kissed her temple and sat back, keeping an arm around her shoulders. "Pennyroyal, rue, comfrey, fenugreek... Some include lavender and Saint John's wort on the list. Pennyroyal tea is safe enough provided you aren't carrying already, and has a good reputation as a preventive, though nothing is entirely effective."

Was there mint in the scent he wore? Lavender? Wrapped close to Casriel, Addy felt as if a Dorset meadow lay behind her windows, not a tiny London garden.

"How do you know this?"

"My father was quite the botanist, and our library at Dorning Hall is rife with all things agrarian. When I became a papa while yet a minor myself, I decided to pay attention to how to avoid future missteps. I shared the information with each of my brothers, at length, repeatedly. I am happy to report that Tabitha has no illegitimate cousins—yet."

To sit like this, discussing the most ungenteel subjects, was intimate in a way Addy hadn't been intimate with her husband.

"You would blame yourself if your brothers had illegitimate children?"

He brushed his fingers over the side of her neck. "Not blame myself, but ultimately, responsibility for the child's care would fall to me, as head of the family. Jacaranda married quite well and will never want for anything. Daisy is much more modestly situated, and I've already had to... Why are we discussing this?"

He'd lent money, or made a gift of money, to his sister's husband.

"Because I like talking to you," Addy said. "I like cuddling up with you, letting the conversation go where it will, while I pet your knee and you stroke my neck."

"I'll bring you the herbal tea," he said. "Next week. If you send your maid to the apothecary, she will wonder why you've suddenly become enamored of a humble meadow tea. We have all manner of meadow teas and herbal stores at Dorning House, because Dorning Hall has entire fields left over from Papa's various experiments. If you ever need a pillow stuffed with lavender or a sachet of spearmint, I'm your man."

The turn of phrase was quaint, also a little unfortunate.

Grey Dorning was *not* Addy's man. "Next week, you will be my lover. I will look forward to that."

"Not half so much as I, my lady."

He turned the topic to his various brothers and neighbors, describing each one with a combination of affection and candor. His sisters were given similar treatment, as were his small nieces and nephews. He was truly the head of his family, which was already large and likely to become enormous.

This was another reason why he would marry Lady Antonia: He had a limitless supply of brothers who would likely sire an army of nephews, and every one of them would expect "Uncle Grey" to find him a post, buy him a commission, or otherwise open professional doors.

That realization was lowering for a vicar's hoyden daughter, though probably for the best. Addy wanted Grey to be happy. As devoted as he was to family, he needed to marry well, and she understood why he could not be happily married to her.

She finished her tea. He finished his. After another kiss behind the locked door, she showed him out, thanking him for all of his work on Aunt Freddy's ailing harp.

CHAPTER NINE

When in London, Grey attended Sunday services at St. George's, which activity consisted of a lot of socializing with a few hymns and a sermon thrown in. Sycamore had remained abed, which in theory could see him fined, but in practice would ensure a better mood later in the day.

Grey walked to and from services, not only to spare the staff having to hitch up a vehicle and loiter away the morning with the horses, but also to afford him an excuse to walk. He missed tramping his fields in Dorset, missed spending most of the day in the fresh air—not that London had any truly fresh air.

He missed stacking hay, damn it.

He missed his siblings too. The Dorning brothers improved the choral offerings of any congregation and enlivened all the conversations in the church yard thereafter. They also kept Grey company on the hike back to Dorning Hall, everybody in good spirits for having taken a little care with his appearance and enjoyed some time with the neighbors—and their daughters.

Grey left the church not in bad spirits, though the sermon on the subject of self-restraint had annoyed him. Why couldn't the preacher have held forth about joy? About the wonders of creation in spring? About the commandment to love one another?

"Your lordship, good morning." Lady Antonia Mainwaring offered him a businesslike curtsey from the walkway. Her Sunday bonnet was no fancier than anything else he'd seen her wear, her smile no more welcoming.

"My lady. A pleasure. I hope you enjoyed the sermon?"

"Frankly, no. We get that harangue every year as the Season reaches its peak. Somebody's darling boy has gambled too much, somebody's wife has run off with a footman. Then comes the sermon about self-restraint. Why does Vicar never preach on the Song of Solomon? It is unique among all Scriptures, a fascinating piece of literature, and yet, we ignore it."

"Excellent point." Also, perhaps, Lady Antonia's version of casting a lure, given the focus of those passages. "Might we discuss other sermon topics while I walk you home?"

In the country, if an unmarried man and woman began walking home from church together, crying of the banns might well follow. In Mayfair, this courtesy was less portentous, though still doubtless noted.

"Perhaps that's for the best." Lady Antonia cast a glance up the walkway, where a maid was in conversation with a footman. "Halpern, McDaniel, his lordship will see me home."

The maid curtseyed. The footman grinned and tipped his hat at her ladyship.

Grey offered his arm and felt like an impostor. He was executing a step in a dance, just as standing up with her ladyship for the supper waltz was a figure in that same dance. The pattern ended at the altar, exactly where he needed it to end.

But did he want it to end there with this woman? Had Addy avoided services because of him?

"I've often wondered," her ladyship said as they walked in the direction of Grosvenor Street, "how services would be different if women managed them. Would the sermons be about heeding the call of adventure rather than self-restraint?"

Her ladyship's stride would get her across any pasture in good time. "I'm not sure I take your meaning."

"Who needs to be reminded to restrain himself? Ladies are taught restraint from when we're in leading strings. We restrain our laughter, our voices, our opinions, our appetites. If lectures regarding restraint have any effect on us, that effect has been gained before we take our first communion."

"Gentlemen are taught restraint as well," Grey said, "though in my case, the lesson was a little late to take hold." She might as well know this now.

Lady Antonia sent him a look from beneath her bonnet brim. "One wonders if you had a misspent youth. Some of the most sober-appearing gentlemen did."

"And if I made a few errors in my younger years?"

Her pace increased. "Then I would tell you to make a few more. One wants an adventure or two to recall in one's dotage. One is dull company otherwise."

Did she find *him* dull? "Have you had adventures about which you don't speak, my lady?"

"Of a certainty. I went out without my parasol last Tuesday. I returned a book to the lending library two days late and wasn't even scolded. I read Bryon, which I'm told is unfit literature for a lady, though his lordship himself is accounted good company." She came to an abrupt halt at a street corner. "Are you considering courting me, Lord Casriel?"

Am I...? She'd ambushed him, though probably without meaning to. "Why do I feel as if my dance partner from the other night has been whisked away by the fairies and a more interesting and unhappy woman has taken her place?"

She dropped his arm and fished in her reticule for something known only to her. "Your legendary good manners must be a burden sometimes, just as my contrary nature is."

"I find you lively rather than contrary. My sister Jacaranda is contrary."

Her ladyship produced a large iron key and started across the street. "She married Worth Kettering. They were said to be a love match."

"They very much are a love match, but first she kept his country house for him. An earl's daughter ran off to take a position in service, because in her words, if she must drudge all day on behalf of a lot of ungrateful males, she'd at least get paid for it."

Lady Antonia came to a halt before the wrought-iron fencing around Grosvenor Square. "You consider that contrary?"

Grey took the key from her. "You don't? I corresponded with her, I kept an eye on the situation, I intervened when the matter required a show of family concern, but had not Kettering fallen arse over teakettle for her, she'd be drudging still out of sheer fixity of purpose."

He opened the gate and bowed the lady through, then gave her back the key. "You asked if I'm courting you. Manners cannot inform my answer, for if I say no, and you were hoping for an affirmative reply, I have hurt you. If I say yes, and you were hoping for a negative reply, I have put you in a very awkward position. As a gentleman, I desire your happiness above my own, so what answer would you prefer?"

"I think I followed that. Shall we sit?"

He did not want to sit beside her and watch the other residents of the square whiling away their day of rest. A dandy with a large dog was allowing his canine to investigate the hedges. A little girl trotted along beside her nurse. All very safe, all fenced in with iron railings to keep out the people truly in need of respite.

Now was too soon to embark on a courtship. Doing so would mean Grey could not call on Addy in the capacity of a lover. He wasn't ready to give up the hope of some intimacy and companionship with her before he consigned himself to being his intended's dutiful swain.

And yet... Sycamore was apparently in difficulties, or soon would be.

Ash's silence from Dorning Hall boded no good for the hay crop.

Fraternal correspondence that went around Grey rather than through him suggested more bad news was on the way—another leaky roof, another draft team gone lame.

He had given up rental income on the town house to facilitate his fortune-hunting, and now he'd lose the rental income from the dower house as well.

"I should marry you," Lady Antonia said, taking a seat on a bench beneath a maple.

Grey's heart physically ached at her words. "Any man would be honored if you looked with favor upon his suit." *Just please, not quite yet. Another week, a fortnight...*

Three days from now, but not yet. His longing was foolish, because parting from Addy after another encounter would be harder than parting from her now. And he *would* part from her.

"Any woman with sense would be pleased for you to pay her addresses, my lord. Any reasonable woman."

Lady Antonia was more rational than most men Grey knew, including at least three of his brothers. He tried for a pleased tone. "Shall I court you then, your ladyship?"

Beatitude, my love. I miss you. I will always miss you.

"I am not only contrary," Lady Antonia said, "I am a romantic."

God have mercy on an impecunious bachelor. Poetry and flowers, then. Moonlit strolls... and beyond that, Grey could not think. Even waltzing with her ladyship was more an athletic undertaking than a pleasurable dance.

"I have not the luxury of a romantic choice," Grey said, "though I will make every effort to show my intended that I esteem her." He did esteem Lady Antonia. He esteemed Mrs. Beauchamp too.

"The realization that I am a romantic is recent and unwelcome,"

Lady Antonia said. "I would rather be an eccentric. I am too homely to be an original and too ancient, but an eccentric is granted a certain latitude that a Long Meg of a spinster is not."

The dandy with the dog went mincing past, his collar points so high they prevented him from turning his head.

"You are neither homely nor ancient, and I will pummel any man who says otherwise."

"That is precisely the problem. Shall we take a turn around the square?"

"I would rather we remain here, my lady, and conclude our discussion. Perhaps you might explain this problem to me?"

In small words, so that a man more upset than he had a right to be could follow them. Grey liked Lady Antonia, he'd exerted himself to charm her, and now they were to court. No giggling Arbuckles, no mercenary Miss Quinlan. He should be pleased and grateful that his aims had been accomplished so easily.

He was, instead, on the verge of shaking his fist at the sky and roaring profanities in public.

"The problem is, you are a good, decent man, and I like you."

"I enjoy your company too, which bodes well for our—"

She touched his arm and shook her head. Because of her blasted bonnet, Grey could not read her expression.

"You frighten me, Lord Casriel."

While she baffled him. "I would never, ever raise my hand to a woman. Not only are you safe with me, my first obligation as a gentleman is to keep you safe from all other perils as well."

She scooted and turned, so he could see her face. She was actually quite pretty, with serious gray eyes and—if a man bothered to look—faint freckles dusting her cheeks.

"I am *afraid* that I will marry you," she said. "You have taken notice of me, the first to do so in at least three years. I've had the same fortune all along, but I'm so..."

"Do not say plain, ancient, or contrary, for you are none of those."

"So unremarkable, that even the fortune hunters now give me a pass. I have become invisible and lonely. Then you strut into the ball-room, all handsome and mannerly, and my resolve weakens. You tempt me. I wish you did not—I wish you *could* not—but you do. I must stand firm against pretty manners and lovely eyes, though, or I will end up even lonelier than I am now."

The impact of her decision settled slowly, a warm blanket of relief in a chill wind of duty. She would not marry him, in other words. She would not compromise her standards or yield to battle weariness.

And right behind his relief came a good quantity of admiration.

"I think you are extraordinarily wise, my lady, and I wish you every happiness." She was also extraordinarily wealthy and could afford to be resolute in her search for a spouse. Still, for a young woman to eschew the married state was a testament to substantial fortitude. "Is there anything I can do?"

She looked away, at the girl now skipping beside her nurse—on the Sabbath. "Do?"

"Anybody you'd like to be introduced to? Any gentleman who has caught your fancy who might benefit from hearing what an amazing conversationalist you are?"

"What they say about you is accurate, then. You are a truly perfect gentleman."

"Not always. Sometimes I curse and kick walls and rant at my brothers. Sometimes, I lose patience with my tenants and nap during sermons."

She regarded him again, all seriousness. "But have you returned a book *two days* late? Perhaps you need an adventure. You mentioned youthful indiscretions. I know about your daughter. She attends school with one of my younger cousins. They both like horticulture."

"Does everybody know about my Tabitha?"

"I like that," Lady Antonia said, rising. "She is *your* Tabitha, and soon you will be back to threatening to pummel the unwary. I like that a very great deal, my lord, but the philosophers leave you bored, and if I were to bring up theology over breakfast, you'd probably spend the rest of the day calling on tenants. We would not suit."

Grey stood and offered his arm. She hesitated, then took it.

"Perhaps we would not suit as spouses, but I think we suit well as friends. Which gentleman has caught your eye? I'll tell you if he gambles excessively, makes stupid wagers, or treats his help badly."

Lady Antonia remained silent until they were once again on the walkway outside the square. "You are rumored to be fortune-hunting, my lord, but you have wealth."

"The Dornings have land," Grey said. "I manage well enough." Not quite true. He managed year to year and gave thanks nightly that a peer could not be jailed for debt. His brothers, however, could be, and he had an entire herd of brothers.

"You have wealth," Lady Antonia said. "You have siblings to spare, and they aid your causes. If you wanted to know about, say, Thomas Blessingstoke's gambling markers, your brothers would correspond with their friends, and soon, you'd know down to the last farthing what the man owes and to whom. That's wealth."

"When you celebrate the holidays at Dorning Hall," she went on, "you can barely fit everybody around the table. That's wealth. When your daughter makes her come out, every other earl's wife will take a kindly interest in her, hoping your countess will do the same for their step-daughters and step-sons. That's wealth."

She was back to walking quickly, leaping from idea to idea. They might have driven each other barmy as husband and wife, though Grey honestly liked the woman.

"The sort of wealth you refer to does not buy many bonnets, my lady. Is this your house?"

They'd turned down a side street, a quiet, shady lane where each house looked almost exactly like the buildings on either side.

"Mine is that one, with the boring blue salvia. Are you wroth with me, Lord Casriel? I did not wait for you to ask, I did not give you the you-do-me-great-honor speech, though I suspect you were about to do me a very great honor, also a great awkwardness."

Lady Antonia was a puzzling woman, half fierce, half vulnerable, and probably something of a mystery to herself. But she had been—ultimately—kind and honest with Grey, for which he was grateful.

"I am pleased to regard you as my friend," he said, taking her hand. "If ever there is a good turn I can do you, you must not hesitate to ask. By being so forthright, you have done me a very great honor, Lady Antonia, and the gentleman who wins your favor will be the luckiest of men."

She withdrew her hand before he'd finished bowing. Then she was up the steps. At the door to her home, she turned to face him where he waited on the walkway.

"Thank you, my lord. For everything."

"Tonight," he said, "when you are leading prayers for the household in the family parlor, read to them from the Song of Solomon."

Her smile was dazzling and a bit intimidating. "Excellent suggestion."

Then she was gone, and Grey was blessedly alone. On the way home, he tried to reconcile himself to proposing to an Arbuckle—Drusilla was the elder—but he could not think past half day with Addy.

Nor did he want to.

"WE MUST DECIDE," Anastasia announced. "Mama has said that Casriel's manners are exquisite, that he has vast acreage, and his title is old and respected. He's not some first Baron of Lesser Thistledown. His sister married a nabob-ish fellow who is rumored to invest on behalf of dear King George. The family has wealth, even if Casriel is pockets to let at present."

Drusilla set aside the latest installment of *The Lady's At-Home*, not that yet another syllabub recipe made for riveting literature. When Anastasia said something must be decided, she usually meant *she* had reached a decision, and Drusilla's role was to agree with her before they presented the matter to Mama.

"What, exactly, are we deciding now?"

"Which one of us will marry Casriel, of course. He's had enough dances with Lady Antonia and played enough cards with Miss Quinlan. We must act, sister dear, and act decisively."

Anastasia paced the parlor in an unladylike fashion, another portent of bad tidings.

"He played cards with us before he played cards with *La Quinlan,* Ana. He walked the lake path with us and declined to accompany Miss Quinlan and her mama." Drusilla had liked his lordship for that, liked how he'd simply done the polite thing and thwarted a woman too intent on her own wishes. Though as to that, Anastasia was sounding rather determined.

"But he did escort Lady Antonia, Dru. She's rather old to fill up his nursery. That's a point against her."

Her ladyship was too wealthy to be discounted, also a decent person. "I think Casriel would make a good papa."

"I knew it!" Anastasia plopped onto the sofa, her skirts billowing then settling like laundry in a breeze. "You regard Casriel the way a woman considers a prospective husband. You should marry him, Dru."

The rumor in the ladies' retiring room was that Casriel *was* a father—only the one by-blow, though.

"One of us should marry him," Drusilla said, "and you would make a more impressive countess than I would." Sometimes, Anastasia could be flattered out of her convictions.

"I cannot argue with you about the countess part, but you will learn to deal with him. He doesn't strike me as a difficult man, provided he's allowed to do whatever it is men get up to when not waltzing or playing cards. Perhaps he votes his seat."

"Papa said Casriel minds his acres. Do you suppose his lordship rides about the shire, looking well mannered and titled?"

Though Casriel did not look all that titled. His dress was conservative to the point of boredom. He wore little jewelry—a ring, a pocket watch with fob, a cravat pin—and he smelled of shaving soap rather than exotic French perfume or imported pomade. He was also a largish fellow, whose complexion bore evidence of having spent time in the sun. Mama called him a dragoon of an earl.

"He'll drive you about the neighborhood if you're his countess," Anastasia said. "You'd like that, playing lady of the manor."

Dru would *be* the lady of the manor if she married Casriel, and that was worth considering. Mama's standards in the husband-hunting department were slipping lately, from a ducal heir, to a widowed marquess, and now this, an earl with more manners than money.

Two years hence, Dru's prospects might be limited to a gouty baronet or spinsterhood. "I am loath to marry and leave you here to contend with Mama all alone."

Anastasia fluffed out her skirts as if arranging her dress for a portrait sitting. "We've discussed that. I'll visit you for much of the year. Who knows? If one of the Dorning brothers is handsome and comes into some money, I might marry him."

Or would Anastasia enjoy being the only Arbuckle heiress in Mayfair?

"You like all the waltzing and card playing," Drusilla said. "As a countess, you could have your own formal balls and dinners. You could invite whom you pleased and have Casriel drive you in Hyde Park."

Drusilla was leery of horses. They stank and left malodorous evidence of their passing, got hair all over a lady's habit, and were dangerous when bad-tempered. Casriel could probably arm-wrestle an equine and give a good account of himself, but Drusilla would rather married life not include a lot of time sitting behind a horse.

Anastasia sent Drusilla a conspiratorial smile. "If you were Casriel's countess, you'd also soon become a mother. An earl must have an heir, and you adore babies."

"Who doesn't adore babies? They are sweet and dear and

precious. Of course I adore babies, and my own babies..." That was the point of the whole business, wasn't it? To have babies to love and cherish and call your own? To have children who loved you back and called you Mama while their papa grumbled about the bills and smiled at you down the length of a noisy breakfast table?

"Your own babies," Anastasia said, "might have the famous Dorning eyes. Your oldest son would have a courtesy title. Your daughters would all be ladies from the moment of birth."

If Drusilla's babies were simply healthy, she'd consider herself well blessed. "You think I should marry him."

Drusilla thought she should too, and yet, she hesitated. Casriel did not love her, if he esteemed her at all, and she barely knew him. A title would be delightful, of course, and he'd certainly put her money to good use, but still... The notion of actually marrying, despite three Seasons of waiting for an offer, was unaccountably daunting.

Marrying Casriel, anyway.

"Dru, dearest, please recall I do not like babies. They drool, and mess, and cry. Nursery maids deal with much of that nonsense, I know, but somebody must hatch the little darlings. I am not keen on the conception part either, which sounds undignified in the extreme to me. You accept that business as part of the bargain, while I would rather not lose my figure just yet."

This difference of opinion was as rare as it was baffling. How anybody could dislike a baby? And of course somebody must hatch the little darlings. Conception, according to Mama, was a matter of five minutes and not that onerous. If men could accomplish child-bearing unassisted, what purpose would that leave for women?

"I still say you would make the better countess, Ana. Perhaps we are overlooking other possibilities."

"If we are overlooking those possibilities, then Mama has overlooked them as well. If either of us is to marry this Season, I fear it's Casriel or a nobody."

Nobodies—handsome charmers with no means and middling pedigrees—were often excellent company, but alas, one could not marry them. Sycamore Dorning was a nobody, for example, and Drusilla found him very good company.

"I'll consider marrying Casriel, then, but even I can't demand a proposal from his lordship. He'd gallop back to Dorset with a proper horror of me."

Anastasia patted her arm, something Mama did that Drusilla abhorred. One petted small children, cats, and the elderly, and they couldn't pet one back.

"If you are willing," Anastasia said, "Casriel will come up to scratch. I have an instinct about these matters. Any man who has worn the same color of waistcoat to three different events needs to find himself an heiress sooner rather than later. You will be his countess, and all will come right."

Anastasia rose, arranged her skirts, and swished out of the parlor, doubtless off to convince Mama that Drusilla was the best possible wife for his lordship. Drusilla would certainly try to be, if he proposed. And a good mother too, of course.

If he proposed.

Which she half-hoped he would not.

ADDY HAD SLEPT BADLY when she'd slept at all. The hours of darkness had dragged by, full of anticipation, worry, and self-doubt. Today was half day, and she'd used some of her morning to pay a call on a drowsy Aunt Freddy.

The housekeeper reported that Aunt Freddy hadn't much appetite and had done little more than move from a chair to the bed to the parlor across the corridor. Aunt remained cheerful, though she'd received no callers other than her solicitor. Lord Casriel had sent Aunt a note and a bouquet of asters and daffodils, also a tisane for aching joints.

Asters were for patience—a reference to the harp project, perhaps—and daffodils were for sincere regard in a chivalrous sense rather than a romantic one. If Casriel were free to send Addy flowers, which ones would he choose?

Did his family's vast herbal include a tisane for an aching heart?

"You didn't eat much breakfast, my lady," Thiel remarked as he opened the parlor drapes. "Perhaps you'd like your luncheon now?"

Was he being considerate? Maneuvering for half day to start early for the kitchen staff? "A tray of sandwiches and some lemonade in my sitting room will do. Have you plans for this afternoon?"

Addy hadn't been raised with servants, beyond a maid-of-all-work at the vicarage. She was doubtless more familiar with her employees than a countess ought to be, but they were also the only other members of her household.

"I'll play a few rounds of skittles at the pub," Thiel said. "I can take a different half day if you'd like to pay calls, ma'am."

"No, thank you. An afternoon at home suits me very well."

Did Thiel favor a particular serving maid? He wrote letters on occasion, all to his family back in the neighborhood of Canmore Court. He was only a few years older than Addy and a handsome blond with merry green eyes.

"Thiel, do you ever consider returning to service at Canmore Court?"

He arranged the velvet drapes so they hung with exact symmetry on either side of the window. "I saw enough of life in the country as a youth, my lady. At a huge place like Canmore Court, I'd be the third or fourth underfootman until I was too old to carry anything more than a vase of flowers. Besides, I'd rather earn my pay than idle about all day."

He bowed and withdrew, leaving Addy restless and out of sorts.

Thiel knew what he wanted. What did Addy want? Not to be married again—that had gone badly the first time—but not to be invisible either.

"I will end up like Freddy, entertaining my solicitor once a week with stories we've been telling each other for decades."

Addy remained in the informal parlor, her embroidery in her lap, until a soft triple rap on the front door woke her. *He's here* popped into her mind at the same time she thought, *I wanted to change into something more flirtatious.*

She tripped over her workbasket, cursed in French, and paused long enough to check her appearance in the mirror in the foyer. She was tired, not dressed for the occasion, and she'd styled her hair in a bun worthy of a vicar's maiden aunt.

What is wrong with me? This was her first venture into merry widowhood, she'd chosen a wonderful partner in pleasure, and today they would consummate their affair.

I should be radiant, full of gleeful abandon. She opened the door to find Casriel standing with his back to her, as if on the point of departure.

"My lord, welcome."

He faced her and swept off his hat. "My lady, good day." His expression was nearly somber, no glee, reckless or otherwise, in his eyes.

"Do come in." Addy avoided, barely, glancing up and down the street to note any neighbors who might have seen the earl paying a call on the household's half day. "Shall I take your hat?"

"Best not."

"You won't be staying?" Disappointment crashed over her, making her out-of-sorts mood positively glum. Had he become engaged already? Been given permission to court? After waiting years to take a wife, he could not put off his betrothal even a few more days?

"I dearly hope I am welcome, but leaving evidence in the foyer that I'm on the premises is not well advised."

Oh. *Oh.* "I see." He was well mannered even about this. "Then let's remove to my sitting room, shall we?"

He looked as if he had some announcement to make. Addy started up the steps rather than learn he was paying his addresses to Lady Antonia. Even behind the locked parlor door, Casriel still made no move to take Addy into his arms, but that was perhaps fortunate, given her lack of inclination to be embraced.

"Have you some news to impart, my lord?"

He set his hat on the sideboard and propped his walking stick near the door. "In fact, I do. Lady Antonia Mainwaring has weighed me in the scales and found me—along with every other man of her acquaintance—lacking as a potential husband."

"You asked to pay her your addresses?" *When you knew we had an assignation today?*

Addy had no right to be angry or hurt, but she did admit to disappointment. Casriel at least had the grace to look uncomfortable.

"To the contrary, I made no such inquiry regarding any such addresses. She took it upon herself to disabuse me of ambitions in that direction and assured me emphatically that we would not suit."

Addy subsided into the armchair. "She told you not to bother? Didn't even wait for you to ask?" *How very decent of her.*

Casriel took the corner of the sofa. "Beatitude, I have no business raising this awkward topic with you at all, and you will think me daft, but I was so relieved I nearly fell to my knees in a public display of gratitude. I am apparently unable to conduct myself as more worldly men do, with one sort of association here and another sort there. I suspect my father was of the same nature, and thus I have many siblings."

"He was faithful?" *Grey would be faithful, and Addy wasn't sure how to feel about that, because his fidelity would be aimed away from her.*

"Papa's second countess strayed at least once. I do not judge their marriage, for times were different, but I do know this: I am very glad that received me today."

Addy poured him a glass of lemonade from the tray on the table, stirring the sweetness up from the bottom.

"Roger kept a mistress and did not deny himself other liaisons. He exercised the privileges of his station to the fullest, and he was a charming rascal." That label was wearing thin, though others had seen him as such.

Casriel held the glass halfway to his lips. "The late earl was a disgrace, if he allowed knowledge of his every peccadillo to find its way to you. A gentleman exercises some discretion."

Addy poured herself a drink and swirled the glass. "Roger was worldly, and in many ways, he and I did not suit, but our regard for one another began as genuine. We simply held different expectations from marriage and muddled on as best we could. Given time, I'm sure our union would have become more settled."

Though she and Roger had had years, and she'd become resigned, not settled. Addy wanted more than muddling on for Grey Dorning, and she did not want to spend the afternoon in sad reflection.

"I am glad you are here today," she said. "Glad we have this time to enjoy each other's company privately. Glad you are not like more worldly men."

"I am glad to be here. How is Mrs. Beauchamp?"

He did not bolt into the bedroom, leaving a trail of discarded clothing, did not fall upon Addy with kisses and caresses. She preferred his more restrained approach to Roger's heedless rutting. Preferred the fiction that they had limitless time and opportunity, rather than a few stolen hours.

"I fear Aunt Freddy is failing. She sleeps more and more. She doesn't mention any unusual pain, doesn't ask for anything, but she grows more pale and has less energy."

"Watch out for a dry cough," Grey said, sipping his drink. "Papa's final decline started out with a slight cough that grew worse when he spoke or tried to overdo. The herb woman said it was evidence of the heart weakening."

"You sent Aunt flowers and a tisane. Thank you for that."

"At Dorning Hall, we have enough herbal stock to fill the shelves of every apothecary in London with a good start on Paris besides. I'm tempted to plow up all of Papa's tea meadows and turn them into pastures, but my brothers would object."

"Have you heard from your siblings?"

Addy and her guest sipped lemonade, they ate half of the sand-wiches, they visited as any pair of friends would, and her low mood dissipated. Grey Dorning was still a free man and still a very attrac-tive man. She was still a widow in need of a diversion, and the after-noon—at least—was still young.

CHAPTER TEN

An intimate affair was supposed to involve sexual congress between the participants. Grey knew this, but he couldn't find the right moment to turn the mood in the direction of desire. His body had no trouble with the notion of taking Addy to bed, but his spirit...

What sort of man—what sort of gentleman—discussed his courting progress and lack thereof with the dear lady who'd embarked on a liaison with him? Other fellows likely did so without a qualm, but Grey was awash in qualms.

His courting apparently needed work, which bothered him not at all, but so did his manners while trysting with Addy, which bothered him significantly.

"You are concerned for your aunt," he said. "Shall I come calling some other day?"

"You have come at the only possible time." She rose and crossed to the bedroom door. "Will you think me very forward if I invite you to make love with me?"

Not *romp*, not *cavort*, not any of the dozens of other trivializing euphemisms for the greatest intimacy two people could share.

"I would think you brave, generous, and irresistible," he said, joining her in the doorway.

She hadn't worn a dress too low-cut for daytime, hadn't come to the door wearing only her dressing gown or with her hair tumbling seductively down her back. She was simply Beatitude, enjoying a widow's freedoms on a quiet afternoon.

And yet, Grey needed for this encounter, perhaps the only one they'd have, to be special, to be memorable and precious.

He looped his arms over her shoulders. "Will you tell me your most secret intimate wishes?"

She curled against his chest. "Will you tell me yours?"

"I have many. I want to learn the scent of you everywhere, want to learn whether the curls between your legs are lighter or darker than the tresses on your head. I want to hilt myself inside you, want to feel your pleasure as it overtakes you. I want—"

She kissed him, which was for the best. He wanted the right to share her bed whenever they pleased, not simply on half day when she wasn't indisposed and he wasn't spoken for. He wanted...

To be foolish. To marry for joy, but how much joy could a couple claim when the family seat became a leaking ruin, siblings were denied opportunities for lack of even modest coin, and a precious daughter had no chance to make a decent match?

"I want to taste you too," Addy said. "I want to fall asleep tonight with the scent of you on my sheets. I want to feel your pleasure as it overtakes you..."

That last was impossible, but a lovely, inspiring thought nonetheless.

Addy was unbuttoning his coat even as she kissed him. Grey got a start on her hooks. He and she would soon make love. He was physically ready—more than ready—and he'd thought of little else for the past week, but still...

This memory might have to last him a long, lonely lifetime.

"What's something I can do for you?" he asked, breaking the kiss to peel out of his coat. "What pleasure can I give you that you've longed for but denied yourself?"

"I know how to... That is, I've learned how to manage on my own."

She was referring to self-gratification. Women did, contrary to the myths propounded by sermonizing buffoons. Perhaps not with the frequency or enthusiasm of the young male of the species, but then, nothing in nature was as fixated on erotic pleasure as the young male.

She sat to toe off her slippers, and Grey knelt before her. "Allow me."

"I can undress myself."

Grey's sisters had explained this to him: Yes, a woman might enjoy the services of a lady's maid when dressing formally, but stays could be tied off in front, dresses dropped over the head, and the last few hooks fastened easily enough. Ladies—again, contrary to Mayfair myth—could dress and undress themselves for most occasions, just as men could.

"Allow me to be the smitten swain, Beatitude. To dote and tease is a lover's right."

Her smile was shy, suggesting he'd stumbled into an approach that worked for her.

"Very well," she said, easing her skirts no higher than her ankles. "You may assist me."

He untied her slippers, left then right, and set them aside. Her garters came next, pink lace confections that made him smile. He set those with her slippers, rolled down her stockings, and rubbed gently at the indentations left by the garters.

"That feels good." She sounded puzzled, a step in the right direction.

Grey explored the muscles of her calves—sturdy—and the bones of her ankles—delicate. Her feet were not ticklish, and her arches weren't particularly high. She had a scar on her right knee.

"I fell from a tree," she said. "Papa forbid me to ever climb that tree again."

"So the next day, you were up a different tree and climbing even higher." Her knee tasted of lavender, and her smile was a little less shy.

She leaned back against the armchair. "You needn't bother with this, you know. I'm not without a married woman's—I like that."

He'd shaped her breasts, confirming that she'd again forgone stays. "Touching you intimately is not a bother, Beatitude, but rather, my dearest fantasy come to life. You, willing and relaxed, the doors locked, the afternoon ours."

He lifted her skirts to her waist and answered one question. The hair on her head was lighter and had less of the reddish hue found in a more intimate location.

He brushed a finger over her curls. "May I?"

"Could I stop you?"

"Of course."

But she didn't. She merely regarded him broodingly, so Grey went exploring and indulged in every wicked impulse ever to delight a healthy man. Addy was slow to arouse, but by inches and sighs, she gave herself up to the moment. By the time she convulsed around his fingers, Grey had lost his boots, his waistcoat, his shirt, and half of his wits.

Addy's legs were draped over his shoulders, Grey's cheek pillowed against her thigh.

"I am... I am..." She trailed her fingers through his hair. "I don't know what I am. I hardly know who I am."

"Are you pleased?"

"Pleasured would be a more accurate term." She gave his hair an affectionate yank. "I will have my revenge. You are forewarned."

He kissed her knee. "That sounds promising. Should I set the sheath to soaking?"

"I am not familiar with sheaths. You must manage without any guidance from me on the matter, and I must somehow find the strength to rise and totter to the bed."

Gone was the articulate, self-possessed Lady Canmore. In her place was an endlessly dear woman somewhat bewildered by sexual satisfaction.

"We'll have none of that tottering business," Grey said, scooping her into his arms. He set her on the bed and let her watch as he undid his falls and stepped free of his breeches. His cock was at parade salute, and while he undid another dozen hooks on Addy's dress, she stroked a finger down the length of his shaft.

"You're so... at home in your body. You like being a man."

He fished the sheath from his coat pocket, poured a glass of water from the pitcher on the washstand, and set the sheath to soak.

"When I'm with you, I adore being a man. Will you leave your hair up?"

He would adore being *her* man, not simply her lover for a brief liaison. She hadn't indicated anything more than a liaison would interest her, though, so why speculate?

"I'll leave it braided, but you can take out my pins."

A treasure hunt ensued, with Grey searching gently for pins, while Addy, seated on the bed, tormented him with casual caresses to his cock, his flanks, his chest, his balls...

"Are you indulging your curiosity, my lady?" He'd set a dozen pins on the table by the bed.

"I am. I have never..." She rested her forehead against his belly. "Your approach to this undertaking is different from what I'm accustomed to."

He brushed his thumb over her nape and ignored a regret: He wished he'd been her first and only, wished she'd been his first and only. Ah well. That would mean no Tabitha, and Grey would never regret having a daughter.

"What are you accustomed to?"

She stood on the bed-step to wiggle out of her dress. "Dispatch, I suppose." She passed him her frock. "Focus, efficiency, purpose. A lusty and pleasurable objective achieved."

They were eye to eye because she remained on the bed-step.

Grey was naked. Addy was in her shift. Her gaze held uncertainty that tore at his heart.

"We do this however you choose, my lady, because my purpose in sharing this time with you is mutual pleasure. If all I want is a few moments of intense sensation, I can bring that about with my own hand. I want *you*."

"Do you?" she asked, ruffling his hair. "Bring pleasure about with your own hand?" She'd been married to a supposed libertine, and yet, her gaze was guardedly curious.

"Not as often as I did in my youth. I was a randy boy." Where had the randy boy gone, and did Grey want any part of him back?

She climbed onto the bed. "Now you are a grown man. How long does the sheath soak?"

"A few minutes. Might I join you?"

Her smile was a little wicked, a little bashful. "Please do," she said, lying back among the pillows.

Grey climbed over her on the bed and took a moment to relish the feel of his body pressed to hers. She was warm, lithe, and generously curved. Her touch was slow and soothing, more an exploration than a caress. He wanted her with an excruciating intensity, and yet, he lay quietly in her arms and let her hands wander over him.

Some fool—some fool of a husband—had rushed her into love-making, as a bride and as a wife. Some idiot had given her the notion she wasn't worth lingering over and cherishing. Addy traced the slope of Grey's nose, while he mentally cursed her late spouse.

If Lord Canmore had made marriage a more pleasurable under-taking for his wife, would Addy have a more charitable view of the institution now? Would she even—in a theoretical sense—entertain the possibility of marrying some worthy fellow who esteemed her greatly?

Such speculation could lead nowhere. Grey waited until Addy's hands stilled, then hitched up to crouch over her and begin a slow kissing tour of her every feature.

"PASS THE DECANTER," Valerian said, wiggling his fingers.

"It's empty," Thorne replied. "Oak, bring the decanter from the library."

Ash had gathered with his brothers in the estate office, though these impromptu meetings had taken on the feel of a wake. If Grey were here, he'd be assigning them tasks so they'd feel useful, minimizing the damage the rain had done to the hay crop, and coming up with another way to squeeze a farthing from thin air.

"It's Ash's turn to fetch the decanter," Oak replied. He was sketching at the sofa, while Hawthorne prowled the room with a glass in his hand. Valerian lounged against the mantel and Ash remained at the window willing Grey's gelding to canter up the drive. The earl would swing from the saddle with characteristic energy, and all of Dorning Hall would feel lighter and happier.

Grey would have been out calling on tenants, inspecting the crops and the calves, enjoying a pint at the posting inn with the local tradesmen, not lurking at the Hall like a sulky boy.

"I've been thinking about something," Ash said.

"Nothing good can come of you attempting to think." Thorne shook the last drops of his brandy into his mouth. "Thinking can lead to brooding, and you do too much of that."

Brooding was the family euphemism for the despair that engulfed Ash regularly. The medical fellows had other names for it. Nobody had a cure other than self-inflicted death, upon which the church at least frowned mightily.

"Think about getting the decanter," Oak said, glancing up from his sketch pad. "Though I'd rather Valerian fetched it. If you move, Ash, the light will shift."

The light at Dorning Hall never shifted enough. "Valerian should finish his damned book," Ash said, which caused Oak and Thorne to exchange a look, before Oak resumed scratching at his sketch pad.

"Oak should sell his paintings," Valerian replied mildly. "Or teach. I could teach as well—deportment for all the gentry sprigs hereabouts—but a gentleman does not engage in trade."

"That wouldn't be trade." Thorne came to a halt behind Grey's chair. "That's not working with your hands, which is what I do best. I should find a post as a steward."

"Stewards are gentlemen," Ash said, leaving unasked the question of what he himself should do for a profession. He'd thought to join Sycamore's enterprise in London, but that wasn't meant to be. He'd declined to continue working as a man of business with his brother-in-law, Worth Kettering, because he'd reasoned Sycamore's need was more pressing. Worth promptly had hired another for the position Ash had vacated.

"We should do *something*," Valerian said. "Grey at this moment is likely subduing a mountain of correspondence, or he's dancing attendance on some sweet young lady who will drive him daft within a year."

The silence that stretched was guilty and frustrated, also much too familiar.

"I've wondered lately," Ash said, "why Grey must send quarterly sums to the Pletchers at the posting inn. His liaison with their daughter was nearly 15 years ago, and he provides lavishly for our Tabby."

Blonk. Thorne set his glass on the sideboard. "Because Grey's conscience is overly active. He despoiled the fair Tansy and must make amends."

Valerian, Oak, and Ash all remained silent. The fair Tansy had more or less despoiled Grey, but even in Grey's absence, Ash would not make that ungentlemanly observation.

"Tansy Pletcher made a good effort to despoil our dear Willow at the same time," Thorne went on, "though I think Will's virtue held firm."

"Of course it did," Ash replied. Will's fraternal devotion had held firm, even if his virtue had been tempted. "Grey is compensating the Pletchers for the loss of Tansy's labor all these years, but she's well into her thirties by now and likely has a parcel of children with her tinker. Why does Grey continue to send her parents money?"

"Because he's Grey," Oak said. "I continue to paint and draw because I'm Oak, and Thorne must regularly apply himself to the forge because he's Thorne."

While Ash sat upon his backside and brooded because he was an idiot. "I cannot abide the notion that Grey will marry some feather-brain who will resent the Hall and her life here more every season."

"Perhaps you should have remained in London bride-hunting yourself," Thorne retorted. "Even I know you left a lady pining for you. Lady Della's settlements might have bought Grey some time."

Nobody discussed Ash's decision to quit London, and he wasn't about to let the topic be aired now.

"I'm off to the posting inn," he said, pushing away from the window.

"You've changed the damned light," Oak snapped.

"I would like to change a lot more than the damned light, but I'll start with the posting inn. I don't want it on my conscience that I did nothing while Grey traded his happiness for my future. That would drive me daft."

Valerian squinted into the empty decanter. "As Papa was driven daft?"

Thorne beat Ash to the door. "As we are all going daft."

GREY DORNING HAD MAGICAL POWERS. He could make time slow, like a conductor bidding an orchestra to play a stately *sara-bande,* or he could make sensations pile up and intensify, a presto finale to a grand symphony of intimate touches, kisses, and pleasures.

He'd kissed and stroked and fondled Addy for a wondrous eter-nity, until she'd been drunk with sensation, utterly passive beneath his hands. He'd never issued a single instruction or command, never grabbed her or put her hands where he wanted her touching him, though he'd let her know that her caresses pleased him.

He liked her fingers winnowing through his hair. He liked when she bit his earlobe.

She liked his mouth on her breasts, and she loved—loved—the maddeningly slow tempo at which he joined his body to hers. The sheath was different, a little cool, a little rough. She'd watched as he'd tied it around his shaft, nothing self-conscious or awkward about the moment.

Amid all the other revelations and insights washing through her, she saved a thought to consider later: *I was married to a selfish boy.*

Grey Dorning was not a selfish boy. He was a generous man, a skilled lover, and a demon when it came to self-restraint.

"You will not—" She'd meant to tell him that he'd not send her into pleasure again without finding satisfaction himself, but the damned man got one big hand under her backside and changed the angle of his hips.

"That is diabolical," she muttered against his neck.

He was taller than Roger, his arms longer, his frame larger. His *everything* was more generously proportioned, and thank God for that. Addy surrendered to satisfaction again, the intensity of the moment nearly equaling a loss of consciousness.

But better, much, much better, than simply fainting.

"You are a fiend," she panted, running her tongue along his collar-bone. "A devil, an imp of the bedroom."

"That sounds more interesting than being an earl." He was pleased with himself, and well he should be.

"You look all gentlemanly and predictable in your various blue waistcoats and sober evening wear, but beneath all that fine tailoring..."

He kissed her temple. "I'm simply a man, Beatitude."

She fell silent, accepting the reminder that she must not develop fancies where he was concerned, though ye heavenly choruses, she had much to think about.

"You are my lover," she said, scissoring her legs around him. "And you have yet to gratify your own desires."

"I have gratified many of my desires in the past hour."

"Gratify one more."

Of course, he could not be selfish even in this, driving Addy before him into a frenzy of fulfillment. To her shock, he withdrew and spent on her belly, despite wearing the sheath. The loss of him was both a physical ache and an emotional distress.

That wasn't how this was supposed to end. "I thought the sheath prevented conception."

He levered up a few inches. "Nothing prevents conception for a certainty. This is the safest approach I know short of limiting one's passion to longing glances and bad poetry."

Laughter was a relief, also precious. Early in the marriage—very early—she and Roger had laughed, though most of his mirth had been directed at her inexperience.

"Shall I untie your ribbon?" she asked, feeling very daring. Roger had never used a sheath, of course, never explained them, never shown her one.

"I can manage."

Grey got off the bed and ambled behind the privacy screen, giving Addy a chance to admire a very well-made man. Sheep farming put the muscle on a fellow, apparently.

"Will you take off that damned shift?" he asked, climbing back onto the bed. "I understand modesty, but you are beautifully constructed, and I treasure the feel of your skin next to mine."

Beautifully constructed. Had Roger ever called anything about her beautiful?

Addy pulled the shift over her head, stuffed it under her pillow, and curled down against Grey's side. "Tell me about Dorset, about your tea meadows and your sheep."

She liked the feel of his voice rumbling forth as she lay against him, liked the sensation of his hands wandering over her neck, shoulders, and arms. She liked the scent of him, shaving soap and man, and the warmth of his body snug up against hers.

She loved being able to bask in his company, delighting in a leisurely tumble, complete with a cuddle afterward.

She did not like at all that some woman would be at his side when he returned to Dorset weeks hence. Some woman would walk those acres with him. Some woman would have years to enjoy his many talents and considerations as a lover.

And that woman would not be her.

TO HOLD Beatitude while she slept was sweet, also painful. Her exhaustion was deep enough that she hadn't stirred for a quarter hour. She curled against Grey's side, skin to skin, giving him time to list regrets.

They all came down to the same lament: *I wish I were free to simply love her.*

If she didn't care to remarry, Grey would content himself with the role of intimate companion and dear friend. Widows were permitted to choose their escorts, so to speak.

"I can feel you thinking," Addy murmured. "Do you never relax, Grey? Never tell the world to go hang while you doze on a blanket amid the fragrance of your tea meadows?"

Oh, what memories he could have made with her. "I haven't napped in my father's botanical gardens for years. Playing the harp was relaxation. I painted some, until it became obvious Oak's talent eclipsed my own."

She tucked the covers over his arm. "Why should that matter?"

"Because Oak would not have pursued his artistic education if he thought in any way that his talent cast my own in the shade."

"He did not want to compete with you. Would to God that Roger had had more of that sensibility."

What etiquette applied for discussing a late spouse with a current lover? Perhaps the etiquette expected of friends would serve.

"You are still unhappy with Lord Canmore."

She rolled to her back. "A widow is allowed to be upset that her spouse has died."

The most recent Countess of Casriel had survived her husband by some years. She'd grieved Papa's passing, but not like this.

Grey shifted to his side, the better to observe his lover. "Do you miss him?"

"I miss having a husband, I miss being the countess, not the late earl's widow. I miss having somebody else who dwelled with me, took the occasional meal with me, provided me the occasional escort rather than trailed at my heels in his livery. In that sense, I miss Roger."

Grey took her hand beneath the covers. "But?"

She stared at the canopy, putting Grey in mind of the stone saints guarding the ruins of the Dorning Hall abbey: eternal long-suffering guarding eternal regrets.

"But I do not miss *him*," she said. "I was the vicar's daughter. Only a tavern maid would have been a less likely countess than I, and in hindsight, I can see that Roger chose me in part to twit his uncles."

"You were dazzled by his charm, too inexperienced to know infatuation from genuine regard, and just well born enough to believe he offered you a love match. I'm surprised you didn't end up hating him." Canmore, if he was the typical aristocratic puppy, had not thought of the pain his twitting would inflict on his young, unsophisticated bride.

Addy shifted again, so Grey was treated to the elegant line of her shoulders and the temptation of her nape.

"I nearly did hate him at times. One can't, of course. Once hate gains a purchase on one's sentiments, it's like dry rot or creeping damp. Nearly impossible to eradicate. Roger regretted marrying me, I know that, but we tried hard to remain civil, and I respected that about my husband."

Grey spooned himself around her, hurting for that young bride, hurting for the widow. "So his death left you feeling both angry and guilty? I certainly felt both when my father died."

She peered at him over her shoulder. "You did? Truly?"

"I would go to Papa's grave and lecture him on the unfairness of having abandoned me, then beg him to tell me what to do. All very dramatic, though I think my histrionics served a purpose."

Addy's backside fit perfectly against the curve of Grey's body, just as this conversation—intimate rather than erotic—also fit with his notion of what lovers could share with each other.

"What productive end could such a display possibly serve?" she asked.

"I sorted myself out," Grey said, searching for words that weren't also pointlessly dramatic. "I admitted to myself, and to a lot of weeds and dead flowers, that I was angry and afraid. From there, I could tackle the matters that were putting me into such a state. I could use the fear to bolster my determination to safeguard my dependents."

Addy laced her fingers with his and brought his knuckles to her lips for a kiss. "Hence, the hard physical labor, I suppose. Perhaps I ought to take up hillwalking."

The hills of Dorset were beautiful. Grey could not say that to her, could not invite her to the Hall as a member of a house-party guest list.

"What one quality are you most annoyed with Roger for? What failing or misstep did he inflict on you that you were simply unable to overlook?"

She was quiet for so long, Grey wondered if she were falling asleep again, then her grip on his hand tightened.

"Roger died when his carriage overturned. He was pinned under the wreckage, and the horses could not get free until his friends arrived. His injuries were internal, and it took him some hours to expire."

Somebody ought to have spared her that knowledge, ought to

have told her that her husband had faded gently from injuries that had caused him no apparent pain.

"You wish he had not been reckless at the reins?"

"He was a skilled whip. I learned a lot from him in that regard. He simply had bad luck, but he also had time to send me a note."

Did Addy ever drive out? Grey was nearly certain she did not. "He was dying, Addy, probably feeling the effects of laudanum, if not laudanum and drink."

"I hadn't considered that. He could hold his liquor, but laudanum..."

Grey was not about to let her dodge off on that rabbit trail. "He wrote to you."

"He wrote to me: *Dearest wife, if you can produce a boy child within the next year, Jason won't get the title. Even a girl will cost him some wealth. Do it for me. Canmore.*"

Addy was motionless, clearly waiting for Grey to react.

"You've never mentioned this note to anybody?"

"Of course not. I still have the note, because I cannot fathom... I cannot believe those were my husband's dying words to me. When I read them, I am again the bewildered bride who could not grasp why her titled spouse laughed at her. The words hurt—reminding me that I had failed entirely as a wife—but even more, they terrify me."

Grey gathered her close, the only comfort he could offer. "In his relatively short and vastly indulged life, Canmore had been denied only one thing. He had wealth, a title, a bride plucked from contented innocence on his whim, a father who doubtless spoiled him from infancy, and a mother who doted on him without ceasing. He did not need an heir of his body, he merely wanted one, and rather than accept that God or fate or his own vices made that boon impossible, he had a protracted and stupid tantrum. He did not deserve you. He was not worthy of the privilege of being your husband."

Addy turned so she was wrapped along Grey's length, face to face. "One should not speak ill—"

"Protect his memory for the sake of others if you must, Beatitude, but we can have truth between us. Roger did not deserve you."

She held on to Grey tightly, her face against his throat, and Grey braced himself for tears. She was entitled to cry. She was entitled to shatter expensive porcelain, to hurl foul oaths and spend money at the shops like a sailor on shore leave. Instead, she'd kept her dignity and been more of a lady than her husband had ever been a gentleman.

"You aren't wrong," she said. "Nobody knew him the way I knew him. Jason probably suspects some of what went on, but he and I have kept our distance. At Roger's wake, in every mourning call, all I heard was what a pity it was that I had nothing *to remember him by*, as if five years of marriage were nothing, as if only a child could have compensated the poor man for taking such as me to wife. I wanted a child simply to love, because I questioned whether my husband could ever love me."

And doubtless, if she'd had a daughter, the lament would have been the lack of a boy child.

"You remind me why I treasure my estate in Dorset. Why a life of practical challenges, beautiful scenery, and family squabbles is preferable to polite society's inanities. You should burn that damned note. At best, it was the fearful and fevered wanderings of a young man facing a pointless death. You doubtless have other happier mementos of the late earl."

"Burn it?"

"Crumple it up, toss it onto a blazing hearth, watch it turn to ash." Grey did not offer to undertake that ritual with her, for he was merely her lover. "Canmore's foolishness does not deserve to trouble you, and whatever else was true about him, in this Canmore was a damned fool."

Addy's hold on him eased. "Burn it. I will think on this."

While Grey had to think of the passing of the hours. He'd left a pile of unopened mail on his desk at the town house, and his evening would be taken up with a soiree. Such thoughts were obscene while

Addy lay naked in his arms, struggling with demons she should never have had to subdue.

Grey rolled, taking her with him so she ended up straddling him.

She regarded her bare breasts. "I seem to have lost my damned shift."

I've lost my damned mind. "The view from where I lie is inspiring. If your ladyship can spare the time, perhaps you'd like another turn on the dance floor?"

She kissed him, her nipples brushing his chest. "A gavotte this time. Cheerful, sprightly, and full of fun."

"A gavotte it shall be." Later, when he was alone with some decent brandy, Grey would allow his heart to sing a silent lament.

CHAPTER ELEVEN

"This is a disaster," Hawthorne muttered.

"It's simply another leaking roof," Ash countered, though if Hawthorne pronounced something a disaster, it likely was. Ash's trip to the posting inn the previous day had proven awkward and ended with Mrs. Pletcher promising to have a discussion with Mr. Pletcher.

Discussions did not leaking attics repair.

"This is a roof that's been leaking for some time," Thorne said, peering at the attic's ceiling. "Why the hell doesn't the housekeeper tour the attics once a quarter as Mama used to?"

"Because we haven't a countess on the premises to tour the attics with the housekeeper." Increasingly, all roads led to acquiring a countess.

Grey would come home when he had a countess, and the myriad debates and decisions relating to management of the estate would fall to him. The tenants would direct their endless stream of woes to him. The task of calling upon neighbors would be taken in hand by the countess, and no more time need be wasted discussing the weather, the crops, or the upcoming assembly with anybody who cared to demand Ash's time in the family parlor.

Oak was too shy to entertain callers on his own and was usually busy with a painting. Valerian worked on his book by the hour. Thorne had no small talk.

"We might not have a countess at the moment," Hawthorne said, scowling at the water stains and peeling plaster on the attic wall, "but we have common sense. Dorning Hall is ancient. The house cannot maintain itself, and just because an attic is empty..."

He stalked off, having to duck beneath the massive roof beams. They at least looked to be holding firm.

"We'll replace a few slates," Ash said. "Clean the gutters, inspect the drainpipes. The roof will stop leaking. The wall will dry."

"Do you know what properly quarried slates cost? Do you know what it takes to get those slates up to the rooftop? How many men we'll need to undertake the labor? And it's not a matter of tossing a few leaves from the drains and gutters. You think the gutter on this side of the house is causing the problem, but the water has found some means to travel by stealth from the other side of the house. A worn soffit, a bad join between the south wing and the east. One does battle with and for a house this old, and Grey knows where all the latest skirmishes were fought."

Latest meaning in the past century, no doubt.

"Then we'll have Oak draw Grey a diagram of the problem and an estimate to put it to rights. I'll tuck in a little explanatory note, and you will add a lecture reminding him that the sooner he finds us a countess, the more likely the house is to be standing when he brings his bride home."

Hawthorne ducked through the low door that led to the stairway. "Valerian is our writer. What does that leave for him to do?"

"He is our charmer. He will recruit assistance from the local tavern and churchyard."

"We cannot pay anybody for anything remotely resembling assistance."

"Why should we have to?" Ash pulled the attic door firmly closed. "We make hay with our neighbors, we shear with them, we harvest with them and dig out drainage ditches with them. We send anybody who asks whatever exotic medicinals they might need at no charge, and every family in the shire gets a generous basket from us at Christmas whether their rent is paid or not. Every wardrobe in the county is scented with our sachets. Our herb woman has the best inventory in the realm. Name me one other peer whose family does as much for their tenants and neighbors."

Thorne pushed the door open. "Let the air circulate, and the wall might begin to dry out. I cannot name you another earl who matches Casriel for generosity and fair dealing with his tenants, and you know it. Papa set a certain standard, and Casriel honors that standard. Times are changing and not necessarily for the better. I respect that Casriel does what he can for our neighbors, but we can't fix a leaking roof with a tisane."

Grey did what he could for the neighbors, the family, the local church, and the staff. "If the House of Lords ever gets him to sit as chairman of some damned committee, we're doomed."

Thorne started down the steps. "Without a countess, we're doomed anyway, though we needn't fear the House of Lords will abduct him. Casriel is a countryman at heart, and he's doubtless doing the pretty, bowing and smiling over perfumed, gloved hands as we speak, but Dorset Hall is his first responsibility. He'll find us a wealthy countess or die in the attempt."

"He shouldn't have to go to such extremes."

Thorne paused on the landing. "As long as you and I and that pair of fops known as Oak and Valerian spend most of our days racketing about the Hall, pretending to be busy and productive, as long as Sycamore kicks his handsome heels pretending to manage a gaming hell while in fact running up bills at the tailor's and bootmaker's, Casriel must marry wealth. In his shoes, any man would do the same."

"Any honorable man."

"And Casriel is honorable."

"Do you ever wish he weren't such a paragon of duty and selfless-ness, Thorne?"

They reached the floor of the house where the brothers' apart-ments were. Each brother had his own suite of rooms, and all of them had lovely views of the Dorset countryside. The Hall was beautiful, considered from the right perspective, though Ash was growing to hate the place.

"I wish Casriel would play the harp again," Thorne said. "I wish he would laugh. I wish he'd go to London because a change of scene can be a pleasant diversion, not because he must parade himself before this Season's crop of heiresses while ignoring the stink of sewers that flow like rivers. I wish he'd find a damned countess who could give him some babies to love and spoil and maybe even distract him from the purgatory that the earldom has become."

For Thorne, that was a third-act monologue. "The Hall needs a countess," Ash said. "Grey needs a wife."

"And I need a drink."

Drinking solved nothing. Ash had learned that lesson in a very hard school.

"Excuse me, Mr. Ash, Mr. Hawthorne." Rawley, their butler, had come up from the floor below. "Vicar is paying a call. I've put him in the guest parlor."

"Why on earth would you do that?" Thorne asked. "The damned man never stays less than an hour and can imitate a plague of locusts over the tea tray with convincing enthusiasm."

"I do apologize, sir, but he heard your voices from the foyer. He knows you are on the premises, and we have turned him away twice in the past two weeks. I did escort him to the guest parlor with all due haste, but he has good hearing."

Ash had been dodging Vicar in the churchyard for the past two Sundays. Grey was responsible for dealing with all matters relating to the local living, another duty the right countess could ease.

"I'll pour him a cup of tea," Ash said. "But, Rawley, you will tell the kitchen to send up half the usual tray, and in thirty minutes—not thirty-five, not forty-two—you will interrupt to inform me of pressing matters requiring my attention at the home farm."

"I would not advise that, sir. As the earl himself has realized, the home farm is in the direction of the vicarage, and you will find yourself escorted thence by your guest. Better to have a pressing issue at the estate brewery. The vicar knows little about how beer and ale are made, and our brewery lies in the opposite direction of the village."

"The brewery it is," Ash said, "and then I'll want to send an express to the earl in London."

"Another express, sir?"

"Another express."

Rawley withdrew, descending the steps at a decorous pace.

"Where are you going?" Thorne asked as Ash took off down the corridor.

"Even I know receiving a man of God with cobwebs in my hair isn't done. I wish Grey had never gone to London." *And I wish I hadn't had to leave.*

"Not quite true," Thorne said, falling in step beside him. "You wish he was back from London. We all do. When you write that express, tell him to snabble the first available heiress and hurry home."

"I've already told him that. Twice."

"Tell him again."

THE MAID HELD up the latest creation from Madam Batiste, a soft green evening dress designed to show off slightly more of Sarah's attributes than was proper for a woman in her first Season.

"I must try it on. Mama, get me out of this rag."

"If the green requires alterations," Mama said, rising from the sofa, "you can wear the blue. Bartles, you may be excused."

The maid folded the dress back into its box, curtseyed, and withdrew. Now Mama would start with her scolds and lectures, unless Sarah took the floor first.

"I cannot wear the blue. I wore blue to Lady Brantmore's do, and I wore blue to the most recent card party."

Mama's hands on Sarah's hooks were slower than Bartles's would have been. "Lord Casriel favors blue waistcoats, my dear. He might think blue dresses are a flattering attempt to complement his attire."

"That is precisely why I must not wear blue. He should be complementing my choices, not the other way around. For the rest of our married life, I will be bound by vows to honor and obey him. In courtship at least, he ought to be honoring and obeying me."

Mama paused in her unhooking. "Has he danced a supper waltz with you?"

"He's a gentleman, and gentlemen must dance with both the plain and the pretty, or they aren't allowed to dance at all. I'm pretty, and he danced with me, thus he was required to dance with less-attractive women at some point."

Mama resumed her progress down to the middle of Sarah's back, though holding still while Mama delivered her little sermon was excruciating.

"Has his lordship walked you home from services?"

"Why would a peer of the realm bother with an antiquated custom even the yeomen no longer put much stock in?"

Mama finally got to Sarah's waist, about which Sarah was not merely proud, she was unapologetically vain. Bartles knew how to cinch in a corset, and the result of a small waist was a bosom that appeared more generous by comparison. Gentlemen did have their little aesthetic preoccupations, after all, and the Creator had neglected to fill Sarah's bodice as well as she might have liked.

"You've been interviewing yeomen, to know their habits of late?" Mama asked. "Lord Casriel owns a good patch of Dorset, so when he walked Lady Antonia home from church, he might well have been indulging in an antiquated custom of some import to him."

Sarah turned. "He walked Lady Antonia home?"

"Arm in arm, conversing as they strolled along and tarried in Grosvenor Square. You were too busy twirling your parasol at Lord Dentwhistle to notice. Casriel and Lady Antonia made a handsome couple."

"You needn't be nasty, Mama, or leap to unjustified conclusions. Perhaps Lady Antonia lives in the same direction as his lordship. Perhaps they share an interest in Italian opera. Help me get this dress off."

"Lord Casriel hasn't been seen at the opera yet this Season, that I know of."

Sarah held still while her mother gathered up skirts and underskirts, carefully raising them over Sarah's waist. This ritual—dressing and undressing—was vaguely annoying. Little children needed to be dressed and undressed. Why did fashion require that grown ladies also have assistance with any wardrobe worth wearing in public?

Though having a maid on hand to deal with pins and ribbons and to take away wrinkled clothing was ever so convenient.

"So Casriel doesn't care for a lot of caterwauling from warbling sopranos and well-fed tenors," Sarah said. "Neither do I."

Mama lifted the dress over Sarah's head. "His lordship might not care for you, Sarah Quinlan."

Why must Mama make that suggestion when Sarah wore only her stays and shift, her meager endowments so clearly pushed up into a semblance of abundance?

"All the gentlemen like me. I'm an Incomparable. Lord Dentwhistle told me so."

"Dentwhistle is a fortune hunter whose grandfather beggared the family with foolish investments. Are you losing weight?"

"Why do you ask? Do I look too skinny?" Sarah turned this way and that, considering her figure in the cheval mirror. The white of her underlinen washed out her complexion and made her dark hair look garish.

I look like a tall, pale, gawky girl. Not confident like Lady Antonia, who truly was tall and gawky. Not generously rounded like those blasted Arbuckles. Not confident, well rounded, *and* pleased with life, like Lady Canmore.

"You do look a little tired," Mama said, holding up the green dress. "You'll have time for a nap before we go out tonight."

Children napped. Sarah obligingly ducked her head and held out her arms so Mama could get her into the green dress. The silk fabric felt deliciously cool and expensive, and the fit was exquisite.

"Tonight," Sarah said, examining her reflection, "I shall cast a *lure* at Lord Casriel."

Mama knelt to straighten the drape of the underskirt. "What an original approach. I'm sure no young lady has ever cast a lure at him. Perhaps instead of drawing and pianoforte, those expensive finishing schools should teach young ladies how to angle for trout."

"Mama, I believe *you* are in need of a nap. Lord Casriel might not understand the language of the fan or the glove. I will have to be subtle but clear."

Mama rose. "Sarah, you must not convince yourself that Casriel will trot to your side because you crook your finger and wink. Lady Antonia enjoys a much higher station than you. The Arbuckles are from older wealth than you and are considered pretty. They can also aid each other should one of them attract his lordship's notice. While you..."

Mama sighed, a sound of exasperation and disappointment.

Over the Arbuckles? The *Arbuckles*? "They are not prettier than I am. They are in their *third* Season."

Mama tugged the dress's bodice upward, which was futile when the waist was so snug. "But, Daughter, even the Arbuckles are more of Casriel's ilk. Their mother's father is a baronet. Do you truly want to spend most of your life in Dorset? You know little of managing a country house."

Why must Mama ruin everything lately? Sarah's joy in the new dress was melting away like the beeswax tapers in a ballroom chandelier.

"Do you think my situation is easy, Mama?" Sarah paced away from the mirror, loving how the silk swished about her ankles and punctuated an angry mood. "You have never endured a London Season. You have never had to stand still for fittings that take hours, never had to befriend women who would as soon knife you in the back as turn pages for you at the pianoforte. I want an earl, and I shall have an earl, and not just any earl. An earl who needs my money will be much easier to manage than one who condescends to offer for me out of a mere passing attraction."

Mama's gaze was on the empty mirror. "The money belongs to your father, and one does not embark upon marriage as if it's a mercantile venture. Many aristocrats take that approach, and a sorrier, sadder lot of human beings you will not find on this earth. We who have had to work for our bread are more discerning than that sort, more genuine. Casriel seems like a decent man, but I'd rather you find a fellow whose motive isn't simply to expand his selection of waistcoats."

Members of the peerage were ruthless about marriage and wealth, which was wonderful. If they weren't, Sarah would never have had a chance at a title.

"I like that some people can approach marriage pragmatically," she said. "Sentimental foolishness fades, while a fortune and a title are permanent comforts. I have the fortune, Casriel has the title, and I like him well enough."

He wasn't too handsome, wasn't too old, wasn't too flirtatious. Casriel would be biddable and grateful, and he'd be polite to Sarah's parents when necessary.

More than she was able to manage lately.

"Sometimes," Mama said, picking up Sarah's discarded day dress, "I don't like you. Be careful, Sarah. You lack the stature to compromise a man like Casriel, and all your father's money cannot rescue your reputation if you throw it away on a lure that misses its mark."

Folding up the dress as any maid would, Mama looked old and weary, though she was barely forty.

"I hadn't thought to compromise his lordship." The notion was intriguing. To trap a famously well-mannered man by using social convention made all the sense in the world. Casriel would probably thank her for sparing him a lot of bother dancing with the wallflowers.

"If you misstep with Casriel, you will find yourself sewing samplers in Cheshire for at least the next five years, Sarah. Your father will not be made a laughingstock, no matter how generous he is with you otherwise."

Mama's mouth was in a pinchy line. Mauve shadows formed half circles beneath her eyes.

I will never look like her. Never, and this time next year, I won't have to listen to her either.

"Mama, you worry for nothing. His lordship needs to marry money, and I am happy to become his countess. That's how these things are done."

"That is not how your father and I did it," Mama said, moving toward the door, "and we manage well enough. I'll send Bartles to help you out of your dress, lest you wrinkle your new frock prancing before the mirror."

Mama closed the door softly, though she had as usual managed to have the last word.

For now.

~

"MY PRIORITIES HAVE CHANGED," Grey said. "Instead of looking for a lady with handsome settlements, I now search for a prospective countess who's an expert on repairing roofs."

In fact, since spending a long afternoon in Lady Canmore's bed last week, Grey had been searching for his sanity, while dodging eligible young women. He'd found safety among the wallflowers, widows, and dowagers and avoided the near occasion of heiresses.

Then Ash's letter had arrived.

"The hour is early," Tresham said, pausing to sniff at a rose. "Have you been at the brandy, Casriel?"

"I cannot afford to *be at the brandy*. Dorning Hall, the edifice in which my family, forty inside servants, and another thirty outside servants shelter, has developed a serious leak in the roof of the east wing, which, naturally, is where the family quarters are."

Tresham sauntered along the garden path, a mastiff trotting at his side. "I thought tenant cottages were famous for leaking roofs?"

"Infamous, and because tenants are forbidden to make improvements to structures on their leaseholds, landlords must perform the needed repairs. I was caught up—I was *almost* caught up—with the tenant cottage and pensioner cottage repairs."

"You can't simply patch a few holes and hope for dry weather?"

The dog paused to lift its leg on a bed of blooming daisies.

"This is England. Summer is as close as we get to dry weather, so the roofs must be repaired now, and no, a patch job seldom works. Dorning Hall will beggar me if the damage is as bad as Ash thinks." *Finish beggaring me.*

"So close off that wing, dismantle it while you can salvage plenty of bricks for resale, and plant a few more trees on that side of the house. In a hundred years, nobody will notice that your façade lacks symmetry. It's an ancestral pile. They'll call it charming and unique."

They'd call it an architectural failure courtesy of the present pathetic excuse for an earl. "Shall we lop off a wing of the Quimbey family seat, Tresham? Sell off the windows and hinges to the builders swarming around London? Is that any way to husband a heritage that's centuries in the making?"

"Let's sit. Caesar is in the mood to investigate today."

Caesar being one of the Quimbey household's canine behemoths. Tresham settled onto a bench, while Grey paced the garden walk.

"Then the vicar," he said, "who well knows the Dorning family circumstances, reports that the church is also in need of a new roof. Not a mere repair either. A new roof. If the previous vicar had installed standing seam tin as Papa had advised, we would not have this problem. But no, a church must be beautiful, said the holy man who is supposed to counsel us against vanity. The church must have a slate roof, and not twenty years later, the damned thing is growing moss on the north side and leaking perilously near the fourth earl's organ."

Tresham was smiling at his dog.

"Not that sort of organ," Grey muttered. "Married life has made you easily distracted."

"I am not the poor fellow who is so beset by a lack of roofing slates that he cannot sit still on a beautiful spring day. You knew when you arrived in London that marrying a fortune was your objective. You knew your roofs would eventually leak. Your fields must eventually be marled. Your ditches and drains cleared, your daughter dowered."

The day was beautiful only to those trapped in London. Here, a fair day meant a yellowish tinge to the sky for much of the morning and a pervasive hint of grit and smoke in the air. When the wind was wrong, the stink off the river made even the clearest of London days unbearably odoriferous. No wonder Londoners suffered so many lung ailments and chest colds.

"Despite the challenges you face," Tresham went on, "at last week's soiree, I saw you evade both the Arbuckles and Miss Quinlan. You didn't even stand up with Lady Antonia, but instead danced with every wallflower ever to sprout in Mayfair. Theodosia is concerned for you."

The dog sniffed at Grey's boots, then wandered over to sit at Tresham's knee.

"A gentleman dances with a variety of partners, if he dances at all."

"You haven't danced with Lady Canmore lately."

Oh yes, Grey had. He'd danced with her in countless dreams. He'd conversed with her in more imaginary discussions than any ballroom could contain. He'd pleasured himself to memories of time spent in her bed, and he was counting the hours until the next half day.

Thirty-six, give or take a few, minutes. "Lady Canmore and I are friends."

Tresham and the dog gave him the same pitying look. "You are smitten, and just when your resolve to marry an heiress is being tested, the roof threatens to cave in back home. If you need a loan, you have merely to tell me."

Despair nearly felled Grey, for offers of loans were made only to friends in the direst circumstances. Tresham's estimation of the Dorning fortunes had apparently eroded from *not that bad* to *nearly hopeless*.

"That offer is most kind of you, Tresham, also embarrassing as hell. If I accepted your loan, when my income and expenses barely balance, how would I repay you? I'd simply dig a hole for my son or heir to dump his prospects into."

"Peers cannot be jailed for debt. You pay back what you can when you can."

Grey took a seat on the hard bench, though he wanted, badly, to kick something—his own backside, for example.

"Peers cannot be jailed for much of anything, which is why a titled man's honor must be sufficient to ensure that he commits as few injustices as possible. He may blunder and stumble, but to willfully exploit the privileges of his station is contemptible."

Tresham pulled gently on the dog's ears. Willow, the Dorning family expert on canines, claimed dogs liked that. When Addy tugged on Grey's ears, it certainly inspired him to wagging his tail and panting.

God save me.

"Casriel, you are the soul of social savoir faire, and yet, you are barely making sense. Is Lady Canmore inspiring you to blunder and stumble?"

Grey took off his hat and set it on the bench. "A gentleman does not bandy a lady's name about."

"Theodosia called on Lady Canmore yesterday. Every other word was 'Casriel this' and 'his lordship that,' punctuated by blushing silences. If she's bandying *your* name, then you can certainly keep a concerned friend informed of your worries."

Addy had perhaps mentioned Grey twice, and one of those mentions would have been prompted by Tresham's wife. Still, blushing silences were all too credible. Grey, in fact, was blushing while Tresham and his damned dog watched.

"Like that, is it?" Tresham said.

"I have created an impossible situation," Grey said. "I care very much for her ladyship, and yet, duty compels me to seek marriage with a woman of means."

Tresham gave the dog a final pat to its massive head. "You can't cut expenses?"

"Dornings are thrifty. There are too many of us for any profligacy. By the time I've lent Will a bit in a lean year, aided Sycamore to get his club on its feet, kept Oak, Thorne, Ash, and Valerian in new boots and riding horses, paid for the parish living, done a bit for charity, looked after my pensioners, caught up Tabitha's bills—"

Tresham held up a hand. "I recall your ledgers. An heiress is the necessary solution if you can't either cut expenses or increase revenue, and the sooner you get your hands on her money, the healthier the earldom will be."

Grey should have stood, thanked Tresham for his damned keen insight, and taken himself away to kick stone walls and curse all leaking roofs. Instead, he remained on the bench.

"My difficulty is that a man is expected to get his hands on his wife from time to time, not simply on her fortune. This is an obligation which I no longer believe to be within my abilities."

The dog cocked his head.

"You are in love," Tresham said gently. "You are smitten with Lady Canmore, and you cannot fathom being intimate with another."

"Cannot fathom... cannot even theoretically admit the necessity. And yet, marriage entitles a woman to expect certain attentions from her husband. I'm not sure why else a wealthy female would take a husband, much less a man whose household includes four grown brothers, not a one of whom can seem to recall that his boots do not belong on the furniture. That reminds me. How is Sycamore faring at The Coventry?"

"You should ask him."

"I have, and he's predictably evasive, suggesting he's in over his head, floundering, and making a bad situation worse. He excels at putting a good face on a disaster, but charm alone will not pay the bills."

The dog wandered over to the fountain, stood on his back legs, and took a noisy drink from the water splashing down from the stone pineapple.

"Sycamore has changed some practices at the club," Tresham said. "I think he could use a brother or two at his side, but it's not my place to tell him that. He seems to be managing."

Grey rose rather than hear more bad news. "When he seems to be managing, when he's doing his best impersonation of a young gentleman in control of his affairs, that's when he's usually top over tail in trouble. Thank you for letting me rant and pout like a toddler."

Tresham eased to his feet. Since marrying Theodosia, the Quimbey heir was more relaxed. He moved more slowly. He smiled more. He was a more congenial host at his monthly Lonely Husbands evenings, and he could occasionally be seen hacking out with Mrs. Tresham on fine mornings.

The changes were modest, visible mostly to friends or family, but Tresham was thriving in the married state. Clearly, husband and wife shared the day's gossip with each other. They spent the occasional evening at home together, and they even stood up with one another for the first waltz of the evening.

Grey envied his friend with an intensity no gentleman could admit to and no honest man could deny.

"What will you do?" Tresham asked. "You cannot offer for a woman in bad faith. One could—some men could—but *you*, Casriel, cannot. You are also incapable of dissembling where Lady Canmore is concerned, and my best guess is that your feelings are reciprocated."

Don't say that. Don't think that. Don't even hint that. "Her ladyship's first husband was a less-than-ideal match for her. She does not view remarriage enthusiastically."

The dog climbed into the fountain with a great splashing leap. The water wasn't deep enough to submerge the entire mastiff, but Grey envied the beast his simple pleasures.

Tresham smiled as the dog behaved like a twelve-stone puppy. "Have you considered asking Lady Canmore to marry you?"

Only a thousand times. "I dare not. If she answered in the affirmative, where would that leave us? I can offer her only poverty and disgrace." And if she accepted his offer, they'd be in a damned, hopeless mess, as opposed to a merely wretched coil.

"Theodosia says Lady Canmore's means are modest, Casriel. I'm sorry."

"Perhaps her ladyship will tire of me." If that happened, Grey would retreat into the role of fond memory and wish the lady well. Then he'd get roaring drunk and kick whomever and whatever he pleased, starting with the vicar and finishing with Papa's headstone.

The dog bounded from the fountain and had the grace to shake vigorously while still some yards off. A dog's life was uncomplicated, his comforts inexpensive and easily found. One of Caesar's few obligations was to attend Georgette, Will's equally stupendous lady mastiff, when she paid her visits.

Oh, to be a hound rather than a peer of the realm.

"Lady Canmore will not tire of you," Tresham said. "She hasn't spared another man so much as a glance since Lord Canmore went to his reward. They were reported to be a love match, you know. If she's put aside his memory to favor you with her company, you are more than a passing fancy for her."

She'd put aside her heartache where Canmore was concerned, or started to. That Grey had been her confidant was more precious to him than all the slate roofs in Dorset.

"And she is much more than a passing fancy to me," Grey said.

"Could one of your brothers perhaps attach an heiress?"

One of Grey's brothers—Ash, by name—was much taken with Lady Della Haddonfield, to whom Tresham had a discreet family connection. She was not an heiress. Ash had engaged the lady's affections to all appearances, and then scarpered back to Dorset, leaving the woman no explanation.

Grey had his suspicions regarding Ash's motivations, but Ash's reasons were his own. He was surrounded by family at Dorning Hall, and that was for the best.

"The only brother with sufficient charm to win an heiress," Grey said, "is Sycamore, and he's much too young to embark on such an objective. Oak is retiring by nature, Valerian a dandy without means. Thorne is charmless and unrefined of sentiment. I at least have a title to offer. The fortune-hunting is best left in my hands."

Tresham delivered a thumping pat to Grey's shoulder. "Perhaps one of those brothers will provide you with your heir. It's the least they can do, considering the sacrifice you're contemplating."

Tresham saw Grey to the back gate, the damp dog panting unfragrantly at his heels, and then Grey was making his way alone through the shaded alleys. The alleys were free of debutantes and matchmakers, which he'd discovered of necessity in the past two weeks.

Alleys were a good place for a man to walk and worry.

In every regard other than consummation of the vows, taking on a wife was arguably a prudent move. The countess would assist with managing Dorning Hall and the earldom's social obligations. She'd take meals with the family. She'd incur some expenses, but also— Grey hoped—provide a guiding hand for what remained of Tabitha's upbringing.

None of which told Grey how he could possibly perform as a husband was expected to on his own wedding night.

CHAPTER TWELVE

"You are brooding," Aunt Freddy said. "This is why you should have applied yourself to the study of the harp, my dear. If you must be pensive and pale, you could at least look pretty doing it."

"I am neither pensive nor pale. I'm trying to be considerate when you are clearly too tired for conversation."

That answer—more snappish than Addy had intended—was proof enough of Aunt's conjecture to have the old woman smiling.

"This is about Casriel, isn't it?" Aunt asked. "He's a fine specimen, and he claims he'll have my harp ready any day." Aunt picked up her tea cup and blew on the contents without taking a sip. Her hand trembled slightly, though she didn't spill.

"If my mood is poor, that's because the Season has reached the dragging-on-interminably stage," Addy said, "and I am approaching the anniversary of Roger's death."

Aunt set down her tea cup. "My poor lamb, I had forgotten, but then, I'm not exactly consulting my calendar regularly. Perhaps you should go down to Canmore Court for a week or two. Take a respite, spend time with your nieces and nephews."

Jason and his countess were up to five children. A third healthy little boy had arrived two months ago. They'd named him Roger and asked Addy to be his godmother.

"I will not impose on my in-laws when they have a newborn in the house. Shall I bring you your knitting?"

"You may do a few rows for me," Aunt said, clearing her throat in the abrupt manner of the elderly. "If you wait until the present Earl of Canmore has no infants in his nursery, you will be nearly as old as I am. Just as the children taper off, the grandchildren start. When that happens, otherwise sensible, mature people lose their remaining wits over a scrap of humanity who weighs no more than a cat."

Casriel would be like that. A doting father who became an adorable grandfather, wise, kind, full of good stories.

Though he would not be doting on Addy's grandchildren. She'd seen him standing up for a quadrille with Miss Quinlan, seen the ambition in the young woman's smiles. Grey's troubles would soon be over, as would Addy's affair with him.

She opened Aunt's workbasket and took out the blue shawl. Nothing had been added to the project since Addy's last visit, not so much as a single row.

"This will be wonderfully warm come autumn," Addy said. "Do you have enough of the blue yarn to finish?"

Aunt took a sip of her tea. "Tell me about Casriel."

Older people could be like this, having trouble following the thread of a conversation. "He's all that is gracious and good company, and I suspect we'll hear an announcement regarding his marital prospects before the Season ends."

She set the needles in motion, trying to quell a growing sense of despair. Her first affair was to have been a lighthearted romp. Not even a stolen pleasure, for widows were expected to romp.

They were *entitled* to romp, in fact.

"You are supposed to knit six and purl six, Addy. Have you fallen in love with the famous Dorning eyes?"

"Don't be ridiculous. His lordship and I are friends. Have a biscuit."

Aunt coughed gently, perhaps to avoid laughing. "Friends don't stand by and watch as a mésalliance forms beneath their noses, my girl. Casriel would suit you splendidly. He's settled, is sufficiently well born, and is every inch a gentleman. You are overdue for some gentlemanliness."

Addy had to go back and count her stitches, for she'd lost track halfway down the row. "Casriel is a gentleman with constrained finances and a strong sense of duty. He'll marry well."

"As *you* married well?"

When had Aunt grown so querulous? "I married far above my station. Too far and at too young an age. Roger was amused with me for a time, but then I failed him in the one aspect of wedlock that mattered to him. Casriel is far kinder than Roger and won't have unreasonable expectations of his bride."

He'd expect much of himself, though.

"You are cross. Women in love, contrary to the myths, can be difficult. They tend to fall in love with men, though not always, and therein lies a great deal of aggravation."

Addy finished the row, though it didn't look right. "Where did I go wrong here?" She held up the knitting for Aunt to examine.

"You fell in love with a good man," Aunt said. "The mistake is understandable, but now you must deal with the consequences of your folly."

Tomorrow was half day. Addy was counting the hours until her next episode of folly. "There can be no consequences, and I have not fallen in love. I know what falling in love is like—I fell in love with Roger. I was giddy at the mention of his name. A glance from him could send me into raptures."

The raptures Casriel engendered were of a different nature, and every one came wrapped in regret. *It wasn't supposed to be like this.*

"Why couldn't you have met Casriel ten years ago, hmmm? I'll tell you why. Because, if he'd had the sense to realize what a treasure you are, he would not have allowed himself to offer for you then either. He would have been just as poor, but too convinced of his ability to remedy his finances with sheer hard work. You would not have had the discernment to realize what a treasure *he* is, because he fiddles with ailing harps, he talks of farming, and he's mannerly rather than gorgeous and wicked. You have it all backward."

"I beg your pardon?"

"You started off the row purling instead of knitting. Perhaps you should propose to Casriel."

How did one repair an entire row done incorrectly? "Ladies do not propose to gentlemen, and I have no fortune. Casriel isn't greedy, but his family looks to him to provide. In five years, when marrying me costs him the ability to dower his Tabitha well, or to keep his brother Sycamore from debtors' prison, he'd resent me just as bitterly as Roger ever did. Do I take out the whole row?"

And probably ruin the shawl doing so.

"You can, or you can simply start a new pattern. For the next forty-seven rows, begin with the purling, then for the next forty-eight after that switch back to beginning with the knitting. Some of my best projects did not go according to—" Another quiet cough, then a throat-clearing. "According to my plans."

This lighthearted affair with Casriel was not going *at all* according to plan. Addy had entrusted him with some of her most bitter memories. She'd fallen asleep in his arms. How often had Roger dozed off after his marital exertions, leaving Addy feeling inexplicably empty and lonely? Casriel had held her. He'd talked to her. He'd *listened.*

Addy could not bear the thought of him married to some empty-headed twit, not because she was jealous, though she was, but because he deserved better.

And that was the essence of her dilemma. She'd resented Roger's mistresses and liaisons, then learned to be indifferent to them. Most men of means did not limit themselves to a wife's attentions. Roger's passions had been quick to rise and swiftly sated, so how important could those other partners have been to him?

Addy had never worried that Roger was unhappy with those

people, never wondered if any of them were taking advantage of him. She'd never fretted that Roger was squandering his time on pursuits that were in some odd way only making him more miserable.

"You should at least have some tea," Addy said. "You're not eating enough to keep a bird alive, Fredericka Beauchamp."

Freddy closed her eyes. "Because it's time I flew away. I have some money, you know. I'm not leaving it to charity."

Not this. Not now. "Aunt, you must do with your funds as you please. You always have, and I am fortunate that my means are adequate for my needs."

"And yet, your life is not adequate. You should go to Canmore Court. Children are always so cheering, and then Casriel would be free to pursue his fortune-hunting with a clear conscience."

Aunt's eyes were closed, but that arrow had been aimed with the skill of a master. "He will end matters soon enough."

"Yes, dear. Of course he will."

Addy knitted and purled, she let the tea grow cold, and she considered Aunt Freddy's advice, which had been meant kindly and had been offered from long experience.

Casriel would *not* end matters. He'd danced with the wallflowers, partnered dowagers in the cardroom, and avoided all but one set's worth of socializing with either the Arbuckles or Miss Quinlan. If Addy cared for the man, and she did, beyond all sense or explanation, she should end this frolic sooner rather than later.

But not just yet.

TOMORROW WAS HALF DAY. Wonderful, delightful, precious half day, but tonight was a musical evening at Lady Dornley's. Fortunately, Grey's hostess did not believe that her guests should have to sit in rows on uncomfortable chairs like schoolchildren serving detention. She'd opened up the public rooms in her house, so guests were free to wander from the buffet under a tent on the terrace to the music room, to the library and parlors.

Addy was not among the guests. He'd looked for her, despite the fanciful notion that he'd feel her presence. Tresham wasn't in evidence either, though both the Arbuckle twins and Miss Quinlan had greeted Grey effusively.

Why did gentlemen never plead a headache and leave a gathering early? Why could a gentleman never tear a handy hem, never take a bad step on a dance floor or garden path?

Why am I whining?

"My lord, good evening!" Drusilla Arbuckle, for once without her twin, beamed up at him. "Are you enjoying the quartet? They are quite good, I think."

"Good evening, Miss Arbuckle. The music is most enjoyable. May I escort you to your mother?" The young lady had come upon him on the terrace, where couples and small groups were conversing under torches. The buffet gave off the aromas of cooked meat, and laughter punctuated the music wafting from the house. The evening should have been pleasant, and yet, Miss Arbuckle's smile foretold Grey's doom.

I should spend the rest of my evening charming her. I should spend at least half an hour winning her favor. I should be willing to devote fifteen damned minutes to... my future bride?

Even thinking the words sat ill with him.

"Mama had to help Anastasia re-pin a hem. I was to wait for them here in the fresh air."

An odd choice, but not improper, given the number of people milling about. "I can keep you company. Shall we sit, or would you like to peruse the buffet?"

She wrapped her arm through his. "I'm told her ladyship's roses are in good form. Let's have a look, shall we?"

No, we shall not. And yet, what choice did Grey have? He wanted to tear free of Miss Arbuckle and stomp across the terrace, bellowing about tomorrow being half day and a man being entitled to a few happy memories before he sold his soul for a mess of roofing slates.

"I believe the roses are to the left," he said. Miss Arbuckle was short and her steps small. The pace she set would have upheld the dignity of an exhausted tortoise.

"Do you miss Dorset, my lord?"

No, to his surprise, he did not miss Dorset per se. Dorset was the Land of Leaking Roofs. He missed Addy. He missed having his days to do with as he pleased, provided he was productive. He missed his brothers, but not as much as he ought to. He missed sheets scented with fresh lavender, a wardrobe redolent of cedar, and the perfume of blooming orchards wafting in his window at night.

The whole stink of London was tired and dutiful, but he could hardly say that to Miss Arbuckle.

"I will be home before long. Now is for enjoying good company and the pleasures of the capital. Do you prefer London or the countryside?"

One step down, two steps down. On the third step, Miss Arbuckle stumbled predictably, leaning on Grey for a moment that some finishing governess had doubtless declared would turn a gentleman's imagination in husbandly directions.

Grey set the lady on her feet and escorted her to the garden walk without further incident.

"I adore the country," Miss Arbuckle said. "I love the fresh air and the... cows. Cows are lovely, don't you think?"

When bovines were admired from upwind, Grey had no objection to them. He liked a well-aged cheese and favored a creamy raspberry fool when the berries were in season.

"I own more sheep than cows, and I do have a fondness for the Dorset breeds. Do you like to ride, Miss Arbuckle?"

She peered up at him, her smile faltering. "Ride? Horses, you mean?"

"We spend a lot of time on horseback at Dorning Hall. The

tenant farms are flung all over the shire, and though I love a good hike, I also like to accomplish as much as I can in the course of a day."

"As do I, my lord. I am much enamored of accomplishing... things."

They had to pause on their progress toward the roses while Miss Arbuckle freed a hem that had snagged on a pot of spent irises.

"How are your brothers, my lord? They must miss you when you're absent from the family seat."

Did they? Or did they enjoy having the run of Dorning Hall without Grey barking at them to get their boots off the hassocks?

"They are grown men who can manage without me. We are not the only guests intent on admiring the roses."

"Roses make me sneeze."

Then why...? He knew exactly why. Miss Arbuckle was providing him an opportunity to declare himself, to ask her permission to pay his addresses. After a few weeks of that purgatory, he'd ask her papa for leave to court her, though his fate would be sealed by the outcome of this evening's conversation.

But tomorrow is half day, and I cannot be any sort of husband to you. "Let's sit by the fountain," Grey suggested. "The sound alone is pleasant."

"Oh yes, I do love a quiet fountain. How many of your siblings bide at Dorning Hall, my lord?"

Too many. "Four brothers at present, and a fifth bides with me in Town."

"That would be Mr. Sycamore Dorning? Or is Mr. Hemlock Dorning biding with you?"

Oh, the symbolism... "Only Sycamore."

"I beg your pardon, my lord. Sycamore. I have stood up with Mr. Sycamore Dorning. He's quite graceful. And the others... Chestnut, Maple... I'm making a hash of this, aren't I?"

Grey handed her onto the bench and took the place one decorous foot to her left, unsure whether to laugh or start splashing in the fountain like Tresham's mastiff.

"Polite conversation is a challenge," he said. "This far into the Season, we've exhausted the weather as a topic of discussion, and even the scandals have lost our interest. Do you really like country life, Miss Arbuckle? You can be honest with me."

"I hardly know, but does that matter? My future is not as a land steward on some large estate. Every young lady of quality aspires to be a wife and mama. I'm rather looking forward to the mama part, and the wife part too, of course."

She was entirely, desperately in earnest.

"You've had enough of waltzing and promenading, soirees, musicales, and Venetian breakfasts?"

Water trickled softly, the quartet lilted along in a sprightly major key, and Miss Arbuckle smoothed a gloved hand over her skirts.

"Anastasia likes the social whirl. She always has, and people like her. I don't mind it, really, but we are *twenty years old*. Almost every young lady who came out with us is engaged or married, and some have babies. I adore babies. Do you adore babies?"

Grey adored *his* baby, though she was growing up too quickly. "Your aspirations do you credit, Miss Arbuckle." *Might as well get on with it.* "Do you know I have a daughter?"

She nodded, blond ringlets bobbing. "Miss Tabitha Dorning. Mama told us and said we were not to remark it. Many gentlemen sow wild oats, and I'm sure she's a very sweet young lady."

Drusilla Arbuckle was a sweet young lady, despite having reached the hoary age of twenty. She deserved better than a man who came sighing to her bed when he dragged himself there at all.

"You are kind to say so," Grey replied.

What did kindness require of him? Family duty and self-interest demanded that he court Miss Arbuckle's favor and her fortune. He could not pursue that course in good conscience, and now Miss Arbuckle reminded him that a husband was expected to *be* a husband.

As if Grey needed reminding of *that*.

He searched his heart, honestly, for some hint of affection toward the young woman who'd risked her dignity to accost him on the terrace. Could he see a time, a year or two hence perhaps, after a long and cordial courtship, when they might be friends?

But, no. Friends brought to mind Addy, curled on his chest, snoring softly. Friends meant the pleasure of winking at Addy across a crowded parlor, while Drusilla attempted to capture Grey's attention.

Grey could not be Drusilla Arbuckle's friend. He could not—heaven defend him—be her husband, but he could be kind to her.

"Might I further prevail on your good nature, Miss Arbuckle? A matter of some delicacy has been on my mind, and you are in a position to offer me good counsel."

She turned toward him, her gaze both hopeful and wary. "A matter of some delicacy, my lord?"

"We've mentioned my brother Sycamore. I am concerned for him."

She sat up straighter. "He's a very good-looking young man, sir. Even my mama admits that much. He has the Dorning eyes and cuts quite a dash. Not that you don't, of course. Cut a dash, that is."

Grey sent up a prayer for forgiveness. "Sycamore has expressed a fondness for a certain young woman to whom I was considering paying my addresses. I love my brother, but he is as yet an unsuitable *parti*. He cannot hope to offer for a lady until he's amassed some means and consequence of his own. You understand why the situation is delicate?"

Miss Arbuckle stared at the silver skeins of water trickling down the side of the fountain. "Your brother might carry a grudge if you offered for the young lady. Anastasia was angry with me for two years because my godmother gave me a kitten and didn't give Anastasia one. We have different godmothers."

The string quartet came to a close amid a gentle smattering of applause.

"Marrying the woman for whom my brother bore a *tendresse* might sting a bit more than being denied a kitten. Young men have such delicate pride, you know. The lady is pretty, gracious, and well dowered. It seems unfair that my suit could prevail while Sycamore must stand silently aside, when—but for the title—he and I are very similarly situated."

Miss Arbuckle smoothed her gloves up her arms. "*Very* similarly situated, my lord?"

"Afraid so, unless you consider the leaking pile I call my ancestral home to be a great advantage on my side of the ledger."

"The roof leaks?"

"Only in the family wing," he said. "So far."

Drusilla studied the fountain, she studied her gloves, she scooted on the bench, and then she studied Grey.

"You never said if you like babies, my lord. I understand that your sentiments toward your brother are very... You care for his feelings, which does you much credit, but don't you want heirs in your nursery?"

She was making a careful choice, which Grey respected. He wasn't sure he could say the same about his own decisions, but neither could he offer her the marriage she had every right to expect.

"I have raised one child, Miss Arbuckle, or begun raising her, and I have noticed something." He stood and offered his hand. "Children are expensive. Children are enormously expensive, and my Tabitha hasn't even had her first Season."

"Papa would agree with you about the expenses." She let Grey draw her to her feet. "No babies, then? You aren't determined to have your heir and spare? Mama said all peers must have an heir of the body."

And look what that thinking had done to Addy's marriage. "I have six brothers, Miss Arbuckle, and they are all in good health. One is very happily married. I suspect the others will be as well, and we have paternal cousins. As much effort as I've put into maintaining the family seat, for one of my brothers to take on the expense and effort of raising the next Earl of Casriel would be a very great help indeed."

Her grip on his arm was light, her progress in the direction of the house brisk. "You don't need an heir. Well. I suppose you should consider Lady Antonia, then, my lord. You're of an age with her, she's quite well fixed and a good sort of person. I think you might suit."

"Lady Antonia?"

"She might even seek a white marriage, though you're not that old and you aren't bad looking. Your manners are positively exquisite, but if you truly don't wish to have children...?"

"I simply don't see the need. I am one of nine, and I hazard that my papa grumbled about expenses a good deal more than yours does."

"Papa grumbles incessantly, then Mama grumbles about Papa's grumbling, and Anastasia gets into a taking about the pair of them, so we must go shopping to settle our nerves."

Mr. Arbuckle had Grey's profound sympathies, but then, so did Drusilla. "That is a lot of grumbling among people who care for each other. You see the problem."

She paused with him at the top of the terrace steps. "Oh, quite. I wish you every success with your situation, my lord, and commend you for considering your brother's feelings. I don't suppose he's among the guests tonight?"

Good for you, Miss Drusilla Arbuckle. Her clarity of purpose relieved Grey's conscience as well, for she was obviously more attached to her future offspring than to the idea of being Grey's countess.

"I last saw Sycamore in the blue parlor. He looked a little lonely, a bit out of his element amid all that fine art." Grey considered adding, *We had to sell most of what was collected at Dorning Hall,* but that would be an exaggeration—Oak's paintings far eclipsed the musty landscapes shipped off to the art brokers—also unnecessary.

Miss Arbuckle had already curtseyed and spun on her heel, taking off at a good clip in the direction of the blue parlor.

Grey returned to the bench by the fountain, pleased with the conversation. He'd not quite dissembled, he'd avoided making Miss Arbuckle a very disappointing husband, and he could enjoy tomorrow with Addy as a man unencumbered by any woman's marital expectations.

And yet, he'd all but sentenced himself to marrying Miss Quinlan. That the union would likely be a white marriage was the smallest and coldest of consolations.

～

ADDY'S BELLY ACHED, her head ached, her heart ached worst of all. She opened the front door and stepped back.

"Greetings, my lady." Grey's smile was hesitant, as if even he knew that she'd come to a decision. "How are you?"

"I am well." *I am dying inside.* "Will you join me in my sitting room?"

"I'd like nothing better." He followed her up the steps as if their routine was of long, comfortable standing. "I missed you at Lady Dornley's last evening."

I miss you all the time. "I'm sure the gathering was pleasant." Addy was equally sure he'd sat with some Arbuckle or other, or possibly with Miss Quinlan. Maybe more heiresses had entered the lists. Handsome, mannerly earls in search of countesses were not exactly thick on the ground.

"How is your aunt?" Grey asked. "I have finished her harp and am adding the last coats of wax. The instrument is lovely and has a more beautiful tone than I would have thought possible."

He'd looked right at Addy when delivering that pronouncement.

"Aunt Freddy will be pleased, though she seems to tire easily lately. If anything might revive her spirits, it's music."

Grey stood in Addy's parlor, still holding his hat and walking stick. "I have failed again." He looked around the room as if to see who had said those words. "With Miss Drusilla Arbuckle. She accosted me..."

He'd *failed* with Miss Arbuckle?

Addy locked the door and took his hat and walking stick. "Have a seat and explain yourself."

Grey flipped out his tails and settled in the corner of the sofa, while Addy put his accessories on the sideboard. He did not look like a man who'd failed.

He looked relieved.

"Miss Arbuckle came upon me out of doors, amid the usual crush, and I offered to escort her to the rosebushes. Her intent was simply to get me as alone as a couple can be at such a gathering. Did you know Lady Dornley's fountain features Cupid nocking his arrow? I found that hilarious."

Addy took the place beside him. "And yet, you are not laughing." *Neither am I.*

He offered his hand, and she took that too. "I have no encumbrances that would prevent me from calling upon you today. That is cause for rejoicing. In the course of my discussion with Miss Arbuckle, she expressed a great fondness for babies and assumed that as a peer without legitimate male issue, filling my nursery would be a priority for me.

"I could not..." He paused to kiss Addy's knuckles. "My lady, I simply *could not*. Not in pitch darkness, not in two years. Not ever, and I should be roundly pummeled for discussing this with you, of all people. Miss Arbuckle wants and deserves a doting husband. She will be a fierce and fine mother, but I simply could not see... She deserves more than I have to offer her, and I am a fool."

Addy was a fool too, for she beamed at her guest. "You did the honorable thing, Grey. How can that be foolish? You and Miss Arbuckle would both have been miserable. A whole nursery full of chortling infants can't compensate for discord between spouses."

Grey cradled her cheek against his hand. "As my father learned. And an empty nursery can fill a marriage with discord. Your example was instructive, Addy. Thank you for that, or I might be a man paying Miss Arbuckle his addresses today."

Addy kissed his palm, though his words only confirmed what

Aunt had said. Grey would not court anybody in earnest as long as Addy shared intimacies with him.

"Shall I pour the tea?" she asked.

He brushed her hair back from her brow. "Perhaps later." He remained beside her, holding her hand.

If Addy were sensible, she would explain to him why their affair must end now, before she let him waste another musicale, literary salon, ball, or rout. She instead straddled his lap.

"Lady Canmore, what are you about?"

She'd made him smile. "I am a widow. We are entitled to our diversions." She kissed him, because she could, because she had to. "Is this a new waistcoat?"

"I'm surprised you noticed."

"The embroidery is more elaborate than on some of your other waistcoats, though the blue is your predictable favorite. Should we put a sheath in water?"

He reached into his coat pocket and passed her a leather packet. This part of being lovers was not romantic, but Addy treasured Grey for his pragmatism and responsibility.

"I feel very sophisticated," she said, rising to pour a glass of water at the sideboard, "knowing how this is done."

"And yet, you still look exactly like my Addy," Grey said, untying his neckcloth. "Pretty, proper, and charmingly ladylike."

"Because I am with you." She dipped the sheath into the water. "Midafternoon intimacies with you and feeling like a lady aren't mutually exclusive. One can have pleasure and respectability, in the right company."

Which was confusing. With Roger, every pleasure—every single one—had to bring with it a hint of wickedness, of rebellion. He could not simply make love with his wife. He had to make love with her on the desk in the study behind an unlocked door.

Grey rose, his neckcloth in hand, the first two buttons of his shirt unfastened. "You are pensive today. Would an allemande suit you?"

Relaxed, calm, soothing. With him, of course that would suit her. "What would suit you?"

Without touching her anywhere else, he kissed her. What started out as a delicate tasting became voracious possession, the hearty, robust male roaring forth from beneath his manners and good breeding.

"You suit me," he said. "I wish to God—"

Addy kissed him rather than hear regrets and dreams that echoed her own. "Take me to bed, Grey. We have now. Let's make the best of it."

He looked like he wanted to argue, but a gentleman never argued with a lady, and Grey Dorning was a gentleman.

"We will take each other to bed. Shall I undo your hooks?"

"I can manage."

They had a sort of race, with Grey yanking off his boots and Addy pulling her dress over her head. His waistcoat and stockings went sailing onto the armchair. Her stockings and garters landed atop them. Grey's shirt followed, then he stood, hands on hips, while Addy debated whether she was brave enough to take off her shift before they'd climbed under the covers.

She would never again have this opportunity with him, never again find an intimate partner who inspired her to feats of courage. She raised the hem of her shift as high as her knees.

Grey wore only his breeches, and while Addy watched, he unbuttoned his falls. The sight of him, tousled, nearly naked, his cock arrowing up along his belly... He crossed his arms, leaned against the bedpost, and waited.

Addy drew her shift higher, to her waist, then over her breasts, then over her head. She tossed the wad of linen onto the pile of clothes and stood naked before her lover.

Grey twirled a finger, and Addy turned, a new feeling blossoming as she slowly pivoted.

This was... He *liked* looking at her. That was plainly evident. The sight of her aroused him, but also pleased him. With Grey, she could shed every pretense, every precaution and stand before him as God had made her.

For the first time in her life, standing naked before a man felt marvelous. Not wicked, not uncomfortable, but joyous. She liked looking at Grey too, and he obliged by stepping out of his breeches and completing the heap of clothing on the chair.

"I'm not..." Addy wasn't young. She wasn't old either, though. "I'm not as..." As firm, trim, round...? Perhaps, but also not as gullible, ignorant, or easily duped. If that was the price of maturity, Addy considered the bargain fair.

"You are perfect," Grey said, stepping close. "You are lovely and dear, and for the next two hours, you are mine and I am yours, and that is all that matters."

CHAPTER THIRTEEN

Grey had never been so upset, and yet, it took until Addy was smiling at him, not a stitch on her lovely person, before he could name his feelings for what they were.

He was furious. Reeling drunk with rage. Not with gentlemanly resentment, frustration, or quiet longing. He was angry enough to march the wilds of Dorset for years, angry enough to lose his soul to the harp and never ransom it back.

Addy was leaving him. He could feel the sorrow in her kisses, see it behind her smiles. She had decided to do him the great service of setting him aside, as a woman set aside a man she treasured because hers was the greater claim to honor.

He could not argue using words, but he could argue with everything else he had to offer. He carried Addy to the bed, skin to skin, heartbeat to heartbeat, and came down over her.

An allemande was a slow, graceful elaboration on a courtly promenade. Grey treated Addy to caresses that meandered over her shoulders, arms, breasts, and belly. He turned her over, glorying in the feminine wonder of her back, elegant curves flaring out to generous hips and a well-rounded derriere.

"I want to devour you." Consume her present, past, and future. He crouched above her and draped his greater length over her from head to foot, reveling in the feel of their bodies pressed so closely together.

She raised her hips. "Do you want...?"

He wanted to bite her nape, though what she was offering became apparent before he'd done more than nibble. Grey had engaged in the usual frolics and depravities at university, albeit sparingly.

He didn't care to engage in them again now, when he and Addy might never make love again.

"Stay right where you are." He was off the bed and back, sheath in place, within the space of half a minute. "The next decision is yours, my lady."

Addy had rolled to her back and lay before him, rosy and naked. Grey had never seen a lovelier nor a more heartbreaking sight. She held out her arms, and he joined her on the bed even as he resolved to locate some damned restraint.

Addy apparently had other plans for him. Her kisses were voracious and unrelenting, her hands were everywhere. She stroked Grey's cock, then undulated against him until his sole defining ambition was to be inside her.

"Grey Dorning, must I beg?"

"Never."

He meant to go slowly. He meant to savor and cherish, as a gentleman ought to when saying an intimate good-bye. Addy arched up into the joining and seized him in a single roll of her hips.

"Be still," he rasped. "For the love of all that's precious, Beatitude, do not move. Do not breathe, and please, I beg you, do not clench at me with your—"

She smiled against his neck—smirked, rather—as she gave him a sound, very intimate squeeze.

He bore that, barely. "I want this to last." *Forever, damn it.*

"Sometimes we get what we need, not what we want."

What followed was excruciating pleasure. Addy, in a mood Grey could not fathom, teased him within an inch of his sanity, until he was a human tuning fork humming to the pitch of mounting desire. Enormous satisfaction lay ahead. He knew that both as a rational conclusion and as a bodily conviction, but on the far side of that satisfaction lay perhaps the worst grief of his adult life.

Addy gently tugged on his chest hair. "Grey, stop being a gentleman. Let me give this to you."

"We give this to each other."

Those were his last coherent words for a good quarter hour. Addy sent him into a maelstrom of physical sensation that overwhelmed all thought, all hope and worry, to the point that he was entirely defined by what he shared with her.

She held nothing back, her passion a ferocious testament to female bravery, and then she was quiet, apparently content to stroke Grey's back and marvel at their lovemaking.

Reality intruded several moments later with all the subtlety of a leaking roof. "I did not withdraw."

"I did not want you to. I used the sponges and vinegar."

He kissed her, grateful beyond words for that consideration, also heartbroken. She should be the mother of his children. He should be the father of hers.

While their bodies cooled, Grey searched in vain for some way to keep Addy by his side. He was the head of his family, given many privileges, but also many responsibilities. Was there no way to meet those responsibilities other than an advantageous match?

"Let's cuddle for a bit," Addy said, stroking his backside, "or steal a short nap."

She offered only *a bit* of cuddling, a *short* nap. Grey knew for a certainty that she'd decided to send him on his way.

"As you wish, my lady." He went behind the privacy screen to deal with the sheath, forcing himself to take the first steps toward the last shared moments. His reflection in the mirror showed a man who'd been thoroughly pleasured, but certainly not a strikingly attractive man. He was healthy, for which God be thanked, but no great physical prize.

He'd found the occasional gray hair near his temples, and if he let his beard grow, more gray would evidence itself there. *Grey is going gray*, as his brothers said.

If he waited another two years to marry, Dorset Hall would be a ruin, he'd be two years older and more worn, two years more deeply in debt. The fiction that he was anything more than an heiress hunter would have grown more worn as well. His brothers would be two years away from the status of young men seeking their way in life and two years closer to being poor relations.

They needed him to marry well. Tabitha needed him to marry well. Dorset Hall and its tenants needed him to marry well. He could kick as many doors as he pleased, and none of that would change.

"Grey, are you coming back to bed?"

"Of course." He used Addy's brush to put his hair halfway to rights, mustered a smile, and returned to her side.

She'd burrowed under the covers—no more gratuitous displays of nature's wonders—and held the sheets up for Grey, then tucked herself against his side.

"You show me new pleasures, Beatitude. Will you allow yourself a respite in my arms?" Or would she deliver the coup de grace while he lay in her bed, naked and replete?

"You must not let me sleep too long," she said, hiking a leg over his thighs. "We have matters to discuss."

She yawned, patted his chest, and drifted into silence, while Grey watched shadows creep up the wall and awaited his doom. When he was certain she was truly asleep, he brushed the hair from her brow, kissed her temple, and allowed himself to whisper one, unassailable, hopeless truth.

"I love you, Beatitude, Lady Canmore."

He felt a butterfly brush of her eyelashes against his chest. "I love you too, Grey Birch Dorning, Earl of Casriel, and that is why our affair has come to an end."

"CASRIEL IS CONCERNED FOR YOU," Tresham said. "He's concerned for all of his family, but especially for you."

Tresham delivered that salvo from the far side of the six-rowed abacus on Sycamore's desk, which gave Cam the sense of being behind horizontal bars. The desk had once been Tresham's, though use of it and the abacus had conveyed to Cam with the leasehold on The Coventry Club.

Sycamore set the abacus on the floor. "Did Casriel tell you he was concerned, or did he merely hint about, seeking information that's none of his business?"

Tresham rose and prowled across the room. The mastiff of the day —Caesar? Comus?—watched him, but didn't bother getting up from the hearth rug. Sycamore had learned from his brother Will that dogs were better at judging human moods than people were. If Tresham were truly agitated, that hound would be anxious, not calmly watchful.

"Casriel has made such general inquiries as one brother can about another, though he certainly hasn't pried. He's worried that you're failing and that you either don't realize it or you won't admit it."

Not quite. "Grey expects me to fail. They all do, with the possible exception of Ash, who I had hoped would throw in with me." Though Ash had problems of his own, and they were not problems likely to be solved by spending every waking hour at a gaming club.

Tresham stalked to the reading table and studied schematics Sycamore had drawn of a plan to pipe water from a roof cistern into the retiring rooms and kitchen.

"If your brothers expect you to fail, Dorning, then you must prove them wrong, of course. That doesn't mean you keep them guessing for no reason."

Sycamore leaned back in his chair and propped his boots on the corner of the desk. "Do you see Casriel coming around of an evening, having a look for himself? Do you see any of my various concerned siblings taking an interest in this place?"

"Maybe they are doing you the courtesy of allowing you some privacy, some time to get on your feet. Maybe they have other challenges comparable to the one you face. Maybe they are engaged in the doomed endeavor of securing a wealthy bride, in case some brother who has never managed a commercial venture should fall upon his skinny, arrogant arse before all of London."

Tresham peered at the drawings, while Sycamore considered his words—his accusations.

"You claim Casriel is marrying for my sake?"

"This is clever," Tresham muttered. "I would not have thought to bring the piping down through the linen closets. The pipe is less likely to freeze if it's within the building, but heaven help you if a pipe bursts."

"Heaven help me if the roof leaks. You should hear Grey hold forth about the eighth biblical plague, the leaking roof."

Tresham rolled up the drawings and rapped Sycamore on the top of his head. "I have, at length. He has nightmares about leaking roofs. Nightmares about his daughter having no dowry. Nightmares about his brothers needing his aid and him being unable to free them from debtors' prison."

Sycamore rose, snatched the plans from his guest, and smacked Tresham soundly across the chest. "I am not a new midshipman to be chastised, even if you are my landlord. Casriel never complains to me. All I hear from him is, 'Let me know if you need a loan.' That's all any of us hear from him, as if we're indigent incompetents rather than well-educated, hardworking fellows."

The dog whined softly from the hearth rug.

"Perhaps you're both," Tresham said. "Well-educated, hardworking, indigent incompetents. I know this, though: Casriel is prepared to prostrate himself on the altar of the advantageous marriage, and that is not because he wants to build a folly by the lake at Dorning

Hall, or because he's developed a sudden infatuation with Miss Sarah Quinlan's eyebrows."

Sycamore set his plans on the desk. "We don't need a folly. We have the real article, an abbey in ruins with a picturesque stream running by in case a fellow needs to do some fishing on a summer morning. If ever I could not find my oldest brother, I knew exactly where to locate him."

"Among the ruins."

Marriage had turned Tresham preachy. "Whiling away a few hours with a fishing pole."

Tresham stepped closer. "Fretting over how he'll afford a decent match for his illegitimate daughter. Worried about replacing the damned roof on Dorning Hall. Distraught that his countess will have no dower house. Guilty because the tenant repairs are not up to the moment. Exhausted because he's the only peer of the realm I know who shears sheep, stacks hay, mucks out ditches, and repairs stone walls."

"Grey likes to work hard." Sycamore had viewed that as an eccentricity, like Papa's preoccupation with horticulture, or Oak's fascination with the visual arts.

"*All the time*, Sycamore? Does he like to work hard from dawn to midnight in every season? I've seen the earldom's books. His staff at the Hall is more pensioners than able-bodied servants because he's cut back as much as he dares. He's let out every acre and building he can rent. He's reduced the stables to only working stock, not a single brood mare. He sells everything, from cheese to jam to wicker baskets, at the local markets, and he hasn't had a new pair of boots for three years."

Tresham paced away, clearly not finished with his tirade. "He's put spinning wheels into every cottage on the property, so the estate can sell not only wool, but also finished yarn, thus keeping more of the proceeds. If he could buy some looms... but he hasn't any working capital. He's too busy sending his brothers to university, repairing roofs, and courting young women who see him only as a title for sale."

The longer Tresham ranted, the more Sycamore felt like an eight-year-old who'd used Mama's best French embroidered coverlet to build a blanket cave.

Not that he'd made that mistake more than once.

"You're saying he's rolled-up. The Earl of Casriel hasn't a feather to fly with."

Tresham braced a hand on the mantel and stared at his boots—shiny, likely not a year old. "He's been shrewd to the point of genius, he's worked harder than any man should have to, and he's denied himself much, but he's one person, Sycamore, with many dependents. While you were frittering away a term at university, he was dredging the millpond at Dorning Hall. I don't mean he was striding about on the bank, giving orders, and offering encouragement. He was in the muck, wielding a shovel."

That picture was easy to imagine, for Sycamore had seen his brother wielding shears, a hay fork, a draft team, a mason's trowel...

"He likes to work hard," Sycamore said again, though he heard doubt in his own voice. "Papa was the same way, always planting this and inspecting that. Putting up another glass house or adding to the conservatory."

Casriel had reduced the size of the conservatory by one-third, selling the enormous glass panes and custom iron framing to a neighbor who'd come into a fortune.

"When Casriel asked me to look over his books," Tresham said, "he gave me the estate journal he's been keeping for the past ten years. I saw, day by day, what filled his time. There's hard work, Sycamore, and there's indentured servitude to a losing proposition. If Casriel had any alternative to marrying for money, he's explored it, probably more than once, and found it inadequate."

"You're saying this marriage scheme is a last resort?" The question was uncomfortable, because last resorts were inherently bad options, which was why they were left for last.

"What do you think?"

The dog rose, came over to Sycamore, and licked the back of his hand. Cam gave the dog a pat for its kindness and then another because petting a dog soothed a troubled soul.

"I think you have never had brothers," Sycamore said, "so you don't understand how complicated fraternal relationships can be."

"Caesar, come." Tresham made a hand gesture, and the dog padded to his side. "I would not have leased you this place unless I believed you'd make a go of it. I know it's early days, but you owe your brother an accurate report of your status. He's making decisions based in part on how his siblings fare and what he anticipates they'll need from him. The least courtesy he's owed is correct information."

Downstairs on the empty club gambling floor, somebody was singing the old Jacobite ditty *Charlie Is My Darling*, though the voice was male. Charlie was the young pretender to the British throne, a Scottish upstart best forgotten by the history books.

"My brothers don't see me, Tresham. They see a young lad always getting into scrapes, one desperate for attention any way he can get it. They don't regard me as particularly bright or hardworking, and they expect me to fail."

And Cam had obliged their expectations on any number of occasions.

Tresham headed for the door, the dog at his heels. He gave Sycamore one last pitying look. "Unless you want Miss Sarah Quinlan redecorating Dorning Hall for the rest of her days, you'd best stop feeling sorry for yourself and take a look at your brothers as they truly are. Casriel has carried the full load on his own for years. You're not little boys anymore, though if you lot are any example of how brothers behave, I'm glad I don't have any."

He left, closing the door softly, taking his hound with him.

LEARNING of Roger's death had hurt terribly. Addy had realized only then that she'd held out hope of seeing her marriage mature into a peaceful union. Perhaps a child would have come along. Perhaps Roger would have reconciled with Jason. Perhaps in time...

But death had stolen all the time she'd had left with her husband, and that had been sad. Sadness had eventually given way to a guilty sort of relief. She and Roger had had years to find peace and had instead annoyed each other more with each passing season.

No child had come along.

The rift with Jason had grown colder and wider as Jason and his wife had had more children, especially a fine healthy son.

What Addy had hoped might become peace had in fact been a balance between resentment and indifference.

And then Roger had hit upon his final scheme to deny Jason the succession...

Lying in Grey's arms, Addy closed her eyes and felt no relief that she was saying farewell to the man she loved. This parting would have no silver lining, no unexpected gifts among the grief.

"Beatitude, I cannot lose you." Grey's touch could not have been more gentle or his tone sadder.

"You never had me," she said. "We have enjoyed a few encounters, but you did not come to London for casual trysts. You must be about your courting, and I am a distraction."

He remained silent when she wanted him to beg. If he begged, she would relent. She would put off the parting. She would bargain with God for more time, a few more weeks, a few more hours.

A waltz, a promenade, anything.

He got an arm under her shoulders and brought her over him, so they could cling to each other. His embrace was everything Addy had ever needed—sheltering, intimate, cherishing, *strong*. Her heart ached, her throat ached, every part of her ached at the loss of him, even as a corner of her mind knew that she'd survive this too.

She would survive the announcement of his engagement, survive hearing that the banns had been cried. She would even survive learning that the Earl of Casriel had an heir in his nursery.

Because she did love him.

"If you cry, I will not be able to leave this house," Grey said, hands trailing over her back. "Please don't cry. Tell me I am a pathetic lover, you are bored with me, you could never care for such a dull man. Don't *cry*."

She cried, at length, and he held her and dried her tears. He assisted her back into her clothing and let her help him dress as well. When he was again the dapper gentleman in his morning attire, and she was a lady with a red nose and puffy eyes, she subsided into sniffles.

He kissed her one final time, with damnable sweetness. "You will send for me if you ever need anything, Addy. Anything. Coin, a roof over your head, a friend. Promise me you will send for me if you are in need."

He held her again, desperately tight, until Addy stepped back. "Thank you, Grey, for more than you will ever know. Be happy."

"A gentleman does not argue with a lady, so I will take my leave of you." He bowed and showed himself out.

Addy went back to bed, drew the covers over her head, and cried some more.

ADDY'S SACRIFICE should not be in vain.

Grey lectured himself to that effect for three days and nights, during which he polished Mrs. Beauchamp's harp to a brilliant shine, caught up on his correspondence, avoided Sycamore, and did not attend a single social event. Three days was not too much to ask when a man's heart was broken beyond all mending.

And yet, he would have made the same choices, even if he'd known how brief his time with Addy would be—though he'd have chosen to embark on the affair sooner.

But, no. Addy had had to seize the initiative in that regard as well.

A triple tap on the study door inspired a scowl. That was

Crevey's knock, and Grey did not want to be taken from thoughts of Addy.

"Come in."

Crevey was his usual, pleasantly unruffled self, which struck Grey as a cardinal injustice.

"Luncheon is ready, my lord. Shall you take another tray in here or use the dining room?"

Another tray. Everybody was a critic. "Is Sycamore awake yet?"

"Some hours ago, sir. In fact, he is from home and sent word from The Coventry not to expect him to return for several days."

Grey rose, his back protesting too many hours in the same chair. "He's removed to his club?" Probably a good thing if Cam was to properly manage the place, though Grey would—eventually —miss him.

"Mr. Sycamore did not say where he was off to, but he took your traveling coach and a small satchel."

Grey did not have a Town coach, that conveyance having been sold to finance Sycamore's time at Oxford.

"He took the only decent closed carriage I brought to Town and did not ask permission to borrow it. Where has he taken it?" This was so like Sycamore. Darting off with no plan, leaving no word, paying no heed to others.

"He did not say, sir."

I will disown my brother. Grey could inquire at The Coventry regarding Cam's whereabouts, but if this was a maneuver to avoid creditors, then sounding the alarm could spell Cam's doom.

"I'm going out, Crevey. I'll be back in time for a light supper."

Crevey's calm slipped to the extent of raised eyebrows. "But your luncheon, my lord. Surely you have time to sample Cook's efforts? The roast fowl is one of her best dishes."

For the past three days, Grey had been eating, or trying to, to appease Cook's vanity, and because he was not entitled to inconvenience the staff with his pining.

"I'm not hungry, and I have a few calls to pay. I'm sure the staff will enjoy the fowl. My brother is likely brewing another scandal just when I need to secure the hand of the next Countess of Casriel."

Crevey stepped away from the door. "The grooms might know where Mr. Sycamore was bound."

"Then please make the appropriate inquiries. Sycamore Dorning at liberty without supervision does not bode well for the peace of the realm."

"Something else you should know, sir."

Not another leaking roof. "Don't keep the news to yourself, Crevey."

"You have received an invitation to the Quinlans' soiree next week. It's among the others awaiting your attention."

Why would Crevey single out that one invitation? "Is this soiree of any particular note?"

"Mr. Quinlan brought it around himself, sir." Crevey studied the seascape of Durdle Door on the opposite wall. "I believe you were *out* at the time."

Grey's last true outing had been to spend time with Addy on half day. Since then, he'd not been at home to callers.

"I'll deal with the invitations when I'm done with today's calls. If Sycamore should return, please tie him to the piano and don't let him leave until I have a chance to question him."

"Very good, my lord."

"You think I'm joking."

"I think you are a very good earl, sir, and an even better brother. Shall I have the gig brought around?"

If Sycamore had taken the team, then only Grey's riding horse remained to pull the gig. The beast was certainly sturdy and well trained enough for any discipline, but he did not care for being driven and made that apparent.

"I'll walk. I'm not going far."

"Doing a bit of shopping? I can send a footman with you."

"No footman, no grooms, no tiger. This is a personal call and nobody's damned business but my own."

Crevey bowed, though he made that courtesy a reproach. Grey left the office and marched straight for the music room before Crevey could ask even one more prying, unhelpful question, or remind Grey of one more hopeless, damnable invitation.

"ARE YOU SURE, BEATITUDE?" Theo's tone hovered between dismay and concern, though her expression, as usual, was composed. She fit in well here at the Quimbey ducal town house, which she was gradually setting to rights after decades of haphazard care. The library was an especially handsome room, though the smiling portraits plucked at Addy's nerves.

Would Dorning Hall need attention from its new countess? Addy's imagination tormented her with questions like that by the hour.

"I have considered my situation for the past week, Theo." A week in which Addy had sat at her bedroom window and watched for Grey walking past her house, not that he'd ever be so callow.

She'd begun, and tossed into the fire, any number of letters to him.

She'd tried to read poetry and ended up reading the journals she'd kept early in her marriage, which left her only more sad and angry.

She'd looked in on Aunt Freddy, who'd been asleep at midday on both occasions, and she'd made arrangements to have Aunt brought to her own home for "some cosseting."

She had not stopped missing Grey. Not at all.

"Does this have to do with Roger's passing?" Theo asked. "He died about this time of year, if I recall."

Theo would remember that. "The anniversary of his accident comes at the end of the month. I do not want to be in London for that occasion. I am making arrangements to leave for Bath before the Season ends."

Theo held up the plate of biscuits. Addy took one to be polite, though food had lost its appeal.

"You have a new nephew, Beatitude, and you are his godmother. Maybe you should make his acquaintance, as difficult as that might be."

Everything was difficult. Waking, sleeping, recalling what day it was, working on Aunt Freddy's shawl while Aunt gently snored her life away in Addy's spare bedroom.

"When Roger died, I knew what to feel. I was a widow. Society tells us what to do when we're bereaved of a spouse: hang crepe, wear weeds, stay home but for services, take down the knocker, and receive only close friends and family until the mourning calls may begin. That dance proceeds along steps known to all of society. We learn the pattern as we mature without even realizing the lesson has been taught."

Addy set her cup and saucer along with the biscuit back onto the tray, though she wanted to pitch the lot of it against the silk-covered walls. The current Duke and Duchess of Quimbey, a love match late in life, beamed at each other in their gilt frame, their portrait mocking everything Addy felt.

"This is about Casriel, then," Theo said, shifting from her armchair to take the place beside Addy on the sofa. "I'm so sorry."

She put an arm around Addy's shoulders, and Addy wanted to both weep noisily on her friend's shoulder and bolt from the room.

"His lordship returned Aunt Freddy's harp to her, Theo. Brought it to her personally. The instrument is beautiful now. All warm, rosy wood. Every string perfectly tuned. It sits by her bed, but there's no one to play it, and Aunt is not awake to hear it played. I've moved her to my house, where there's more staff to look in on her."

The mercy of Aunt's decline was that she could no longer deliver lectures or scolds. The heartache was that Addy missed even Aunt's tart tongue. The shawl would soon be complete, though Aunt might not live long enough to wear it.

"You were hoping..." Theo gave Addy a squeeze and sat back. "You thought Casriel would return the harp to you?"

Addy rose, compelled by an urge to wrench off her slipper and hurl it at the window. "He is a gentleman, Theo. I gave him his congé. He was all that was decent and kind, and he took himself off without any drama or importuning."

On his part.

"How awful of him, to be so mannerly at such a time."

Awful, and entirely, absolutely Grey. "I trust you will keep an eye on him?" Addy turned her back on the smiling, besotted pair above the mantel, only to face instead a recent portrait of Theo and her husband.

Everywhere, besotted smiling couples. Grey, I miss you more than I can bear.

Theo took a bite of Addy's biscuit. "By that, you mean I am to tell you when he becomes engaged. The Quinlans are holding a soiree later this week. Casriel hasn't been seen in public for days, and Jonathan mentioned that Sycamore Dorning has left Town. Your swain might be rethinking his plan to marry wealth."

"He's not my swain, and he's not rethinking his plan. If he had any other choice, he would have explored it." Of that, Addy was confident, or she would never have let him go.

Never have all but pushed him out the door, rather.

Theo rose, brushing crumbs from her bodice. "I want you to know something, Beatitude."

"Not a lecture, please, Theo. I cannot bear one more lecture, reproach, or second thought. I cannot leave Town while Aunt needs me, but I cannot bear to sit by and watch..."

While Grey Dorning sacrificed his happiness for the sake of duty.

"I will inform you of developments here in Town if that's what you need me to do, but I will also remain your friend if you and the earl elope to Gretna Green, live in scandal, or defy all common sense to live in genteel ruin. Nobody took my part when my husband died except you, Beatitude. You sent me to a banker who could be trusted with my secrets. You kept the creditors from my door until I could think again. You warned me of the realities Society pretends widows need not face. You are more fierce and magnificent than you know, and you will always, always be my friend."

Addy was grateful for that stirring declaration, also surprised by it. At any other time, she would have reciprocated with a recitation of all Theo had meant to her, and what Theo still meant to her.

Instead, she endured a hug, said polite thank-you's and farewells, promised to write if she left London, and made it from the Quimbey town house with her dignity nominally intact. She eschewed Thiel's proffered arm, though, and returned home without yielding to the temptation to walk past Grey's town house.

CHAPTER FOURTEEN

"I will have my earl by this time next week," Sarah said. "See if I don't."

Her parents exchanged a look she'd seen frequently of late, though she could not fathom its meaning. Papa had come home early, perhaps to ensure all was in readiness for the upcoming soiree.

Mama had been oddly subdued all day, even as Sarah had endured her final fitting for her newest evening gown.

Now, Papa sat reading yet another newspaper, while Mama embroidered a handkerchief.

"Soon, Casriel will ask me if he can pay me his addresses," Sarah went on. "I'll wear blue, for pity's sake, and the Arbuckles are on the scent of a viscount. Lady Antonia hasn't stood up with the earl once in the past week."

"Nobody has stood up with him lately, child," Mama said without looking up from her hoop.

"Is he ill?" Casriel's timing was wretched if that was the case, and Sarah had no desire for a sickly husband, even if he was an earl.

"His lordship has not gone out," Papa said, turning the pages of his paper. "His youngest brother has turned up missing, and Casriel has not left his town house for nearly a week, other than to ride in the park at dawn. He hasn't even taken dinner at his clubs."

Mama and Papa had to be worried. They'd invited half the eligible titles in London to this soiree, and very few had refused the invitation. Some would come to gawk at a cit, others to gawk at the cit's beautiful daughter.

Let them gawk, Sarah would soon be a countess and wear any blasted color she pleased.

She stalked to the window, which looked down between leafy boughs to the street below. "Has his lordship sent regrets?" If Casriel had sent regrets, Sarah and Mama would call upon him the day after the soiree and express concern for his health. That was the Christian, sociable thing to do.

"He has accepted," Mama said. "He's the only earl who has, the highest title we'll entertain. Lord Dentwhistle has also accepted."

The day was sunny, which made Sarah long to join the carriage parade in Hyde Park. She had not arranged for a handsome gentleman to drive her, though, in case her dress required more than a morning's attention from the modiste.

"Dentwhistle is a mere viscount," she said. "I'm not settling for a viscount."

Papa turned another page of his paper. "Since when did young ladies do the proposing, Sarah Jane?"

How she *hated* her middle name. "Casriel needs my settlements, and if he won't propose to me, he'll propose to my fortune." Sarah did not mistake her intended for a greedy man, though a greedy husband would have been even simpler to manage. The settlements would spell out Sarah's pin money, and Papa would ensure every penny of it was made available to her.

Casriel needed coin to support his family and his dependents, priorities Papa respected. Sarah could appeal to Casriel's honor if he became clutch-fisted about her decorating scheme for Dorning Hall or her entertainments.

"He won't propose to anybody or anything," Papa said, "unless and until he asks my permission to court you."

A tall man in morning attire strode up the walk. Between the leaves of the plane tree, Sarah spied the blue of his waistcoat.

"Perhaps that's why his lordship is approaching our front door right now," Sarah said. "Because he seeks leave to court me."

Mama rolled up her embroidery. "He'll ask if he can pay you his addresses first, Sarah. A proper man like that will observe the niceties."

Despite knowing that Casriel's suit was inevitable, Sarah was pleased. He was here, even before he'd seen her in the blue gown and at a time when no other gentlemen were on the premises.

"Order the tea tray," Papa said. "Use the best everyday rather than the silver, lest he think we put on airs. I'll leave Casriel to you ladies for now." Papa rose, tucked the newspaper under his arm, paused to kiss Sarah on the forehead, and left.

"Are you nervous?" Mama asked, closing the lid on her workbasket. "A touch of nerves is to be expected, Sarah. He is an earl and much respected."

That Mama and Papa were cowed by a man's title was both annoying—Casriel was a fortune hunter, the same as the rest of the bachelors admiring Sarah's eyes—and gratifying. Sarah would soon be a countess, a lady by title, and she'd be among those doing the cowing.

"I have made my choice," Sarah said, peering at her reflection in the mirror beside the parlor door, "and his lordship is sensible enough to agree with me. I am not nervous."

Neither was she pale, tired, or anything else unattractive, thanks to constant vigilance and a determination to be ready for the moment when her intended presented himself. She was not wearing blue, but like Papa's advice to save back the good silver, that was probably for the best.

Mama gave Sarah's bodice an upward tug. "You are not nervous, and you apparently aren't burdened by an excess of humility either.

Perhaps his lordship is stopping by to offer his regrets for our soiree. Perhaps his brother has encountered difficulties, and Casriel will be leaving Town. You are not the only pretty heiress in Mayfair, my girl, and Casriel is far from smitten with you."

"He's smitten with my settlements, and I'm smitten with his title. That's how these matters are handled."

Mama glanced at herself in the mirror. Her dress was positively drab and her hair styled in a simple bun. Sarah loved her mother, but in the name of all that was stylish, was a bit of rice powder or a few ringlets too much to ask?

"I'll greet his lordship in the formal parlor," Mama said. "Come along in a few minutes, and then I'll find a reason to leave you and the earl alone for a short while. Be sure the door remains open, Sarah Jane, or Casriel might well revise his opinion of your settlements."

An impecunious earl with marriage on his mind waited one floor below, and still Mama must lecture.

"Yes, Mama, and I won't interrupt his speech about tender sentiments and dearest hopes. I do intend to be a good countess, you know —a good wife."

Mama's lips compressed into a line that did nothing to enhance her unfortunately plain visage. "That's the least you'll owe him if he offers for you." She left with her usual quiet air of martyrdom.

Sarah waited the count of ten, then gave her bodice a stout downward wiggle.

GREY HAD WAITED THREE DAYS, waited for a note from Addy, waited for his resolve to fail, waited for a miracle that would never happen. He'd sent an acceptance to the Quinlan soiree, and despair had moved aside only far enough to be joined by desperation.

He needed to marry well and soon. If he did not set his feet on that course now, Addy's sacrifice would be wasted, for he'd never again find the determination to come to Town and search for a bride.

He'd spend the rest of his life exactly as his father had, wandering the Dorset hills, ignoring financial realities, and exhausting himself in fruitless rural pursuits while his family slid toward ruin.

Grey rapped on the door of the Quinlan town house when every particle of his being wanted to call on Beatitude instead. Not for another afternoon in bed, but simply to assure himself she was bearing up. To hear her voice, to see her, to bow over her gloved hand.

"My lord." A suitably distinguished, balding butler stepped back from the open door and bowed. "May I take your hat?"

Grey did not want to surrender his hat, his walking stick, or his freedom, but he turned over the first two articles and steeled himself to part with the third.

"Is the family at home?" *Please, say no.*

"If you'd accompany me to the green salon, I will inquire, my lord." The old fellow toddled down the corridor, and Grey trailed dutifully behind. In midafternoon, most of Mayfair was at home, and Grey hadn't expected the Quinlans would be any different. He'd called early enough that driving Miss Quinlan in the park at the fashionable hour would have been a possibility, if only Sycamore hadn't absconded with the carriage team.

Thank heavens for Sycamore's impulses.

The Quinlan town house was decorated in painfully good taste. No excess of art, no superfluous gilding, no ostentation of any kind was visible, which in itself commented on the family's ambitions. Dorning Hall, by contrast, featured an ancient fowling piece with a nine-foot barrel mounted over the front door, a relic of the eighth earl's travels in Scotland.

The marble floor in the Hall's foyer had been scored in one corner where, as boys, Ash and Valerian had carved a treasure map for Oak to find. An enormous fern stood over the damage, and every footman knew why the plant sat off-center, two feet from the nearest window.

The Quinlan dwelling was a folly, a caricature of its intended purpose, and Grey would be calling here often.

The green parlor was more of the same, with exquisite oriental-themed silk wallpaper sporting peacocks, flowered vines, and butter-flies. Grey could never in his wildest imaginings have afforded such décor, though his countess would probably demand—and her father would pay for—even finer appointments than this.

Dorning Hall would become a showplace, and that pink marble in the foyer would be replaced with a pristine black and white parquet pattern in the latest fashion.

What the hell am I doing here?

"The ladies are happy to receive you, my lord."

The butler had known they would be, else he would have offered a guest refreshment. Grey was led down another perfectly appointed corridor and wondered if this was how sheep felt when they were herded toward the shearing shed. Resigned, resentful, determined to endure the coming indignities.

He gave himself a mental kick at that thought, for such senti-ments hardly flattered Miss Quinlan, who deserved a husband's regard no matter that she saw him merely as a title.

The formal parlor faced the street, and the gold draperies had been drawn all the way back. Here, the Quinlans had overshot the mark of good taste. The pier glass over the sideboard was framed in gilding worthy of a palace. The porcelain in the curio cabinet was crowded too closely together. Where a vase of roses might have sat on the piano, a bouquet at least three feet tall featuring orchids and ferns stood instead.

Grey did not judge the family for trying too hard. He was trying hard as well.

"Mrs. Quinlan, Miss Quinlan." He gave them his best bows, they curtseyed, and while Mrs. Quinlan's smile was genuinely friendly, Sarah was *sparkling* at him. She'd worn gold earbobs during the day, as well as a thin gold necklace that ended in a locket nestled right above her cleavage.

All three were blunders, did she but know it—the earbobs, the necklace dangling just so, the display of cleavage by day that would have been considered daringly fashionable in the evening.

"This is quite an honor," Sarah said, touching pale fingers to the locket. "Mama, do send for a tray so we might entice his lordship to stay for the requisite two cups. He prefers gunpowder, if I recall."

Grey would prefer a double helping of brandy.

"I am not particular regarding my tea. One pays calls for the company to be enjoyed." He'd offered that line on occasion previously and passed it to his brothers to smooth over a moment when the tea disappointed. What or who, exactly, was disappointing him now?

"Shall we be seated?" Mrs. Quinlan said. "Sarah and I were putting the finishing touches on our plans for the upcoming soiree. My daughter could likely manage the whole affair herself, but what would that leave for me to do?"

Mother and daughter beamed at each other. Grey took a seat in a wing chair.

"Are you enjoying London, Mrs. Quinlan? Even in springtime, I find the air in much of the city less than salubrious compared to Dorset." Even this overly beautiful parlor bore a faint scent of cooking odors and coal smoke.

Sarah settled on the end of the sofa closest to Grey's chair, leaning forward slightly as if to remind him to stare at her locket. Mrs. Quinlan took the center of the sofa and didn't rustle about, arranging her skirts as if to say, *Notice me! Attend me!*

"I do miss Cheshire," Mrs. Quinlan said. "London is very busy, though for bad air, Manchester must take top honors."

"Mama," Sarah muttered, her smile slipping. "His lordship won't be impressed by complaints about a city he's never seen."

"I have been to Manchester, as it happens," Grey said. "The air might be unfortunate, but the city is undeniably a center of industry. Much is accomplished there, and the realm richer for it. Progress always seems to come at a cost, though."

As did happiness.

"How is your family, my lord?" Sarah asked, a complete non sequitur that suggested she was nervous.

Good. Grey's nerves were less than settled, though Lady Antonia's words came back to him, about having wealth he'd failed to appreciate.

"I am very fortunate in my family. Four of my brothers are at Dorning Hall, making it easier for me to enjoy myself in London. My sisters are taken up with raising my nieces and nephews, all of whom provoke an uncle into doting and dandling. Have you family in the north?"

"None worth mentioning," Sarah said. "I am the sole offshoot of this branch of the Quinlan family tree."

The sole heiress, in other words.

Mrs. Quinlan sat up straighter. "I have a sister in Leeds, married to a vicar. Mr. Quinlan is without other family and thus is given to doting on our Sarah. I'd best see what's keeping the tea tray."

Leaving Grey alone with all of Miss Quinlan's sparkling ambition. He was abruptly in need of a fast horse pointed toward Dorset, for this was a precipitous step on a path he'd hoped to tread slowly.

Mrs. Quinlan left the door open, which did nothing to stop Sarah from leaning yet closer and patting Grey's knee.

"We can be honest with one another, my lord," she said. "You are here to start the courting dance. I am amenable to your suit."

Grey should have been relieved. He instead crossed his legs. "You are very confident of your conclusions, miss. Perhaps I am here to assess whether to *start* the courting dance." He leavened that comment with a smile. Miss Quinlan was young, she was nervous, and with her forthrightness, she was only trying to spare him effort and time.

"Assess all you like," she said, sitting back and squaring her shoulders. This had the effect of stretching her bodice over her bosom. Grey enjoyed feminine pulchritude as much as the next man, but he did not enjoy a woman reducing herself to the status of breeding stock. He rose and pretended to study a painting of a hermit's grotto positioned near the piano.

"I have assessed you as well," she said. "You aren't bad looking, you have an old and respected title, Papa can address your family's impoverishment, and I'm young enough to provide you an heir and a spare, and perhaps—I am ignorant of certain realities, you know—a daughter or two. We'll have to see about that."

She slanted him a look that was doubtless intended to be flirtatious.

Grey moved on to peruse the overstuffed curio cabinet. German, French, and English porcelain had all been jumbled together, shepherdesses and angels, sheep and empty vases crammed next to one another.

"As it happens, Miss Quinlan, my countess—assuming I choose to marry anybody—will not be burdened with securing the succession. I have a plethora of male relations, both brothers and cousins. I'd trust any one of them to raise a future earl, for they are all gentlemen."

Grey was being honest. For no inducement, under no circumstances, could he foresee becoming intimate with the young lady regarding him quizzically from the sofa.

"You seek a white marriage, my lord?"

"I might well, though of course I'd expect a cordial union regardless of the details. Let us turn the topic to you, Miss Quinlan. How are you finding your first Season?"

Ambitious or not, she was unable to resist the lure of that question. Raptures and effusions were still pouring forth when Mrs. Quinlan returned, a footman pushing a tea cart in her wake.

Grey stayed for the requisite two cups, trying to label the emotions this encounter engendered. A sliver of reluctant amusement threaded through everything else. Miss Quinlan thought herself quite sophisticated and cunning, but if she became Grey's countess, part of his responsibility would be preserving her from myriad social blunders.

She truly would be marrying him for his manners, whether she appreciated that or not.

But amusement was a thin skein amid a tangle of darker feelings. Sarah Quinlan was the worst possible spouse he could choose. Tansy Pletcher had honestly liked him and desired him, and had, in fact, disdained his title.

Lady Antonia had offered him ferocious honesty, a gift usually exchanged only between friends.

Even Drusilla Arbuckle had grasped that she was entitled to certain expectations of a husband and set Grey aside when he'd disappointed those expectations.

And yet, Sarah Quinlan had money. Damned, impossible, bloody money.

"Ladies," Grey said, rising, "I thank you for a pleasant visit, and I'll look forward to seeing you both at the soiree."

He dreaded the very thought.

"You need not wait until then," Sarah said, popping to her feet so vigorously, her bosom jiggled. "As it happens, I have nobody to drive me in the park this afternoon."

Her mother's wince was impossible to miss. "Perhaps his lordship has plans, Sarah. We must not presume."

"Who's presuming?" Sarah asked, fingering her locket. "I merely state an oversight on my part. You are welcome to ride with Mama and me, my lord. Our new vis-à-vis is quite the crack."

"Language, Sarah," Mrs. Quinlan murmured.

Grey ought to accept. He ought to just get the shearing over with, ought to go quietly to his fate. That course was even tempting, in a grim, hopeless sort of way.

But Sarah Quinlan would be an awkward fit as a countess. She'd need much guidance and support from her husband and his family if she was to become an earl's bride without polite society making her an object of contempt and ridicule.

If he was considering marrying her—and he was—then he owed it to her to establish his authority regarding social matters before she appointed herself an expert in that regard too. She did not want Grey in any personal sense, but she wanted social standing and a countess's consequence. Her papa's money was a liability when considered from the perspective of what she truly desired.

"Your mother has the right of it," Grey said. "I am unfortunately unable to oblige as an escort this afternoon. Perhaps you'd like to ride in the park with me early Monday morning?"

Nobody stayed out late on Sunday. Even an Incomparable ought to be well rested on Monday morning.

"You do have a new habit," Mrs. Quinlan said. "The pretty blue one, remember?"

"You are right, Mama. Very well. Out of appreciation for my modiste's latest creation, I will accept your offer, my lord. I shall meet you at the gates on Park Lane at sunrise on Monday."

She stuck out her hand, which Grey bowed over, though he had every confidence that no blue riding habit yet existed. Miss Quinlan wore a fair amount of blue, now that he thought about it, a less than ideal choice for a woman with green eyes.

"I will look forward to our ride, and if rain should befall us, we can try again on Tuesday."

"I will hope for fine weather," Miss Quinlan said, touching her locket again. "I'll hope for it very earnestly."

While Grey would pray for rain.

GREY HAD BEEN RIGHT. A dry cough had presaged Aunt Freddy's final decline, and Addy was torn between the need for her truest ally to find peace, and outrage that Aunt should be taken from her now.

"You can stop offering me tea," Aunt said from her bed. "Tea has never been as much of a comfort as brandy. Fine stuff, brandy. I took the Corsican into dislike not so much because he waged war over hill and dale—we English seem to need our wars, provided they aren't on home soil—but because his antics made brandy so lucrative for the coastal trade."

This speech, the longest Freddy had made all evening, ended in a spate of gentle coughing.

"Would you like a sip of brandy, Aunt?"

They were alone in the bedchamber Addy had set up as a sickroom. Night had fallen, and the house was quiet.

"Please, and don't you be slipping any of the poppy into my drink, Beatitude. A few aches are an old woman's right. That is such a lovely harp."

Aunt's staff kept the collection at her home covered in Holland cloths for the most part, but Aunt had asked that the latest addition, the one Casriel had restored, accompany her to Addy's house.

"Casriel knew what he was about, apparently," Addy said, pouring a scant measure of brandy from the decanter on the vanity. "The instrument is beautiful."

She slipped an arm around Aunt's shoulders and held the glass so Aunt could touch her lips to the brandy. This too caused a few coughs.

Aunt lay back amid the pillows stacked at her back. "You stock good brandy. Is that to have on hand when Casriel comes around?"

"I doubt he'll come around again." Addy set the glass on the bedside table and took up Aunt's knitting. The shawl would soon be finished, though the pattern had changed down the midline thanks to Addy's forgetfulness.

"Who will play my beautiful harp, Beatitude? I would truly like to hear it again before I die."

Addy didn't bother protesting. Aunt had not eaten to speak of for several days, hadn't left her bed except with Addy's assistance. She was fading as gracefully as a woman could, while Addy knitted and grieved and longed for the sound of Grey Dorning's voice.

"I could try to pluck out a few airs," Addy said.

"I want music, my girl. Beautiful, lush, magical—" She coughed, turning her head to the side, too weak apparently even to hold a handkerchief.

Not now, Addy silently wailed. *Please don't leave me now.* "You must save your strength, Aunt. No more lectures. I can have the kitchen send up a tea tray with some biscuits."

Not for dear Aunt Freddy, but for Addy to have something to do, something to fuss over. Addy rose from the chair she'd had Thiel set beside the bed and went to the corridor. Thiel sat across from the door, his livery for once less than pristine.

"Is anybody awake in the kitchen, Thiel?"

He rose and straightened his coat. "Somebody is awake in the parlor, my lady. When you changed into your nightclothes, Mrs. Beauchamp asked me to fetch Lord Casriel. He's been waiting for the past hour. Said not to disturb you unless Mrs. Beauchamp asked for him again."

Oh, Aunt. "She sent for him directly?"

"Said I wasn't to tell you. 'Just bring the earl here, and don't argue with a dying woman.' I am very sorry, my lady."

"You did as Aunt wished, Thiel. I suppose you'd better send Casriel up."

Addy considered changing back into a proper outfit, but she was more decently covered in a plain dressing gown than she would be fully clothed. Aunt could slip away at any moment, and this was not a time for observing conventions.

"Do you need a tray, my lady? The kitchen is keeping vigil with you."

Aunt would take so much as a sip. "No tray, and you may seek your bed, Thiel. There's nothing more for you to do." Nothing for anybody to do but wait and mourn.

"I'll bide in my chair for a while yet, if your ladyship has no objection. Allenway will take my place in another hour or so, and I'll relieve him at dawn."

Even more than Aunt's cough, this consideration from the staff confirmed that Addy was soon to be alone, that she was indeed keeping a final vigil.

"I heard voices." Grey Dorning stood in evening attire at the top of the stairs. "I apologize if I'm intruding at such an hour, but Mrs. Beauchamp apparently asked for me. I hope I am not too late."

The sound of his voice, the sight of him, the knowledge that he was near... Those realities filled Addy with a comfort and relief disproportionate to all sense.

"I am glad you've come, my lord. Aunt Freddy longs to hear her harp played. Perhaps you could oblige?"

Thiel retreated down the steps, though Addy didn't dare touch her guest. She didn't need to, because his presence was miracle enough.

His lordship closed the distance between them. "You are exhausted, my lady. I can sit with Mrs. Beauchamp. I'm no stranger to sickrooms, and I'd count it an honor to allow you some rest."

And miss the chance to spend these few remaining hours with Aunt Freddy? Miss the chance to spend that time with Casriel? Very likely, Aunt had asked for the earl in part to put him in the same room with Addy, and Addy had not the fortitude to thwart that plan.

"I can rest later, my lord. Aunt Freddy will be very pleased you've come."

They stood simply gazing at each other, alone in the shadows cast by the sconce. The moment was intimate and precious beyond telling, an unlooked-for gift from a true friend and gentleman.

Grey opened the bedroom door. "Mrs. Beauchamp, good evening."

A smile wafted across Aunt's pale features. "You came. Good of you, my lord, but then, one hears much about your faultless manners. I have a harp that wants playing, and you have been neglecting your music. Beatitude, take his—" The dratted cough plagued her.

Grey sat on the edge of the bed, slid a gentle hand behind Aunt's shoulders, and held the water glass to her lips, suggesting he truly had attended an invalid or two.

"Take his coat," Aunt said, sinking back into the pillows when the coughing spell had passed. "The harp does not tolerate Bond Street vanities."

Grey passed Addy his coat and moved the harp and its stool closer to the bed. "What shall I play?" he asked, taking a seat and positioning the harp against his shoulder. "Simple tunes at first, I think, because my skills are rusty."

"Beatitude, don't neglect my knitting," Aunt said. "To have a pleasant tune for my ears, my dear niece at my side, is all I could wish for."

Aunt was saying she was happy. In a peculiar way, that gave Addy permission to take not joy from the moment, but peace, perhaps—something good. Grey had said that Addy could call on him at any time, and in the capacity of friend, he'd not fail her.

He'd meant that. Clearly, honestly, with all the considerable honor in him, he'd meant that.

"An old-fashioned air to start with," Addy said. "Something from Aunt Freddy's youth, in a major key but not too sprightly."

"A lullaby," Grey said, stroking an arpeggio from the harp. "As it happens, I know more than a few. I used to play them for my Tabby."

He set his hands on the strings, random notes at first, a test of the tuning, a bow and curtsey between instrument and musician. Aunt closed her eyes. Addy took up the knitting, draping the soft blue wool over her knees.

And Grey began to play.

CHAPTER FIFTEEN

Grey's musical technique had faded from disuse, but as he reacquainted himself with the soft strains of lullabies, his mind wandered as it hadn't since the last time he'd fished the stream beside the abbey ruins.

He'd given up his music because Tabitha's skill had been approaching his own. He'd set aside a treasured pastime to make room for his daughter's ambition.

He'd set aside his painting—one of the finest ways he knew to solve problems without thinking of them directly—when Oak's talent became obvious.

He'd delegated many of a steward's tasks to Thorne, who had an aptitude for farming. Care of the land and livestock was one aspect of being the earl that Grey enjoyed, and yet, he'd passed those responsibilities to his brother because Thorne needed to feel useful.

As surely as Aunt Freddy was fading on the bed, Grey had been letting parts of himself slip from his own notice. This insight changed nothing, but he had at least put together causes and effects in his own heart.

Addy was snoring in her chair, a swath of blue knitting draped over her knees. Mrs. Beauchamp was asleep as well, or in the untroubled twilight wherein many awaited death. Grey recalled his grandfather's last hours being spent in a similar state, as had his father's.

Had those men been at peace? Had they regretted a short-lived affair that should have been the love of a lifetime? Grey did not regret his encounters with Addy. Just the opposite. He was profoundly grateful to have been allowed even those brief interludes to be himself, not the earl, not the head of the family, not the fortune hunter.

Himself.

He played on, and Aunt Freddy's breathing changed, becoming more audible.

Addy's eyes opened, and when Grey would have brought the tune to a close, she shook her head. "She should leave us while lovely music fills the air."

Addy took her aunt's hand, though the old lady gave no sign she was aware of the gesture. For the space of two soft, sweet choruses, Mrs. Beauchamp continued to breathe, while Addy held her hand.

Then... nothing. No sound of breathing came from the bed. No movement of the covers suggested life yet lingered. Fredericka Beauchamp had departed the mortal realm, a pretty tune in the air, her niece at her side. Grey could not be sad for the old woman, but his heart broke for Addy.

"Play one more," Addy said. "I need you to play one more lullaby for her."

Grey did not play for Mrs. Beauchamp. He played for Addy. His music was offered as a consolation, a promise of peace, and the only gift he could give her. When he'd played the piece through twice, he rose and set the harp back in its corner.

"You'll want some time to make your farewells," he said. "I'll let the household know you are not to be disturbed and have word sent to Mrs. Beauchamp's domestics."

Addy remained seated, the blue knitting still in her lap. "Are you leaving?"

Grey knew exactly the state of her mind, both because he'd lost many older relations and because he knew *her*. Addy appeared calm and accepting of the realities, but on a level beneath words, she was dealing with a blow.

Nothing would be the same. A loss had to be grieved.

"I'm going to the kitchen to let your staff know of your aunt's passing. I will write a note to Mrs. Beauchamp's solicitor and send for her senior staff. They will want to assist with what comes next. I will not leave the house without bidding you a proper farewell. If you have no crepe, I can lend you my stores."

"I have crepe," Addy said, gaze on the small, still form in the bed. "Mr. Ickles has offices near the Inns of Court. I'd not thought... I'd forgotten how much effort a death can be."

An aunt need not be mourned as a spouse or parent was mourned, but this aunt had been dear to Addy. The rituals would be observed out of respect rather than duty.

"I'll return shortly." Grey longed to take Addy in his arms, wanted to at least hold her hand, but he had not the right.

The staff took the news with sadness and relief—a lingering invalid could turn a household upside down for months—and despite dawn being two hours away, Grey jotted off notes to Mrs. Beauchamp's housekeeper and to her lawyer. The message to her vicar could wait until morning and should be penned in Addy's hand.

Grey collected a tea tray from the kitchen, waved away a tired footman, and took the food upstairs himself. Addy's housekeeper, in nightgown and cap, trundled at his side, occasionally sniffing into a handkerchief.

"You're most kind to trouble over us, my lord. Most kind."

"If mourning cannot inspire friends to kindness, then what can?" He set the tray in Addy's sitting room and accompanied the house-keeper to the sickroom.

"Mrs. Fortnam," Addy said, rising from her chair. "Aunt Freddy has left us."

"His lordship said as much, my lady. I am so sorry, and I know Mrs. Richards will want to pay her respects as soon as may be. I can sit with Mrs. Beauchamp now, if you'd like to rest."

Addy rose, gathering the blue knitting into a bunch. "I don't want to leave her."

Grey knew that feeling too. "If you choose one of Mrs. Beauchamp's favorite frocks, Mrs. Fortnam and Mrs. Richards will see that she's laid out in it."

Addy's composure faltered. She blinked several times and clutched the knitting more tightly. "I would... I would appreciate that. The green dress with the pink embroidery, then. Aunt had it made in Paris. It's delicate. You will be careful?"

"Very careful, my lady. I promise." The housekeeper sent Grey a look: *For pity's sake, help her.*

"A tea tray waits across the corridor," Grey said. "I could use a cup, even if your reserves of energy have yet to fail."

Addy spared the bed one final glance, bit her lip, blinked, and nodded.

Grey resigned himself to pouring out another pot of tea nobody much wanted, and held the door rather than take Addy's hand.

"MRS. QUINLAN, I suspect we have a small problem."

Charles raised this small problem at breakfast, for Sarah had not deigned to join them at such an early hour, thank God.

"I am plagued by small problems," Edna replied, "such as a modiste who has forgotten the meaning of modesty. Madam claims fashion all but requires a young lady's attributes to fall from her bodice, and Sarah abets her."

Sarah was at the heart of most of the household's difficulties, though Charles honestly did not care how many new riding habits his daughter demanded or how many slippers she threw. He cared very much that Edna hadn't smiled at him for three days.

"Sarah is worried that she won't bag her earl," he said. "Quinlans are ambitious by nature, and I don't apologize for that."

Edna took a sip of her coffee. She liked it black and strong, as did Charles. "I fear Sarah did not make a good impression on her earl—if Casriel is hers. She's convinced they are off to a roaring start, but nobody was smiling when I returned to the formal parlor."

Charles did not care for the formal parlor. Sarah, aided by her finishing governess, had seen to the decorations, and they struck Charles as gaudy. Edna had said not to criticize Sarah's first efforts at shaping a household, and he'd held his peace.

"Casriel was not at Lady Bellefonte's do last night," Charles said, sawing off a bite of steak. "He has a family connection to the Haddonfields. His brother Willow is married to a Haddonfield, and you'd think Casriel would put in an appearance."

Charles had nothing against music, but evenings spent with caterwauling sopranos or young couples too besotted to stumble through a duet at the pianoforte were an annoying waste of time.

"The earl has not been socializing much lately," Edna said, peering at her coffee. "Sarah claims that's because he's made his choice, and he'll soon declare himself."

"Does Sarah know that Casriel spent all of last night with Lady Canmore?"

Edna set down her cup, carefully. "He's an aristocrat, as is her ladyship. They regard marriage differently than we do."

"Lady Canmore's auntie apparently expired in the middle of the night, but what does it say that a pretty widow sends for Sarah's earl when the hour is well past midnight, and the damned man arrives on the instant and hasn't left the premises as we speak?"

The hour was quite early—Charles did not believe in wasting daylight—but sending for an undertaker and ordering the servants to hang crepe did not take all night. Casriel's affections were clearly engaged, and so were Lady Canmore's.

"Mr. Quinlan, are you having Sarah's earl followed?"

No judgment colored Edna's question. Much was learned simply by observing a potential business associate from a discreet distance. A future son-in-law merited at least the same scrutiny.

"Of course I am. Wish I'd had the younger brother followed. That one hasn't taken ship, so where the devil is he, and what's he about?"

Edna selected a triangle of buttered toast from the rack at her elbow. "Perhaps he's enjoying the hospitality of a sponging house. More likely, Sycamore Dorning has gone home to Dorset for a respite from London's pleasures. Lord knows, I've had enough of this place."

And that was why Sarah must have her earl. Charles's daughter would be miserable if she failed to land a titled husband, but Edna was miserable now. The hunt needed to come to an end, before Edna lost patience with the whole endeavor, or Sarah made a complete fool of herself.

For his own part, Charles expected polite society's snickers and whispers, but for his daughter, he demanded better.

"We won't be here much longer, Mrs. Quinlan. I do not begrudge a bachelor and a widow their diversions, but staying the night is not done, no matter who has gone to their reward. Casriel needs to understand that he'll be a faithful husband, or I'll have a thing or two to say about it."

Edna dipped her toast in her coffee. She would not have done that if a footman had hovered at the sideboard.

"Casriel is not of our ilk, Charles. You cannot expect him to behave like a besotted yeoman when he's an earl making an advantageous match. Earls keep mistresses. They have affairs. He already has a by-blow and makes no secret of it. Sarah likely won't care what he gets up to, provided she can continue to spend your money."

That last observation was not intended to compliment Sarah—or her father.

"Say what's on your mind, Mrs. Quinlan. We have ever been honest with each other, one of many things I treasure about you."

Edna munched her toast, and Charles waited. His wife was slow with her judgments, also thoughtful and shrewd. Her insights frequently astounded him.

"Ever since Sarah came back from that fancy finishing school," Edna said, "I have felt as if I do not know her. She speaks French when she knows I can't understand a word of it. She was a good girl, Charles. I want my good girl back, not this preening twit. We sent her off with a good opinion of herself, and she came home determined to look down on her own upbringing."

Charles's steak had grown cold, which bothered him not at all. There had been a time when steak hadn't been on even his Sunday menu.

"She should look down on her own upbringing. We're common as dirt, despite all of our money. My Sarah does not have to be common, and my granddaughters will have the title lady. My grandson will be an earl, and nobody will dare look down on him. That's what Sarah wants, so I'll see that she gets it."

Edna took another bite of soggy toast. "I would far rather my grandchildren be happy than titled, and I suspect Sarah has simply adopted her father's priorities when it comes to progeny and titles. Sarah is setting herself up for an empty marriage, among people she won't understand. She is not of the aristocracy, and she knows little of the gentry. Country life will leave her bored and lonely, and resentment is sure to follow. I want better for her. I want her to have what I have—a wonderful man who is her best friend and intimate companion."

Edna on the scent of truth was a fearless warrior, but Charles understood ambition, and thus their daughter, in a way Edna did not.

"*Sarah* wants a title," he said, "and Casriel in particular. He's a bird in the hand, Edna. If I send him packing, Sarah will be impossible. She'll be the butt of unkind talk, and then we'll never get back to Cheshire."

Edna poured herself more coffee, but Charles was not fooled. She was *allowing* him the last word. She was unhappy, she did not agree with him, and she was not entirely wrong.

"If it becomes necessary," Charles said, "I'll have a word with Casriel. He'll not play Sarah false. To the extent an earl can make his wife happy, Casriel will exert himself to that end, or I'll ruin him."

Edna blew gently on her coffee. "Sarah will be his *countess*, Charles. Not merely his wife, perhaps not his wife in any meaningful sense, but his countess. You cannot ruin him without also ruining her."

THE SUN WAS RISING, as the sun always did. In early widowhood, Addy had clung to that evidence of life going forward. The sun rose, and Addy had risen from her bed. The sun traveled across the sky. Addy had dressed, eaten, received friends, eventually received the mourning callers. She'd traveled across first and second mourning and into the terrain of the proper, settled widow.

"I think some part of me was always anticipating Roger's death," she said.

Grey had led her to the back garden, an oasis of green a mere dozen yards wide and three times as long. Just enough of a garden to attract birds at daybreak and grow one stately shade tree.

"You anticipated Roger's death because he was reckless?"

"That word... Yes, he was reckless. Let's sit beneath my maple."

Gnarled roots lifted the soil at the base of the tree, canting the white wrought-iron bench slightly higher at one end. Addy often took a pillow out here and read. She'd been beneath this tree, trying to compose a letter to her sister-in-law, when word of Roger's death had reached her.

"You should take a nap," Grey said, coming down beside her on the bench. "Grief destroys our natural rhythms, and you barely slept last night."

Addy did not recall falling asleep. She'd been sitting on her sofa one moment, prattling to Grey about who among Aunt's friends would need to be notified of her death. The next, she'd been aware of

Grey lifting her feet to the cushions, stuffing a pillow beneath her head, and retrieving a quilt from her bedroom.

While she'd dozed, he'd been busy, for Addy had awoken to a house draped in crepe, the knocker off the door, the mirrors covered, and fragrant lilies in the windows of the formal parlor.

The scent of those flowers made real that Aunt had died, but how had Grey procured lilies before the sun had properly risen? From the kitchen had come the aroma of fresh bread, and the voices wafting up the stairs suggested Aunt's senior staff was on hand to join in the mourning.

Grey had done what needed doing, though soon he needed to leave.

"I must deal with the vicar." Addy had sent the note, though Grey had had to remind her. His presence beside her on the bench steadied her. They'd barely touched since last night, but she'd leaned on him shamelessly.

And that had felt natural and right, damn it all to Hades.

"The vicar can do little," Grey said. "He'll swill tea and cite biblical passages meant to be comforting, though they are flimsy consolation against the loss of a loved one. He'll encourage you to attend services, and you'll go, Beatitude, because it's the only way you're allowed to leave your house and all the wretched crepe staring you in the face during first mourning. Why am I telling you these things? You are a widow. I am merely recalling the loss of parents, aunts, grandparents, uncles, a pair of cousins..."

He ran a hand through his hair, and that small gesture revealed that death upset him as well.

"You inherited the title when your Papa died. Did you want it?"

"Of course not. What fool wants a title when an earldom means he loses his only surviving parent and becomes responsible for scores of people who have every right to look to him for sustenance? He must husband thousands of acres, flocks and herds, forests, mead-ows... Anybody who views a title as a mere license to frolic doesn't deserve membership in the peerage. My father understood that and made sure I did as well."

Hence, Grey's need to marry well. Even through the weight of grief, Addy could spare plenty of resentment for his circumstances.

"You don't want your son to have to feel that way, though. You want him to have the means he needs to be a good earl."

Grey crossed his feet at the ankles and leaned back so his head rested against the tree. "*I* want to have the means to be a good earl, but Addy—"

She put her hand over his mouth. "You are a good earl. You are a very good earl, a good brother, a good cousin, a good neighbor, a good friend. Thank you from the bottom of my heart for your company, Grey Dorning. I might have called on Theodosia, but she is not... She has become Mrs. Tresham, a duchess-in-waiting. She could not have played that harp. She would never have taken matters in hand as you have. I am in your debt and always will be."

That was Grey's cue to rise and leave quietly through the back gate. Instead, he took Addy's hand.

"I will alert Mrs. Tresham to developments here," he said. "But, Beatitude, I'd like you to do something for me."

He'd never asked her for anything, though she'd given him her heart. "Name it."

"I want you to go to Canmore Court once you've tended to Mrs. Beauchamp's affairs. Leave Town and spend time with your family. You have nieces and nephews, you have a right to a dower house, and you should at least see that it's maintained to your standards."

His hand was warm around hers, but he was letting her go—again. *Leave Town* was a kind way to inform Addy that he'd soon be back at his courting game, if he hadn't already embarked upon it.

"I had thought to go to Bath," Addy said. "Aunt's friends are there, and they will be solicitous of my loss."

Those friends would speak about an Aunt Freddy whom Addy had never known, a young, vivacious, pretty lady who'd nonetheless never quite settled into the narrow role society created for intelligent, opinionated women.

"Please, not Bath, Beatitude. The elderly congregate there with the infirm. Your aunt would want you to enjoy the company of family, to be around children, and to go for mad gallops as a vicar's hoyden daughter used to do. Climb a few trees, tear your hems in the raspberry patch. Nap in a hammock or two while reading Byron's racy prose. I need to know that you will not be toppled by grief."

Toppled by grief *when Grey took a wife*, as he must. How delicately he dealt with the impossibly painful.

"I don't want to go to Canmore Court. They will try to discuss Roger."

Grey clasped her hand in both of his. "Then discuss him. He was a selfish fool who appreciated neither his wife nor his brother nor the children who would continue the succession. You and the present earl have common ground, and you likely have common guilt as well. Put it behind you and move on to happier pursuits. Aunt Freddy would tell you the same."

Addy leaned into him, and he settled an arm around her shoulders. What he asked was too much, a parting in truth, not merely a decision to avoid each other. Grey was all but ordering her to find somebody else to fall in love with, but that would not happen.

"Thank you for being my friend, Grey Dorning. I will think about your suggestion." Addy would resist, but soon—with a few days at most—she'd leave Town as he'd asked her to. Casriel was not a man to issue warnings for the sake of filling a silence.

"Thank you for being my friend, Addy. I will miss you."

Addy pressed close, and to blazes with anybody spying out of the neighbors' windows. She was exhausted, she'd suffered a blow—two blows—and was entitled to a small lapse in decorum.

Grey let her be the one to sit up.

"Be well, Grey, and if you can, be happy."

He said nothing, merely pressed his lips to her temple, rose, and departed quietly through the back gate.

"WHERE THE HELL HAVE YOU BEEN?" Grey was relieved to see Sycamore, hale, whole, and casually strolling into the town house office.

And Grey was furious with a sibling who lacked the consideration to leave word of his whereabouts. But then, since parting from Addy two days ago, Grey had been furious most of the time.

"Took a jaunt down to Dorning Hall," Sycamore said, hands in pockets, not a care in the world. "Everybody sends their love. Have you cried any banns yet?"

"You took a jaunt..." Grey rose, lest he pound his fist on the desk. He'd rather pound on his baby brother. "Did it not occur to you to ask me for use of the traveling coach? Did it not occur to you to let me know you'd taken a sudden notion to ruralize? Could you not be bothered to send a note reassuring me that you'd not been taken up for debt?"

Sycamore looked him up and down. "What has you in a pet?"

"I had visions of you selling your cravat pins for food in Calais, or fleeing for your life because a patron at The Coventry conceived a notion to do you an injury. One funeral a week is one too many."

Sycamore took down the abacus that hung on the wall near the landscape of Durdle Door. "Who died?"

"Mrs. Beauchamp." And thank God convention decreed that women typically did not attend graveside services, or Grey would have snatched Addy by the hand and... "Did you purloin the traveling coach to prevent me from eloping with Lady Canmore?"

"Casriel, I'd buy you a coach if you promised to steal away in it with her ladyship. I simply wanted to see my other brothers and thought perhaps you'd appreciate an eyewitness report of doings at the Hall."

"Report, then, and be quick about it. I must change for an evening out."

"Where?"

"None of your damned business."

Sycamore gave him another look, much like the looks Grey had been enduring from his staff for the past several days.

"You leave," Grey said, "and tell no one of your plans, but you expect me to consult you regarding my social calendar. The Quinlans are hosting a soiree this evening."

"*Not La Quinlan*, Grey. You cannot... Is this your way to evict the brothers from the Hall? She'll drive them all screaming for the Royal Navy within a fortnight. Send your regrets, for I've brought money."

Sycamore withdrew a folded paper from his coat pocket and set it on the desk. His gaze gave away nothing, suggesting the money did not have a respectable provenance.

Grey opened the paper, which was a duly executed bank draft. "This is signed by Aloysius Pletcher." A good amount of blunt. Enough to repair many roofs, not nearly enough to prevent an engagement to Miss Quinlan. "How did you come by it?"

"Ash came by it. The lovely Miss Tansy Pletcher became Mrs. Hammond Barclay ten years ago. Left her tinker for a well-to-do tannery owner and is a respectable goodwife over in Exmoor. The Pletchers used the money you'd given them until that time as a dowry for the fair Tansy."

Grey sank into the chair behind the desk. "And they've been collecting additional money from me for *ten years?*"

He'd consumed countless pints of ale at the Pletchers' tables, kept them informed regarding Tabby's progress at school, shared many of her letters with them, and encouraged her to both write to them and spend time with them. He considered the Pletchers extended family of a sort, though they clearly considered him something else entirely.

"I don't understand, Cam. They took money they didn't need, money Tansy didn't need, and never said a word to me of her marriage." While Grey had sold his father's Italian glass panes to buy hay for the shire's flocks. That wasn't wrong, exactly, but the sense of having been taken advantage of remained.

"They saved this money for Tabby," Sycamore said, propping a hip against the desk, "or so they claimed when Ash pressed them. I don't know the particulars, don't know how much you've been sending them, but they haven't any means to invest the money. You do. Ash pointed that out to them and also made plain that Tansy's frolic with you left her none the worse for the experience, while you've taken responsibility for Tabby without a word of complaint."

Grey stared at the bank draft, a small fortune that had come from his conscience and his own pockets. "*Of course I did*. She is my daughter."

"Nothing compels even a gentleman to support both a daughter *and* her well-situated mother ten years on, Grey. You will take that money, or I'll hand it over to Worth Kettering for investment in one of his magical schemes."

Jacaranda's husband was a genius with investments. Out of pride, Grey had avoided imposing on him, though Sycamore would do exactly as threatened.

"I'll take it to Kettering," Grey said. "This sum is not the dowry an earl's daughter should have, but it's something. In five years, it will be more, particularly if Kettering manages it. Please tell Ash—"

Sycamore shoved away from the desk. "Tell him not to meddle in your affairs? Tell him yourself." Cam was angry, though unlike Grey, he was managing to conceal his ire.

"I'll give him my thanks in person then," Grey said. "I would never have thought to ask the Pletchers to account for the funds. I'll thank them as well, and now I must change for the evening."

"You'll keep the money?"

"You'll not go haring off without letting me know I needn't worry?"

Cam shrugged. "I was homesick. I'm coming with you to the Quinlans'."

Of all Grey's brothers, Cam was the most determined, which was saying something. "Sycamore, I don't need a chaperone. I won't spill my punch or make drunken pronouncements. Miss Quinlan and I are approaching an understanding of the marital variety, and that does not require your assistance."

Grey had fallen into a bleak sense of inevitability where Miss Quinlan was concerned. With Mrs. Beauchamp's final obsequies having been tended to, Addy had no reason to linger in Town.

And Grey had no excuse for putting off his courting.

"Grey, how much is enough?" Sycamore asked, marching up to the desk. "Ash takes a notion to chase down money that's been leaking from your pocket for years, and a goodly sum lands on your desk as a result. That means you needn't consign yourself to marriage with a vain, spoiled young woman who will be—not coincidentally— miserable as your countess."

"I will do my utmost to make her happy."

Cam slapped both palms on the desk. "You cannot *make* another person happy. You cannot buy all of Oak's paintings, make Valerian's book a wild success, give Thorne tenants of his own, or make my gaming hell thrive. You cannot make Sarah Quinlan happy, but you damned sure ought to be spending more time seeing to your own joy in life."

Grey rose, standing eye to eye with Cam, the bank draft on the blotter between them. "Our father would disagree with you. With a title comes a responsibility to manage the head of the family's duties. Those duties were imposed on him as a result of present company, and I will do at least as much as he did to uphold the honor of the earldom."

The anger faded from Sycamore's eyes. "What the hell are you talking about?"

"Papa had to marry because I was on the way. My mother was a decent young woman, not a tavern owner's wayward daughter, and Papa and Mama had no choice but to marry."

"Which he well knew when he was frolicking with your mother, and which she knew too. You are not the reason they married, Grey. I come by my impulsive nature honestly. Don't burden your brothers with your own misplaced guilt. Marry because you damned well want to marry, and do not wed a woman who will bring you nothing but suffering."

The bank draft sat open on the desk, a reproach of some sort, though Grey could not fathom for what. He should not have trifled with Tansy, but neither should he have blindly continued to send money to her parents when they nor she had need of it.

And Tabby did.

"This is Tabby's money," Grey said, stuffing the bank draft into his pocket. "I'm exceedingly grateful to have it, but it changes nothing about my own circumstances. How are our brothers?"

Cam wanted to argue. Grey saw that in the compressed line of his brother's lips, the mulish glint in his eyes.

"They are managing. They would be loath to see you marry a carping twit who will turn Dorning Hall into Versailles-on-the-Winterbourne. Ash pressed the Pletchers for these funds because he knows what a desperate situation you're facing."

"Ash declined to return to Town with you?"

Sycamore sidled away to study the landscape of Dorning Hall with the ruins in the distance. "Oak, Valerian, and Thorne keep an eye on him. He's getting dressed each day, taking meals, that sort of thing."

Drifting, in other words. When autumn came, Ash typically threw himself into the harvest, but inevitably, winter saw his spirits plunge. Cam's words echoed: *You cannot make another person happy,* though Grey would and could keep Ash safe.

"If you're coming with me this evening, you must promise not to act on any impulses, Sycamore. The key to our brothers' fortunes, as well as to those of half the tenants in the shire, lies in my ability to win Miss Quinlan's hand in marriage. She's amenable to my suit, and I owe her the niceties."

"She told you that?"

"She knows her mind."

"But does she know your heart?" Cam left the office on that question, moving too quickly for Grey to land a punch.

CHAPTER SIXTEEN

Grey had donned his finest waistcoat for the occasion of the Quin-lans' soiree—blue silk the hue of a Dorset summer sky shot through with green and gold embroidery. Those colors put him in mind of ripe wheat fields and lush hedgerows. He doubted Miss Quinlan would notice, but this was as close to shining armor as he possessed.

"My lord." Miss Quinlan's curtsey threatened to put the contents of her bodice on display before the whole receiving line. "A pleasure to see you."

"A pleasure to be here, particularly on so fine an evening. You know my brother Mr. Sycamore Dorning, I believe?"

Sycamore took hold of the lady's proffered glove and bowed smartly. "An honor, Miss Quinlan, and might I say, that is a beautiful locket? Whose images do you carry so close to your heart?"

She simpered, letting Cam keep hold of her hand. "That is for me to know, Mr. Dorning, though I might confide that secret to his lord-ship some fine day. Enjoy the punch, and don't forget to admire the roses. They are coming into their full glory at *such* an obliging time."

A headache started a dull tattoo at the base of Grey's skull. "Come along, Sycamore. Roses in bloom are not to be missed."

Miss Quinlan sent him an arch look, as if he'd meant that observation flirtatiously.

Which he had *not*. As the evening lumbered along, Grey was the object of more arch looks from Miss Quinlan. Drusilla Arbuckle merely smiled at him, and Lady Antonia spared him the merest nod while she gestured emphatically at Lord Dentwhistle in a corner of the terrace.

Even Lady Antonia's philosopher nuns held more appeal for Grey than Miss Quinlan's melting glances and simpering.

Beatitude, I miss you. He'd no sooner allowed himself that single, vastly understated thought than Miss Quinlan attached herself to his arm.

"Papa has a Gainsborough. It's time you admired it."

Papa also had a very forward daughter. Grey stayed where he was, amid the crowd milling on the torchlit terrace. "A sporting portrait?"

"Some skinny horse with its tail bobbed short. Come to the library and see."

She was giving an order, not offering an invitation. Across the terrace, Sycamore watched, his gaze solemn to the point of sadness.

"I enjoy good art," Grey said, yielding to the pressure Miss Quinlan exerted on his arm. "Have you ever taken in a royal exhibition? The array of talent we have among our English painters is impressive." Oak should submit some of his landscapes to the Royal Academy, though such was his modesty that he'd never made the attempt.

"I dabble in watercolors myself," Miss Quinlan said. "Oils are so intense. Give me a pretty garden scene or a peaceful landscape and I'm happy."

She dragooned Grey back into the house, past the music room where a quartet sawed away, past the formal parlor with overdone gilt and porcelain. The library was quiet, as Grey had known it would be, and devoid of other guests.

"We should leave the door open, Miss Quinlan. I've no wish to cause talk."

She turned the lock on the latch. "This is my home, my lord. I can go where I please, and nobody will say anything to it. Haven't you a declaration to make? A speech? Something?"

She was smiling at him, but Grey was put in mind of a younger Sycamore, full of bravado and hubris, and just perceptive enough to know his confidence rang a bit false.

"How are you?" Grey asked, a gentleman's inquiry of any acquaintance. *And can I leave this library without becoming a doomed man?*

"I am waiting for you to get on with it, my lord. I've told you your suit will be acceptable to me, and I'd very much like a big, sparkly ring to wear every time I enjoy the carriage parade. You may drive me on Tuesdays and Fridays, though I will have my other gallants attend me as I see fit on the remaining days of the week. We will walk home from services together starting this Sunday, and you will—"

Grey wanted to clap his hand over her pretty mouth. Instead, he smiled.

"I have not yet asked to pay you my addresses, Miss Quinlan." But he would. He most definitely would. That was a Gainsborough on the wall, a Richard Wilson landscape hanging beside it. The shelves of the library were full of bound books, which in themselves attested to wealth. The carpet was Axminster. The fireplace looked to be Italian marble. A reading balcony projected over the fireplace, the railing intricately carved to match the spiral staircase that curved between floors.

She frowned at him. "Do you want to kiss me? Is that it? I thought you said *that* part of marriage holds no interest for you. I'm not averse to affection between husband and wife, I suppose. You said you have no need of an heir, and I certainly have no need to lose my figure filling a nursery."

While Beatitude had longed for a child, just one child, to love.

"I am free of any craving for your kisses." Grey was also making a hash of this interview, which should have been simple enough.

Miss Quinlan, I esteem you greatly and have reason to hope that my feelings might be reciprocated. Please indicate whether in the fullness of time I might aspire to be more than a friend to you, and you will make me the happiest of men.

The speech wasn't complicated, but it did involve falsehoods. A gentleman was kind, but he was also *honest*, and those falsehoods... Grey did *not* esteem this woman, he wasn't *even* her friend, and marriage would make them *both* miserable.

"Do you prefer boys?" Miss Quinlan asked. "I'm not supposed to know about that, but at school we had nothing to do but talk—mostly in French, so the younger girls wouldn't understand—and Carlotta Dormioni had an uncle who consorted with a cata... cata... I forget the word. It's scandalous."

This conversation was going from bad to worse. "Miss Quinlan, might we admire the artwork? I've always thought Wilson an underappreciated talent."

"Your job is to admire *me*, my lord. Now make your declaration, and then you may kiss me." She touched her cheek with a gloved finger. "Right here. I won't mind."

Tap-tap-tap against her pale cheek, like the hand gestures Tresham used to communicate with his dogs.

Grey stared at the spot on her cheek and thought of his daughter, who needed a larger dowry than she had. He thought of Dorning Hall, slowly crumbling beneath a leaking roof. He thought of Oak, who by rights should have been painting up a storm in Paris. Valerian had the soul of a Town dandy. Thorne deserved his own estate.

Ash... Ash would need the Hall as his refuge, and Miss Quinlan would regard him as pathetic. Grey thought his brother heroic, for who could battle melancholia year after year and never once complain?

Grey bent near to her and closed his eyes, for he had no wish to view the treasures Miss Quinlan was determined to display. Her scent was as overdone as the gilt in her mama's formal parlor—a cloying freesia fragrance that nonetheless held a hint of sour wine. She exuded not eagerness, but impatience, which was likely a harbinger of the emotional signature the entire marriage would take on.

You cannot make another person happy.

Beatitude had never asked him for happiness. She'd asked him for *himself*, the true man, the fellow who was happy to shear sheep and fork hay, the man who worried for his daughter and his family.

A gentleman was kind *and honest*.

"Miss Quinlan, I regret that I must inform you that we would not suit." The admission was reckless—a challenge tossed at life that could end very, very badly—also freeing. She deserved better, but *so did Grey.*

He deserved a woman who respected and desired him, a woman who would support his aims and talk sense to him when sense was needed. Such a woman existed. She'd been in his arms and had taken up residence in his heart.

He might never have a future with Addy, but he deserved better than a spoiled heiress.

Grey straightened, even as a thousand recriminations urged him to take back his words. A thousand and one memories of Beatitude kept the retraction behind his teeth.

"I've worn blue for you," Miss Quinlan retorted. "We will suit quite well, and we will have an understanding that begins this evening, Lord Casriel. You need my money, and I want your title."

"But we do not want each other," Grey said, gently, because the young lady was clearly at sea. "A gentleman is considerate of others and truthful. I cannot allow you to marry into a circumstance that will result in misery for us both."

"Your allowing doesn't come into it," she snapped. "If I can't marry an earl, what am I to do? That leaves only barons and viscounts, and they are not to be borne. My daughters must be ladies. My son must have a courtesy title."

Her voice rose, suggesting Grey was about to be treated to a display of hysterics. He welcomed them, because the longer she ranted, the more resolved he became.

"I told you not to expect any children from me, Miss Quinlan. With you, that sort of marriage would not have been possible. I suggest you return to your guests, and I will wish you every happiness."

"Damn you, *I wore blue*. I am prepared to allow you liberties. I let you have a dance. I let you maunder on about paintings, and—"

"Sarah." A masculine voice sounded from the balcony over the fireplace. "You will excuse his lordship and me." Charles Quinlan stood at the railing, his expression pleasant. He descended the spiral steps at a leisurely pace.

"I will be a countess, Papa," Sarah said. "I don't care what you have to do to make Casriel see reason. He and I would suit. I'll make sure of it."

She jerked the locket from around her neck and threw it to the floor, which display her papa allowed without a word of rebuke. She flounced out of the library, slamming the door in her wake.

"My lord, I understand your reluctance," Quinlan said. "Shall I pour you a brandy? You'll probably need it."

"Thank you, no," Grey said. "I will take my leave of you, with apologies for that regrettable scene." He would pack for Dorset and be gone by sunup if he had to walk the entire distance. First, he'd pay a call on Beatitude and apologize to her for ever thinking that he could love one woman while embarking on a courtship of another.

What an ass, what a complete, muttonheaded—

Quinlan held up a serving of brandy. "Sarah has made her choice. My lot is to see that she gets what she wants."

Grey didn't touch the brandy. "A husband is a who, not a what, and I will not be that man. I'll bid you good night."

"You will sit," Quinlan said mildly. "And you will marry my daughter."

Never.

And yet, Grey did not spin on his heel and bolt from the room either. Quinlan had the physique of an ironmonger, despite his fine tailoring. His shoulders and chest were burly, and he had height as well. He was built to wrestle heavy loads in stifling heat, and his demeanor said he was utterly confident that he could manage one polite earl.

"I cannot marry your daughter," Grey said. "I would make her a terrible husband. She would make me an awful wife, meaning no disrespect. All the snug roofs and fat dowries in the world cannot compensate a couple for knowingly making a bad match."

"Sarah wants a title, and a title she will have." Quinlan took a sip of the brandy he'd poured for Grey. "I cannot ruin you—you're a peer and a decent sort. Your kind take more ruining than my kind can accomplish. You don't gamble, you don't drink to excess, you have no family members courting disaster at present, though Mr. Sycamore Dorning bears watching. You do, however, care for a certain widow."

Another slow sip of brandy followed that observation.

"Lady Canmore and I are friends. Why should that interest you?"

"I can ruin her," Quinlan said. "Polite society is vicious toward its womenfolk. In the villages and towns where I come from, we don't expect women to be kept like so many porcelain shepherdesses in a glass case. They work alongside their menfolk. They toil in their way as much as any man, half the time with a babe at the breast, another clinging to their skirts. We don't cast them out for being human. You lot..." Quinlan finished his brandy and set the glass on the sideboard.

"Sarah wants to be the porcelain lady," he went on, "so I'll buy her an earl. If I have to ruin a countess to make him come willingly to Sarah's side, I'll ruin a countess. I look after my own, Casriel."

"You condemn your daughter to a fate you abhor," Grey said, stalking across the library. "You think she's lonely here, surrounded by other young women, some of whom she met at school. In Dorset, she'll know not a soul. They will criticize her finishing-school accent, her affected French, and her too-fancy gowns. She cannot shoot, cannot manage a country dance. She likely tires in the saddle in the first five miles of a morning hack. The smell of raw wool will make her bilious, while to me and mine, that is the scent of success. You cannot do this to your own daughter and claim it's for her benefit."

And yet, what had Grey been doing with his brothers? Keeping them half imprisoned at Dorning Hall in the name of protecting them from... what? Failure? Every man fell on his arse at some point, and a brother's job was to commiserate, not to make sure the ground was strewn with satin pillows.

"She'll adjust," Quinlan said. "I'll hold you responsible for seeing to it that she adjusts happily."

Grey swiped the discarded locket from the carpet. "You haven't been able to make her happy in eighteen years of trying. What makes you think I'll have any greater success?"

"She wants a title," Quinlan bit out. "You can give her that, and no, she probably won't be happy, but her daughters will be ladies, and perhaps they can be happy. You will offer for Sarah, my lord, or I will make you regret the decision not to."

Quinlan's reasoning was flawed. Grey could grasp that much, but working out the fallacy would have to wait for another day. Something about unhappy parents seldom raising happy children.

I will regret ever allowing Beatitude to send me on my way.

"I shall not, ever, offer for Miss Quinlan." A gentleman did not engage in falsehoods, but for the love of his life, he could bluff. "And if you think to threaten me into revising that decision, be assured that I can, thoroughly, politely, and with every evidence of good manners, *ruin your daughter* if her headstrong foolishness doesn't accomplish that aim before this evening is concluded."

Grey would *never* ruin another person on purpose—Beatitude would be ashamed of him, and he'd be ashamed of himself for abusing his station like that—but Sarah and her father had to be dissuaded from pursuing a disastrous course. Quinlan thought he was being a conscientious papa, but he was consigning his beloved offspring to a wasted life.

The locket in Grey's hand was open, the clasp having come undone. Inside, two plain gold surfaces lay facing each other like the interior of a clamshell. No miniature portraits beaming at each other, no pleasant pastoral scene, no wise saying embellished with tiny flowers.

"Think carefully before you make your choice," Grey said, tossing the locket at Quinlan's chest. "A gentleman does not make idle threats, nor does he tolerate them from others."

He left the library at a dignified stroll, finally free of the urge to kick something. Instead, he wanted to leap for joy, find Beatitude, and hug her until harvesttime. The Dornings might be headed for ruin, but that ruin would be honorable.

First, however, he had siblings to sort out and an estate to rescue.

Even an earl could not court the love of his life without having something to offer her besides a leaking roof and a lot of smelly, bleating sheep.

"HE WAS AT THE QUINLANS' soiree last night," Theodosia said. "Lord Casriel, I mean. Your earl."

Addy had received her friend in the garden, and they sat in the sun along the lavender border. Since Grey's final parting, Addy had avoided the shady bench beneath the maple.

"He is not my earl. If he went to the Quinlans' soiree, he will never be my earl." No peace followed that admission, no sense of wishing a friend well, despite all.

"So you are dodging off to Bath," Theo replied, plucking a sprig of lavender. The tiny purple flowers would not appear until summer had fully arrived, but even the foliage gave off a pungent fragrance.

"You will embark upon the path your aunt trod, half out of step with polite society, never complaining, always gracious."

What mood was this? "You trod that path with me for years, Theo, and we don't embark upon it. Society grabs us by our widow's weeds and shoves us onto it."

Theo twirled her lavender sprig. "How will you settle Aunt Freddy's affairs if you nip off to Bath? Jonathan says estates can be complicated, even simple estates, and he's ready to assist in any manner."

In the corner of Addy's mind not overcome with grief, she knew what Theo hoped to accomplish. She was trying to keep Addy in Town, trying to keep hope alive. Losing Aunt Freddy had been inevitable and sad.

Losing Grey... *I never really had him. I was not enough for him.*

"Aunt had money in the funds, and she had her house, nothing more. Mr. Ickles has assured me the house is mine to sell, rent out, or maintain for my own use, and he'll manage whatever disposition she made for her funds. I'll likely sell her house and this property as well." *And never come back.*

"A London town house in a fine neighborhood would make a nice little dowry, Addy. If Casriel is short of funds, that might be a consideration."

Oh, Theo. She'd been married to a mere mister, albeit one in expectation of a title. Her marriage to Tresham was recent and hadn't even involved a visit to the Quimbey family seat yet.

"My husband was an earl, Theo. I know what thousands of acres, multiple houses, tenant farms, an ancestral pile, and pensioned retainers do to a family's means. One modest house in a decent neighborhood won't make much difference. I'll likely sell both of my London properties and travel for a time."

"Why are you doing this?" Theo asked, tossing the lavender into the bed from which she'd plucked it. "Why are you turning tail and giving up? Casriel is a decent fellow. He's done what nobody else could do and tempted you away from worshipping at Roger's grave.

Now, you all but shove Casriel into the arms of a hopeless gudgeon when you know she'll make him no sort of countess."

Theo meant well. She always meant well.

"You set Tresham aside when your differences seemed insurmountable, Theo. And I do not worship at Roger's grave. I thought my marriage to him ruined me for all other entanglements, but Casriel…"

"You and Roger were a love match." Theo patted Addy's arm. "Of course you feel disloyal to his memory when Casriel attaches your affections, but Roger would be the last person to begrudge you a chance at a future with Casriel."

Roger again. Roger, always Roger. "Theo, by the time my husband died, I nearly hated him. We argued constantly, then we barely spoke. When he passed away…"

I was relieved. Not the sad relief Aunt Freddy's death engendered, not an acceptance that a loved one was at peace. The relief of a soldier at the end of a long, hard march.

"Every marriage hits rough patches," Theo said. "You would have come through it, I'm sure. You loved your husband, that was plain to anybody."

But he did not love me. The words emerged from Addy's mind with the clarity of a tolling bell. Maybe at the beginning of the marriage, Roger had regarded her affectionately, but by the end… He'd been willing to sacrifice her happiness, her very place in the world, for his own ends. Casriel was willing to sacrifice his happiness for the sake of others.

The contrast was stark and freed Addy of the last, lingering need to dissemble where Roger was concerned.

"I tried to love my husband," Addy said. "I was not equal to the challenge." And now she'd all but heaved Grey Dorning into an equally hopeless match.

He was not married yet, though. Not quite.

"Perhaps Roger was incapable of fidelity," Theo said, "but he was loyal to you, Beatitude. He maintained his households with you, stood up with you for the occasional dance, flirted with you in public. Many husbands can't be bothered with that much."

Addy sat very still, because this conversation was shifting the foundations of mental edifices she'd been building for years. She felt as if, should she move, some arrow of insight would land two inches off the mark, and she was long overdue for insights.

"If your dear Mr. Tresham limited his dealings with you to an occasional dance, some public flirtation, and sleeping under the same roof most nights—punctuated with hasty couplings any time and place he chose—would you consider that loyalty?"

Theo's brows drew down. "I'd consider that... I'm sorry. If it was like that, I'm sorry."

Addy was sorry too. Sorry she'd ever married Roger, sorry she'd sent Grey away. Regrets solved nothing, though, and time was of the essence.

"I have a call to pay," Addy said, rising. "I can walk you home."

"The hour is early for paying calls. I didn't want unkind talk to bring you word that Casriel was at the Quinlans' last night."

"I can hear about it from the earl himself," Addy said. "You didn't see an announcement of any engagement in the morning papers?"

"I doubt matters have progressed that far, but there's something else you should know."

Addy was in a tearing hurry to see Grey Dorning, to let him know that a lady had changed her mind, and a gentleman was not to argue with her. They'd muddle through the financial mess, put Aunt's little bequest to work, economize, spend a few years living cheaply in Paris...

"What else do I need to know?"

"Casriel was alone with Miss Quinlan in the library behind a closed door, and the young lady rejoined her guests at the end of the interview smiling like a cat who'd puzzled out how to open the bird-cage. Her father and Casriel apparently had some discussion there-after, though nobody knows whether any agreements were reached."

"Then there's still time," Addy said, striding for the back door. "I still have a little time, and I must call upon Grey this instant. May I borrow your traveling coach if the need arises?"

Theo stopped her at the door to the house and wrapped her in a tight hug. "Of course you may. You absolutely may take every vehicle in my carriage house."

When Addy arrived to Casriel's town house, she was received by Mr. Sycamore Dorning, who ushered her into the same cozy parlor where she'd called upon Grey weeks ago.

"He's not here," Mr. Dorning said. "I can ring for tea, I can offer you biscuits, and discuss the weather if you insist, but Casriel left at first light."

"Left?" *Now?* Where would he go and why? "He left Town?"

"He was in a tearing hurry to get back to Dorning Hall." Mr. Dorning studied the parlor's molding, which could do with a good dusting. "You know he attended the Quinlan soiree last evening?"

Such kind eyes he had, much like Grey's, and how that gaze hurt Addy's heart. "I'd heard as much. And now his lordship has quit Town?"

Mr. Dorning looked as if he longed to offer confidences but he refused to betray his brother. "I doubt Casriel will return here in the immediate future, my lady. Mind you, he didn't confide the whole of his plans to me, but I gather his reasons for tarrying in London no longer apply."

Grey was engaged then, or as good as. Hope died, for no gentleman would ever, ever cry off once his suit was tendered.

"I am too late," Addy said, rising. "Thank you for receiving me." The heartache was spreading through her again, more painful and heavier than before. Grey was lost to her, truly and forever.

"Shall I escort you home, my lady?"

The youngest Dorning brother had learned from Grey's gentlemanly example after all. "No thank you. I came by carriage, and can see myself home."

Addy didn't even cry after Thiel had handed her up into her

town coach. There was nothing left to do, but return home and resume packing.

"HE'S COME HOME," Oak said, pushing aside the curtains in the study. "That's Casriel galloping up the drive, or Sycamore has stolen his lordship's horse this time instead of his coach."

Sycamore had descended from London like the wrath of Boudicca and put the fear of a certain prospective countess in his brothers. The sum Ash had produced from the Pletchers wasn't likely to have warded off disaster, but perhaps it had given Casriel some time to develop alternatives.

Ash had racked his brain for what more they could do, but every scheme and plan required Grey's imprimatur, and he was off waltzing to his doom in London.

"That is Grey," Valerian said, joining Oak at the window. "Sycamore hasn't as good a seat. I do hope our brother has not been sent packing by the fair heiress."

"I hope he has," Ash retorted. "Cam described her as a horror of the first water."

"Casriel would not comport himself in any manner a lady could object to," Thorne said. "Not on purpose."

Perhaps Grey hadn't had a choice. Ash kept those words to himself, because he well knew the guilt that came with disappointing a woman who'd done nothing to deserve it. Lady Della Haddonfield had written to him—not quite a breach of propriety, given the family connection—and hoped he was well.

He was not well, though his affliction was of the mind rather than the body. Perhaps he should simply tell her that.

"Casriel's been riding hard," Oak said as the horseman cantered into the circular driveway. "Dusty from head to foot, the horse lathered. I suspect he has an announcement, and the Hall is about to get a thorough cleaning in anticipation of the nuptials."

"We can't clean away a leaking roof," Thorne muttered.

A groom scampered out of the stables and took Casriel's horse, which would require walking for some time. The day was warm and sunny, and the plume of dust Casriel's arrival had raised on the drive drifted in a mild breeze.

Dorning Hall was so pretty, and yet, it was also beginning to feel like a prison. Did the other brothers feel the same way? Would they admit as much even to themselves?

"Let's greet the prodigal," Thorne said. "He doubtless has news for us."

Did he have news of Lady Della? Another letter, perhaps? Ash followed his brothers down the main staircase and out onto the drive. Grey sat on the mounting block removing his spurs, for a gentleman did not wear spurs indoors.

"Welcome home," Thorne said, whacking Grey on the back. "We left the Hall standing despite all temptation to the contrary. The corn's doing well after all that rain, but the hay came in on the stemmy side."

"Have you news?" Oak asked, taking the dusty hat Grey passed to him. "Sycamore dispensed all manner of doom and gossip, then tore back to London without so much as a by your leave."

Grey rose, for once looking less than dapper and well turned out. His face below where his hat had been bore a fine coating of dust, as did the creases of his riding jacket. His boots were a disgrace—even for him—and his linen was positively wrinkled.

"I have news," he said. "Give me five minutes with a basin and a towel, and let's meet in the study. I'm exhausted, famished, and filthy, but it's wonderful to be home with my family."

He passed Ash his spurs and strode into the house, bellowing for Rawley to send enough sandwiches for an army up to the estate office, then draw a bath, and for pity's sake lay out clean clothes before a man expired from his own stink.

"He's back," Valerian said, staring at the front door. "He's back for two minutes, looking like he's been dragged through a hedge in a high wind, and already, the Hall feels more lively. How does he do that?"

"He loves this place," Ash said. "He loves us. He meant what he said. For him, it's wonderful to be here."

Thorne started up the steps. "Let's hope his countess feels the same way, for increasingly, I do not."

CHAPTER SEVENTEEN

Grey would rest later, but for now, he needed to begin as he intended to go on. Addy sat in London in her house of mourning, which at least would keep gossip from reaching her ears.

Perhaps.

Even those who mourned attended services, and churchyards were nothing if not filled with talk. Grey had tucked a note for her among his outgoing correspondence—ostensibly a condolence, which anybody was allowed to send to the newly aggrieved—but he hadn't had time to say much.

Off to Dorset. Back soon. Will call when I return. Ever your servant, Casriel.

He'd had more than a hundred miles to berate himself for such a pathetic epistle, but had he started on anything more substantive, he'd still be in London crossing out *I love you* and blotting over *please forgive me.*

A leaking roof waited for no earl.

He took time to change his shirt and wash off. His clean clothes smelled fresher at the Hall, because the laundresses laid his shirts on the lavender borders to dry. The cedar-paneled wardrobe was scented with sachets from their own meadow gardens, and the air was free of London's coal smoke.

"What the hell was I about?" he asked his reflection in the mirror over the washstand. "London would destroy any man's spirits." Though, he'd met Addy there, a point forever in London's favor.

He shrugged into a waistcoat and clean jacket, pulled on an older pair of boots, and joined his brothers in the estate office. An enormous plate of sandwiches sat on the desk, along with a tray bearing a pitcher of cider and five tankards.

"Am I the king," Grey asked, taking the chair behind the desk, "that nobody can eat until I've been seated at the high table?"

Thorne grabbed a sandwich, Oak and Valerian followed. Ash hung back, which was worrisome. He tended to lose his appetite when the dark mood was upon him, though his clothing was tidy and he looked rested.

"What's the news?" Oak asked, pouring a round of cider. "Are we to have a countess?"

"I don't know about a countess, but I do know you all need to be about gainful employment."

Uneasy glances flew about the room.

"We stay busy," Valerian said, taking a seat on the sofa. "I have my book, Oak paints and sketches, Thorne has been overseeing the stewards. Ash..."

Ash had *taken action,* prying a small fortune loose from the Pletchers.

"I have a proposition for you," Grey said. "First, take these." The bank drafts were much creased, but the signatures were still legible. "Sycamore repaid the loans I've made him in recent years. The Coventry is solvent, for now, and he wanted to clear his debts. I'm dividing the sum among you lot, and you are to regard it as the last largesse the earldom can spare you."

More uneasy glances.

"I thought..." Oak took a reading chair and regarded the bank draft as if he couldn't place the artist. "Did you or did you not go up to Town to marry a fortune?"

"I found riches beyond imagining, but no fortune. I have a proposal for you gentlemen, which you may accept or reject, but either way, you will quit the Hall by Michaelmas and find other lodgings."

That left the brothers more than four months to find their feet. By then, Grey would either have the countess of his dreams or a broken heart.

"You're kicking us out?" Thorne asked, pocketing his bank draft and reaching for another sandwich.

"I am helping you to get your start in the world," Grey said. "If you want a recommendation as a steward, I will write you the most convincing character a man has ever penned. Oak can use his funds to set up a studio in Paris, or submit his work to the Royal Academy. Valerian can finish his book, and Ash..."

Ash was studying the worn carpet.

"I'll leave," he said. "Oak has spoken endlessly of Paris's charms and its affordability. I'll be gone."

"You are the linchpin in our new venture," Grey said. "If you want to manage the business from Paris, that is entirely up to you, or you can leave the lot of us to muddle on as best we can, assuming you all approve of my plans. I'd take it as a kindness if you'd personally keep an eye on Sycamore, though. His head is above water at The Coventry, but with Sycamore, the calm never lasts."

Ash's melancholias were temporary as well. They doubtless felt eternal to him, though. Grey worried most about Ash, when he wasn't worrying most about Sycamore, or Thorne, or Valerian, or Oak.

And yet, none of those worries came close to his concern regarding Addy. Had she received his note? Would she be angry with him? Would Tresham do as he'd promised and help settle Mrs. Beauchamp's affairs?

"You mentioned a proposal," Thorne said around a mouthful of sandwich.

"That involves all of us," Oak added. "I am only good for painting and sketching and staring at blank pages."

"I know the horticulture and livestock," Thorne said.

"I'm handsome and charming," Valerian added. "Not much of a skill, but there you have it."

"And Ash," Grey said, "is handsome and charming, he is thoroughly acquainted with Dorning Hall and its holdings, his aesthetic sense is that of a gentleman, and he's good with numbers."

Ash stared at his cider. "Not much to boast of. Money comes in, money goes out. Fairly straightforward. Sycamore has more of a head for figures than I do."

"Sycamore has a head for figures," Grey retorted, "but I suspect you have the better head for business. You can think on a topic for days as Oak considers a composition. You can turn an idea over in your mind until it lies in pieces at your mental feet."

Ash brooded too, but he had powers of concentration to equal the rest of the family's combined.

"So what is the great scheme you're hatching?" Thorne asked, "and will it make money?"

"That aspect of the undertaking will depend on you," Grey said. "All I know is London reeks. It stinks, it smells, it leaves a strong man gagging when a certain wind blows from the river in summertime. A gentleman is always clean about his person, but in London, that challenge is nearly impossible."

Ash looked up from his cider. "We're going into *trade*? A gentleman does not get his hands dirty. We're gentlemen."

"Harvesting the bounty of the land has always been a gentlemanly pursuit," Grey said, "and I frankly do not care where polite society wants to draw lines after that. We have the most fragrant meadows in England. London has the worst stench this side of the Pit. We have enough mature medicinals to stock every apothecary in the realm, and London is the capital of illness and misery as well as

the seat of government. We owe it to England to address those problems as best we can."

Ash plucked a sandwich from the plate. "It is a fact that the
stench of London has to be smelled to be believed."

"Paris isn't exactly fragrant," Oak said. "We have acres of herbs
and flowers, though. Casriel is right about that."

"Don't say that." Valerian brushed crumbs from his cravat. "Don't
say Casriel is right about something. He'll get a swelled head."

"All I ask you to do is think about it." Grey snatched a pair of
sandwiches and left his brothers bickering, which they could do
without any help from him. In fact, they would have to learn to bicker
without him, because he had an earldom to see to, and—God and
Lady Canmore willing—a countess to cosset.

Thorne trailed him into the corridor.

"What about the great heiress hunt?" Thorne asked. "We still
have no dower house, the vicar is clamoring for a new roof, and the
Hall needs work. We can set up a scent, sachet, and soap business,
but that will take time."

"We can have products on the London shelves well before Yule-
tide," Grey said. "The salvage from the dower house can be used to
construct the workshop, and the women from the village will likely
be happy to earn some coin there."

"Women?"

"They work hard, they have delicate noses, and they are less
likely to squander coin on drink and gaming. Why not women?"

Thorne took a sip of his cider. "I like women well enough. What
other ideas has this trip to London germinated in your fertile brain?"

"I have many ideas. What bricks and beams we don't use to
construct a workshop should be sold for coin. Our dear neighbor Mr.
Bulwaring, who has enough blunt to build a conservatory with Papa's
Italian glass, can also take on a portion of the burden of repairing the
church roof. With my brothers housed elsewhere—Complaisance
Cottage sits empty, for example—I can demolish the family wing,

which has never been quite sound. I'll sell the salvage to any local builder and be able to undercut London prices substantially."

Thorne studied him, and Grey had the sense his brother was seeing him anew, as Grey had been seeing anew since leaving London.

"Wouldn't it be easier simply to marry money?" Thorne asked. "It's done all the time and allows families with means to become families with titles."

"Then you do it," Grey said. "You talk yourself into plighting your troth for coin, to the point that your mind ceases to see every other opportunity for you or your family. You accept the rote answer to maintaining aristocratic standards, though it means your soul is forever tarnished and cheapened. When I finally set aside the notion of an advantageous match, only then did I see the wealth we have, Hawthorne."

"Sycamore was right, then."

Grey needed to soak in a hot bath, he needed to write a true letter to Addy—a love letter—and he needed to catch up on all the business of the estate.

"Sycamore is frequently right. We simply ignore him much of the time. In what particular way was he correct?"

"The young lady whom you had chosen to court must have been a true nightmare."

That wasn't fair. Sarah Quinlan was likely exactly the daughter she'd been raised to be, which wasn't her fault. Grey was also the son he'd been raised to be, or he had been for too long.

"It's more accurate to say that the lady whom I have chosen to court is the woman of my dreams. I and Dorning Hall must be worthy of her esteem, or I have no business asking for her hand."

Thorne shoved Grey's shoulder and offered a rare smile. "I can't wait to meet her."

"She hasn't said yes. In fact, I haven't even asked permission to pay my addresses."

Though he soon would, provided Addy was willing to receive him.

DAY BY DAY, Jason and Clarinda were less careful around Addy. The children, bless them, had accepted her as Aunt Addy from the moment she'd stepped down from Tresham's traveling coach. She was required to read fairy tales by the hour, play catch and blind man's bluff, roll down a hill with her skirts twisting about her legs, and generally impersonate a hoyden.

The family also left her alone to wander Canmore Court's grounds, or to retreat with a book to some secluded stream bank, where she took off her boots and trailed her toes in cool water.

Grey had been right. The company of the children was a much-needed tonic. The fresh air helped, and mad gallops still had the power to raise her spirits.

As Tresham's traveling coach had swayed through London's crowded streets, Addy had considered chasing Grey to Dorset. That, alas, would have provoked scandal. While a gentleman could not cry off, a lady could. If Miss Quinlan backed out of the engagement, Grey would be disgraced and impoverished.

He deserved better, and if his heiress did not exert herself in every regard to make him happy...

Addy would do nothing, for Grey would not want her to meddle.

She turned a page of Theo's book about women's health, though the point of escaping to the porch of the estate's fishing cottage was not necessarily to read. The point of all Addy's idle time at Canmore Court had been to miss Grey, to concoct letters to him that would never be sent, and to be furious with Roger.

The missing Grey felt awful. The anger felt... right.

"I was told I'd find you here, though the current Countess of Canmore nearly inspected my back teeth before she parted with that information."

Grey Dorning stood on the steps of the porch, his hat in his hand.

Addy set aside her book, slowly, lest she blink and he disappear. "My lord, good day."

"May I have a seat?"

Always polite, always dear. "Not if you are an engaged man. If you have plighted your troth, you will do me the kindness of leaving and staying gone."

Where had she found the strength to say those words?

"As it happens,"—he came up the steps—"I am not yet engaged." The swing creaked as Grey took the place to Addy's right. "How are you?"

Not *yet* engaged? Hope and despair battled in Addy's heart. "You aren't wearing a blue waistcoat. You always wear a blue waistcoat, but that one matches your eyes."

Almost blue, nearly blue, but veering toward lavender or periwinkle, and beautiful. The change was subtle, though it complemented his coloring marvelously.

"I used to wear blue because my father wore blue, and nobody dislikes it. Sarah Quinlan has taken me very much into dislike." He set the swing to gently rocking.

Addy closed her book around a scrap of silk. "I will not believe you offended her on purpose." But he *had* offended the most eligible heiress in London. Why, and was the insult permanent?

"She ordered me to kiss her cheek. I could not oblige. Not very gentlemanly of me."

His smile wasn't gentlemanly either. It was mischievous, pleased, a touch arrogant. He looked like Sycamore when he smiled like that.

"Grey, please be honest with me. What have you done?"

"Well, that's the point, isn't it? A gentleman is honest. I honestly could not commit my future to a woman who sees me as only a title. I could not vow to love and honor her, to be a true husband to her. Miss Quinlan was not appreciative of those admissions when I conveyed them to her, but in time, she might be."

Addy set her book aside. "I am appreciative of them."

Grey rested an arm along the back of the swing. "Her papa was a bit put out."

"An enraged father is nobody to trifle with."

"An enraged earl is even more formidable. Quinlan threatened to tarnish your reputation if I failed to marry his daughter. He did me the very great service of reminding me that wealth isn't the only resource that matters, and that we sometimes go astray when attempting to do our best for our loved ones. Will you marry me, Beatitude?"

The words ambushed Addy's thinking mind. "I beg your pardon?"

"That came out wrong, or too soon. I was an idiot to embark on a liaison with you that was anything less than honorable, but I cannot regret being that idiot. I love you, I will never love another, and if that makes me an idiot in love, so be it. Money can be earned and made and inherited, but you... You are all the treasure I will ever need."

She scooted closer and rested her head on his shoulder. His arm came around her, and the moment was perfect.

"I am an idiot in love too, Grey Dorning. I went to your town house to tell you so, but you had left for Dorset. I assumed your course was set, and was prepared to hear an announcement."

"So you will marry me? Be my countess? Holler at me when I track mud into the Hall? Bring me a nooning when I'm in the shearing shed impersonating a farmer?"

How prosaic his version of wedded life was, and how precious. "Of course, and you will read to our children, flirt with me before our neighbors, and host noisy holiday gatherings for your whole family."

His embrace became more snug. "We don't need heirs, my love, and to be truthful, I'd rather you never faced the risk and ordeal of childbed."

Addy closed her eyes, the better to revel in Grey's warmth and scent. "I've learned something."

"Tell me."

"Roger's physicians were absolutely, unequivocally wrong in the advice they gave me. I've been reading a book Theo lent me, and the midwife is very clear about when conception is most likely and that English physicians have it all backward."

"Truly? Backward?"

"Any farmer could probably have puzzled that out, but who was I to contradict Roger's learned physicians? We might well have children, Grey."

"Then we have children, and because they are our children, we will love them endlessly."

She had to kiss him for that, which somehow led to straddling his lap and kissing him some more.

When she had kissed him almost enough—for now—Addy looped her arms around Grey's neck and pillowed her cheek on his shoulder.

"Roger was threatening to set me aside because I was barren." She hadn't meant to say words, or hadn't meant to say them at that precise moment. Even here, amid the bucolic splendor of Canmore Court, even in Grey's arms, the betrayal was infuriating.

What peer would so disgrace his own wife?

Grey gathered her close. "And then he died, and you were expected to mourn a man who sought to cast you off. How did you ever...? I know how. You are a lady, and you allowed his memory to rest in peace."

"He offered me a quiet dissolution of the marriage, an annulment if the bishops were amenable. The notion was raised as a jest at first, but with increasing frequency. I don't know if he would have followed through, but I do know that being set aside was increasingly appealing. Jason was privy to most of this—men gossip, and the brothers had a few mutual acquaintances—but Jason hasn't known quite what to say."

"He should say, 'Roger was a wretched scoundrel who didn't deserve you.'"

"Roger was an earl, well liked, wealthy, charming... but he was no gentleman. I lacked the sophistication to see that. I spent my first three days here marching around by his grave, shouting at him, and airing vocabulary no vicar's daughter should know."

Grey stroked her hair. "Good. I hope wherever he is, he heard your tirades and was shamed by them. He did not deserve you. I hope I do deserve you—you must be the judge—and I promise, should you look with favor upon my suit, I will bend all of my being to maintaining your regard for me."

"I love it when you turn up all speech-y and earl-ish."

He framed her face with his hands. "I am an earl, I can't help that, but these speeches come from a man who's in love with you. Will you marry me, Beatitude? I've given my brothers a deadline for leaving the nest—should have done that years ago—and set them on a commercial venture that has a good chance of success. I'm planning on reducing the size of the Hall, both to sell the salvage and because we'll need a smaller staff that way. I'll pass responsibility for the local living on to a wealthy neighbor, and thanks be to Providence, I've made a start on Tabby's dowry. I wrote to you about that."

"I did not receive your letter. I left Town shortly after you did, which suggests you did not get my letter either. Aunt left her funds to your Tabitha and her harps to you. The sum is quite respectable, to my surprise, and Aunt's man of business said the harps are worth a fair bit as well."

Grey kissed her, and amid all of this discussion, Addy was aware of rising desire on his part—also on hers.

"Tabby inherited from Mrs. Beauchamp?"

Addy whispered an amount into his ear, because whispering in his ear was lovely.

"Ye gods, my daughter will soon be an heiress."

"And she will have a double countess for a step-mama," Addy said, nipping at Grey's earlobe. "There's a lovely little bedchamber inside this fishing cottage, my lord. Might we celebrate our engagement privately?"

Grey rose with Addy in his arms. "You will soon be a double countess. I am a peer of the realm, and you suggest we tryst in a lowly fishing cottage. Madam, have you no thought for the consequence of our station?" His smile would have outshone the Dorset summer sun.

"I love you. That's all I can think about, Grey Dorning."

"I love you too, and thank the heavenly powers that a gentleman never, *ever* argues with a lady."

He dipped his knees so Addy could manage the door latch, and for the next two hours, nobody in the fishing cottage argued with anybody about anything, *at all*.

Nine months to the day after the happy couple's nuptials, Lady Fredericka Gardenia Dorning made her appearance in the Dorning Hall nursery. She argued with everybody about everything, but then, a lady with three younger brothers and six protective uncles was entitled to be a bit contrary.

TO MY DEAR READERS

To My Dear Readers,

I hope you had fun reading Grey and Addy's story. Their tale was a delight to write, and I hope to see more of them in future **True Gentlemen** titles (and yes, more of Sycamore too, I suppose...). I expect to have a story done for Ash and Della in early 2019, but the exact timing is up to them.

My next exciting adventure is the release of my first **Rogues to Riches** tale, **My One and Only Duke**, which comes out Nov. 6, aka Election Day. Please vote (if you're in the US), and then treat yourself to an HEA for the least likely duke and duchess ever to meet in Newgate's accursed halls. I've included an excerpt from Quinn and Jane's story below.

I've also tucked in an exclusive excerpt from Kelly Bowen's latest, **_Last Night with the Earl_**, which released Sept. 25, 2018 (what a coincidence!). Kelly is a double-RITA winner, and writes Regencies full steam, snappy repartee, and clever plotting. If you haven't read her before, you are in for a treat.

If you'd like a little break from all things Regency, I just released a contemporary romance, **_Scotland to the Max_**, that puts an

American engineer skilled at real estate development at the helm of a Scottish castle renovation project. Max Maitland is thwarted by everything from crooked investors to a pair of legendarily besotted castle ghosts, and he needs single mom Jeannie Cromarty to keep the job from ending in disaster. He does *not* need to fall in love with Jeannie, but romance is in the very air at Castle Brodie, and has been for generations. Wheeee!

Excerpt below.

I have more projects in the pipeline, including ***Tis the Season***, a multi-author anthology of holiday short stories coming out Oct. 23, 2018. My next **Rogues to Riches, *When A Duchess Says I Do*** (Duncan's story, April 2019) is also already available for pre-order. You can never have too many HEAs!

If you'd like to receive a short email notifying you of pre-orders, deals, and new releases, following me on **Bookbub** is the simplest way to set that up. If you want the kitten pics and coming attractions reel, then please do sign up for my **newsletter**. I've also recently taken a stab at **Instagram**, and I like it!

Happy reading!

Grace Burrowes

My One and Only Duke by Grace Burrowes, **Rogues to Riches** Book One (Nov. 6, 2018)

When Quinn Wentworth and Jane Winston spoke their wedding vows in Newgate prison, neither expected the result would be a lasting union. But here they are, a month later, no longer in Newgate, very much in love, and not at all sure what to do about it...

Having no alternative, Quinn went about removing his clothes, handing them to Jane who hung up his shirt and folded his cravat as if they'd spent the last twenty years chatting while the bath water cooled.

Quinn was down to his underlinen, hoping for a miracle, when

Jane went to the door to get the dinner tray. He used her absence to shed the last of his clothing and slip into the steaming tub. She returned bearing the food, which she set on the counterpane.

"Shall I wash your hair, Quinn?"

"I'll scrub off first. Tell me how you occupied yourself while I was gone."

She held a sandwich out for him to take a bite. "This and that. The staff has a schedule, the carpets have all been taken up and beaten, Constance's cats are separated by two floors until Persephone is no longer feeling amorous."

Quinn was feeling amorous. He'd traveled to York and back, endured Mrs. Daugherty's gushing, and Ned's endless questions, and pondered possibilities and plots—who had put him Newgate and why?—but neither time nor distance had dampened his interest in his new wife one iota.

Jane's fingers massaging his scalp and neck didn't help his cause, and when she leaned down to scrub his chest, and her breasts pressed against Quinn's shoulders, his interest became an ache.

The water cooled, Jane fed him sandwiches, and Quinn accepted that the time had come to make love with his wife. He rose from the tub, water sluicing away, as Jane held out a bath sheet. Her gaze wandered over him in frank, marital assessment, then caught, held, and ignited a smile he hadn't seen from her before.

"Why Mr. Wentworth, you did miss me after all." She passed him the bath sheet, and locked the parlor door and the bedroom door, while Quinn stood before the fire and dried off.

"I missed you too," Jane said, taking the towel from him and tossing it over a chair. "Rather a lot."

Quinn made one last attempt to dodge the intimacy Jane was owed, one last try for honesty. "Jane, we have matters to discuss. Matters that relate to my travels." And to his past, for that past was putting a claim in his future, and Jane deserved to know the truth.

"We'll talk later all you like, Quinn. For now, please take me to bed."

She kissed him, and he was lost.

Order your copy of *My One and Only Duke*!

Read on for an exclusive sneak peek from Kelly Bowen's *Last Night With the Earl*!

Earl. War hero. Notorious rake. After the Battle of Waterloo, Eli Dawes was presumed dead—and would have happily stayed that way. He's no longer the reckless young man he once was, and he's not half as pretty either. All he wants is to hide away in his country home, where no one can see his scars. But when he tries to sneak into his old bedroom in the middle of the night, he's shocked to find someone already there...

"Don't move."

Eli froze at the voice. He turned his head slightly, only to feel the tip of a knife prick the skin at his neck.

"I asked you not to move."

Eli clenched his teeth. It was a feminine voice, he thought. Or perhaps that of a very young boy, though the authority it carried suggested the former. A maid, then. Perhaps she had been up, or perhaps he had woken her. He supposed that this was what he deserved for sneaking into a house unannounced and unexpected. It was, in truth, his house now, but nevertheless, the last thing he needed was for her to start shrieking for help and summon the entire household. He wasn't ready to face that just yet.

"I'm not going to hurt you," he said clearly.

"Not on your knees with my knife at your neck, I agree." The knife tip twisted, though it didn't break the skin.

"There is a reasonable explanation." He fought back frustration. Dammit, but he just wanted to be left alone.

"I'm sure. But the silverware is downstairs," the voice almost sneered. "In case you missed it."

"I'm not a thief." He felt his brow crease slightly. Something about that voice was oddly familiar.

"Ah." The response was measured, though there was as slight waver to it. "I'll scream this bloody house down before I allow you to touch me or any of the girls."

"I'm not touching anyone," he snapped, with far more force than was necessary, before he abruptly stopped. Any of the girls? What the hell did that mean?

The knife tip pressed down a little harder, and Eli winced. He could hear rapid breathing, and a new scent reached him, one unmistakably feminine. Soap, he realized, the fragrance exotic and faintly floral. Something that one wouldn't expect from a maid.

"Who are you?" she demanded.

"I might ask the same."

"Criminals don't have that privilege."

Eli bit back another curse. This was ridiculous. His knees were getting sore, he was chilled to the bone and exhausted from travel, and he was in his own damn house. If he had to endure England, it would not be like this.

In a fluid motion, he dropped flat against the floor and rolled immediately to the side, sweeping his arm up to knock that of his attacker. He heard her utter a strangled gasp as the knife fell to the floor and she stumbled forward, caught off balance. Eli was on his knees instantly, his hands catching hers as they flailed at him. He pinned her wrists, twisting her body so it was she who was on the floor, on her back, with Eli hovering over her. She sucked in a breath, and he yanked a hand away to cover her mouth, stopping her scream before it ever escaped.

"Again," he said between clenched teeth, "I am not going to hurt you." Beneath his hand her head jerked from side to side. She had fine features, he realized. In fact, all of her felt tiny, from the bones in her wrists to the small frame that was struggling beneath him. It made him feel suddenly protective. As if he held something infinitely fragile that was his to care for.

Though a woman who brandished a knife in such a manner couldn't be that fragile. He tightened his hold. "If you recall, it was you who had me at a disadvantage with a knife at my neck. I will not make any apologies for removing myself from that position. Nor will I make any apologies for my presence at Avondale. I have every right to be here."

Her struggles stilled.

Eli tried to make out her features in the darkness, but it was impossible. "If I take my hand away, will you scream?"

He felt her shake her head.

"Promise?"

She made a furious noise in the back of her throat in response.

Very slowly Eli removed his hand. She blew out a breath but kept her word and didn't scream. He released her wrists and pushed himself back on his heels. He heard the rustle of fabric, and the air stirred as she pushed herself away. Her scent swirled around him before fading.

"You're not a maid," he said.

"What?" Her confusion was clear. "No."

"Then who are you?" he demanded. "And why are you in my rooms?"

"Your rooms?" Now there was disbelief. "I don't know who you think you are or where you think you are, but I can assure you that these are not your rooms."

Eli swallowed, a sudden thought making his stomach sink unpleasantly. Had Avondale been sold? Had he had broken into a house that, in truth, he no longer owned? It wasn't impossible. It might even be probable. He had been away a long time.

"Is it my brother you are looking for? Is someone hurt?"

The question caught him off guard. "I beg your pardon?"

"Do you need a doctor?"

Eli found himself scowling fiercely, completely at a loss. Nothing since he had pushed open that door had made any sort of sense. "Who owns Avondale?"

"What?" Now it was her turn to sound stymied.

"This house—was it sold? Do you own it?"

"No. We've leased Avondale from the Earl of Rivers for years. From his estate now, I suppose, until they decide what to do with it." Suspicion seeped from every syllable. "Did you know him before he died? The old earl?"

Eli opened his mouth before closing it. He finally settled on, "Yes."

"Then you're what? A friend of the family? Relative?"

"Something like that."

"Which one?"

Eli drew in a breath that wasn't wholly steady. He tried to work his tongue around the words that would forever commit him to this place. That would effectively sever any retreat.

He cleared his throat. "I am the Earl of Rivers."

Order your copy of **Last Night with the Earl**!

*And finally, **Scotland to the Max,** for a change of scene from ye olde Regency... Max Maitland is in Scotland to turn Brodie Castle into an international honeymoon destination. The project's success is far from assured, and the last thing—the last, last, very last thing—Max needs is to be distracted by the lady who's held the whole endeavor together prior to his arrival. Jeannie Cromarty is determined to move on, and Max is determined to let her.... mostly.*

"Jeannie, can we get one thing straight?" Max asked, shifting the baby-pack so Henry's little foot stopped digging into Max's back.

Jeannie moved off a few yards, to the edge of the clearing. "A fling is a fling. I know that, Max. I have enough on my plate without trying to... without romantic complications. One doesn't want to make a fool of oneself, though."

The angle of her chin was determined, the set of her shoulders resolute. Everything about her posture radiated independence, which only made her more dear.

Max walked up to her and wrapped his arms around her from

behind. "I am in trouble, okay? I went for years without being tempted, then I ran into a woman I thought was everything I'd ever wanted in a partner. She was smart, funny, ambitious, attractive in ways beyond the physical, and she said she was equally gone on me. Better still, she knew my line of work and talked shop with me by the hour. It didn't work out, so I went for a few more years without being tempted."

As Max spoke, an insight emerged: He'd been devastated when Shayla had turned him down and walked away. The greater blow had been not to his heart, but to his pride. He'd been conned, thoroughly, and like most well-chosen marks, he hadn't had a clue he was being played until the damage had been done.

Jeannie turned and wrapped her arms around him. "You're in trouble?"

Over her shoulder, the castle's curtain wall rose against the blue summer sky. A pennant flapped in the breeze, not the flag of the Earl of Strathdee, because the owner of the castle was far away, enjoying wedded bliss in Damson Valley, and building a different sort of castle.

"I want to go tomato shopping with you," Max said, as Henry twined small fingers into Max's hair. "I want the pillow fights and parenting discussions, the stupid arguments that teach us how to make up and be better partners. I want the long nights and the... I want treasures I have no business wanting, Jeannie. I'll settle for a sunset, maybe even a sunset every so often for the next few months, but that's all I can offer."

God, she felt good in his arms. Warm and lovely, fresh and feminine.

Henry whacked Max on the ear. Jeannie smiled.

"Let's get back to the Hall," she said, "and get a certain unruly young man ready for his nap." She kissed Max on the cheek and strode off down the path.

Order your copy of *Scotland to the Max*!

Made in the USA
San Bernardino, CA
20 March 2019